The Jesus Trial

Kathleen Keithley

and

Daniel T. Doyle

ISBN: 9781499382792

US Copyright Pending

Publish: Amazon Books 2019

Dedicated to our friends and family who have supported us and those who love to blend fiction with reality and imagine what if...

Table of Contents

Chapter 1
The Arrest

The hour just before dawn found members of a small band of men asleep in the forest just outside the city walls. The olive trees released a gentle fragrance into the night air that was cool and heavy with fog. The men had grown fatigued from their full stomachs and the wine they had consumed at a late supper the night before. Only one among the group, the holy man named Jesus, was awake... away and waiting. He knelt in a clearing, a garden, away from the others. He looked to the heavens and quietly prayed.

The flickering of torches signaled the approach of an escadrille of the Guards of the Sanhedrin. One of the holy man's followers led the guards to the man and identified him. Jesus's other followers awoke from the commotion and defended him. In the scuffle, one of the disciples, Simon Peter, wielded a sword and leveled it against Maluch, the guard commander. In a flash, the glistening blade tracked down the side of Maluch's face and nearly sliced off his ear. He fell to his knees grasping his wound from which bright red blood streamed and spewed. Jesus rushed to Maluch and clutched his head in his hands. He gazed intensely into Maluch's eyes until another guard pulled him away. Astonished, Maluch felt his ear which was now reattached and healed.

The violence and bloodshed ensued but the guards ultimately prevailed. Jesus was soon surrounded, apprehended and bound. Meshek, the second in command of the Sanhedrin guard, rushed to Maluch who was still on his knees in the grove, confused and bewildered.

"Rise, man! We must take the holy man to Caiaphas!" Meshek shouted.

Maluch stared back at Meshek, almost as if he didn't know him.

"Go… leave me."

Maluch watched as Jesus was taken away. He leaned his head back and squeezed his eyes shut forcing the tears that were brimming in his eyes to run down his face.

The streets of Jerusalem began to come alive as the sun peeked over the walls that fortified the city. The narrow cobbled streets of the city were dappled with the soft light of dawn and were quiet and largely abandoned. But as the day gained in strength, merchants and food vendors began to emerge en masse onto the bright sunlit streets. Shoppers were soon surveying the vendors' ware and bickering over prices with the merchants.

As the throng of citizens grew in number, there was a sudden commotion when a contingent of Jewish guards burst onto the scene. Meshek led his men, armed with spears and swords, through the crowded streets. As they walked, the guards surrounded Jesus, a tall, slender figure dressed all in white who presented a stark contrast to the short swarthy men who had arrested him. The holy man's hands were tied behind his back. A large rope was wrapped around his neck and secured with a heavy chain. His white robe was splotched with blood. Although Jesus showed no signs of resistance, he was frequently flogged and kicked as the odd procession made its way through the streets. After one particularly heavy blow, Jesus fell to his knees from the sheer force of the assault. The holy man struggled to stand but his bound hands stopped him. One of the guards grabbed him, pulled him to his feet by yanking on his long, dark hair and then shoved him forward.

As the guards and their captive passed through the streets, curiosity grew among the populous. One woman, who was carrying a basketful of fruit and vegetables, took a large juicy fig from it and secreted it in her hand. Just as the soldiers and the arrested man came into close range, the woman hurled the fig hitting Jesus on the side of his head. The squashed fruit splattered and slid down his face evoking smiles and laughter from those watching. One man stepped out from the crowd as the guards and the accused neared him.

"Why, this is Jesus of Nazareth!" the man proclaimed, "Our lord and savior." Bitter sarcasm dripped from the man's every word.

"How can the Messiah save us when he can't even save himself!?" another man shouted over the noisy crowd.

As they continued walking with Jesus, one of the guards stepped out of the procession and shoved some of the bothersome curiosity seekers out of their path. One man stood defiantly in front of the guard. But his defiance was short-lived. As soon as the guard drew his gleaming sword, the man apologized and with great dispatch quickly lost himself in the crowd. The guards pushed Jesus onward to the courthouse where he would soon be facing formal charges.

The guards delivered the accused to the Second Temple where the Great Sanhedrin Council of the Jewish High Court of Jerusalem resided. The council had jurisdiction only over religious matters and had some civil powers but could not hand down or enforce punishments. Jesus was escorted to an inner room known as the Chamber of Hewn Stone where the council met. As the guards brought Jesus before the council, there were scores of chief priests, elders and scribes already assembled. A hush fell over the room as Caiaphas, the Jewish High Priest who presided over the council, entered the room and took his seat at the head of the council table. Caiaphas wore a dark blue wool tunic over a lighter under garment. As Caiaphas walked, the small golden bells that hung alternately between the rose-colored pomegranates that decorated the scalloped hem of his dress, gently chimed.

"May I offer my gratitude to you, Meshek," Caiaphas said as he bowed his head slightly toward the leader of the guards.

"We found him in a garden. One of his own men led us to him," Meshek said, proud of his successful mission.

"Thirty pieces of silver have never been spent more wisely," Caiaphas responded.

Caiaphas now turned his attention to the arrested man. "Jesus of Nazareth, the Council has assembled to defend you from the testimony by witnesses who have sworn that you claim to be the Messiah," Caiaphas began. "What evidence do you have that those statements are untrue?"

"None," Jesus responded, looking directly at Caiaphas.

"I hear that you are the son of a carpenter not of a god. But others say you are a king. If that is true, where is your kingdom?" Caiaphas demanded.

"I am a teacher," Jesus responded quietly.

Caiaphas, a smock frozen on his face, scanned the faces of the great council.

"The man is a hypocrite! He cures with the help of devils yet he claims to cast them out!" Hozai, another high priest, shouted angrily. "And he claims to be the bread of life! The man speaks evil!"

"What evil words have I uttered?" Jesus asked.

"There are witnesses who have testified that you promised them eternal life if they followed you," Caiaphas responded. "And if that isn't preposterous enough, some have testified that you boasted that you could destroy the holy temple and then rebuild it in just three days!" Caiaphas boomed.

Caiaphas' face reddened slightly. His patience was wearing thin with this beggar. If the accused refuted the claims, he could walk away.

"If you deny the charges, the Council will consider dismissing your case. You would be free to go," Caiaphas said slyly. "In the name of the living God, I now put you on oath: tell us if you are the Messiah, the Son of God!"

"So say you," Jesus responded. "But I tell all of you: from this time on you will see the Son of Man sitting at the right side of the Almighty, and coming on the clouds of heaven!"

"Blasphemy!" Caiaphas raged as he glared at Jesus.

There was a stir among the council members who expressed their shock and dismay at Jesus's statement. Caiaphas's eyes narrowed in anger as he focused on Jesus. He banged his gavel repeatedly to bring silence over the chamber.

"By your own words then, Jesus of Nazareth, you are guilty of blasphemy, the ultimate crime against God," Caiaphas snarled. "Since the Council does not have authority to administer the appropriate punishment—the punishment that God demands— we must refer your case to the Roman Court where this Council will serve as the prosecution."

Caiaphas pounded his gavel to signal the end of the court's session. The guards surrounded Jesus to escort him to the court of Pontius Pilate.

***

At the same time that Jesus was being taken through the streets as criminal, Pontius Pilate was just arriving at the Roman courthouse. Pilate was the Roman Prefect of Judaea—the Governor of Jerusalem—and in that capacity also served as the presiding high judge of the Roman Court in Jerusalem. Pilate was tall and elegant. His thick black hair was peppered with gray strands which enhanced his authoritative presence. Pilate was prepared for his usual full day in court. He was wearing official garb that consisted of a long white tunic covered by a deep blue formal robe. On his head, he wore a crown of golden leaves which depicted his exalted position in the Roman government, the foreign power that occupied and ruled the city of Jerusalem. As usual, Pilate would be deciding on the jurisprudence of many cases. Most cases would involve those charged with petty theft, failure to pay their debts and other minor offenses. There could be some cases holding slightly more interest for Pilate—those of a more salacious nature that involved men or woman accused of committing adultery. But for the most part, Pilate's court days were routine and monotonous. Although Pilate took his duties seriously, the tedium even challenged his stellar work ethic; he was known on occasion to drift off during a proceeding. Pilate was less than enthused at the prospect of another long, dreary day of new cases that promised to be identical to those of the day before that had been identical to those of the day before that.

Just a short walk from his personal residence, Pilate entered the courthouse through the back entrance and made his way to his private chambers located behind the main courtroom. The floor of the room was covered in white marble which contrasted to his gleaming ebony desk that took up a large portion of the room. But its size was merited for it was a very important desk; it was the desk where evidence was weighed and punishments were handed down.

A large window overlooked the streets below. A servant, barefoot and wearing a tattered, dingy tunic, rushed in with a silver tray containing a jug of water, a jewel-encrusted golden goblet and a platter featuring an array of bread, cheese and fruit. Pilate excused the servant after he poured a glass of water for him. Pilate stood and pushed open the shutters that covered his chamber's window. He frowned, curious about the crowd that had gathered around a group of Jewish guards who was escorting an arrested man to the court. He wondered to himself if that man had stolen a loaf of bread or perhaps… someone's wife.

Out on the street, Jesus was being shoved and prodded toward the court's main entrance. The guards perceived themselves to be displaying their mettle by their blatant abuse of the arrested man. Jesus was not resisting his arrest; rather, he inexplicably was resigned to it. There was no reason for the guards to abuse the peaceful, non-combative man other than to demonstrate their virility to the masses.

By the time the guards reached the Roman Court, Jesus was suffering—exhausted and in pain. The soldiers burst into the empty courtroom, shoving the broken man to his knees at the base of Pilate's bench. Meshek sent the guards back to their battalion. He removed his helmet and headed for the passageway that led to Pilate's chambers and to the apartment where Captain Gennadius was temporarily headquartered. Meshek had parting instructions for the Roman guards standing watch before he left the room.

"I'll be turning this brigand over to Captain Gennadius," Meshek shouted to the guards. "Keep an eye on this fellow," he told them. A slight smile crossed his face as he observed Jesus who was on his knees with his head bowed so low that his forehead nearly touched the wooden floor. "He's a miracle worker. He might disappear on us."

The Roman soldiers laughed at Meshek's comments. To demonstrate a spirit of cooperation, one of the soldiers approached Jesus and gave him a hearty kick in the side. The soldiers seemed surprised when Jesus did not cry out. Meshek's face turned stoic as he quickly rushed from the room.

***

Captain Seneca Gennadius, Commander of the Roman soldiers, stood before Pilate's chamber and rapped lightly on the massive door. Gennadius drew his ear close to the door to listen for Pilate's response. He knew that the Prefect of Judaea would not be inclined to stand and open the door himself. After a few moments, Gennadius knocked again, this time a little more robustly. He listened again and heard the muffled response of Pilate.

"Enter!" Pilate yelled through the door, annoyed that his day was officially about to begin.

Gennadius opened the door and quickly entered. He greeted the esteemed potentate with the official Roman greeting.

"Hail, Caesar."

But Pilate would have none of that. He waved the guard's salute off dismissively, completely disinterested in paying homage to Caesar. Pilate, who was busy reading from a stack of documents on his desk, spoke to the commander without looking up.

"What is it, commander?" Pilate asked.

"Your honor, we have a new prisoner…" the commander responded but was interrupted.

"Another petty thief or public drunk?" Pilate asked. "Why do you come to me with such drivel?"

"Sir, the Jewish guard brought the man in," Gennadius responded.

"Did the man dare to cut his hair or fail to go to temple?" Pilate asked sardonically.

"The man is a holy man," Gennadius answered.

Pilate looked up at Gennadius for the first time, a scowl on his face.

"A holy man? What are the charges?"

Gennadius' face reddened.

"He was dispatched by order of Caiaphas. I do not know the nature of the charges against him," Gennadius said.

Pilate stood and glared at Gennadius. "Where's your mind! You should have known the charges before you disrupted my work, Commander."

"I'll speak with Caiaphas immediately, sir," the humiliated commander replied. "Caiaphas can explain all the charges." Gennadius, bowed, turned and rushed out the door. He was angry with himself. He should have gotten word of the charges from Meshek. Gennadius had recently been promoted to commander of the contingent of soldiers assigned to the courthouse. He wanted to impress Pilate and convince him that he had made the right choice in advancing him. Now he had failed miserably and had angered Pilate. He rushed through the courtroom where Jesus was still on his knees.

"Primus! Find Caiaphas!" Gennadius shouted to one of the soldiers. "I need to meet with him immediately! I'll be in my quarters at the Principia."

Primus saluted and rushed out. Gennadius focused on Jesus and slowly approached him.

"Holy man, you are not making my day very pleasant," Gennadius snarled. "I will do my best to see you pay for my misery."

Gennadius placed his helmet back on his head and rushed out of the courtroom door.

***

The courtroom began to fill with court officials and attorneys. Liberius, Pilate's court clerk, appeared from a back hallway and immediately spotted the bound man who was kneeling before the bench. Liberius frowned as he observed the blood on the man's tattered robe. He knew that such a display of abuse and disrespect for a holy man would damage Pilate's reputation and would foster even more resentment for the Roman occupation among a segment of Jerusalem's Jewish populace.

Liberius scanned the room and spotted the three soldiers at the back of the courtroom. It was apparent to Liberius that the holy man must be in their charge. These oafs had no concern with the image of the Roman court, Liberius thought to himself. Not wanting to draw more attention to the situation, Liberius made his way back to the soldiers through the throng of court officers and spectators which was growing larger by the minute. As Liberius neared the guards, his pique was escalated when he observed that one of the soldiers had violated protocol by sitting down on a visitor's bench during his watch. And worse, he had plopped his dirty feet and dusty sandals on the bench in front of him, displaying complete and utter disdain for the Roman Court. When the soldiers realized that Pilate's scowling and powerful court officer was heading for them, they hurriedly stood at attention to greet him.

"The man in front of the bench," Liberius began, "is he in your custody?"

The guard with the dusty sandals spoke up. "The Jews brought him. It was by order of Caiaphas."

"A good soldier may act on his own simply because it is the right thing to do," Liberius responded.

The soldiers' blank faces told Liberius that his attempt to instruct them on the virtue of high-mindedness was completely lost on them. "The holy man must immediately be unbound and allowed to stand erect before the bench as the other accused will do. An abused holy man is not the image that His Honor wants to present."

"Yes, sir," one of the guards responded.

Liberius turned to go but then hesitated. "I suggest you do this immediately. Judge Pilate will soon appear on the bench to view those who have been indicted and are scheduled to appear before his court today."

With great dispatch, one of the guards headed for Jesus and soon the rope that had tied his hands was removed. The guard pulled the man to his feet as Liberius, satisfied that his actions had avoided a potential problem for Pilate.

The holy man who now stood before the bench was soon joined by others accused of crimes, some of whom were accompanied by counsel. The courtroom had filled to capacity with citizens, relatives of the accused, attorneys, scribes and the curious. No one was present to represent or support Jesus.

Those accused of crimes were required to line up alongside Jesus. There were beggars and thieves and liars and cheaters, all aligned in front of the towering judge's bench where Pilate would soon hold court. Most cases would either be dismissed or receive a perfunctory punishment that would immediately be handed out by the high judge. Some of the accused were nervously awaiting the arrival of the arbiter of their fate while other, more experienced criminals, seemed unconcerned. The punishments generally handed out by Pilate for petty crimes ranged from a night or two in a cell or a few dozen lashes with a flagellum. The hardened criminals were made of tough stock and did not fear a whipping or confinement in a rat-infested cell. When their punishment ended, they would lick their wounds and return to the streets and to their foul, wayward lives.

As the more than dozen accused citizens stood before the bench, the squeak of a door was heard in the now-silenced room as Liberius stood in front of the bench and proclaimed the arrival of Pontius Pilate so all could hear.

"All rise!"

In his gold and blue splendor, Pilate entered a hushed courtroom. He strode to his bench and pounded his gavel which indicated the official beginning of the day's court session. The mere presence of the Prefect of Judaea garnered both fear and respect. The Romans were incredibly unpopular among the Jews who saw them as oppressive occupiers. Pilate was the most loathed of the Romans since he had the authority to punish the Jews if he deemed evidence warranted it. Pilate was not reluctant to use that authority and mete out punishment to the full extent of the law. As the room remained quiet and still, Pilate opened several scrolls which contained the day's docket agenda. It was often Pilate's practice to observe the accused up close and he was known to leave the bench and confront them directly as he reviewed the charges against them. This day was one of those days.

Pilate descended the short staircase that led from the bench to the courtroom floor, carrying the docket with him. Pilate asked each man about his crime. Most responded that they were not guilty. He reviewed the charges and the evidence. Pilate instantly dismissed several cases and just as quickly sentenced others. He made several accused men very happy as they ran from the courtroom to freedom while others were hauled away to a cell. By not holding any of these men over for trial, the day would be less cumbersome and more bearable. But there was one case that ultimately would be carried over to his court.

Pilate came to Jesus who was the last man in the line. He discovered that he had no documents for this accused man. Liberius, wanting to save Pilate from confusion, approached him and explained that this was the man who the Jewish guards had arrested. Pilate looked at the young man for a few moments before he returned to the bench.

"I have ordered Gennadius to provide me with evidence of the charges," Pilate said. "Take him away... for now."

Pilate's eyes lingered on Jesus as the court officers escorted him out of the courtroom.

***

Gennadius lounged in his quarters at the Principia. He had taken off his metal breastplate and weapons. His helmet had been tossed on the floor. The commander's sandaled feet were propped up on the dining table before him. A metal tray strewn with cheese and fruit rested before him on the dining table. Just as he poured red wine from a flask into his ornate goblet, there was a light rapping on the door.

"Come!" Gennadius shouted.

The heavy door pushed opened slowly. Gennadius turned to look at his visitor. Caiaphas bowed slightly to the commander.

"Ah, Caiaphas!" Gennadius sneered, "You bring a criminal without the crime! Pilate demands to know the charges against the prisoner you arrested today."

"I will most assuredly provide His Honor with the evidence against the man and will do so at once," Caiaphas responded in an even tone although his darkened eyes belied the disdain he held for the Prefect of Judaea at the mere mention of his name.

Caiaphas turned to go but was stopped by Gennadius. Caiaphas hid his annoyance that this buffoon was delaying him further. But Caiaphas was a master of deception. Although the weather was oppressive, Caiaphas remained cool in his heavy wool apparel—not a drop of perspiration on his brow. He turned his attention back to Gennadius.

"What is the nature of this man's offenses?" Gennadius was not asking in an official capacity but merely to satisfy his own curiosity.

"He thinks he's god."

Gennadius chuckled. "So does Pilate."

Caiaphas looked intensely at Gennadius. "The charge against Jesus of Nazareth is not a metaphorical one. The man claims to be god."

"You should see him now. He is nothing like a god. He is bent and bloodied and broken."

Chapter 2
The Charges

Caiaphas hurried out of Gennadius's quarters. It was important that he see Pilate as soon as possible. Caiaphas was aware that a chance to speak directly to the imperial Governor of Judaea was a rare opportunity, and the importance of the meeting was heightened by the seriousness of the matter—one that was of ultimate importance to the Jewish High Council. Caiaphas scurried out of the guard's garrison and onto the narrow streets of Jerusalem now crowded with its citizens and sweltering from the oppressive mid-day heat. He made his way through the streets crowded with merchants, shoppers and groups of children at play. Had it been another day, Caiaphas would have been annoyed by the bedlam created by the bickering merchants and their customers, the singing and dancing and game playing of the children and the clatter of rickety carts on the cobblestone streets. But today, his mission was single-minded and its importance overwhelmed such trivial distractions. Caiaphas was a man with one mission, a mission he viewed as the most important of his life. He pushed his way through the crowds, ignoring the bows and greetings of members of his congregation he passed; there were more important things on his mind.

Caiaphas arrived at the large building that housed the Roman Court of Jerusalem, its limestone exterior resplendent with a golden replica of the Roman Empire's coat of arms. Two centurions were guarding the door, the older officer leaning against the wall, the other standing at attention. The younger soldier spotted Caiaphas and took several steps forward. It was a rare sight to see one of the Jewish High Priests visiting the Roman Court. Immediately, the soldiers were wary of the approaching Caiaphas. As he began to ascend the stairway that led to the court, he was stopped and questioned.

"What business have you here today, your holiness?" the younger soldier asked sardonically.

Caiaphas, wise and experienced in dealing with the hostile Roman guards, made sure that his manner remained respectful. He tilted his head and bowed slightly to the soldier.

"Kind sir," Caiaphas began in his most respectful tone, "His honor, Judge Pilate, has requested information that I possess. It is urgent that I meet with his highness."

The other officer, who apparently was of higher rank, approached Caiaphas.

"What could his honor, Pontius Pilate, learn from you, Caiaphas?" The sergeant asked, sparing no contempt for Caiaphas's feelings.

"It is crucial evidence," Caiaphas responded. "It involves a case that is to be heard today. And, I understand that his imperial highness must have this information in order to proceed with this important legal matter."

The sergeant's eyes narrowed as he looked Caiaphas over slowly. Making the mistake of allowing the wrong person in to see Pilate would not be a prudent move on his part. If this Jew was lying, his commander would have it in for him. Yet, if the Jew was telling the truth, he might be punished viciously for not allowing important information to reach Pilate. Perhaps it was Caiaphas's steady gaze—a look that appeared to be honest and sincere—that swayed the sergeant to allow him to have entry. The sergeant nodded to his underling who swiftly opened the large oaken door that led to the courtroom.

Liberius was just emerging from the interior chambers when he spotted the small figure of Caiaphas entering the darkened rear section of the courtroom.

"Caiaphas!" Liberius shouted out. "What business have you in this courtroom?" he asked in a bold and insolent manner.

Caiaphas bowed to Liberius who was Pilate's most trusted court clerk. The Jewish priest understood the importance of staying on his good side.

"My kind sir," Caiaphas began, "I am here on court business. I have evidence in the case of Jesus of Nazareth."

"Evidence?" Liberius asked. "Where is this evidence? I see you are without documents or scrolls?"

"It is the knowledge if have, kind Liberius," Caiaphas responded. "It is information that I must relate to his honor directly."

"You are the evidence," Liberius restated Caiaphas's words with a slightly different bent. A nearly imperceptible smile stretched across his face. "His honor will be quite impressed I assure you." Liberius turned to leave but then hesitated and looked back the small man who seemed even smaller in the large and abandoned courtroom. Liberius nodded to the back benches of the gallery. "You may sit in the back there while you wait."

Caiaphas bowed to show his gratitude as the corners of his mouth drooped downward. He took a seat as Liberius suggested, in the last bench in the room, to wait for the arrogant and overbearing Pilate who Caiaphas viewed as another individual who confused himself with God.

Liberius rushed to Pilate's private chambers. After the morning court cases were heard, Pilate, as was his custom, retired to his chambers for food, wine and a short nap before returning for the afternoon session. Between the heat, the tedium of holding court and a full belly, it was sometimes all Pilate could do to rise and walk to his mat. If the drowsiness overwhelmed him, he would sometimes lay his head on his table and nap there. Liberius was compelled by the knowledge of his superior's routine to hurry back to Pilate before he had succumbed to the allure of sleep. Pilate would be enraged if he were to face Jesus once again without documentation of the charges. He would be infuriated and would not be above taking it out on his trusty court clerk.

Liberius rapped several times on Pilate's large chamber door. He was growing old and his hearing had suffered. So, rather than try to do the impossible and hear through the thick door, Liberius was in the habit of pushing the door open after a few knocks. He peered in the bright room and could see signs that Pilate was growing drowsy.

"Your honor," Liberius called quietly to him as he peeked around the door. "Caiaphas is here. He has the evidence in the case against Jesus of Nazareth, the Jew prisoner."

Pilate turned and glared at Liberius. "Does he now?" he asked rhetorically. "The Jew has evidence on another Jew. Delightful! They are turning against each other, Liberius. The last thing I need is for civil unrest to break out."

Pilate sat motionless for several moments. He recalled his encounters with Caiaphas who he had always found duplicitous and ruthless. Now the Jewish High Priest was eagerly seeking the prosecution of one of his own. Pilate considered having Liberius order him to leave. He didn't relish the idea of conversing with the Pharisee. But there was a curiosity that lingered within Pilate about the accused. The man seemed humble and certainly not threatening. What charges did Caiaphas have against him and what was the urgency, Pilate wondered to himself. Pilate felt somewhat put upon that the Jew was pushing one of his problems off on him. But Pilate was an ethical man and would fulfill his responsibilities. If Caiaphas felt the matter should be heard in the Roman Court, and if the charges had merit, he would allow it to be heard in his courtroom. He had more important matters than to settle a squabble between two Jews, but he would not shirk his duties no matter how distasteful. With haste, Liberius returned to the courtroom.

"Caiaphas, his honor will grant you a brief audience," Liberius called loudly across the courtroom. "Quickly!"

Caiaphas immediately rose and with his staff in hand, clattered to the front of the court house as quickly as he could in an attempt to follow the fast-moving Liberius who was disappearing down one of the interior hallways. Moving hurriedly down the hall, Caiaphas found Liberius standing dutifully beside a large wooden door that he was holding open for him.

"You may enter," Liberius said quietly to Caiaphas in an almost reverent tone.

Caiaphas bowed slightly to Liberius and entered the private chambers of the Prefect of Judaea. Pilate, sprawled in his large throne-like chair, did not bother to rise to greet his visitor nor did he offer him a seat. But to maintain proprieties, Caiaphas bowed deeply to Pontius Pilate despite the disdain he held in his heart for the man.

"My gratitude for allowing me to speak with your honor," Caiaphas began. "It is with great respect that I come to you and…"

Pontius interrupted, waving his hand in the air. "Save all that," Pilate said. "I have no interest in or time for all these empty formalities."

"Yes, your honor," Caiaphas said as he bowed again.

"Can you begin to fathom—are you able to grasp at even a layman's level just how crowded the docket for the court is each day?" Pilate asked angrily but didn't wait for a response. "Do you understand my responsibilities, the pressure that is put upon me to hear all the cases that befall this court?" Pilate rose and stretched and walked to his window. He gazed out over the afternoon activities taking place in the street below.

"Despite these pressures, each day I am charged with the ethical disposition of my office and must fulfill my duties," Pilate continued as he turned and glared at Caiaphas. "And what do I find this morning but one of your people unceremoniously deposited in my court with no supporting documents and no apparent charges. Do you realize the inconvenience that this type of situation caused me?"

"My humble apologies, your honor," Caiaphas responded. "It was inconsiderate of me but it was with great urgency and import that the case was referred to the Court of the Romans."

Pilate surveyed Caiaphas for a moment. "Explain," Pilate ordered.

"The man you refer to, the man I asked the guards to bring to your court, is Jesus of Nazareth," Caiaphas began.

"That much I knew, Caiaphas," Pilate snapped.

"At my request the guards arrested this man before dawn and brought him to the Council to face the charges against him." Caiaphas explained.

"I do not pretend to possess an expertise in Jewish laws, Caiaphas, but was it not irresponsible, even sacrilegious, to arrest the man before sunrise?" Pilate asked, displaying his acumen in the religious laws of the Jews despite his disclaimer. "I understood that it was against your laws to arrest someone during the night time hour. Do you fear that the actions you have taken may ultimately be cause for appeal or, indeed, even dismissal?"

"It was an unusual circumstance and, as I indicated, it was a matter of great urgency," Caiaphas responded, his hand trembling slightly indicating that dealing with the might of Pilate was not quite as painless as he may have first thought. "Jesus was a wanted man and had to be apprehended whenever the opportunity presented itself. I and the other Jewish High Priests had to act on information we were given about his whereabouts. It was a matter of circumstance over protocol."

"I'll remember those words if he's found guilty of the charges and they come back on appeal," Pilate responded reproachfully.

"With all due respect," Caiaphas responded, "the matter was of such importance to our people and our religion that the actions we were forced to take are most defendable."

"I am finding the defense of your actions tedious and irrelevant," Pilate replied, his voice fatigued and his tone irreverent. "Get to the heart of the matter, what is this man accused of?" Pilate asked pointedly.

"Jesus of Nazareth thinks he's a god," Caiaphas said in a quiet and deliberate manner.

Pilate found the news absurd and laughed heartily. "The man thinks he's a god?!" Pilate responded after he recovered his sober demeanor. He turned back to the window and pointed to the crowd below. "I could probably have my soldiers stop and interview any number of Jews who are daft enough to think they're gods. What's the harm? An insane man is not responsible for the crazy words he says or the grandiose image he might have of himself."

Caiaphas eyes darkened and a slight tension could be detected across his face as he absorbed the misguided words of Pilate. "The case of Jesus of Nazareth is different, your honor," Caiaphas responded in a tone most serious. "This man has a ministry. He is not irrationally in the usual sense of the term. Jesus is able to think and function normally. If he has a mental disorder—if the man is deranged as you suggest—he is merely crazed by the power he covets. Jesus is ministering to devoted Jews. He has a following, a growing following. Jesus is... dangerous."

"Ah, I see," Pilate responded, as a smile stretched across his face. "He is a threat to your position, to your power and authority."

"Forgive me, sir, but that is not the case," Caiaphas responded. "This is not a personal matter. His crime is far more serious than an effrontery to me. Jesus of Nazareth is violating the laws of God—it is God's honor that is being wounded. And by so doing, Jesus has been deemed to be guilty of blasphemy, the most serious of all crimes."

Pilate sank back down in his seat as he took in the words of the Pharisee. Even though Caiaphas presented his case in what appeared to be a sincere manner, Pilate was not impressed. To Pilate it was a silly matter that could be smoothed over with a few words by a religious leader who had the authority and skill to do so. But Caiaphas was known to be a prideful man who relished his high position within the Jewish community. Pilate did not trust Caiaphas's intentions. He was sure that the High Priest felt threatened by the apparent rise of Jesus and his ministry. Pilate resented Caiaphas's presumption that the exalted Roman Court should be used for such a trivial issue.

After several contemplative moments, Pilate refocused on Caiaphas. "It is but a simple matter. As a leader of your people, it seems as though you should be able to resolve this matter yourself without bringing in the Court of the Roman Empire. It seems that you yourself are dishonoring your god by your unwillingness or sheer inability to defend him."

"Jesus was given every opportunity to deny the charges, but he would not," Caiaphas responded. "With all respect, your honor, our laws are subservient to those of Rome. The Council is restricted from meting out the appropriate punishment for this man's crimes."

"Punishment?!" Pilate responded. "So that's where the fly in the ointment is. I can't begin to visualize the appropriate punishment for the crime of purporting to be a god. Let's see, I would think you would want him thrown in a cell to see if this god could survive without food and water. That could be the true test but a risk for you. If Jesus escaped from the irons that bind him, he would prove that he indeed is a god. That would very damaging ballyhoo for you, would it not, Caiaphas?"

Caiaphas bowed his head slightly and offered no response. Pilate whose already thin patience was being challenged further, rose and paced back and forth before his visitor.

"I warn you, his punishment could be harsh under our laws, Caiaphas," Pilate said. "Are you willing to take that risk?" Pilate was certain he could convince Caiaphas to take care of his own by threatening him with the dire fate that might await Jesus. "He could be sentenced to be beaten and be thrown in a dark hole for days with no sunlight, food or water."

Still Caiaphas did not respond.

"Your silence is deafening and your cowardice is nauseating," Pilate said. "Go on with you. I will take it under consideration."

"Your honor, if I may," Caiaphas responded. "There is another very delicate matter that I fear will trouble you but one that you should have full knowledge of."

"Now what on earth could that be?" Pilate asked rhetorically. "My endurance is waning, Caiaphas. You are eating into my nap time. Out with it, man!"

"As I told you the followers of Jesus are growing in numbers," Caiaphas began. "I have it on good authority that he is encouraging his devotees to abandon the tributes they are required to pay to Rome." Caiaphas locked eyes with Pilate as he allowed his words to linger in the air.

"Are you saying that Jesus is advising his followers not to pay the taxes to which they are legally bound?" Pilate asked, his face reddening ever so slightly.

Caiaphas bowed again but all the while kept a watchful eye on Pilate. Although what he just told Pilate was untrue, Caiaphas felt justified in his lie. After all, he was attempting to bring the sinner to justice. To Caiaphas, it was expedient for one man to die so that a nation might not perish. Contrary to what Pilate had said, Caiaphas *was* defending his god. If it took a harmless falsehood to bring him justice, Caiaphas was sure he would be forgiven for this noble transgression.

"Please also know, sir, that most of my people support Jesus's prosecution," Caiaphas said, his voice lowered in a conspiratorial tone. "Anger is growing. I would hate to imagine a riot in the streets. There could be bloodshed if things got out of hand. One and all would be at risk. No one would be safe."

The inference that he himself would be in danger was not lost on Pilate. He chose not to engage in such speculation. After a long hesitation, Pilate headed for his mat again. "I will take this all under advisement," he said quietly.

"Your honor, shall I appear in the court session scheduled for this afternoon?" Caiaphas asked.

"Fine!" Pilate responded. "I'll have a decision by then."

Pilate stretched and yawned as Caiaphas bowed to him and backed out of the door.

Just as Pilate was heading to his mat, Liberius stuck his head in the door. "Sir, did Caiaphas provide adequate evidence of the charges against Jesus of Nazareth?" Liberius knew that Pilate was probably by now cantankerous. He was no doubt drowsy and in a bad frame of mind after having to deal with Caiaphas. But Liberius had to set up the docket for the afternoon and it was essential that he learn whether Jesus would be brought before the bench to face his charges.

"You too, Liberius?" Pilate lamented. "I am a good and honest man with great responsibility. Yet, I am denied a few moments of rest. All I want is a brief nap to be refreshed in order to face the afternoon that will mirror exactly the tedious morning I just endured. Please leave me."

"Should I put Jesus on the docket?" Liberius asked although he knew that he was pushing Pilate to the end of his patience.

"You are a pest, Liberius," Pilate responded as he walked toward his mat. "Yes, put the man on the docket. I have not decided if I will take the case. It is a flimsy, preposterous charge. The Jews are playing games. I have yet to decide if I will play with them. I will sleep on it. Perhaps the answer will come to me in my dreams."

***

The afternoon court session was delayed almost an hour. It seems that Pilate had fallen into a deep sleep and refused to be roused at the urging of his loyal aide. Finally, refreshed from his respite, Pilate appeared in the courtroom with no explanation for the delay.

Since Jesus's case was delayed from the morning docket, he would be the first to appear before Pilate who had the option of finding for an immediate disposition of the case which included its dismissal. The Roman soldiers escorted Jesus into the courtroom. The judge's bench had been empty when they entered. Liberius ordered the soldiers to deposit the bound and chained man in front of the bench. He was so spent from the abusive treatment he had been subjected to that he fell exhausted to his knees where he bowed his head in silent prayer. Liberius made the quick decision to abandon his order that Jesus stand before Pilate unbound. After all, he was a convicted criminal. The shackles about his ankles and the hemp about his neck and that constrained his hands had been well-deserved.

There was a stir in the courtroom as the spectators stepped aside to allow Caiaphas to enter the room. He solemnly made his way, clicking and clacking his staff on the wooden planks, to the prosecutor's table and took a seat, all the while eyeing the accused who was still on his knees in front of the bench. Caiaphas had been informed by Liberius that Pilate would hear the formal charges against Jesus. If the hearing evolved into a full court trial, Caiaphas would prosecute the case against Jesus since the alleged crimes were violations of Jewish religious laws.

Jesus startled when the court clerk suddenly shouted, "All Rise," as the chief judge, Pontius Pilate, entered the courtroom. Jesus, bound and weak and reeling, was unable to stand on his own. Several of the Roman soldiers who had remained in the courtroom pulled him forcibly to his feet.

After Pilate took his seat on the bench, he stared at the accused before him. "Raise your head, defendant and look into my eyes." Jesus focused on Pilate who was slightly taken aback by the man's clear intense eyes, eyes that gazed at him with intelligence and kindness. Pilate quickly averted his eyes from the intensity of the man's penetrating stare.

"Court clerk, who is the man standing before me?" Pilate shouted, although he knew the answer.

The clerk scurried to the front and bowed before Pilate. "Your honor, this man is Jesus of Nazareth."

A look of chagrin registered on Pilate's face. "So, this is Jesus. He is a god, is he not?"

Laughter was heard from a few of the spectators at Pilate's acerbic words.

"What is Jesus of Nazareth accused of?"

Caiaphas rose from the prosecutor's table and walked slowly toward the bench. He made a wide berth around Jesus, staring at him as if he was a pariah. Pilate, who was not particularly pleased that he would be dealing with the pompous Caiaphas again, remained silent and waited for the official charges to be read publicly in court for all to hear. Caiaphas consulted the document he carried with him.

"Your honor, if it pleases the court, Jesus of Nazareth has been found guilty by the Jewish High Council of committing blasphemy," Caiaphas announced in a detached and even tone.

"And, Caiaphas, what evidence do you have of this crime?" Pilate demanded.

"This man, this Jesus person, claims to be a God," Caiaphas replied, his words now tinged with bitterness.

"And, I assume that you deem him not to be a God but a liar and a pretender," Pilate replied, expecting that his words would rile the arrogant priest.

"This man is not a God," Caiaphas offered, his calm tone had returned.

Disappointed that he was unable to rattle Caiaphas, Pilate glared at the accused. "And if this court concurs in your finding, what punishment would this fraud, this faker receive?" Pilate asked with a slight smile on his face. He was certain that this ragged vagabond before him was unimportant and non-threatening. Perhaps the man was crazed and a few weeks in a dark cell would return his sanity to him.

Caiaphas held a steady gaze on Pilate as he responded. "Death, sir. The punishment is death."

Pilate was adept at not displaying his emotions in court but a shiver went down his spine as he absorbed the words of the Jewish priest.

Chapter 3
Legal Advice

Pilate was angry with himself. He should never have allowed Caiaphas to publicly lay out the evidence in his court! Caiaphas claimed that the Roman Court of Jerusalem had jurisdiction in the case of Jesus of Nazareth. But Caiaphas was not to be trusted. After he reluctantly agreed to hear the evidence, Pilate was taken by complete surprise when Caiaphas indicated that the prescribed punishment for this man's crime was death. He burned with the recognition that Caiaphas had deceived him, angered that the sly Jew had withheld the severity of the punishment in their private discussion about the man's crime. He should have known better and should not have been surprised by the crafty Jew who was known to bend his words and shade the truth.

After Caiaphas's claim that Jewish laws called for death as punishment for Jesus's crimes, Pilate did not want any part of the trial. He decided that the best way to avoid the trial, and the ugly aftermath that would surely follow, was to prove Caiaphas to be a liar and a fraud. After Caiaphas proclaimed that a punishment of death was appropriate for Jesus's crimes, Pilate called a brief recess. He retired to his chambers and summoned the court scribe, Titus, to meet with him.

Titus entered Pilate's chamber and stood dutifully before him with his parchment and stylus in hand.

"Sit, Titus," Pilate ordered.

Titus took a seat before Pilate who was bent on out-maneuvering the deceitful prosecutor.

"The Jewish High Priest Caiaphas has proclaimed that Jewish law demands that a defendant who is convicted of blasphemy be put to death," Pilate said. He peered closely at Titus. "Do you think that punishment appropriate or indeed rational?"

"Sire, I do not pretend to know the religious laws of the Jews," Titus began. "I am not on a par with Caiaphas when it comes to such matters."

"Of course not, Titus," Pilate glared at him. "Nor am I. But do you think the sentence of death for imagining yourself to be a god is reasonable, man?!" Pilate's temper was simmering, ready to boil over.

Titus bowed to Pilate. "I do not, sir," Titus responded meekly. "But it is the Jews who have handed out this punished— they are not known for being reasonable."

Pilate laughed. It was a good answer and summarized how Pilate felt about the haughty Caiaphas and the rest of the Jewish troublemakers.

"I will outsmart this provocateur, Titus, and keep this trash out of my court," Pilate said. "I want you to conduct a thorough search of the official archives and study the laws of the Jews. Find if there is a precedent for such punishment. Provide proof, Titus. Cite the cases. And in the remote possibility that death is indeed the stipulated punishment, find me the legal basis that the Roman Court has no jurisdiction in the matter. Provide me solid argument where the appropriate jurisdiction lies for this asinine case."

Titus rose and bowed to Pilate who stopped him before he left.

"This is important, Titus," Pilate said. "Our relationship with the Jews is fragile. I do not want to be responsible for the execution of one of their holy men. It could cause unrest, serious problems."

Pilate stopped a moment, reflecting on the potential for a simple, meaningless case such as this one of turning into a profound disaster. "In his subtle charming way, Caiaphas has warned me that the streets could turn to blood if the religious laws of the Jews are not enforced. He had the unmitigated gall to infer that danger could be in store for me personally if it appears that the Roman Empire does not show due respect for their edicts."

Titus remained silent. Pilate would never knowingly take any action that would bring a threat to him or his family. Although he thought that Jesus was being persecuted by his own kind, he would not place himself or his family in danger to defend him.

"Do your best," Pilate said after his thoughts returned to the matter at hand. "Tell Liberius to announce that court will resume in the morning. After I receive your arguments, I will make my ruling. If all things go well, this court will not be trying the case of Jesus of Nazareth."

***

The next morning, Titus was waiting at Pilate's door before the judge's arrival. He had worked through the night to confirm the proper punishment and jurisdiction for the crime. He felt satisfied that he had done a thorough job. Titus had many answers for Pilate and, as his honor had ordered, he cited case law. Pilate would readily accept some of the answers but would not find others very pleasant. Titus nervously awaited Pilate for their meeting.

Pilate entered the courthouse and headed down the dark hallway to his private chambers. He bid a good morning to Titus but told the scribe that he would have to wait a bit longer. Pilate needed to go over some documents and, of course, have his morning meal. Titus, fatigued from overwork and lack of sleep, leaned against the wall for the longer wait as the court servant brought a platter of cheese and grapes and a flask of goat's milk to Pilate. After Pilate ate his meal and settled in, he summoned Titus to discuss his findings.

"From the weary look on your face, Titus, I would imagine that you worked very long hours on your case study," Pilate said as Titus entered with his red eyes and stack of parchments.

"Yes, your honor," Titus responded. "I had quite an evening. There were many cases to study and much material that was new to me, especially the scrolls of Jewish law which were written in Hebrew. I did as thorough a job as possible."

"I am confident that you did," Pilate responded. "Now, tell me, what were your findings?"

"First, sir, Caiaphas is correct about the Jewish laws. The punishment attached to a Jew convicted of blasphemy is the death sentence," Titus began but was immediately interrupted by a disappointed Pilate.

Pilate slammed his fist down on his table, scattering the last of the dark red grapes that rolled and dropped to the floor. "So I am forced to hand down an unfair sentence? The Jews are subservient to the Romans so it follows that their laws should be as well."

"But sire, nowhere in Roman law or precedent could I find a charge or conviction for blasphemy," Titus said. "Blasphemy is not a crime in Rome. It is only a crime if committed by a Jew in Jerusalem. It is a religious law of the Jews."

"And so the pious and sanctimonious Jews want to force this ludicrous case into Roman hands," Pilate replied, his eyes narrowed in contempt. "It is the Jewish High Priests who are behind this farce, yet it will be the Romans who will be blamed for the man's death." Pilate's face was reddening as the anger within him began to boil to the surface. "Caiaphas is pulling the strings and we are his puppets. He will eliminate a threat to his power and shift the blame for a Jew's death to Pilate and his court. Was there nothing else, Titus?! Is there no law to protect us from this devious man? Are we helpless to counter his selfish actions?"

"There is some good news, your honor," Titus responded quietly.

"Tell me, man! What is it?" Pilate said hopefully.

"Firstly, there are cases that can be cited that support the thesis that perhaps Jesus did not commit the crime of blasphemy," Titus told Pilate.

"But he's already been convicted of the crime, Titus," Pilate interjected. "Caiaphas claims he was found guilty in the hearing at the Jewish Council last night."

"Ah, that is true and it brings up another point," Titus continued. "The Jewish council is a lower court. If evidence is presented in the higher court to prove that Jesus, in fact, did not commit blasphemy and therefore is not guilty of violating Jewish laws, the conviction could be reversed and therefore the associated punishment in the matter would be a moot point."

Pilate smiled. "We could be beating Caiaphas and the Jews at their own game," he said. "What was the other point my query raised?"

"The Jews are guilty of violating their own laws," Titus said.

"Yes, they arrested Jesus at night," Pilate said. "I mentioned as much to Caiaphas. He defended their actions, claiming an exception. It was an urgent matter, the Jew alleged, and the criminal had to be captured as soon as he was found."

"But it is written by Jewish law that a citizen cannot be arrested in the dark," Titus said. "No matter what excuse Caiaphas has—whether feeble or meritorious—it does not change the fact that the Pharisees were guilty of breaking their own laws."

Pilate was smiling again. "And therefore, my brilliant scribe," Pilate said, "The case could be reversed on the basis that a citizen was denied his rights prescribed by law. And, adding more dimension to our cause, the Jews are guilty of breaking the law—their own laws! Cause for dismissal. I would relish throwing that in Caiaphas' face." Pilate laughed. "On top of that, perhaps with my authority, I can cite precedent and hand down an appropriate punishment to Caiaphas himself! Twenty lashes for arresting a lunatic who thinks he's a god at an illegal time of day." Pilate laughed at the absurdity of the premise. "Study that angle, Titus! But not tonight. You need to catch up on your sleep."

"But if the case should wind up in your court, Judge Pilate," Titus continued. "There is another way to avoid dealing with Caiaphas's petition that Jesus be put to death." Titus leaned closer. "Jesus could plead insanity."

Pilate erupted into laughter. "Brilliant!" he roared. "Titus, you have my sincere gratitude for your ingenuity and hard work."

"If we are forced to trial and an insanity plea seems the optimum strategy," Titus continued. "We may have to hire an attorney..."

"And pay him well, eh Titus?" Pilate interrupted. "I am confident that with all the weapons we have at our disposal, we will defeat the clever Caiaphas and avoid the death sentence for this harmless but misguided man. And we can avoid unrest so that I can live in peace and tranquility among the trash and rubble who call themselves Jews.

"You know, Titus I have been in this position for eleven years and soon will return to Rome. My tenure here has been its own kind of punishment. I was hoping to complete this assignment before a serious incident would arise with the Jews. If we are smart and stay one step ahead of Caiaphas, it looks like my aspirations will come true."

"There is yet one more angle, sire—that of jurisdiction. There is case law and precedent that the Roman court may not legally have jurisdiction in the case of a Jew violating Jewish law," Titus responded. "Although Jerusalem is ruled under the authority of the Roman Empire, Jesus of Nazareth is accused of breaking Jewish laws—not Roman. There are several remote cases that I have uncovered in which a Jew—a Galilean which I presume Jesus to be—who violated Jewish religious laws was tried under the jurisdiction of the ruler of the Jews."

Pilate smiled. "Ah… what you are saying, my dear Titus, is that Jesus of Nazareth while a citizen of Rome is also a subject of Jewish authorities and should be tried accordingly," Pilate said. "If this is true, and I trust it is, it is Herod who has the responsibility of meting out judgments and punishments against his own kind. Jesus is Herod's case! He is Herod's problem!"

Pilate rose from his chair and pulled on his robe for his entry into court. "You have done well, Titus," he told his scribe. "You have presented a veritable banquet of ways to elude this distasteful case." Pilate looked somber for a moment. "I have a nagging feeling that this case should not be heard in the Roman Court. Perhaps that will not be an issue after everything you have discovered. You have done very well, indeed. We have other arrows in our quiver should they be needed, but I believe I will proclaim my finding to be that the Roman Court does not have jurisdiction in this case. But to show my full consideration for the accused, I will have a private discussion with him."

Titus bowed to Pilate and backed out of Pilate's chambers. Pilate placed his golden crown of leaves on his head and headed for the morning session of court. He was ready to deal with this holy man, this Jesus of Nazareth.

Just as Pilate swept into court, Liberius ordered that everyone rise in his honor. Pilate immediately spotted Jesus who was standing silently and alone in front of the bench. He was still bound and chained and the roughly hewn hemp rope remained about his neck. Pilate was relieved to see that Jesus did not seem to have any new wounds from the night in a cell. Pilate did not want any of his soldiers to be responsible for beating him without authority. The last thing Pilate needed was to have a controversial incident that would place him in a bad light and sabotage his plans.

Pilate also spotted Caiaphas and Annas, another self-important Jewish High Priest, standing near the front of the court. Pilate looked forward to seeing the haughty looks on their faces dissipate when they realize that he was thwarting their plans to murder this man.

Pilate banged his gavel to mark the beginning of the morning session.

"What case do I have before me, Liberius?" Pilate asked as a formality. Pilate was a stickler for conducting his court by the book.

"Your honor, it is the case of Jesus of Nazareth," Liberius responded. "The man standing there before you, sire."

"Ah, yes, I have seen this man before," Pilate said. "I believe it was yesterday was it not?" he asked rhetorically.

Caiaphas took a few steps forward to speak but Pilate cut him off.

"I believe it was the honorable Caiaphas, the Jewish High Priest, who had proclaimed charges against him, was it not, Liberius?" Pilate said, abandoning any subtleties in toying with Caiaphas.

This time Caiaphas stepped forward more boldly and was determined to speak. "Your worship, it is I, Caiaphas, who possess the official charges against this man as well as documents attesting to the guilty verdict that was rendered against him at the Council just two mornings past." Caiaphas said as he bowed slightly toward Pilate.

"Morning?" Pilate said in mock astonishment. "Morning, Liberius? Did you hear the gentle Caiaphas? He said morning. I was led to believe that the arrest occurred before the sun rose. Oh, but that couldn't be, could it, Caiaphas? That would be a violation of your own law."

Pilate was getting under Caiaphas' skin—just where Pilate wanted to be. "Sir, as I explained. We acted under very unusual conditions. It was an important emergency. An exception that the law allows."

"The court clerk will make a note of that," Pilate responded, off-handedly. "Liberius, please step forward to my sidebar."

Liberius rushed to the bench. Pilate spoke in hushed tones to his chief assistant. "I will leave the bench now and wait just beyond the entrance in the hallway. Lead Jesus back to me. I will talk with him privately."

Liberius slightly surprised by Pilate's words, bowed and immediately headed for the front of the bench.

"All rise," Liberius proclaimed loudly as Pilate left the bench.

Liberius walked up to Jesus whose head was bowed and whose shoulders were slumped from the weight of the irons across his chest and around his hands. Liberius spoke quietly to him. "Follow me, Jesus," he said. "His honor wishes to afford you a private audience."

Liberius walked quickly toward the hall but then turned and waited for Jesus who was much slower moving due to the shackles about his ankles. After Jesus caught up with him, Liberius guided Jesus to the hallway where Pilate awaited his arrival. Liberius left the two men alone.

"Jesus, the Jewish High Priests want you executed," Pilate began. "They are petitioning this court to carry out that punishment. They tell me that you have been convicted in the lower court of a crime against Jewish laws—that you have committed blasphemy. Caiaphas tells me that you claim to be a god. What say you, Jesus? Are you a king? A god?" Pilate's tone and demeanor was not mocking. His countenance was kind.

"My kingdom is not of this world," Jesus responded.

"Not of this world?" Pilate repeated Jesus's words. "From that I assume that you are making no claim to a kingdom in this city or region. You are claiming no territory or power." Pilate was not interested in some other-worldly kingdom that this delusional man thought he ruled over.

Jesus remained silent but looked intensely at the Pilate.

"Is it true that you are a Galilean, that you hail from Galilee?" Pilate asked Jesus.

Jesus nodded his affirmation.

"Liberius!" Pilate called to his aide. "Escort the suspect back before the bench."

Liberius escorted Jesus back to the courtroom and announced the return of Pilate who swiftly took his seat at the bench. He banged his gavel several times.

"I am now prepared to hand down my ruling in the case of the man, Jesus of Nazareth, who stands before me," Pilate announced.

Caiaphas advanced from the prosecutor's table, eager to hear the ruling that he hoped would be in his favor and end the disruption that Jesus was causing once and for all.

"Having reviewed precedent and case law and under the rules of stare decisis, I am obliged to recognize those precedents as established law," Pilate began. "I have also interviewed the suspect who has answered my questions satisfactorily. Taking everything into account, I find no cause for guilt."

Caiaphas' eyes darkened and his face reflected his anger and disappointment. The spectators reacted in a boisterous manner causing Pilate to rise and bang his gavel repeatedly. Liberius called for silence in the court.

"Further, it is my considered opinion that the Court of Rome does not have jurisdiction in the case of Jesus of Nazareth."

More angry voices erupted.

Pilate banged his gavel again. "My decision is final," he proclaimed. "Jesus of Nazareth is a Galilean and a subject of King Herod. I find no cause for guilt but if you wish to pursue your prosecution of this man, you must take him to Herod. His fate will be decided in the court of Herod."

For once, Caiaphas was having a difficult time hiding the rage that was simmering within. Annas saw that Caiaphas was on the verge of exploding. It would not be beneficial for Caiaphas to engage in a shouting match with Pilate. They were in Pilate's court and it was Pilate who was in control—at least for the time being. Annas touched Caiaphas's arm to calm him. Caiaphas immediately recovered his stoic demeanor sensing that the fight may not be over. He accepted that they must now take the criminal to King Herod. Since it was widely known that Herod was an incompetent ruler and made a mockery of his religion by the sinful lifestyle he led, Herod was not really in a position to judge anyone. But to Herod they would go.

"Remove the accused from my courtroom at once," Pilate ordered.

As Caiaphas watched Jesus being taken from the courtroom by the Jewish guards, he felt confident that all was not lost. Ultimately, he would have his way. Herod was more interested in drinking and carousing with perverts than defending God and his laws. Herod lived in the fog of wine and the haze of opium and, if anything, would be annoyed that Pilate interrupted his debauchery with the case of Jesus of Nazareth. If Herod rejected the case, it would be remanded back to Pilate. Pilate was duty-bound and took his responsibilities seriously. His own ethics and the unrest in the street—that Caiaphas would orchestrate if necessary—would force the Roman to take the case.

The Jewish guards pushed the bound man down the front steps of the Roman Court. He fell to the ground and wretched in pain from the rope that tightened around his neck. Two guards yanked him to his feet and pushed him forward. They set out for the long walk to Herod's palace that was more than a kilometer away. Caiaphas and Annas accompanied the guards to make sure that nothing happened to prevent the next step in Jesus's journey to judgment.

Crowds of spectators watched as Jesus was marched through the streets. Mary, Jesus's mother, and Simon Peter and Mary Magdalene, two of his devotees, were devastated by Jesus's arrest. Fear over his fate was reflected on their faces. They fought their way through the crowds to stay up with the procession. Also in the crowd was Joseph of Arimathea who was shocked by the arrest of the holy man. Joseph only knew Jesus by reputation but was certain that he was a good and kind man who would do no one harm. He was intrigued by the drama that was taking place before him. Why was this gentle man arrested? What could he have been accused of and why was he chained and bound like a dangerous criminal? Joseph had many questions and the image of Jesus bound and dragged through the streets lingered in his mind.

Chapter 4
King Herod

Jesus was delivered to King Herod's massive Temple to God. The temple was more like a fortress than a place of worship. There were guards stationed atop the four turrets that protected the entry to the main courtyard of the extravagant structure. The temple was constructed of imported white marble which gleamed in the noon-day sun. After stating their business at the main gate, the Jewish guards were allowed to enter into Herod's courtyard with the bound and chained Jesus. The courtyard was vast and crowded, a virtual bazaar with scores of vendors and shoppers. The interior of the temple matched the opulence of the exterior with its décor of exotic marble and inlaid gold. At the rear of the courtyard was an ornate throne on a raised platform where King Herod conducted public business when his mood dictated.

On this day, Herod would not be pleased when he received word that Pontius Pilate had referred a criminal matter to him. Herod was no more a fan of Pilate than Pilate was of him. Herod was suffering from an aching head from too much wine the evening before. That last thing he wanted to hear was that the arrogant Roman, who presumed to have authority over him, had handed down a task to him.

The captain of the temple guards asked Herod's trusted man servant, Ezekial, to inform the King that he had been requested by Pilate to oversee the penalty phase of a case in which a man, a Jewish man and therefore one of his subjects, had been convicted in the court of the Jewish Council. The guard insisted that the matter was urgent and that a quick resolution was needed. Apparently, it was Caiaphas who had found the man guilty. Although the sun had risen hours before, when Ezekial approached his private living quarters, Herod still snored away, sleeping off the celebration from the night before which mirrored the activities of the vast majority of Herod's evenings. Although Herod had constructed the Temple to God, everything that happened in that temple was for the pleasure and entertainment of Herod and certainly not for the worship of god.

Ezekial quietly slipped into the large sleeping chambers of King Herod. The room was nearly pitch black, shuttered against the bright Jerusalem sunlight. He observed that there were two chamber ladies in the King's room. One was in his bed and another was on the floor next to his bed. Ezekial carefully stepped over the naked woman on the floor as he neared the king's raised bed and bent down close to him.

"Your worship," Ezekial whispered in his practiced stage whisper.

The king began to stir, moaning his displeasure at being woken from his slumber.

"Your majesty, Governor Pilate has sent over a man, one of our kind, for your judgment," Ezekial told him.

Herod's bulging dark eyes blinked open. A scowl immediately settled on his face.

"What on god's earth are you screaming in my ear about?" Herod roared.

"Sir, Pilate has sent over a convicted man. He was convicted by Caiaphas and the Jewish Council," Ezekial said.

"Why doesn't the honorable Governor of Jerusalem do his own job?" Herod demanded.

"Apparently, Pilate has found that the case lies within your own jurisdiction, sire," Ezekial responded. "He is one of your subjects."

"I thought the pompous Pilate thought all the Jews in Jerusalem were his subjects, including me," Herod replied.

"I pray that the governor of Jerusalem is not that bereft of the truth," Ezekial responded, fully aware of the contention that existed between the two men.

"Who is this man?" Herod asked.

"His name is Jesus of Nazareth," Ezekial replied.

Herod's eyes lit up in recognition.

"Jesus Christ, the man who claims to be the real king of the Jews" Herod responded. "This will be quite a royal experience, Ezekial. Do you think Jesus Christ expects me to bow to him?"

***

The Jewish guards surrounded Jesus who stood at the foot of King Herod's platform awaiting the King's appearance. A small crowd of curiosity seekers began to grow around the guards and their captive. Jesus had only been in Jerusalem a mere six days, but already his reputation had spread. Most Jews did not believe the accounts they heard about him—that he was the long-awaited Messiah and the Son of God. Most thought it was absurd. Looking at the bound, slender man who was surrounded by armed guards, he seemed anything but all-powerful. He certainly didn't appear to be a god in most people's eyes. Those who were skeptical to begin with felt vindicated in their original assessment of him. Being bound and facing a penalty to be handed down by Herod was well-deserved—the man was committing blasphemy with the claims of holiness that swirled around him. However, there was a small but a growing number of citizens who began to feel the man's spirit and to believe in him, some were already devoted to him. To those who believed in him, it was a sad sight to see him bound, shackled and bloodied.

When he finally appeared, Herod was donned in an elaborate tunic of gold brocade and jewels—fit for a king, of course. In stark comparison, Jesus's white garb was now filthy from the dusty streets and from his own splattered blood. The contrast would not be lost on Herod. Herod had entered the courtyard from the temple's interior to the ringing of gentle hand-held bells. His demeanor would prove to be in sharp contrast to the softness of the muted chimes that marked his entrance to the courtyard.

Silence fell over the crowd as Herod's appearance was always an intimidating event. He slurped a drink of wine from his goblet and as he plopped it down on the stand next to him, the goblet toppled over and the remaining wine spilled and spread out on Herod's platform. Herod stared at the red wine and then immediately at Jesus, the accused man before him. Troubling images of devils and fiends ran through Herod's mind. Herod's face colored as he screamed at Ezekial to have the slaves clean up the spill. On no occasion would Herod ever talk directly to a slave, unless it was a comely woman who he ordered to his bed.

"Why do your slaves, hesitate, Ezekial?" Herod demanded.

Ezekial shoved several male slaves toward the spill and ordered them to clean it up. A female slave hurried to the spot with rags to sop up the wine.

Finally, Herod faced the man who had been convicted in the Jewish High Council. As he stared at the lithe figure before him, Herod noticed the pious Caiaphas was emerging from the crowd. Caiaphas, with his large staff in hand, stood before Herod expectantly. Herod nodded to Ezekial who escorted Caiaphas up the platform to speak privately with the King.

Caiaphas made sure to bow deeply to Herod. He did not want to fuel the resentment that Herod felt for Caiaphas and the other high priests. Herod was aware that they disapproved of his behavior and had no respect for him. But Caiaphas needed Herod now and it was essential that everything go smoothly. The wise and experienced Caiaphas was quite certain that Herod, who was cowardly beneath his outward bluster, would not chance the criticism that would result from sentencing Jesus, a fellow Jew, to death. In the off-chance he did, he would fail to carry it out. It was crucial that Pilate be forced to rule on the case. Caiaphas was sure that he was reading Herod correctly when he concluded that the dunce king would return Jesus to Pilate and allow the Roman to kill the Jew. It would be a safe tactic and would permit Herod to shirk his duties and a difficult aspect of the responsibilities of his position.

"What brings you to my court on this sun-filled day, Caiaphas?" Herod began the conversation.

"Your majesty, it is a matter of utmost importance," Caiaphas responded. "This man, Jesus of Nazareth, has committed the vilest crime against our God and our laws."

Herod smirked. "This is Jesus Christ, is it not?" Herod asked without allowing Caiaphas to answer. "This is the man who just recently wandered into our city and claimed to be a god, is it not?"

"The offense he committed is even worse than that, if you can imagine, sire," Caiaphas said. He leaned a bit closer to Herod as if the words he was about to speak would summon Satan himself. "He claims to be the Son of God, our Living God," Caiaphas whispered to the Jewish monarch.

"A crime against God to be sure. And what is he convicted of?" Herod asked.

"Blasphemy," Caiaphas answered simply.

"I understand that Pilate threw the case out," Herod snarled. "Is that true?"

"Yes, sire," Caiaphas said, bowing again and careful not to reveal too much information too soon in order to draw the chicken-hearted ruler in.

"I am sure I can handle what Pilate could not!" Herod proclaimed. "And... what is the prescribed punishment. A lashing... time in a rat-infested cell?"

"As I am sure you may recall, sir," Caiaphas began as he readied the hammer that he would bring down on Herod's royal crown. "Our laws require that on conviction of blasphemy, the most vile and contemptible crime imaginable, that the punishment is death."

"Death?" Herod asked rather loudly—loud enough to stir the attention of several attendants nearby.

Caiaphas did not respond, only remained in a respectable bow.

"I see. Well, that is fine and acceptable—you… you know God's laws," Herod said, rather tentatively.

Caiaphas bowed and walked back a few steps, ready to depart from the platform.

"Oh, Caiaphas," Herod called to him. "Before I follow through on this sentencing, I am duty-bound to ensure that the conviction of Jesus of Nazareth is a valid one. You know, reflecting on the matter, I am beginning to have some doubts. I will interview Jesus myself after which I will make my determination."

"Of course, sir," Caiaphas responded, silently taking note of Herod's reneging.

"And Caiaphas" Herod continued, "If I find that he is not guilty of the crime of blasphemy, I will remand him back to the court of the Romans who shall either mete out the charges of a lesser crime or decide to agree with your finding and hand down the… the punishment of which you speak."

Caiaphas grew serious. "There is no doubt, your majesty," he said. "The man committed blasphemy on multiple occasions."

Herod had lost his patience. He rose towering over the diminutive Caiaphas. "I am the King of the Jews and I will make that determination! You, Caiaphas, are a Pharisee and a pious busybody. I will not tolerate your attempt to override my authority."

Although, at first blush, it would appear as though Caiaphas lost the battle of words with Herod, he had actually won. He knew that Herod would never have the temerity to execute

Jesus. It would fall to Pilate, who was thorough and dedicated in the dispatch of his duties, to execute Jesus.

Caiaphas was excused as Herod descended the short flight of stairs from the platform to the ground. He was now eye to eye with Jesus.

"So, this is the great Jesus Christ," Herod began, closely eyeing Jesus whose head was slightly bowed.

Jesus did not respond.

"Are you a king, Jesus?" Herod asked. "If you are, what is your source of power? Where is your kingdom?" Herod continued, then hesitated for a few moments. "Or, are you more than a king?"

Again, Jesus remained silent.

"Are you, as some contend, the Messiah?" Herod continued. "Was your birth foretold? "

Caiaphas and Annas, surrounded by their scribes, advanced a few steps forward from the crowd. They wanted to keep up the pressure and not allow the nonserious Herod who was known far and wide for his frivolity to make a mockery of the case. However, they did not mind when Herod and his aides began to make a mockery of Jesus himself.

"I understand that you are capable of simply amazing feats, miracles in fact I am told," Herod continued. "I can only judge your godly abilities if you demonstrate your prowess." Herod's mouth turned down in a smirk. "Show me a miracle!"

Caiaphas felt it was an opportune time to speak up. "There are rumors that he can heal the sick just by laying his hands on the afflicted," he offered.

"That's nothing, Caiaphas," Herod responded. "I have heard accounts that he can make the blind see, the lame walk and even raise the dead from their graves!" Herod approached Jesus. "Look at me, man!"

Jesus looked up at Herod who, like anyone else who was the focus of his gaze, immediately felt the intensity and depth of the man. Herod took a few steps back but he did not back off from his verbal assault of the holy man.

"I want to be entertained!" Herod taunted. "Show me a miracle!"

Jesus just looked at Herod, his shoulders slumped from the weight of his chains, physically exhausted by the abuse he had suffered over the last day and night.

"Ah! I know the problem!" Herod shouted in a mocking tone. "Look at the king's robe. It is splashed with mud and streaked with blood. No king, not even I, could fulfill his duties in such a ragged and soiled garment. This king needs a robe that befits his lofty and dynamic position!"

"Ezekial!" Herod boomed. "Deliver to Jesus here apparel appropriate for a Messiah. The Persian rug in the parlor would be ideal. It is colored in red and purple and embellished with gold. Fit for a king! Dispatch the slaves to gather it up and place it upon our new king's shoulders."

Ezekial ordered two of his slaves to bring the carpet to the courtyard just as Herod had ordered. The two slaves soon appeared in the courtyard with the rug much to the glee and delight of Herod and his court.

"Place the robe on King Jesus!" Ezekial demanded.

The two slaves approached Jesus and hoisted the heavy carpet onto the bound and chained Jesus. The weight of the rug added to the burden from which Jesus's body was already suffering. His shoulders slumped further down under the additional strain.

"Now, ladies and gentlemen," Herod boomed. "Be ready to be amazed!"

Jesus, near collapse, just stood and gazed at Herod. But Herod wasn't done with his fun yet.

"I feel like some wine, Ezekial. You know I spilled mine," Herod said. "Take this pitcher of water to his highness so he can turn it into wine." Herod motioned toward a large pitcher of water nearby.

After it was clear that no miracles were forthcoming, Herod continued his lampoon.

"It seems as though the king is not as gifted as we have heard," Herod said. He and his court had a good laugh. Suddenly Herod became serious and the laughter quieted down at once.

"Caiaphas, I have reached my decision," Herod announced. "I have determined that this man, this pretender, is a fraud to be sure. But what's more, he is not in his right mind. I find him guilty only of being demented. What a shame he has no real powers. If he did, perhaps he could lay hands on his royal head and heal himself."

Herod turned amid the laughter and cajoling of his court. He ascended the stairs and sat on his throne. Jesus had grown weak, his knees buckling under the strain. He slumped to the ground.

"Remove him!" Herod bellowed. "I find no cause for his confinement or punishment. Caiaphas, I order you take him back to Pilate and appeal to his court. If he should see fit to mete out the punishment as you suggest, that is his decision but I have no part in it. Get the man out of my sight!" Herod ordered. "And guards… don't let him take my carpet away with him," he added much to the delight of his giddy court.

Caiaphas nodded to Meshek who ordered his guards to once again surround Jesus. They threw off the carpet and pulled him to his feet, prodding him toward the large gate of the courtyard. More beleaguered than ever, it was becoming more and more difficult for Jesus to walk but he had no choice. The guards surrounding Jesus were followed out of Herod's courtyard by Caiaphas and Annas and their scribes. They would not miss a moment of Jesus's march toward his end. The carpet that was cast off from Jesus was picked up by one of Herod's court attendants. The attendant's hand had been deformed from an accident years before. After holding the carpet, the attendant was astonished to see that his hand was healed. When Herod heard of the phenomenon, he forbade the attendant to speak of the incident or risk death.

The city was now embraced in the afternoon sun. The vendors had retired for the day and the children were home with their mothers. It was quieter now as Jesus was once again pushed and shoved down the narrow, cobblestone streets back to the Roman Court. It seemed as though no one could properly dispatch of Jesus Christ. He presented a problem for everyone. The Jewish High Priests wanted to execute him for his crimes but did not have the authority. Herod had the authority but was reluctant to exercise it because of his cowardly nature and innate fear of criticism, although he cloaked this timidity in disdain. Pilate did not believe the case belonged in his court and did not feel the crime warranted the death sentence. However, Pilate was the only one of the three who had final authority and had exercised it in the past. Caiaphas knew that Pilate was his best chance to permanently eliminate his problem.

As Jesus moved along laden with his bound hands, his chains and the rope tied around his neck, his step was slow. His body cried for rest and his exhaustion was near unbearable. But the guards were merciless, pushing him and prodding him along unconcerned that the man was near collapse. Caiaphas and Annas, followed by a group of loyal scribes, walked behind to ensure that the important delivery for Pilate was accomplished. Although the streets were not crowded as they were earlier, as Jesus and his guards walked along a crowd began to gather behind them. There were jeers and cat-calls directed at Jesus—some brave souls who felt buoyed by tormenting a tortured man. Some of Jesus's close devotees were in the crowds as well. His mother Mary, Simon Peter, Mary Magdalene and John walked in tandem with him whispering to him, expressing their love and support for. Jesus was able to muster a smile when he his eyes met the soft dark eyes of his mother.

Joseph of Arimathea had departed for his legal office after he had watched the strange site of Jesus bound and in chains leaving the Roman Court. After Joseph arrived at his office, he became involved in some urgent legal matters and thoughts of Jesus faded from his mind. Joseph's office was located on the second floor of a sand-colored limestone building that hugged a narrow alley-like passage way that was located just a stone's throw from the Roman Court. Joseph was poring over a scroll that contained the sworn statements of witnesses who were scheduled to appear at an important trial in which Joseph was the defending attorney. The noise from a commotion that stirred in the pathway beneath his office drew his attention. He frowned as he rushed to the window to pull in the shutters to drown out the noise. Just as he was pulling one of the shutters to, he noticed that the Jewish guards were once again escorting the bound and chained Jesus back toward the Roman Court.

"What are they doing to this man?" Joseph asked himself. "How is he able to cope with this ordeal?"

Joseph allowed the shutters to stay open as he craned his neck and watched Jesus being led to the Roman Court. He watched as long as he could until the strange procession was out of his sight.

Joseph immediately returned to the case he was preparing for but was distracted. The image of Jesus in his ragged tunic, soiled with mud and stained with blood, remained in his mind. The more Joseph tried to concentrate, the less he was able to. Thoughts of Jesus lingered in his mind. Finally, Joseph gave up. He rolled up his scrolls and tossed them in a basket on the floor that was already stuffed with many others. Joseph was a successful lawyer and had a robust business. He did not need one more case; in fact, he had been forced to turn some new cases down. Joseph decided to run down to the Court to learn what Jesus was being accused of. It was just a matter of curiosity and would only take him a short while. He would be back at work within the hour.

Joseph rushed down the narrow pathway that led to the main street and then to the entrance of the Roman Court. The guards at the door recognized Joseph as an officer of the court and immediately allowed him entry. As he quietly walked into the courtroom, he noticed some of the same people he had seen earlier in the crowd that morning. He did not know it at the time but they were devout followers of Jesus and that pleasant looking woman with the intense eyes was his mother.

Joseph walked forward and sat a few rows behind Jesus who stood before the bench. After just a short time, Liberius appeared and ordered everyone in the court to rise as Pilate entered to take the bench. Joseph was certain he detected a look on Pilate's face that seemed to be a blend of surprise and disappointment when he saw that Jesus was standing before him. Joseph had served for the defense in many cases in Pilate's Court. It was out of character for the usually stoic Pilate to reveal any emotions in the presence of a defendant.

Much to Joseph's surprise, Caiaphas emerged from the back of the courtroom and stood adjacent to Jesus.

"Your honor," Caiaphas began. "King Herod returned Jesus to your court. He rejected the case. I believe it is Roman law that this court hears any cases that cannot be resolved within the Jewish community. Am I correct, sir?"

Pilate was slow to answer as he glared at Caiaphas. In the end, he chose to ignore the Jewish High Priest's question.

"Who represents you, Jesus?"

"No one," Jesus answered softly.

A pang went through Joseph's heart. His soul cried for the man.

Chapter 5
Pilate's Problem

Standing before Pilate's bench Jesus was withering from the physical abuse he had been subjected to all day. His legs were feeling the strain and his knees were growing weak. Finally, his body could take no more and he fell exhausted to his knees and bowed his head in silent prayer.

"What are the formal charges against this man and who shall submit them?" Pilate asked the open court. Pilate already knew the answers to both his questions. But just as Pilate expected those in his court to follow its rules, he subjected himself to those very same standards. Now that the case of Jesus of Nazareth had landed back in his court and there were no further options, Pilate was being forced to hear the case. He still felt convinced that the outcome would not result in the execution of Jesus. There were always many twists and turns in any case. This one would be no exception and the law—the Roman law—was on his side. Pilate would watch the proceedings carefully and not allow Caiaphas to skirt any of the court's rules or violate any Roman laws in his prosecution of Jesus. Pilate held the strong belief that Caiaphas would see the conviction of Jesus at any cost—even breaking the law himself. Caiaphas would not do that in Pilate's court.

Caiaphas once again emerged from the crowded room as the spectators stepped aside to allow him passage. Caiaphas was dressed all in black and wore a tall silk rabbi's miter that denoted his lofty position as a Jewish High Priest. He made his way to the prosecutor's table, all the while eyeing the accused who was still on his knees in front of the bench. It was official, Caiaphas would be the head prosecutor in the case against Jesus. The room was silent as the diminutive figure of the Jewish High Priest advanced toward the bench. The click-clack of his staff on the wooden floor was the only sound in the large room.

"Caiaphas, there you are once again," Pilate began, the frustration in his voice was apparent. Although he knew it was now inevitable, Pilate decided that before he allowed the formal charges against Jesus to be read into the official court record, he would taunt Caiaphas for a bit. "What did his highness, the most royal King Herod, decree in the case against Jesus?"

"Your Honor, King Herod declared that this man's crime does not fall under his jurisdiction," Caiaphas explained although his response was a lie of omission by failing to reveal that Herod had deemed the case to have no merit.

Pilate glared at Caiaphas. There was something fundamental about the rabbi that Pilate found reprehensible. Pilate felt that underneath his pious exterior, there existed a narrow, mean-spirited man.

"Is your King shrinking from his duties, afraid to judge a fellow Jew?" Pilate asked.

Caiaphas displayed his usual cool exterior and refrained from answering Pilate's obviously sardonic question. He would take his verbal abuse knowing that the scrupulous Pilate would see his duties through.

"What is your business here, Caiaphas?" Pilate asked, slightly annoyed that he'd been unsuccessful at angering the rabbi.

"Your honor," Caiaphas addressed the court, "I, Caiaphas, Jewish High Priest of the Jewish Council, bring to your court formal charges against Jesus of Nazareth."

"And what are these charges and what evidence supports them?" Pilate asked.

"The High Priests of the Jewish Council have found Jesus of Nazareth guilty of the highest-most crime against Jewish laws, that of blasphemy," Caiaphas replied.

"And what is your evidence?" Pilate probed Caiaphas.

"The Council acted as Jesus's defense. We asked him to testify to his innocence but he would not," Caiaphas responded.

"The charges that had been brought against him by others in our community were all consistent with the commission of blasphemy. He refused to deny one and all."

"Provide the court with the individual crimes," Pilate ordered.

Caiaphas consulted the scroll that he now carried with him. His hands trembled slightly as he unfurled the document.

"Your honor, I submit to the Roman court the following charges against this man," Caiaphas responded. "Count one, blasphemy, in that the accused, Jesus of Nazareth, claimed to be the Son of the Living God. Count two, blasphemy, in that the accused, Jesus of Nazareth, claimed to be the Messiah. Count three, blasphemy, in that the accused, Jesus of Nazareth, threatened to destroy the holy temple and with his divine powers rebuild it in three days. Count four, blasphemy, in that the accused, Jesus of Nazareth, claimed to possess the ability to beget miracles that could only be associated with God. Count five, fraud, in that the accused, Jesus of Nazareth, used lies and trickery to convince his followers of his godly powers. Count six, betrayal of fundamental Jewish laws that forbid the forming of a separate ministry that lures Jews to follow it and abandon their religion; thus, leading them to sin against our laws."

"Are you quite finished?" Pilate asked.

Caiaphas bowed. "Yes, your honor," Caiaphas responded. "These are the charges to which the Council found Jesus of Nazareth guilty."

"Who defended him at the Council?" Pilate asked.

"In the Jewish Council, sire," Caiaphas replied, "charges are brought against an accused by the public. They are the prosecutor. The Jewish High Priests served as defense."

Pilate's eyebrows arched in pique. "You, Caiaphas, were his defense?" he asked not expecting an answer. "I'm sure you gave him every benefit of your legal expertise. But it does seem odd that you are now vigorously prosecuting him. In fact, you seem to be licking your chops, if I may be so crude. But, of course, I am not fully cognizant of your laws. It seems you had the man coming and going. And if it was your mission to persecute him—pardon me, prosecute him, that is—if appears he may have had a very weak defense. You must admit that it does seem duplicitous."

A slight reddening of Caiaphas' checks was barely detectible. Pilate was unnerving him but he wasn't about to allow his annoyance to show. The trial could be quite long and Caiaphas was determined not to lose sight of his goal by allowing his resentment for Pilate to become an obstacle to that end.

"Sir, as you indicate yourself, you are not familiar with Jewish law," Caiaphas began, his face stoic and his voice strong yet respectful. "If I may, I would like to enlighten you about the subject that you have presented. If you will indulge me, Judge Pilate, I will take a few moments to explain the structure of the court. I, as Jewish High Priest, am a trusted and honored member of the Council. As such, I have sworn to uphold the law and treat the accused who come before the Council with the utmost respect and fairness. And…"

"Fairness is one thing, Caiaphas," Pilate interrupted. "How can the same man—especially one who holds obvious bias against the accused—be capable of both defending and prosecuting the accused? You see, I'm just trying to understand your laws which so far I would venture to say are not very understandable."

The court stirred. There were a few stifled laughs which compelled Pilate to bring the gavel down on his bench a few times. "Silence!"

Caiaphas locked eyes with Pilate for a few moments.

"If I may continue," Caiaphas said, as he bowed slightly to Pilate. "I am ordained from God as a rabbi in his temple. As such, it is impossible for me to allow any personal opinions I may have about a person to interfere in the dispatch of my duties. If I were not scrupulous and honest in carrying out my responsibilities and adhering to my obligations, God himself would remove me from my position."

"God would do that?" Pilate asked, a slight smile curling his lips.

Some in the gallery were close to laughter but thought better of it as Pilate glared from the bench.

"Do I have to worry about God removing me from the bench?" Pilate asked.

"Only if my god is yours," Caiaphas responded quietly

"Point well taken, Caiaphas," Pilate replied. "So, we are to assume that since you are ordained from on high that you do not have your own motivations whether defending or prosecuting the same suspect. In other words you are incapable of any biases and only seek the truth. Is that correct?"

"Yes, sir, that is an accurate description of the burden that I have been given from God. And, in the case of Jesus of Nazareth, I have found the truth."

"So you say, Caiaphas," Pilate replied, "so you say. Now if I might have a moment to explain Roman law. It is required that the accused of a serious crime be tried in open court. It is the court's responsibility to see that all subjects receive a fair hearing, a right of every citizen. The prosecution must provide evidence and witnesses that prove his guilt. The defense must respond to the indictment and present evidence and witnesses that counter the charges. A jury of the accused's peers will render final judgment. And I, as judge, will hand down the punishment as prescribed by Roman law."

"In all respect, sire," Caiaphas began, "In this case all that—a prosecution and defense and a trial by jury—is not at all necessary. You see...."

Pilate, anger and resentment coloring his face, would not allow Caiaphas to finish his thought. "You do not tell me what is or is not necessary in my court!" Pilate's voice was raised to a timbre that rattled even the seasoned Liberius. Pilate worked at controlling the rage that simmered within for a moment then continued in a calm voice. "Jesus of Nazareth shall have a trial. It is the law and it is his right."

Caiaphas remained silent but even the drunken subjects standing in the back of the courtroom awaiting sentencing knew that Caiaphas was enraged by this unexpected outcome. Dismayed as he was about this turn of events, he was confident that Jesus would be found guilty and that Pilate would have no option but to sentence the holy man to death as required by Jewish Law.

Pilate then focused on Jesus standing before him with head bowed.

"Jesus of Nazareth, you have heard the charges brought before this court from the prosecution represented by your former defender the Pharisee, Caiaphas," Pilate began. "Now, we must hear from the defendant. How do you plead to these charges, Jesus?"

Jesus looked up at Pilate. The intensity from Jesus's eyes that had jarred Pilate at his first court appearance had not lessened. Pilate sensed that Jesus was a match for Caiaphas's venom—in fact he sensed that the defendant had strength beyond that of the Jewish High Priest.

For the first time since he returned to the court, Jesus spoke. His voice was soft and sincere. "Only that those are his words," he responded.

There was a stir in the gallery, hushed voices spread throughout the room.

Pilate crashed his gavel down. "I'll have no editorial comments from the spectators or they shall be banned from my court!" Pilate bellowed.

Pilate felt a dark cloud was forming over him. He was beginning to sense that this case could burgeon out of control and into something that was beyond what it ostensibly seemed to be. His instincts told him that he needed to take control of the proceeding so that it would not come back to haunt him. He would soon be able to leave this sweltering desert and return to his temperate homeland. He did not want anything to stand in his way, especially such a minor case such as the one against Jesus—a wretched, well-intended holy man who was only attempting to spread the word of his god in his own way. If Caiaphas pursued this case, if he actually would follow through on his contention that the punishment for the crimes was death, it would be he—Caiaphas—who would be held accountable for overreach. Pilate's job was to see that there was compliance to the law in this or any proceeding in his court. By doing so, there would be no controversy about his role—no blame would fall upon his shoulders. In Pilate's court, Jesus would be given every opportunity for a proper defense. Pilate's sentiment led him to press the accused.

"You offer no defense, man?" Pilate shouted. "If you are in your right mind, would you not have a counsel standing there at your side?"

"My counsel is God, kind sir," he said.

Pilate smirked. The man must be daft, he thought. He doesn't seem to understand the proceedings. If there was ever an accused man who needed counsel, it was obviously this man. "So, how is this God telling you to plead?"

There was laughter followed by the pounding of Pilate's gavel.

"Jesus, since you informed the court that you have no defender, I assume you choose to defend yourself in this proceeding?" Pilate asked.

"I offer no defense of myself," Jesus replied.

Pilate's eyes flashed. The man did not have a defender and refused to defend himself! What was Pilate to do? Perhaps Jesus of Nazareth was not aware of the consequences.

"Do you realize what is at stake in this case, Jesus?" Pilate asked, barely able to control his anger and frustration. "Do you realize that Caiaphas is seeking the death penalty on the charges against you? Do you?"

"So you say, sir," Jesus responded.

"I am charged with conducting my court in a fair and lawful manner. Roman law demands that there be a balance of opportunity in any proceeding held in this venue for both the prosecution and defense to present their cases," Pilate said in frustration to the court at large. "Roman law dictates that any defendant facing prosecution in its courts must have legal representation. If the accused does not have an attorney, he is expected to defend himself."

Pilate focused on Caiaphas. "So you see Caiaphas, not only has Jesus violated Jewish law according to you at least, he has violated Roman law by refusing a defense," Pilate said.

"I supposed I could threaten Jesus with contempt of court for refusing to provide any defense at all but I have the strong sense that if the threat of death is hanging over one's head, the risk of contempt of court would be as insignificant as a mosquito on the tail of an elephant."

Pilate sighed deeply, signaling his total frustration.

"With no defense, no trepidation about or even a basic understanding of the consequences of a conviction by the defendant, how on earth am I to see that justice is done?" Pilate asked no one in particular.

All the while, Joseph who had again felt drawn to the gallery, watched as Jesus's plight seemed to worsen by the minute. He feared that Jesus could be overwhelmed by the legal process and, even if he was an innocent man, could ultimately and unfairly be found guilty if no defense was presented. It could not be ignored that Caiaphas was an influential figure and a revered religious leader. Any jury chosen to hear Jesus's case would be affected by Caiaphas's powerful position. The repercussions of crossing him were well known among the public. There mere presence of the diminutive Pharisee was intimidating.

Joseph was a cautious man but he was beginning to feel something within him urging him to reach out to Jesus. But for the moment, he decided not to give into those stirrings. He was an attorney of good standing and taking sides on a controversial case such as the one against Jesus could damage his reputation and his career. Joseph had come a long way from his humble beginnings as a law clerk and defending a figure like Jesus who was apparently hated by the Jewish Council would be risking a lot.

For the time being, the trial of Jesus and his plight remained Pilate's problem. Pilate sighed and declared the court in recess until the next morning. He needed time to research the problem that faced him. He needed to learn what options the judge of a Roman Court had when a defendant refused to defend himself and remained unresponsive to the court's counsel. It was time for more help from Titus.

***

The courtroom cleared, with Jesus's mother and his followers among the last to leave. Joseph stood in the shadows at the back of the courtroom and observed the apparent misery and fear that Jesus's loved ones were suffering. He silently wished that he could stop their pain. Jesus was taken from the courtroom by two Roman soldiers who treated him just as brutally at day's end as they had during the morning session. The hope flashed through Joseph's mind that the court and jury would have more mercy on Jesus than did the cruel soldiers. As soon as Jesus was marched away, Mary, Simon Peter and Mary Magdalene left the courthouse. Joseph watched them walk by and felt great empathy for their plight.

Joseph left the courthouse to return to his office. Although it was late, the work was still waiting for him and he felt duty-bound to fulfill his daily obligations. He walked quickly down the small pathway that led to his office. A balmy breeze was blowing up, finally providing relief from the oppressive heat. He thought of Jesus again and hoped that he might rest comfortably during the night. Tomorrow promised to be just as harrowing for him as today. What, Joseph wondered, would be in store for the humble, peaceful man who obviously meant no harm to anyone?

Although Joseph had nothing but good intentions and felt fully committed to completing his work, he found his mind drifting as he dug into his scrolls and documents. His thoughts returned to the Roman courtroom. Joseph was a fast study and had quickly noted that there was an adversarial relationship between Pilate and Caiaphas. Joseph was not surprised by the revelation. Both men were powerful and prideful—one from his governmental position and one from his spiritual role.

After struggling with the legal issues before him for close to an hour, Joseph finally gave up. He flung the documents and scrolls off his desk. There was always tomorrow. He knew the remedy for catching up with his work the next day was to stay clear of the courtroom. But Joseph knew deep down that he would only be fooling himself if he vowed not to visit the court and learn the next step in Jesus's trial. Joseph sighed and began to close up his shop. He needed to go home and rest. Although he had not put in many hours of work, he felt extremely fatigued—more so than if he had worked his usual ten hour day. The prospect of Jesus's fate had been physically and emotionally draining.

As Joseph began to pull the wooden shutters over on his window, he stopped for a moment. It was now early evening and the moon and starts were beginning to appear. He smiled as he saw what looked to be a shooting star in the sky. He felt an unexpected comfort from the experience. That night Joseph slept very soundly. But he dreamed. He dreamed of happy children and flowers and light—a soft beautiful light that covered everything.

***

After Pilate left the courtroom, he headed for his chambers. Liberius, who followed him, was instructed to locate Titus and have him come immediately to Pilate's office. Pilate did not want to spend the evening away from his family speculating about what pratfalls may lay ahead as the trial of Jesus proceeded. Of course, he didn't mind piling a matter onto Titus that would require him to work through the night. That was the reality of their respective roles. Pilate had been impressed with the research Titus conducted on the question of appropriate jurisdiction for the case. Although it had not worked out exactly the way Pilate had planned and hoped, Titus had still done a thorough job and had come up with possible reasons to dismiss the case, declare a mistrial or, if it went that far, to have a verdict reversed in the superior court in Rome. Today, Pilate needed to discuss with Titus what options he had when a defendant refused to defend himself or ask for counsel.

Pilate removed his outer cloak, the dark blue official robe he wore in court. He would be much more comfortable for his meeting with Titus in the loose tunic that he wore underneath it. Pilate poured himself a goblet of wine and took a large gulp. It was dusk and Pilate's stomach told him it was past his dinnertime. Pilate yelled to Liberius.

"Liberius!"

The dutiful Liberius who was never more than a step away, soon peeked his head in the door.

"Sir?"

"Have one of the attendants bring me some cheese and fruit," Pilate told him. "I am near starvation."

"Right away, your honor," Liberius responded. "Titus is on his way, sir."

Liberius bowed slightly and scurried out the door. In just a few moments, a man servant brought in a platter of figs and goat's cheese.

Pilate dug into the delectable treat before he sat down. And just as he sunk into his comfortable leather chair that was lined with sheep's wool, there was a light rapping on the door. Ah, Titus, he thought.

"Come!" Pilate called out.

Titus entered and bowed to Pilate. This time, Pilate offered Titus a seat across from him. Pilate immediately got to the point.

"Titus, I need your worthy legal mind to delve into another matter," Pilate said.

"Of course, sir," Titus responded. "What issue do you need me to pursue?"

"The trial of this Jewish demi-god—or whatever the man thinks he is—is beginning to grate on my soul," Pilate began. Pilate gestured dramatically with his hand. "It's one disturbing issue after another with this man."

"I heard that Herod rejected his case," Titus said. He looked down and sighed. "I am sorry that my research did not prove out."

"For god's sake, Titus, you weren't the problem," Pilate replied. "Your research was accurate. It was the crazy King of the Jews who supplied the bump in the road. Herod was too cowardly to take on a case involving one of his own people. So it came back to rest with me, of course. I am the only responsible one within shouting distance, Liberius. Perhaps I should be King of the Jews."

When Pilate laughed at his own characterization of Herod and the absurdity that he should be the King of the Jews, it signaled to Titus that it was acceptable for him to join in the merriment. Titus did find Pilate's remark quite funny. But soon Pilate quickly grew serious again.

"Titus, I want you to study the law books to learn what my options and responsibilities are when a defendant refuses to be defended," Pilate said. "Jesus of Nazareth is nothing if he is not stubborn. He refuses to be defended or offer his own defense. Yet I am charged with the responsibility of seeing to it that all the cases before my court are tried in a neutral manner, without bias and in an environment where both sides of an issue are evenly and publically aired."

Pilate slammed his goblet down and sloshed the last of his wine out onto his table. "What am I to do with this man?" Pilate asked. "Oh, almost forgot," Pilate added mockingly. "He does have defense after all. He claims god is his counsel."

Chapter 6
Titus, Law Clerk

Titus left Pilate's office after a lengthy meeting. He carried with him his heavy parchment book in which he had taken notes that outlined what Pilate had expected him to learn. Titus was a young man but the sun was setting and he was feeling the fatigue of the long hours he had spent in court. Titus was also famished, his appetite particularly piqued as he sat before Pilate while he snacked on cheese and fruit.

As weary and hungry as he was, Titus's day was far from over. Pilate had piled a huge task on him at the end of the day when he had envisioned himself relaxing at the springs and joining some friends for a late supper at a favorite dining hall. But that was not meant to be. Pilate wanted answers by the time he arrived in the morning. Titus would never voice his resentment, but he pictured the well-rested Pilate arriving the next morning and himself near collapse from overwork and lack of sleep. But any resentment he held for Pilate soon dissipated. Pilate was an important man and had a huge responsibility. Although the Prefect of Judaea was demanding and imperial in demeanor, he demonstrated trust in Titus's work. And even if Pilate was short on gratitude, Titus knew that Pilate appreciated his effort and the results of his work. Pilate was a good man and an excellent administrator. Titus was proud of the position he held in the Roman court and grateful that Pilate trusted in him.

Titus dropped his heavy notebook off in his small office that was located on the far side of the court opposite Pilate's chambers. On his way there, Titus took a slight detour so that he would pass by the kitchen. He peered into the large kitchen and was startled by a noise. The food there was for Pilate and his guests and officers of the court, not for lowly clerks like Titus. But hunger drove him. He smiled when he saw the source of the noise wasn't a cook who would order him out; rather, it was a house cat that was chasing a good-sized rat.

Titus sneaked into the darkened room and headed for the pantry that held fruit and cheese. Titus felt like a thief—which in essence he was—but Titus was famished. Had he asked permission, Pilate would have allowed him to gather some food for himself but Titus was too shy and humble to ask for such a favor. Titus knew his place and was happy to have it. A small mouse was in the pantry, feasting on a chunk of cheese. Titus chased the mouse off and from the clatter that sounded from the rear of the pantry, he knew that the mouse had family and friends. Titus grabbed the piece of cheese that the mouse had chewed off from the large wheel. He threw the cheese and a crust of bread from another shelf into the pouch he carried at his waist. He saw a generous pile of grapes that had somewhat withered in the heat but were still edible and threw them in his carrier as well. Titus took a leaky and battered looking wooden goblet and dipped it into a small vat of stagnant water. The drink would be warm but at least it would be wet and could help wash down his meal.

Back in the small space that served as Titus's office, he ate every bit of food that he had taken. It wasn't enough to truly sate his hunger but it would tide him over. It was actually better that he not have a huge meal lest he'd become groggy. After drinking down the last bit of warm water, he was ready to begin his night's work.

Titus picked up his notebook and began to scan his notes. Pilate was specific about what he wanted. The overarching issue before him was how to deal with the controversial Jesus of Nazareth in general; and, his defense, or lack thereof, in particular. The man was a subject of Rome but was a Jewish citizen. He had been accused and convicted of violating Jewish religious laws by the Jewish Council. Their dilemma was that the Jewish religious leaders could not carry out the prescribed punishment for blasphemy—death—since execution was not permitted outside the jurisprudence of the Roman court. Pilate was not particularly inclined to carry out an execution for the conviction of a crime that he considered minor, even absurd. But Pilate was scrupulous about his work and was an ethical man. He had to pursue a legal remedy around the execution of Jesus so that Caiaphas would not complain and cause an uproar and accuse Pilate of not fulfilling his responsibilities.

Titus looked out the opened window into the dark clear night. Although it wasn't encompassed in the task he was given by Pilate, Titus could not help but wonder why the punishment had to be so harsh. Titus thought back to his homeland. In Rome, many people proclaimed to be gods. Such a claim did not necessarily upset anyone. If others cared to believe these lunatics, their fancy was harmless. Titus had seen Jesus close-up several times. He seemed a humble man and certainly innocuous. If he was mentally imbalanced, he could be thrown in a jail until he decided to abandon his outrageous claims and admit that he was not a god or, if not, he could waste away confined.

Oh, well. That was not Titus's problem. And it was not an approach that would yield any results. He had witnessed the haughty and immovable Caiaphas who was determined to see Jesus executed. Sitting in the back of the courtroom, he had observed Pilate try his best to convince Caiaphas that Jesus's crimes—if they indeed were crimes—were of a minor nature and did not warrant the ultimate penalty. But Caiaphas had been adamant and Pilate apparently had decided, probably out of political concerns, not to trump the rabbi's wishes.

Titus pored over the legal scrolls in the law library, a large room that was adjacent to both the courtroom and Pilate's office suite. As the sun disappeared, Titus lit two candles that were encased in beveled glass containers that served to illuminate the candlelight. Titus was finding only bad news as far as Pilate's responsibility for the client. It was the judge's duty to see to it that each individual accused of a crime was able to present a defense before the public court. The accused had the option to present his own defense if he did not have an attorney or could not afford one. But if in the end if the defendant had no defense, it did not alleviate Pilate's responsibility. Consulting various legal sources, Titus could find very little, if any, wiggle room that would allow Pilate to legally abandon that responsibility.

After hours of study, Titus began flipping back through the tomes trying to discover any remote, obscure legal way for Titus to deal with the Jesus problem but he came up with nothing substantial. He decided to change his approach. Scanning one block of ancient Jewish law, Titus spotted something that could possibly free his superior of having to re-try Jesus and ultimately enforce the punishment handed down by the Jewish Council. Titus discovered there were several cases in which a convicted individual could be given his freedom and escape his penalty if a more dangerous criminal could be executed in his place. Despite the severity of the punishment, there was a standing Passover exception followed by Jerusalem Jews that would allow Pilate, in his role as Governor of Judaea, to commute one prisoner's death penalty by acclimation. Titus was struck by the potential provided by this tradition. His interpretation was that Pilate could possibly have someone take Jesus's place in the crucifixion.

Although there were less than a handful of such cases in the annals of Roman law, there was enough to establish precedence. Thus, Pilate could legally show leniency to a convicted individual who he felt was innocent or was being given a punishment too harsh to fit the crime. This act of mercy could be adjudicated by a form of transference. A judge would be able to select a convicted criminal who was serving cell time and have that individual executed in place of another convicted person who the judge saw as having received a punishment that was too severe, one that did not match the crime. Ah ha, Titus thought— there is Pilate's out! Titus knew there was any number of individuals in the cells of Jerusalem who were much more deserving of the death penalty than the quiet, humble Jesus of Nazareth.

Titus continued his research and found another case in which a judge had appointed one of the officers of the court to defend an accused man. The cost of the attorney was absorbed by the Roman government. It was Titus's sense that ordering an attorney to defend Jesus would not appeal to Pilate. Doing so would be a sensitive political matter. A Roman attorney would have no interest in defending a Jewish holy man with whom he had no connection—it would be beneath him. Assigning a Jewish lawyer as Jesus's defense counsel would have its obvious complications and controversies. Titus could not imagine a Jewish attorney who would be willing to go against his community's top religious leader. None the less, Titus planned to include this approach in his final report to Pilate.

Just as dawn was beginning to peak over the horizon, Titus decided that there was nothing else within the many tomes that could provide any options for Judge Pilate to skirt his responsibility to see that Jesus had a viable defense. Titus was weary and leaned back in his the stiff uncomfortable wooden chair and shut his eyes. He had no intention of dozing off, but fatigue overtook him.

The sun was bright when Titus' eyes snapped open to see Liberius standing over him in the bright light that now flooded the law library. Titus, his eyes wide, shot straight up.

"I must have fallen off," Titus said, defending himself to Pilate's top aide.

"Apparently," Liberius responded, "Is your report completed?" he asked, already knowing the answer.

"I have completed the research," Titus responded. "All I have to do is scratch it down on a parchment."

"Well, I suggest that doing so would be a good idea and soon," Liberius responded with a judgmental tone. "His honor will soon be here and will be expecting his report as soon as he arrives."

"Yes, sir!" Titus replied.

Titus grabbed his notes and one large tome and was out the door. Liberius watched his underling, shaking his head in a derisive manner. It was Liberius' responsibility to see that Titus completed the task that was assigned to him. Pilate would not be forgiving if Titus's report was late especially if he was advised that Titus was caught asleep. Liberius would not hesitate to inform Pilate of that detail if he placed blame on Liberius for not seeing to it that Titus did his job.

Titus was young and Liberius had issues with his underling being late to his job and slow, at times, in producing results. But that would not be an issue—not this time. Since Pilate had tapped Titus to work closely with him, the young law clerk had begun to show a new maturity and ethic. Of course, Pilate's mere presence was usually enough incentive for anyone to do their best.

Titus scurried back to his desk and hurriedly wrote down in a clear and concise form what he had gleaned from the law books and case archives. It hadn't been an easy hunt, but Titus felt satisfied that his work was thorough and that he had left no stone unturned. As he made the finishing touches on the document he would share with Pilate, Titus felt certain that he was providing the best advice to his superior. Just as Titus leaned back in his chair to relax a moment, that moment of rest wasn't to be. Liberius stuck his head in Titus' doorway.

"Titus, Pilate has arrived in his office," Liberius proclaimed loudly. He continued in a tone that was at once reproachful and demanding. "He will want to see you within the quarter hour. Are you prepared for this meeting?"

Titus shot straight up and stood at attention. "Yes, sir," he responded. "I have the full report for his honor."

"I assume that you researched every possible answer and consideration for Pilate?" Liberius asked, maintaining an obviously skeptical posture.

"Yes, sir," Titus responded. "I am sure that Pilate will feel fully informed."

"Will the information please him?" Liberius asked.

"To the extent that any law can please any judge," Titus replied.

Confusion registered on Liberius's face. He was not a legal expert by any stretch of imagination. But he was a prideful man and did not like being in a position in which a subordinate such as the young Liberius was superior to him in any way. Although Liberius did not understand the complexities of the legal profession, he would certainly not confess such shortcoming to the youngster. However, his lack of knowledge was blatantly clear—something that Titus would not dare highlight.

"Remember that Pilate has you consulting the law books to support his views," Liberius responded.

Titus bowed slightly to Liberius but did not respond. He knew how wrong Liberius was and that Pilate was a honorable justice who respected the law and would follow it and not create his own interpretation to suit his personal needs.

Titus decided not to wait for the call from Pilate. Instead, he grabbed the scroll that contained his legal findings and hurried down the long hallway that led to Pilate's chambers. He stood a respectable distance from Pilate's door—he did not want it to appear that he was eavesdropping by standing too near the door. Titus was happy to stand and wait and looked forward to a day that would hopefully end when the sun set.

It was closer to a half-hour before Liberius was called to Pilate's office and ordered to send Titus in. Liberius had not seen Titus standing in the darkened hallway when he entered Pilate's office and was surprised to see him standing just a few feet away from the door when he exited.

"Oh, there you are," Liberius said. "Looks like you're as anxious for his honor to review your findings as he is. He is ready for you now."

"Thank you, sir," Titus responded as he passed Liberius and headed for Pilate's office.

Titus rapped lightly on Pilate's door.

"Come!" was the muffled response from within.

Pilate had finished a morning snack and the remnants of his meal were still sitting before him. It reminded Titus that he had not eaten since the evening before—albeit it was a meal that did not deserve to be remembered. Perhaps he would sleep that evening on a full belly and would not have to share his meal with a rodent, Titus thought to himself. Hopefully, fortune would look down over him and not present Pilate with another legal dilemma that Titus would have to wrestle with through the night.

"Have a seat, Titus," Pilate said. "I hope you have good news for me and if not good news at least some news."

"Yes, sir," Titus responded. "My research revealed several interesting and potentially useful case studies in the archives."

"That is a positive start to my day, Titus," Pilate said, a slight smile on his face. "Show me."

Titus opened his scroll so he could refer to his notes as he related his findings to Pilate who eyed the lengthy parchment filled with Titus' scratching.

"Well, looks as though you weren't idle," Pilate noted.

"Yes, sir," Titus responded. "Following your directions to find a way around the burdensome responsibility you have to carry out the punishment of an accused man who you feel has been treated unfairly by a jury or council, I have found some relevant archival material. Of course, in the current case, it was the Jewish Council who tried and convicted Jesus of Nazareth of blasphemy. The prescribed punishment, at least according to Jewish religious laws, is death. You have stated your abhorrence to this sentence and that you do not feel comfortable in seeing this sentencing through. "

"You have successfully summarized my predicament," Pilate said. "Now, what do I do about it?"

"I was just getting to that, your honor," Titus replied, sensing that Pilate was growing anxious to hear results—he was more aware than anyone of the problem.

"Sir, there are a few cases in Jewish law, a Passover custom in fact, wherein an accused person was viewed by the authorities to have been the victim of an unfair punishment and the judges in these cases was successfully able to avert that eventuality. In these cases, the judges satisfied the hunger of the prosecution to have retribution for the state or victims of the crime by transferring the penalty to another."

Pilate was taken aback. "Please continue," he said, "I am puzzled by your words."

"Your honor, these judges were able to satisfy both their constituency and the laws by selecting a criminal who was almost the diametric opposite of the convicted. The judges chose criminals who, in their views, had committed far more heinous crimes but had received what they perceived to be inadequate sentences. These cases closely parallel the current matter that is confronting you. In one case, a man who was convicted of the murders of several villagers was punished with the sentence of a spending the rest of his life in a solitary cell within a Roman prison. The man had evaded execution—the appropriate sentence for his crimes—by confessing his guilt. The judges and prosecution gave him a lenient sentence since his confession saved the state the cost of a lengthy investigation and trial. But the families of the victims and the citizenry in general were outraged that the killer got away with his life."

"Very interesting," Pilate said, "But please get to the point as to how this case would benefit my situation." Pilate's famous impatience was starting to emerge.

"Sorry, sir. I'll get right to that. I'm sure you'll realize the relevance," Titus responded.

"Yes, the relevance is what I'm most interested in, of course," Pilate said. "Proceed with that. Let's get to that. My day is about to begin."

"The judge suggested that the man who was wrongfully sentenced to death after having only been convicted of a seemingly minor crime—if memory serves me, it was thievery and assault—could have his sentence exchanged for that of the man guilty of multiple murderers. The judge felt the switch could have a two-fold benefit: the man with the lesser crime could be given a more reasonable punishment and the murderer could be appropriately executed which would have the residual effect of making the judge more popular in the eyes of his constituency since they had been outraged by the killer's lenient sentence."

"Ah… I'm beginning to see where you're going," Pilate said, now fully engaged.

"The judge in question did much as you did, your honor," Titus continued with enthusiasm, buoyed by Pilate's obvious interest. "He researched the matter and found no settled law that would prohibit him from such an action."

"Yes," Pilate said, "I see the utility of following this course of action. I would just have to select the unfortunate felon who could take Jesus's place on the cross." Pilate mused about the potential of taking the action for a few moments. But the morning session was about to begin and he was running out of time. "You indicated there was another path that we could take.

"In several of the cases in the archives, judges faced the same dilemma as you. They found before them a defendant who had no defense. In all of those cases, either the defendant was indigent and could not afford an attorney or the defendant was daft and could not adequately speak for himself. In those cases, the judge saw fit to assign counsel to represent the accused which the state paid for."

"Oh, I see. Such an action would serve to fulfill my responsibility to ensure that the accused is defended," Pilate responded. He remained silent for a moment before he continued. "But there could be sanctions from Rome for expending state funds for the defense of an unimportant Jew. I believe the first choice is the more desirable of the two."

Liberius poked his head in the door. "Your honor, it is time for the morning session to begin."

"I must go then," Pilate responded. He rose and focused on Titus who stood as well. "I will think about those options... I am leaning toward the first one you presented. I will think about it during the morning decision and make my decision."

Pilate headed for the door but then turned and looked back at Titus. "Good job, Titus." Pilate then rushed out the door.

***

Titus was walking down the dark hall as the day came to an end. His stomach sank when he heard Liberius' voice.

"Titus, Pilate wants to see you immediately," he said.

Another long night, Titus thought to himself as he trudged toward Pilate's office. Pilate's door was open and he waved Titus in when he spotted him. Pilate was smiling which confounded Titus not knowing if it signaled good news he could go home or bad news he'd have to stay again and read through the legal tomes with eyes blurred from overuse and exhaustion.

"Just wanted to let you know that I have selected a man to potentially keep Jesus's appointment with the executioners," Pilate told Titus. "I plan to put a slightly different turn to the scenario however. I will avoid any political ramifications by allowing the people to decide the fate of both men."

Pilate rose and paced in front of his window that looked out over the darkening city.

"Tomorrow morning, I will call the citizenry to the courtyard and present to them an option," Pilate said with a smile. "And, young Titus, I am quite certain how the crowd will react."

Titus smiled sensing that his hard work had pleased Pilate.

"I will give the Jews an option to either allow Jesus to go free or permit a mass murderer to be liberated and return to their community," Pilate spoke enthusiastically. He spun around and looked directly at Titus.

"The Jews will have the choice of sending Jesus to the executioner or freeing him and allowing the convicted mass murder Barabbas to take his place on the cross!"

Chapter 7
The Choice

Was it by some eerie coincidence that it was Barabbas, whose Aramaic name, "Bar Abbas" meant "Son of the Father" who was selected by Pilate as the sacrificial lamb to save the Lamb of God? Or, were there other wonders at work? As much as Pilate was determined to change the course of the events before him, he was frustrated at every turn. Pilate's clever legal maneuver to exchange Jesus's life for that of a murderous criminal would be no exception. But it was with great confidence that Pilate chose Barabbas to replace Jesus on the cross. Pilate had no doubt that the Jews of Jerusalem would elect to save Jesus's life by forcing them to choose between him and the vile Barabbas. The Jews would not want the mass murderer back on their streets to kill again.

As soon as Pilate arrived at the courthouse, he called Liberius into his private chambers.

"Liberius, have the guards gather the populace," Pilate ordered. "Make it clear to Captain Gennadius that the soldiers are not to mistreat or abuse the people. Tell him that I merely need the people to gather in the courtyard for an important matter for which their presence is necessary."

Liberius looked slightly stunned and didn't immediately move as was his usual reaction to an order from Pilate. Pilate took note and was charitable that morning.

"I do not owe you an explanation, Liberius, but I will sate your curiosity" Pilate offered gently. "The High Jewish Priests are passing their problem off on the Roman Court so I, in turn, will pass it back to their congregation. I have out-maneuvered the crafty Caiaphas."

"Yes, sir," Liberius replied quickly, embarrassed by his inappropriate behavior. "Right away!"

With that, Liberius was off and running and out the courthouse door heading to Captain Gennadius's private chambers at the principia. The morning sun was already beating down on Liberius as he scurried down the dusty road to the Roman soldiers' stronghold. The old Roman was sweaty and huffing by the time he stood before the oaken door of the Captain's apartment. A servant opened the Captain's chamber door and silently stared at Liberius who was struggling to recover his wind.

"Uh… I'm Liberius from Judge Pilate's court," Liberius said after he was finally able to speak. "I must see the Captain on orders from his honor."

With that, Captain Gennadius, who heard every word that Liberius had uttered, rose from his breakfast table and strode across the room, pushing aside his servant.

"And what does his honor, Pontius Pilate, demand of me this morning?" Gennadius said enthusiastically. Gennadius was eager to make up for his misstep when Jesus was first arrested and was anxious have another chance to please Pilate.

"Sir," Liberius bowed slightly, "his honor orders that you gather the Jews from the street and have them assemble in the courtyard immediately."

"Have the citizenry done something to disturb his honor?" Gennadius asked.

"No, they have no blame," Liberius responded. "Judge Pilate needs their assistance in an important manner. Find as many Jews as you can."

Liberius turned to leave but then looked back at Gennadius with a word of caution. "Be warned that your men are not to mistreat the people or abuse them. They should be brought peacefully to the courtyard."

***

***

The courtroom as usual was crowded with those accused of crime, their supporters and detractors as well as curious spectators.

"All rise," Liberius said, his deep voice resonating throughout the large courtroom.

The room quieted and one and all were on their feet.

The morning was bright and matched Pilate's mood as he walked briskly from his office and called the court to order.

Liberius turned on his heel and raced to the window overlooking the courtyard. He was relieved when he saw the yard filled with scores of Jewish citizens. He noted with relief that Captain Gennadius had heeded his word and that he and his soldiers were taking a non-combative posture toward the people. Liberius rushed back to the court so he could assure Pilate that the courtyard would be fully populated as he expected it would be.

"Normal business is hereby recessed whilst I conduct business with the citizenry of Jerusalem in the courtyard," Pilate announced from the bench.

There were gasps and whispers within the courtroom. Some spectators high-tailed it out of the room to observe or be part of whatever would be taking place outside.

***

The crowded courtyard was abuzz and a carnival-like ambiance was in the air. There were not many times when the poor and assiduous Jews of Jerusalem enjoyed a departure from their long work-days and endless chores. There was much speculation as to what the Governor of Judaea could want with them. What could the poor and down-trodden people of Jerusalem do for Pilate? Why would he call upon them? He had at his disposal a league of assistants and staff not to mention an entire army. From the relatively gentle treatment they received from the soldiers, the people sensed that there was no reason to be frightened by Pilate's summoning. When Pilate emerged onto the upper platform of the courtyard, the crowd erupted into cheers. The blare of the trumpets announcing his entry added to the ardor. Pilate was not generally met with a joyful greeting from the Jews but today was different. There was a light mood in the air and Pilate did make quite an impressive figure. There was an imperial aura about the judge in his official white and navy apparel and his golden crown that glistened in the bright sunlight.

Pilate gazed over those who had gathered and was pleased to see that there was quite a turnout. The ever-present Liberius began to sense that Pilate's pleasure with the crowd would be short-lived. Pilate was not a man of the moment; he was an industrious, dedicated justice whose desire it was to get to the business at hand—particularly on this day when the momentum in the case against Jesus of Nazareth finally seemed to be leaning his way.

As celebratory as the crowd was in anticipation of Pilate and as jubilant as it was at his arrival, a hush fell over the crowd as two Roman soldiers quietly escorted Jesus to the platform, marching him to a spot a few feet behind Pilate. Jesus, still donning the chains and restraining ropes, kept his head bowed as he stood before his people. Jesus stood in stark contrast behind the Roman leader. Pilate's brilliant colors made Jesus tattered robe appear all the more dingy. His bloodied vestments testified to the abuse that the Jewish guards had subjected him to. Pilate turned slightly and glanced at Jesus. Seeing the chained man and the blood that had been drawn was unsettling to him, slightly deflating his otherwise victorious demeanor.

After the crowd adjusted to the presence of Jesus, whispers and speculation abounded as to what would be taking place. Some wondered if the execution itself was about to begin—sending chills through some of the citizens. Others thought that Jesus would be excoriated publically by Pilate for his sins, which many in the courtyard would find satisfying. But they were all wrong. No one could have guessed who was about to join the two men on the platform.

Pilate's attention—and everyone else's for the matter—was drawn to the rear of the platform from the sound of a scuffle and a spate of angry words that were laced with profanity. Three Roman guards were tugging and pulling at a combative man who was quite a handful despite the fact that he was tied and chained. Two of the guards gave their subject a final shove and the burly man came tumbling forward. He almost fell at Pilate's feet but his physical strength was such that he was able to stop himself from toppling over. The man stood erectly at Pilate's side, rising to his full height which was fully five centimeters taller than Pilate. The crowd literally took a few steps back in unison when they realized that the man standing there with Pilate and Jesus was the notorious killer Barabbas.

Barabbas opened his nearly toothless mouth in a wide grin which was really more like a grimace. One of his bulging eyes was black while the other one, his blind eye, had a filmy gray opaque covering it. Barabbas could not have had a bath in months which became exceedingly clear to Pilate who turned away from him ashen-faced when he got a good whiff of him.

The crowd was now completely stumped. What could the presence of the three men before them mean? But the three men on the platform were not to be the last celebrity to participate in the large outdoor meeting. The sound of a wooden staff clicking on the dry brittle clay caused the crowd to part and make way for a late arrival. Caiaphas dressed warmly on this warm day headed to the front of the crowd. The slightly reddened patches on the old rabbi's cheeks signaled his anger over the latest turn of events in the case of Jesus of Nazareth. Whatever Pilate was up to, Caiaphas would do his part to sabotage it.

Pilate was ready to proceed with his plans and nodded to Liberius to make it official.

"Here ye, all" Liberius proclaimed loudly. "The honorable Governor of Judaea and Judge of the Roman Court of

Jerusalem, the imperial Pontius Pilate, now demands your undivided attention to a very important matter for both Rome and the Jews."

Everyone had quieted down but it seemed that the quiet somehow increased with Liberius' words. Anticipation was at its highest point.

"I appreciate your participation in this important matter," Pilate raised his voice so that it would reach all corners of the courtyard. He turned and looked at Jesus but could not bring himself to look again at the disgusting piece of humanity that was Barabbas. Pilate's gaze fell upon Caiaphas who was front and center. No one was more attentive to Pilate's words than the Jewish Priest.

"It is a religious law of the Jews, in fact it is a law of Passover, that a convicted man, set to be executed, can escape his fate if another criminal whose crimes were far viler in nature replaces him," Pilate announced.

There was a buzz of speculation in the air. Caiaphas's face visibly dropped as he began to realize what the imperial governor was plotting. Pilate nodded to Captain Gennadius who immediately poked his spear at Barabbas prodding him to the edge of the platform for all to see.

"I offer you the murderous Barabbas," Pilate, now shouting.

The crowd became loud and matched Pilate's apparent fervor. Gennadius escorted Jesus forward a few steps. And, in a quiet voice, Pilate continued.

"I now I offer you Jesus of Nazareth," he said.

There was little reaction from the crowd. Only one person spoke up.

"Will you state this man's crime before the populace?" Caiaphas asked from the courtyard.

Pilate hesitated for a moment as he shot daggers at the rabbi.

"Jesus was convicted—not in this court but in the court of Caiaphas—of the purported crime of blasphemy," he said, his tone still soft.

"I hereby give you, the people of Jerusalem, the responsibility of deciding whether Jesus dies or lives. It is up to you," Pilate said, scanning the crowd, beseeching them with his eyes. "If it is your word that he lives, Barabbas dies in his place."

The crowd erupted in catcalls and shouts. Caiaphas banged his cane angrily on the ground.

"Silence!" Pilate literally screamed, bringing forth the soldiers who, with spears in hand, moved menacingly through the crowd, returning it to order.

"But if you decide that Jesus is to be crucified, then this murdering pile of reeking flesh will go free to walk among you," Pilate said, finishing the details of his proposition.

Caiaphas spun around and faced the crowd. His angry face dared the people to defy him.

"I warn you, that it is your soul that is lost forever if you defy the laws of God," Caiaphas shrieked. He swung his cane at a few Jews who seemed to think the situation was humorous. They quickly exchanged their smiles for more sober countenances, ones that matched that of their religious leader.

Pilate had the sinking feeling that things were getting out of control and that the momentum shift that he had so welcomed was once again careening away from him. In Pilate's mind, Caiaphas was a maven of evil and was determined to destroy his clever legal strategy. Pilate wanted to resolve the matter quickly before the old rabbi could wield his influence throughout the crowd.

"How say you?" Pilate shouted. "Is it Jesus or Barabbas who dies?"

Caiaphas turned and looked at the crowd. "I support neither man," Caiaphas bellowed. "I follow only the word of God who has decreed that it is Jesus of Nazareth who has committed the ultimate crime and must receive the ultimate punishment. Those who choose to discard God's word will be found guilty of blasphemy themselves!"

Although there were looks of sadness in the eyes of some and confusion on the faces of others, the people felt compelled to side with Caiaphas. They were afraid not to. Not only would they receive the wrath of Caiaphas, worse yet, they would receive the wrath of God.

One man stepped forward and said, "Let his blood be upon us and upon our children."

The man was followed by others who echoed the same sentiment and soon the entire crowd was chanting the words in unison, "Let his blood be upon us and upon our children."

The words were prophetic as the blame fell upon the Jews for all time.

Although Jesus's expression did not change, a sad and angry look came over Pilate's face. But the decision had been made. Liberius ordered the soldiers to release Barabbas who was laughing gleefully. As Barabbas made his way down the stairs to join the people who just freed him, Pilate glared at them.

"May your sleep at night time not be disturbed by this heinous animal entering your dwelling with a long knife," Pilate said bitterly. "You have not only chosen Jesus's fate, you have chosen your own! Sleep well, citizens of Jerusalem!"

***

Back inside the courtroom, Pilate realized that he was out of options. Titus had found every available law and case possible to avoid the re-trying of Jesus in his court to confirm the penalty handed down by the Jews. The only way out was for evidence to be presented in the Roman trial that would rescind the conviction in the Jewish High Council. But Jesus had no defense counsel and refused to speak for himself. Jesus was doomed but the prospect of ultimately carrying out the sentence against Jesus sent a chill down Pilate's body. He felt he was doomed as well.

Joseph of Arimathea watched as Jesus stood alone before Pilate's bench. He seemed so alone, so apart from everyone. Joseph was experiencing a tenderness in his heart like never before. It was a feeling that was at once comforting and powerful. Something was changing within him and that something was about to change his day, even his life. The image of his desk stacked with documents and baskets full of scrolls flashed before him momentarily but quickly disappeared. Although he had planned to return to his duties after feeding his curiosity about Jesus, those plans began to have less meaning. Their importance shrunk in comparison to the drama that was taking place before him. Jesus was so alone. The solemn figure of Jesus tugged at his heart and his aloneness struck at Joseph's very soul. It hurt him. Joseph could not let Jesus face the odds against him alone. Joseph was feeling a need to defend him. The usually carefully thought out day of Joseph of Arimathea was abandoned. It was not like Joseph to cast aside his schedule but for the first time in his life he felt he was truly being called. His heart was being taken over by a spirit that he could not explain but that could not be ignored.

Joseph was closely watching the proceedings, emotion building within him. Finally, it seemed the circumstances demanded that he speak up. Joseph made his way through the large gathering and walked slowly to the front. He stood next to Jesus.

Pilate watched Joseph walk forward. He recognized the well-known attorney and officer of the court. Was Pilate's hope for a fair trial for Jesus still within his grasp?

"The court recognizes Joseph of Arimathea," Pilate proclaimed as he brought down his gavel several times to stifle the outbreak of whispers.

"Your honor," Joseph said in a pleasing yet strong voice, "I, Joseph of Arimathea, will defend Jesus of Nazareth."

Jesus turned his head quickly and looked at Joseph but did not say a word.

"You are willing to take on the defense of Jesus who does not even seem to what to defend himself?" Pilate asked.

"Yes, sir. I fear that the defendant may not fully understand what the charges mean and what rights he has as a citizen of Jerusalem and in the honorable Roman Court," Joseph responded, bowing slightly.

"Perhaps you will have more luck than I have had, Joseph or perhaps you are more talented," Pilate replied. "I seemed to have failed in convincing the man of the seriousness of this situation."

"I humbly submit that I, in no way, possess the legal skills that could in anyway compare to your own, Judge Pilate," Joseph offered. "I just have the hope that once I can have the chance to counsel with the defendant privately that I will be able to convey to him the gravity of what he is facing."

Pilate focused on Jesus once again. "Jesus of Nazareth, do you accept the defense of this gentleman, Joseph of Arimathea, who so generously has offered his skills as defense counsel on your behalf?"

"I am grateful to Joseph of Arimathea for his kind offer," Jesus responded.

"Well. . . does that mean you accept his offer?" Pilate asked, hoping that Jesus would have enough sense to accept the help.

"I cannot," Jesus responded.

Whispers were heard around the room. This time Pilate didn't try to stop them. The scarlet glowing on Pilate's face reflected his total frustration.

"You leave me no choice, Jesus, but to take this matter into my own hands," Pilate began. "Since you are in Jerusalem, Jesus, you are a subject of Rome. In my position as the Roman governor of Jerusalem, I will take the burden of your defense as my responsibilities."

Joseph stood at attention, listening to every word from Pilate while Jesus stood with his head slightly bowed as though he was merely riding in the hand of God the Father and would be taken where God wanted him to go.

"And so I proclaim with the powers vested in me by the Roman Empire, it is ordered that Joseph of Arimathea, an accredited attorney and officer of the court, defend the accused, Jesus of Nazareth, who stands before this court. In defending this man, you, Joseph Arimathea, are charged with providing the accused with the best counsel and advice within your abilities. Are you willing to confirm and accept the provisions I have set forth?"

"I humbly accept the responsibility as you have set forth, your honor," Joseph responded.

Caiaphas trembled slightly. He had not expected that Jesus would have defense counsel. He glared at Joseph as he stood there before the bench by his new client. Caiaphas was familiar with Joseph's work and reputation. Joseph was an able and successful attorney. He had made quite a name for himself and had accumulated quite a cache of gold for defending wealthy men in legal matters involving their businesses. Why on earth would a man of such standing take on the case of Jesus, Caiaphas bitterly thought to himself. After finally getting Jesus to the appropriate court—the court that would be required to carry out the punishment he deserved—Caiaphas thought his struggles were over. One of Jerusalem's most prestigious lawyers stepping up to defend Jesus had never been even a slight consideration in his mind. It was proving to be a difficult challenge to rid the city of the scourge that was Jesus. But Caiaphas was confident that in the end he would prevail. Of course, he had no idea that his success was preordained. Had he known what was really taking place, he would not have been so eager to be a part of it.

Joseph had no idea either what larger event was taking place. But his heart had been moved by Jesus's plight and he felt an immediate dedication to see the trial through and save Jesus's life. No stakes could have been higher.

"Liberius, I need your assistance in my chambers," Pilate told his court officer.

As Pilate rose to leave, Liberius ordered that everyone rise at his departure. After Pilate and Liberius exited the courtroom, Jesus and Joseph remained standing before the bench awaiting Pilate's next direction. Jesus turned slightly toward his counselor, a slight smile came over his face.

"I am honored by your kindness, Joseph," Jesus said softly. "But I cannot accept your offer."

"Why do you say that?" Joseph asked, stunned that Jesus was apparently determined to face execution.

"I am a minister," Jesus responded. "I have no money to pay you."

Joseph smiled, relieved that Jesus's objection was not a true obstacle in having the defense he was entitled to. "Jesus, I expect no payment. In fact, even if you had a few shekels to rub together, I would not accept them."

Jesus gazed silently at Joseph for a few moments. His gaze made Joseph feel at once comforted and in awe in the same instant.

"Why, Joseph?" Jesus asked. "Why do you want to defend me?"

"I feel... I feel I must, Jesus," Joseph responded. "It's something within me that compels me. I cannot adequately describe what seems to move me nor do I understand it."

"But I do," Jesus responded and turned his head back to await Pilate's return.

Joseph continued to look at Jesus, feeling all the more committed.

Chapter 8
In Defense of Jesus

While Joseph was becoming acquainted with his new client, Pilate was weighing his legal requirements in conducting this rather unusual case in his court. He also had many political concerns about holding court on the case against Jesus. How would his superiors in Rome view his acceptance of the case? Would they see him as weak in his legal battle with both Herod and Caiaphas? Both Jews had outsmarted him thus far. Pilate feared that he would look foolish and no longer be perceived as effective. It was nearing the time that Pilate would be ending his tour of duty in Jerusalem. He wanted to return to Rome in victory not with his tail between his legs. He looked forward to being honored upon his return and promoted to an important position in the Emperor's inner circle. If the case of an unimportant Jew redounded back to the Emperor in a manner that he interpreted to be politically injurious, Pilate could well be demoted... or worse. Instead of retiring as an important and distinguished member of the Roman Empire, he could be relegated to depart in shame, humiliation and failure.

But Pilate was a dedicated justice and could only be guided by law. Titus had thoroughly reviewed the laws of both the Romans and the Jews. His legal clerk found options but Pilate had been stopped at every turn. Pilate was out of options. He would have to try Jesus in his court on the same charges on which he had been tried and convicted in the Jewish High Council. He would be tried by a panel of his peers—his fellow citizens of Jerusalem, Jews like him. What fault could Pilate have in that? What loomed before him was whether he would use his power as judge and Governor of Judaea to reduce the punishment or indeed reverse the finding of the jury.

***

While Pilate brooded over what the future would hold for him and how this trial may affect his career and even his personal life, Joseph of Arimathea sat alone in the abandoned courtroom.

He was awaiting word from Liberius that he could visit with his new client. As in any new venture that has obvious pratfalls Joseph mirrored Pilate's mood, brooding over his future and whether he was making a huge misstep. Now that he was away from the courtroom drama and its emotion, Joseph wondered what he had gotten into. He was a successful attorney, a respected litigant, now he was freely offering his services for a man who wanted no part of it. For Joseph, it was a time of reflection; doubts began to overwhelm his thoughts. He knew he was doing nothing that would further his career but would his standing sustain permanent damage? Had he completely lost his senses and turned his future over to a toss of the magical dendrites? Joseph rose from the hard bench deciding whether to stay or go when Liberius appeared from the entrance that led to the jail. It was too late to leave. The decision had been made for him.

Joseph followed Liberius down the dark, dank halls that spiraled down below the courthouse. As they walked, Joseph found himself in a new world one that he would never have dreamed he'd ever be part of. Joseph's clientele were wealthy men who he met with in luxurious spas or posh dining halls. Joseph noticed that his long cloak was brushing over the many puddles of filthy stagnant water along the way. He was repulsed by the large population of vermin and insects in the jail section of the courthouse that apparently were so accustomed to humans that they didn't scurry off. Joseph gagged on the horrendous odor that was thick in the air. Those earlier doubts he had experienced began to flood Joseph's thoughts again.

As Joseph followed behind Liberius, he tried to keep his eyes straight ahead but they would often wonder toward the dark cells where men were sitting or lying on the ground. Men in some of the cells would crawl toward their bars or rise and rush to them. Several grabbed the bars and shook them with all their might, outraged at their fate. Some reached out to Joseph, begging for help and mercy. Others, the angry ones, snarled their filthy faces and spate out vile words of hate and venom.

"The ones we are coming upon are in the death knell, all scheduled for execution," Liberius attempted to whisper but his naturally loud voice rang out in the silent passageway.

As they passed through death row, Joseph espied a few of the men who, unlike most men, knew when and how their lives would end; their soulless eyes gazing impassionedly at two men who were allowed to walk about freely. As Joseph glanced at them, he saw no sign of hope, only an acceptance of their fates.

The men came to a confined area with cells that seemed particularly small. It was the holding area, Liberius explained. Convicted felons who had not yet been sentenced were incarcerated in the cells there. As they approached, Liberius called to a soldier who was on duty at the guard station.

"Soldier, this man, Joseph of Arimathea, has the permission of Judge Pilate to visit in the cell with his client, Jesus of Nazareth," Liberius said.

The soldier rose from his bench and, with a smirk on his face, walked toward the cells.

"The Son of God has a visitor we can see, eh?" The soldier asked snidely. "He usually is in there talking to his invisible friends."

"It's not your place to judge," Liberius snapped. "We leave that to his honor."

The soldier knew he had overstepped his bounds. His cheeks reddened as he fumbled with the large ring of keys, clanging them awkwardly until he finally opened the cell. The soldier held open the cell and Liberius stepped aside and motioned Joseph to enter the darkened hole in the wall. Liberius bowed dutifully as Joseph slowly entered.

Had it not been for the whites of his eyes and the relative lightness of his dingy white robe, Jesus would have been almost invisible. He sat with his hands on his knees on the earthen floor against the dark back wall of the windowless cell. As the guard started to close the cell door to lock it behind Joseph, Liberius stopped him. He grabbed a small wooden stool that was on the floor nearby and offered it to Joseph. Joseph reluctantly took the stool and looked at Jesus sitting in dirt. He turned back toward Liberius who knew what he was about to ask.

"There is only one stool, sir," Liberius answered his silent question.

Joseph turned and entered the cell without responding to Liberius. The hair stood up on the back of his neck as the loud iron door slammed behind him. A chill went through him thinking how these men must feel to be locked up—especially when they were innocent. Such misery was unfathomable.

Joseph approached Jesus and sat the stool down in front of him.

"I've been sitting all day, Jesus," Joseph said softly. "Please, sit on the stool. I need to stand to stretch my legs."

Jesus only smiled and remained where he was. "You are a kind man, Joseph of Arimathea."

Suddenly, tears brimmed in Joseph's eyes. It confounded him because he had no reason to weep. He felt a little absurd and gathered himself quickly. He was a professional man and needed to get to the business at hand.

Joseph lowered himself to the small stool so that he could be in direct eye contact with Jesus. All the doubts that had been building in the empty courtroom and during the long walk through the horrid courthouse jail disappeared. Gazing into Jesus's kind face and soft though intense eyes told Joseph he was doing the right thing. From that point on, regardless of what would transpire, Joseph never again doubted his involvement, never looked back.

"Jesus, I want to do my best for you, for your cause," Joseph began in a gentle tone. "To do so, I will need your help. I will need your words."

"Joseph, once some things are set in motion, nothing can turn them around," Jesus said.

"I don't understand what you mean," Joseph responded, perplexed.

"You are a good man, Joseph of Arimathea," Jesus said, "But my fate is decided."

"Jesus, please, don't be resolved to defeat," Joseph pleaded.

"My fate will not be a defeat," Jesus responded.

"That's the spirit! There is always hope," was Joseph's reply.

Jesus smiled warmly. "Yes, Joseph, there is always hope."

***

Joseph was not able to make any progress with Jesus that first afternoon. He felt that Jesus was in a depressed state, resigned to his own end—his ultimate crucifixion. He had pointed out to Jesus that the Roman Court was a more powerful entity than the Jewish High Council and could reverse the decision of Caiaphas and the others. Joseph sensed that during the entire time he met with his new client Jesus was listening politely but was discarding his advice, resolved to a certain fate that he believed awaited him.

The sad and distraught faces of Jesus's mother and his small band of supporters came to Joseph's mind as he attempted to formulate a defense for him. Even though the defendant would not defend himself, surely his loved ones would. He sensed that though there was sadness in their eyes, there was hope and resolve in their hearts that Jesus could be saved.

Keithley & Doyle

It was dark by the time Joseph left the courthouse and padded down the narrow pathway toward his office. He needed to clean up some normal business issues which had been neglected the entire day. When Joseph entered his second-floor office, his shoulders slumped and he sighed heavily. His desk was covered with new scrolls and stacked with parchments that his legal assistant presumably piled up in his absence. Joseph didn't expect the deluge of paperwork that he saw on his desk. But standing there staring at the pile of work wouldn't get it done. Joseph walked quickly to his desk and dove in. He worked several hours organizing and dispatching some of the work, much of which he decided to relegate to a junior partner who had recently joined the firm. He was intentionally clearing his schedule so that he could devote the majority of his time and effort into the defense of Jesus of Nazareth.

All the while he worked Joseph was strategizing. He would seek out Mary, mother of Jesus, about her son's defense. Learn things about Jesus and his ministry that Jesus himself was not willing to discuss. Joseph sensed he would have an ally in Mary. He was beginning to fully understand the challenge of defending a man who refused to speak for his own cause. Although he was frustrated and perplexed with Jesus's attitude, he was all the more determined to defend the man. The short time he had been with him, he felt inspired and more certain than ever that the gentle man who he was representing did not deserve to face the ordeal that awaited him on the cross.

***

On very little sleep, Joseph was up early the next morning and determined to speak with Jesus's family and allies. He stretched and yawned as he pulled on his tunic and robe, threw some cold water on his face and headed to the kitchen of the family's roomy house. His wife, Irit, sleepy-eyed and averting her eyes from the morning sun streaming through the open shudder, entered the kitchen and gathered a sack of food for her husband to take with him. She knew that he was on a new case and, as was his pattern, becoming totally absorbed in it. Joseph hadn't given

Irit any details about the case but she assumed that it was one of the wealthy money-changers or business owners who comprised his usual clientele.

"Joseph, I have gathered some cheese and fruit for you to take," Irit said. "I assume you have no time for a decent cup of tea and crust of bread in advance of your long day?"

"Irit, as usual, you are right," Joseph responded. "I have a very difficult case before me."

"They're all difficult," Irit responded coyly. "Or at least that's what my husband tells me."

Joseph smiled and took the sack of food from Irit. He gave his wife a hug and kiss on the cheek.

"They are all difficult, my dear—each in its own way. But this one promises to be particularly difficult."

"How so?" Irit asked warily, a slight smile on her face. She was accustomed to her husband's hyperbole which was designed to garner sympathy from her.

"This man wants no defense. In fact, he refused to even say definitively that he's not guilty of the charges," Joseph replied, knowing that his very bright wife's curiosity was piqued.

"That's absurd. Why would a man pay good money to one of Jerusalem's top attorneys yet want no defense?" Irit asked.

A slight smile came over Joseph's face as he headed toward the door. "I forgot to mention, Irit, that this man is paying no fee."

With that Joseph was gone. Irit was completely confounded. Had her husband gone daft? What compelled him to take a case with no reward? The more she thought about it, the angrier she became. She'd confront him that evening about his odd turn toward charity cases. Maintaining her household with five children and five servants was not an easy task. If her husband began working for free, there would be hell to pay for him!

***

Joseph had to chuckle to himself as he strode down the dusty path that led to his office. He knew that Irit was fuming by now. She was a good woman—a loyal wife and dedicated mother—though she did tend to be on the bossy side especially when it came to her household. He earned the money and she dispensed it. He knew that she was not happy to hear that he was diving into a case that would yield not one shekel. Irit had a good heart, however, when she fully understood the case, he was sure that she would come around.

***

Joseph was the first to arrive in his office that morning. When his legal assistant, Yakir, arrived he was surprised to see his boss already at work as was his new junior partner, Hadas, who peeked his head in Joseph's office when he arrived.

"Joseph, good morning to you."

Joseph barely looked up from his work and did not respond in kind.

"Please, sit, Hadas," Joseph said, motioning Hadas to sit at the chair by his desk.

"I will be passing over most of my routine work to you," Joseph began.

Hadas looked a little stunned. He had only just come on board and was taken aback by Joseph's words.

Joseph looked intensely at Hadas. "Now, if there is a new case and you need my assistance, have Yakir get a message to me," Joseph stopped and sighed. He realized that his words were overwhelming the young attorney. "Perhaps I should explain what exactly is going on. I have taken on the case of Jesus of Nazareth."

"A business client?" Hadas asked.

"Not at all." Joseph replied, "He is a young man who has a ministry and has tangled with the Jewish High Priest—Caiaphas, you may have heard of him—and gotten himself in a heap of trouble."

"What has he done?"

"Nothing. Nothing, that is, that warrants the death penalty," Joseph responded. "I plan to throw all my time and energies into that case. It's a matter of life and death."

"I didn't realize the firm took on criminal cases," Hadas said.

Joseph rose from his seat, signaling that their meeting was over. "You're correct, Hadas, I am not a criminal lawyer. But this is a case that goes beyond any normal parameters."

Hadas rose from his chair. "Good luck, sir, with the case."

"I feel I will need the luck that you offer, Hadas. In fact, I could use a miracle."

Joseph followed Hadas out of his office and yelled for his assistant. Yakir rushed over to Joseph.

"How can I help you, sir?" Yakir asked.

"Find me Mary, the mother of Jesus of Nazareth. Tell her that I must speak to her immediately.

***

Yakir was street-wise and knew his way around Jerusalem. Acting upon Joseph's orders, he rushed out on the busy streets and after asking a few questions to a vendor here and a woman there, he learned where Mary lived. He delivered Joseph's message; Mary told Yakir that she would await Joseph's visit that afternoon. Although Yakir did not tell Mary what Joseph wanted to see her about, Mary knew in her heart that Joseph was going to speak to her about her son. She waited patiently. Waited and prayed.

Mary went about her normal chores and straightened her modest home. Since an important guest was coming, she would be sure to have a cup of herb tea and a biscuit to offer him. When Mary heard the light rapping on her door that afternoon, she smoothed her dress and pulled her shawl over her head. Mary opened the door. The deep intensity that Joseph saw in her eyes recalled to him the same gaze in the eyes of her son. She bowed in respect and showed him in.

"Thank you for seeing me, Mary," Joseph began after politely accepting the refreshments that Mary kindly offered him.

"It is my honor, sir," Mary responded in a voice that was soft and gentle.

Mary took a seat across from the important man who wanted to speak with her. She was relieved that Joseph, the well-known attorney for the wealthy, seemed to be a kindly man and that he treated her with respect. As Joseph took a sip of tea and a bite of biscuit, Mary remained silent patiently waiting for him to begin their discussion.

Joseph wiped his face with a cloth and smiled at her with light brown eyes that danced and twinkled.

"I'm sure you have probably guessed that my visit to you today is in regard to your son, Jesus of Nazareth," Joseph said.

"I did assume so, sir," Mary responded.

"Let me assure you that my intentions with regard to your son are nothing but the best," Joseph began. "The Roman court has taken the case that was referred to it by the Jewish Council led by Caiaphas." Joseph dropped his eyes and continued in a hesitant tone. "You are aware of the sentence that he received?"

Mary became overcome with emotion. She was embarrassed by her inability to speak. But it mattered not. The single tear that ran down one of her cheeks confirmed to Joseph that Mary was aware that her son was given the death sentence. Joseph was immediately sorry that he made the nice woman cry.

"Well, we don't have to dwell on that, do we?" "Joseph said, trying to step away from the terrible reality of his words. "We are going to rectify that injustice."

Mary had let her tea grow cold and she did not touch her biscuit. She wanted nothing to distract her from Joseph's words.

"The Roman law requires that any defendant that is tried within its court system be duly represented by counsel or if the individual so chooses, he may represent himself," Joseph told Mary. He hesitated before he began again, weighing his words so they would bring no harm. "As you may be aware, your son hired no counsel for his defense and… it uh… seems he wishes not to defend himself. I'm not sure why that is but it's actually irrelevant at this point. What I mean to tell you, good woman, is that I have volunteered to defend Jesus at no cost."

The tears flowed now. Mary grasped Joseph's hands and looked intensely into his eyes. "You are a good man, Joseph of Arimathea. A very good man," Mary choked through her words. After she gathered herself, she continued. "I appreciate what you are doing for my son. I know it is out of the goodness of your heart. You are a benevolent man. You may not receive compensation now, but you will receive your reward someday."

Joseph was appreciative of Mary's gratitude, in fact, he was even a little embarrassed. He was not defending Jesus in a prideful way. This was not about him. He sincerely saw the sentencing as an injustice and wanted to rectify it. The most important thing was that he wanted to save his life.

Mary poured more tea for Joseph and offered him another biscuit.

"Please, kind lady, according to my good wife I am already too stout as it is." Joseph's smile engendered a slight smile on Mary's face, the first one since his arrival.

Very quickly, Mary grew serious again. "Don't you think it true, sir, that there are sometimes things already in motion that there is no stopping them?"

"Hmm... your son said something very similar to that," Joseph said then thought for a moment. "Be assured that I will do everything a man can do to reverse Jesus's fate."

"Sometimes that which man can do is not enough," said Mary.

Chapter 9
Mary's Story

Joseph talked to Mary for many hours during which time his reaction ranged from sympathetic and understanding to astonished and disbelieving. But since he was a seasoned attorney and remained devoted to his client's cause, he did not reveal his skepticism. Besides, he respected women and he would not insult the kind woman who was in despair over her son's fate.

Joseph scribbled quick notes on his parchment with his stylus as Mary told him of her son's life and the special gift she felt he had. That was not a surprise. All mothers felt their sons were special and gifted. He understood a mother's love. His own mother beamed with pride about his talents which she felt were far and above those of any other and, in his opinion, far above what they actually were. But Mary's claims took a mother's pride to a whole new level.

Mary told Joseph that she had been visited by Gabriel an angel and messenger from God who told her that she would conceive a child through the actions of the Holy Spirit the son she would have was sent from God. Mary told Joseph how as a young wife, she had traveled with her husband, Joseph of Nazareth, to Bethlehem, her husband's ancestral home, to give birth to her son. It was the law that her child be registered there in the census of Quirinius. At one point during her discourse, she stopped and lowered her eyes as she spoke.

"The birth of my son, Jesus, was a virgin birth," Mary said quietly. "He is the Son of God."

Well, that statement was stunning and beyond any boast that his own mother had made about him. But Joseph did not allow his exterior to belie his astonishment. Mary was under a great strain. The "Son of God" talk was surely impacting the frail and beleaguered woman. Without question, Joseph knew that if he called Mary to the stand, her testimony would be fodder for Caiaphas's venom. The remarkable statement she just made would be exceedingly inflammatory and only serve to harm his client. As Mary spoke, Joseph was assessing the viability of having Mary as a witness. Perhaps he would not call her but if Caiaphas had an inkling of her account, he would be eager to call her as a hostile witness for the prosecution. More worries for Joseph. But he could not help but wonder what Joseph of Nazareth, her husband, thought about the child she was carrying.

"But, ma'am," Joseph said in a soft voice, "I want in no way to seem indelicate, but the question comes to mind about your husband. How did he feel about the child that his young wife was having that... uh... obviously was not his own?"

"There was some distress early on," Mary replied, "But angels visited my husband on three separate occasions to assure him that the child was the Son of God and that his conception was a blessing from the Holy Spirit for all of mankind."

"I see," Joseph replied quietly, although he really didn't "see" but made a note of her husband's reaction to Mary's claim about the unusual birth.

As the day wore on, Joseph listened attentively but grew all the more dubious. Three wealthy men from the East, kings Mary alleged, had come to Bethlehem to honor the coming of the new Messiah. On that night, now some thirty-three years before, a bright star that marked his birth had shined over Bethlehem to show the kings the way. Joseph quickly thought back and recalled hearing word of a bright star some years before—probably around the time Jesus was born. But that the shining star had anything to do with the birth of this peasant woman's child would be quite another story. As far as the wealthy kings coming to pay homage to the poor couple's child—the story totally lacked credibility in his opinion, one that he did not share with Mary.

What struck Joseph as he listened to the gracious woman's tale was that this story was known to Caiaphas and the Jewish Council and was surely what had sent them reeling. Joseph acquiesced that a claim to be a god or the Son of the Living God was certainly blasphemy according to Jewish law with which he had intimate knowledge. On the other hand, a certain curiosity nagged at Joseph. Why had the religious leaders, the rabbis of the very temple that Joseph belonged to himself, been so closed to the possibility that Jesus was in fact what he and others apparently claimed him to be—the Son of God. While Joseph was not a devout member of his temple, he had been raised as a Jew. Since his very first memories studying Hebrew as a child at the temple, it had always been the hope of every devout Jew that the Messiah would come. David the King would come to rule the earth. As Joseph matured, he began to silently come to his own conclusions about the Messiah and believed that it was probably a legend and wishful thinking on the part of the religious leaders and zealots that a god would descend upon the earth. But why had the believers been so adamant that Jesus could not be that deity?

Despite his personal opinions and concerns about Mary's story, he continued to record her words. He looked at the kind woman with tender eyes. The reality came over Joseph that if Mary testified in open court and recounted this tale, she too could be accused of blasphemy—which added another dimension of risk to the entire situation. His heart sank thinking of seeing this gentle lady facing the executioner.

The odds against using Mary's testimony on behalf of her son began to fade all the more when she recounted how the three powerful rulers from the East had traveled to give her son gifts and call him king. Did those kings believe that the baby was the savior or were they just establishing political cover for themselves in the event he was the Messiah? Oh dear, he thought, would he have to depose these men if he could find them if they did indeed exist? Joseph looked kindly upon Mary but recalled how a Jewish doctor who dealt with people who had apparently lost their minds felt that such insanity could be passed down from parent to child. What in the world had he gotten himself into? The more he learned, the more a strong and credible defense of Jesus seemed impossible.

Mary continued and spoke of the time when she and Joseph and the two-year-old Jesus fled to Egypt.

"Old King Herod heard about the Wise Men visiting my son and honoring him as the Savior," Mary said. "My son was in danger of being slaughtered by the King's army. Perhaps you have heard of the incident?"

Joseph nodded. "The massacre of the innocents." Joseph was stunned, knowing the tale of the incident very well.

"Herod feared that the Messiah had come and ordered that all male children age two and under in Bethlehem be slain. It was a very harrowing time, Joseph. We fled to Egypt and only returned when the old King passed. We settled in Nazareth, my husband's homeland, to avoid the new king's vengeance." Mary looked off in the distance as if she was reliving those early years. Then she turned and looked directly at Joseph.

"You see, my son was blessed by God yet cursed by man ever since his birth," Mary said, her eyes sad, reflecting the decades of torment that she had lived under.

A reassuring smile crossed Joseph's face. "It seems as though his patron is more powerful than his adversaries."

***

Mary literally glowed when she recalled Jesus's childhood and how sweet-natured and obviously bright he was even as a young boy. Now she sounded liked his mother, Joseph thought. Mary explained that she had raised Jesus alone after losing her husband when her son was just a very young child. Joseph gained more understanding of the woman who clung to the story of her son's origin, alone and having to fend for herself in a harsh world that undoubtedly had seemed to be against her. He had a growing empathy for Mary.

As an attorney, the thought struck him that one defense that could be constructed around Jesus was that he was raised to think he was the Son of God by a poor and isolated widow woman whose whole life had turned around her son. But as a man, he rejected the thought as soon as it crossed his mind. He would never pit this good woman against her own son.

As Joseph listened to the story of Jesus's life, that feeling that he had experienced when he was in Jesus's presence returned to him. A warm sensation washed over him, assuring him that by helping Jesus and Mary that he was doing the right thing.

To stay clear of Herod, Mary kept a low profile and stayed in Nazareth in Galilee with her gifted son. Mary told of one day when she lost Jesus in the crowded market. She panicked, of course, thinking that perhaps Herod's men had followed them and nabbed her son and was spiriting him off to Jerusalem for execution. But to her delight, she found her son at the temple where, to the astonishment of everyone but Mary, he was teaching the elders about God.

As Jesus matured, he became a carpenter. He wanted to be one with the people and know what it was to toil and work with his hands. Mary felt it gave him a real connection with the poor people who needed him and who he was destined to lead. Joseph could envision the tall, lean Jesus in such a physical role as he looked down slightly embarrassed by his own swelled middle, the result of too much food and too little mobility.

Mary told Joseph how her son had been moved by the Holy Spirit to begin his own ministry three years before, when he was thirty-years old. She talked of how happy he was as his message began to resonate with the people of Nazareth. Mary and Jesus had just recently moved to Jerusalem because the Holy Spirit was urging him there. And, of course, there was the recent trouble. Mary, sighed, recalling the anguish of those days.

"Madam, can you provide me with anything else in your son's defense?" Joseph asked.

"Only that he is a kind and good man," Mary said, her eyes glistening with the tears she struggled to keep from falling. "But it seems as though that defense is not an adequate one."

Gently, Joseph pushed ahead. "Can you supply me the names of others who know him and will defend him?"

Mary brightened. "Yes, Jesus has great friends. Most are his dedicated disciples who believe in him and his mission. Mary Magdalene is a devotee as is Simon Peter."

"Where can I find them?"

"They congregate—or they did—in the woods just outside the Garden of Gethsemane. Perhaps you may find them there. Simon Peter can give you the names of all the others."

Mary's story was brought to the present day. The two remained silent for a few moments, each lost in their own thoughts. Finally, Mary looked intently at Joseph.

"Sir, please know that destiny is powerful and determined."

Joseph rose to leave. He bowed to Mary and gently took her hand in his.

"You have been kind and patient with me, dear lady," Joseph began. "Please know that I may not be powerful but I am determined and up for the challenge."

Mary smiled wanly, bowed and clutched both her hands around Joseph's.

***

Joseph hurried from Mary's small home back toward his office. He would have rather turned toward home but he feared that Hadas may have been overwhelmed from being on his own all afternoon. It was only fair, he felt, to stop by and offer his support. He also wanted to review the notes he took from his meeting with Mary. He feared he wouldn't be able to use Mary as a witness for the defense since she actually proved the prosecution's contentions. But it was good to know her story in the off-chance Caiaphas intended to call Mary to the stand.

As soon as Joseph entered his office, a trembling Hadas rushed in.

"Sir, a Roman soldier was here to see you," Hadas said with a quivering voice.

Joseph wasn't disturbed and proceeded to go through the stack of parchments and scrolls that had amassed there since he left.

"Really? What did he want?"

"He left word that the honorable Pontius Pilate wants to see you first thing in the morning," Hadas said, now relieved that a burden had been lifted from him.

Hadas's words got Joseph's attention.

"Hmm," Joseph murmured and thought for a few moments. "Very well. If Judge Pilate wants to see me, then see me he will."

***

The next morning, Joseph of Arimathea waited in the courtroom for nearly an hour before Pilate was ready to meet with him. Joseph had arrived bright and early and assumed from what he had gathered about the imperial Pilate that he'd be in for a good wait. Pilate liked to keep others waiting but no one dared to detain him for even the time it took to inhale half a breath, or so Joseph had heard. But Joseph was unperturbed. He wasn't a man who was into a battle of the egos. He preferred to wage his battles in the courtroom.

Just as Joseph had somehow miraculously gotten comfortable on the hard bench in the back of the room where Liberius had instructed him to wait, the old court clerk emerged from the back hall. In a discordant voice with a tone somewhere between the bleat of a camel and cawing of the masked shrike, Liberius instructed Joseph to follow him.

Joseph shot up and scurried after the fast-moving court clerk. Joseph cursed his too-generous belly as he struggled to keep sight of Liberius. Finally, out of breath he arrived at the door held open by Liberius who gestured for Joseph to enter. Joseph had never been in Pilate's chambers before but was not surprised by the opulence he observed despite the fact that the chamber was a government office. The taxpayers of Jerusalem were paying for Pilate's leather chair and lamb's wool throw as well as his golden tray and goblet, Joseph thought to himself. But Joseph was not there to judge—after all, that was Pilate's job.

"Sit," Pilate said without looking up from the parchment he was poring over.

Joseph complied and sat silently until Pilate was ready to discuss whatever it was he wanted to discuss. When Pilate was in the room everyone else was less important and felt it. Finally, Pilate looked up sober-faced at Joseph.

"First, I admire your courage and dedication to the law for offering to defend Jesus of Nazareth," Pilate began.

Joseph nodded slightly to show his respect but he was quite stunned that the Prefect of Judaea was thanking him for taking on Jesus's defense—or for that matter, thanking him for anything at all. Perhaps his worship was more human than the legend that preceded him.

"Unfortunately, thanks may be the only form of compensation that I will be able to offer you," Pilate said, finally arriving at the actual point of his comment.

"Your honor, while your gratitude is appreciated, it is not necessary," Joseph replied honestly. "I never expected to be paid. I take on this task willingly and with every sincerity to provide the best defense possible."

Pilate looked intently at Joseph. "Why?" Pilate's tone was placid and his curiosity earnest.

"The man needs a defense and Roman law dictates that he has one," Joseph replied in a lawyerly response.

"Is there something more?" Pilate asked, his eyes searching Joseph's face.

"Yes, your honor. There is something more," Joseph responded. "Have you felt it as well?"

"I know not of what you speak, "Pilate responded. He frowned and shoved the golden plate sitting on his table aside and into a spin, sending it clattering to the floor.

Pilate seemed to be engrossed in something on a parchment again. After a moment he collected himself and changed the subject. "I'm certain you're aware that Roman law requires that you inform the court of how the accused plans to plead along with your fundamental defense strategy. It all needs to be publicly recorded."

"Yes, sire," Joseph responded. "I currently am formulating the defense plan which I will provide to you in a timely manner. Please do not concern yourself with that."

"What I do have concern about on this morning is the length of this trial," Pilate explained. "How many days do you envision your preliminary work will require?"

"My research and deposition work and strategizing I'm assuming you refer to?" Joseph replied.

"Of course, what else?" Pilate countered.

"Yes... uh... I would need perhaps another seven days to feel prepared for trial, your honor," Joseph responded.

"Hmm. I suppose that's reasonable," Pilate said. "You feel a certainty that that is sufficient time to prepare? I don't want something to come back and haunt me someday. You know, if he is convicted an appeal from the defense that it was rushed to trial. Do I have reason for those kinds of worries, Joseph?"

"Not at all. My honest assessment is that one week will be sufficient. I will work long hours every day to ensure that I am equipped to provide the best defense."

"That's what I like to hear. Now I must prepare for court," Pilate said as he rose from his chair.

Joseph followed suit and stood. "Uh, there is but one more item that has occurred to me."

Pilate's eyebrow arched as his eyes locked onto the attorney. "Go on, man. I am pressed for time."

"I am aware that women are generally not allowed to testify publically in court," Joseph began. "I beg your honor to waive that standard for there are several women whose testimony may be crucial to the defense. I may elect not to use them but in the event I do…"

Pilate thought for a few moments and then responded. "I will trust your word, Joseph that these women are essential. I will allow their testimony."

"My gratitude, your honor," Joseph replied. "I would further ask that you instruct the jury to hold the testimony of these women in the same esteem as that of men."

"Is there anything else I can do for you?" Pilate asked. "It seems as though I exist for you and you alone on this morning."

"I do apologize for my rudeness and do genuinely appreciate your generosity," Joseph responded. Joseph turned to go but stopped at the door. He stood there remaining silent.

Pilate sensed that Joseph was lingering. He sighed. "What is it Joseph? You are testing my good nature."

"Sir, I am not prepared to make a formal request of the court at this time but in speaking with Mary, the mother of Jesus, I fear that her testimony could present a culpability issue. Her publically spoken words could lead to her own prosecution for blasphemy."

"For the love of Caesar! That's all I need—the trial and execution of a peasant woman! A martyr's mother!" Pilate exclaimed.

"As I mentioned, I contemplate the possibility of making a motion to the court. I wanted to give you advance notice that I may ask for immunity for Mary of Nazareth and possibly some of Jesus's other supporters—if I decide to call them or if the prosecution elects to call them as hostile witnesses."

"I see." Pilate plopped back down in his chair, an intense look of concern on his face. He ran the issue of immunity through his mind. Yet another legal entanglement, he thought. He was grateful to have advance warning that Joseph would possibly make such a motion. He would be prepared. Yet another task for Titus, he thought to himself.

***

It was dark when Joseph finally walked up the steep hill to his sprawling house. Joseph paused on the front portico before he entered the house that night. The city below was dark with a twinkling light here and there. He knew he would get an earful from Irit for being so late and decided to take a moment to take a few deep breaths of the air that had finally cooled and think about his day with Mary and his plans for the next day. He leaned against the stucco wall and looked off into the distance.

Mary had given Joseph the names of some of Jesus's close associates who he wanted to depose. He was told the area in which they could be found. He squeezed his eyes shut as he pressed hard to recall their names.

Ah, yes, Joseph thought to himself, there was another Mary. Let's see Mary Monica... no that wasn't it. Mary Margaret... no that wasn't it either. His brain and strength had been challenged that day. He was too fatigued to remember. He'd written it down and would get the name right tomorrow. He planned to have Hadas and Yakir discover her location and arrange for Joseph to meet with her. There was also the name of Peter Simon... or rather it was Simon Peter, he believed. This man and woman were apparently both ardent followers of Jesus. Joseph would have this man tracked down. Mary indicated that Simon Peter could give him many other names.

Joseph was shaken from his thoughts by the squeak of the front door as Irit pushed it open and spotted Joseph at the end of the portico.

"You spend all day making no money with your new client then you come home in the dark and visit the portico without the respect of saying good evening to your family!" Irit was giving Joseph that earful that he knew would be coming his way. "Now, I suppose you want to eat!"

Joseph smiled. He knew his wife so well. She snarled like a jackal but she rarely bit.

"I was just going to come inside and see if there was anything I could do to help my precious wife," Joseph said, displaying his renowned glibness.

"Ha! I'm sure," Irit responded, a slight smile curling on her lip.

"You're the mother of my children, Are you not, Irit?"

"Of course! Why do you ask such a foolish question? Perhaps you're going daft which would explain why you work for nothing."

Joseph walked toward Irit and extended his arm to her. She took it.

"Come inside with me, my love," Joseph said, "And let me tell you about a mother and her son."

Irit gazed at her husband perplexed, as she walked into the house with her husband.

***

Joseph and Irit talked for several hours even though it was late and neither one would be allowed much sleep time. But as Joseph had known all along, the kind-hearted Irit became fully engaged in the story of Jesus and his mother, Mary. She felt much empathy for the widow and her son who had been sentenced to death. She protested—the *punishment did not fit the crime. He was just a misguided young man.* Irit knew as a mother herself that the execution of her son would destroy Mary. Finally, as the sky began to lighten, Joseph was too exhausted to continue.

"Let us get at least an hour or two of sleep," Joseph said as he stood and helped Irit from her chair.

"Fine, we'll sleep now," Irit responded. "Joseph, you make sure to do everything you can do for that young man. And, oh, that poor woman! How can she endure that? Joseph, you need to..."

Joseph listened politely as Irit droned on, giving him advise on how to save Jesus's life and how to spare Mary the anguish that loomed.

"Yes, dear... yes, dear," Joseph's tired voice trailed off as they walked down the hallway to their sleeping chambers.

Chapter 10
Witnesses for the Defense

After Joseph checked into his office the next morning, he leaned back in his wooden chair and thought about the day ahead of him. Hadas and Yakir had found Simon Peter, just as Mary had suggested, in the Garden of Gethsemane. From his assistants, Joseph learned that Simon Peter, who according to Mary was a devout follower of Jesus, seemed to be little reluctant to speak with him. Joseph frowned trying to reconcile the man's apparent recalcitrance to provide support for Jesus given his demonstrated devotion to him. Why wouldn't he want to help him? The more Joseph delved into the case of Jesus of Nazareth, the more daunting it appeared. It seemed as though one barrier was being placed before him after another. He sighed. It would be a very long day.

Simon Peter insisted that if the meeting were to take place, it would have to be in the garden where he and his cronies spent much of their time. Joseph would be out in the heat at the most oppressive time of the day and he already felt fatigued from his lack of sleep the night before thanks to Irit's intent interest in the case. Joseph hoped that he could reap the benefit of perhaps meeting with some of Jesus's other followers who may also be in the garden. There were no guarantees; Simon Peter hadn't promised Hadas that any of the others would be there. But at least it was a possibility. Joseph would think positive.

Joseph made his way down the dusty road that led to the Garden of Gethsemane. His leather sandals were filled with dust and pebbles and he was perspiring by the time he reached the edge of the garden. He took a breather while he pulled off one sandal then the other and shook the debris out of them. He proceeded into the garden and as soon as he did he felt the luxury of the cooler air from the shade of the many trees he passed under. He craned his neck and saw in the distance a lone man sitting on the ground in a clearing. It seemed as though he might be talking to himself or, perhaps he was praying. Joseph, out of respect for the man, approached slowly. When the man grew silent and rested his head on his bent knees, Joseph cautiously drew closer.

"Simon Peter?"

The man's head shot up quickly and focused his attention on the source of the voice.

"Yes? Do I know you, sir?" Simon Peter asked.

"No, sir. We do not know each other," Joseph responded with a slight smile. "But I do hope we get to know each other."

Simon Peter's stoic face now reflected concern. "Your words intrigue me. What need do we have to know each other?"

Joseph didn't want to waste any more time with game playing. "Sir, I am Joseph of Arimathea. I believe my assistant Hadas spoke with you yesterday?"

Now Simon Peter's face changed again. He looked troubled but did not speak.

"May I sit, kind sir?" Joseph asked Simon Peter.

Simon Peter remained silent. Joseph, never the one to be overly conciliatory, took it upon himself to sit down on the ground beside Simon Peter. Joseph picked up some parched weeds and began to pull the dead leaves off the stalk and throw them into the windless air.

"You do know that I defend your friend, Jesus of Nazareth?" Joseph asked.

Simon Peter nodded.

Well, Joseph thought, his travels had taken him from a woman who would give her soul for the life of Jesus to a friend who apparently was reluctant to utter even a word. Joseph realized that though his body and brain were taxed beyond their capabilities, he was going to have to dig deep for this deposition that would not transpire with ease. But he was up for the task.

"You do know Jesus of Nazareth, sir?"

"Of course," Simon Peter said. "He is beloved to me."

"Very well. That is news that rests lightly on my ears," Joseph responded. "What is your relationship with him?"

"I am a devotee. He is the Messiah, Son of the Living God," Simon Peter responded, now without hesitation.

This could be yet another case of blasphemy for the prosecution, Joseph thought to himself. He began to recognize that he may have to request a blanket immunity for most of the defense witnesses.

"Yes, I talked with Mary, mother of Jesus," Joseph responded. "She told me the story of his birth and life."

Simon Peter looked pointedly at Joseph. "Do you believe in Him?"

"My personal opinions and beliefs are not part of this case."

"How can you defend someone you don't believe in?" Simon Peter implored.

"I'll provide legal defense for Jesus of Nazareth. I do not have to be a follower to do that," Joseph answered sternly. "What's important is that I am an expert in Roman and Jewish laws. Jesus doesn't need another follower right now. He needs a skilled attorney."

Simon Peter turned away from Joseph and returned to his stoic demeanor. It occurred to Joseph that something was bothering this man beyond the fact that his idol was incarcerated and sentenced by the Jews to be executed. Joseph quickly assessed the situation and determined that it would be better to start off with questions about Simon Peter's own life. It was Joseph's experience that most people like to talk about themselves. This man would probably prove to be no different.

"Tell me about yourself, Peter... please."

Just as Joseph had guessed, Peter was completely willing to talk about himself.

"I am the son of Jonah of Zebedee. I am a simple fisherman, devoted to my family. My brother, Andrew, and I work hard at our fishing business in Bethsaida in order to support our families," Peter told Joseph."

Joseph took note of Peter's biographical information and remained patient for Peter to reveal in his own time what his relationship was with Jesus. Peter talked on for quite a while longer about his life and family and work. Finally, he came to a stop. Joseph assumed that Peter had come up to the time in his life in which he became involved with Jesus. Finally, he seemed willing to talk about that.

"Now, I will tell you about my relationship with Jesus of Nazareth," Peter offered.

"As you wish, sir," Joseph replied.

"I first became aware of Jesus from my brother, Andrew, who was a follower of John the Baptist," Simon Peter began.

"I have heard of this man," Joseph said.

"He was a good man and told my brother that he had baptized a man called Jesus who was of Galilee," Simon Peter told Joseph. He turned and looked intently at Joseph. "John the Baptist called Jesus the Lamb of God."

"I see. And how did you feel about that?"

"My tendency was to believe the words since John the Baptist was a man of God and a truth-teller," Simon Peter answered. "My brother Andrew became a follower of Jesus and beckoned me to come with him. He told me we had found the Messiah."

"Were you... uh... at all skeptical, sir?" Joseph asked gently.

"Any doubt was dashed when Jesus told Andrew and I to change the height of our nets so that we would catch more fish," Simon Peter responded.

"What was your response?" Joseph asked, intrigued.

"We adjusted the nets to the height he suggested."

"What happened?" Joseph asked, somewhat perplexed.

"We caught hundreds more fish each day!" Simon Peter responded emphatically.

"That is a miracle, isn't it," Joseph responded, thinking to himself that the fish story wasn't exactly the type of thing a legend was built upon.

"But that was nothing," Simon Peter responded sensing that Joseph was dubious about Jesus's powers. "He cured my wife's mother who was on her deathbed. Now she walks around like the young."

Joseph scratched furiously on his parchment as Simon Peter recounted an incident that could certainly be attributed to god.

For the first time since they met, Simon Peter smiled. "After he healed my wife's mother, I was blessed to have him use my boat for his missionaries along the shore of Lake Gennesaret. I became a follower and one of his first disciples and the first apostle to be ordained by Jesus. He named me Peter."

"What was the significance of that?" Joseph asked.

"He named me father of his ministry," Peter recalled.

"Quite an honor, I'd say," Joseph responded.

The two men fell silent for a moment. Joseph strongly sensed that Peter was about to reveal something that was heartfelt and perhaps difficult to speak about. Joseph knew from experience to remain silent in such instances and allow the one being deposed to speak in his own time and comfort rather than for the questioner to pull it out of him.

"I have shamed myself before God," Peter began.

Ah, Joseph thought to himself, finally we're getting to the crux of the matter. It could be important for the case.

"At the last supper that the disciples shared with him, Jesus asked that I watch over him but I was filled with wine and food and fell into a deep sleep," Peter said sadly. "That's when he was arrested. I failed him."

"But that's understandable, man," Joseph countered.

"Ah... but there's worse yet. You see, as close as I was to him, I... denied I even knew him," Peter said.

This wasn't exactly what Joseph was expecting and he was somewhat taken aback by Peter's words not knowing exactly where they may lead. But again, Joseph remained patient.

Peter turned and looked intently at Joseph. "He told me I would."

"You mean that Jesus predicted you would deny knowing him?" Joseph asked but didn't wait for a response. "Exactly under what circumstances did you deny knowing him?"

"You seem to hold no judgment on me," Peter said.

"I'm not in that business, Peter."

"To answer your question, at the last supper with His Lord, he told me that before morning—aye e'en before the cock crowed—that I would deny him and deny him thrice," Peter said, his eyes reflecting the sadness in recounting the moment. "I assured Jesus that I would never deny him and would even die with him but he looked at me with those intense eyes..."

"I've experienced those eyes first-hand," Joseph offered.

"But surely as the sky was dark that night he was arrested, I denied I knew him. As the people crowded around him as he was taken to the High Temple, three people pointed to me and said that I knew Jesus," Peter said, a faraway look in his eyes. "I claimed again and again and again that I didn't know the man!"

Joseph feared that Joseph's testimony could be detrimental to Jesus. How could he reconcile to the jury the testimony of a witness who claimed to be a devotee of Jesus yet publically denied even knowing him?

"I am not sure to this day why I did that. I've asked myself why a thousand times. Was I afraid of being arrested? Was it cowardice?" Peter said as a slight glimmer began to creep into his eyes. He turned and looked at Joseph. "But I heard the cock crow and suddenly repentance came over my body and soul. Jesus forgave me just like he'll forgive all men who follow him. Perhaps my denial had deeper meaning. Perhaps it was destiny, pre-ordained."

Joseph responded but it was almost more to himself than to Peter. "I'm beginning to think there's a lot about this case that's pre-ordained."

***

The head of Jesus's ministry gave Joseph more headaches. It would be another case of possible blasphemy were Joseph to call Simon Peter to the stand. Joseph was all tangled up with defeatist thoughts when yet another one occurred to him. Thinking through everything that Peter told him, there could be a corroborating witness to make the case that Jesus was very special, even god-like—the woman he saved, Simon Peter's mother-in-law. Joseph frowned and shook his head. What was he thinking? Was it plausible that Joseph could wage the defense that Jesus was in fact the Messiah? Joseph grimaced. He might be up on charges of blasphemy himself. He would give it some thought but if the old woman, Simon Peter's wife's mother, were still alive, she could testify that Jesus saved her or that she thought he had. Joseph had a glancing hope that Jesus's miracle had a long-lasting effect and that the woman had not passed yet. But was mysticism the direction in which Joseph wanted to take this trial? Joseph was a principled man. He had to believe in any defense he presented. One of miracles and angels and virgin births would not fall into that category.

***

Peter told Joseph where he could find one of Jesus's most devoted followers, Mary Magdalene. The name had some familiarity to Joseph but he couldn't recall where he'd heard it before. This woman would be the second Mary in the case but Joseph hoped that she might be more help than the first Mary. With any luck, the account of her relationship with Jesus wouldn't be filled with tales of miracles and visits from angels. Since Mary Magdalene was a much younger woman than Jesus's mother Joseph was hopeful that she would have a grasp on just how high the stakes in the case against Jesus were and would tailor her deposition accordingly.

Joseph walked from the Garden of Gethsemane toward an upscale neighborhood that was not far from his own. That was, he was told by Simon Peter, where he would find Mary Magdalene. As with Mary, Mother of Jesus, Joseph would have to deal with the reality that women were not, in the main, considered credible witnesses in legal proceedings. But even if he didn't call the women himself, he knew that Caiaphas would have that option. Joseph had to be prepared for what each woman's testimony might be. He had not ruled out calling the women himself. But if he did decide to use their testimony, he certainly would discuss the credibility of their testimony and beseech Pilate to instruct the jury to heed their words as they would that of men.

After a few wrong turns, Joseph asked some citizens to help him locate Mary Magdalene. When he asked a woman where he could find her, she turned her nose in the air and walked quickly away in a huff. Her reaction was inexplicable to Joseph. Perhaps the perspiration from his walk had made it difficult for others to stand near him. Then he stopped a man who, with a big smile on his face, pointed the way to Mary Magdalene's dwelling. Well, that little study in humanity told him that men were definitely more helpful when it came to assisting a stranger trying to find his way. He'd have to tell Irit about his experience. She was always so quick to say that women were the kinder sex.

Joseph rapped on Mary Magdalene's door and was surprised and actually pleased to be greeted by a very comely young woman. She had large shining dark eyes and wavy hair that cascaded down her back almost to her waist. Peter had gotten word to her that Joseph was coming. She greeted him warmly and asked him to come inside. But Joseph hesitated at the doorway.

"Miss, unless your mother is home with you, I prefer to speak with you outside on the veranda," Joseph said.

Joseph did not want to besmirch the young woman's name by being alone with a gentleman inside her apartment. Mary Magdalene took it differently but her response confounded Joseph.

"As you wish, sir," Mary Magdalene replied, "But I am no longer plagued by the demons. Jesus cleansed me of them."

Joseph maintained an even demeanor as he turned and walked toward the veranda thinking to himself that apparently angels and miracles weren't enough, now he had to contend with demons.

***

Mary Magdalene told Joseph of her devotion to Jesus and how he had inspired her life. She was very upset by the current circumstances but, like the others Joseph had talked with, she seemed to understand a certain destiny about him. From what he could tell from his conversation with Simon Peter, there were no other women who were close followers of Jesus. Joseph was curious about that.

"If I may, Mary Magdalene, were there other female devotees of Jesus in addition to yourself?" Joseph asked.

"There are women who are believers, sir, but I am unique in that I am within his inner circle," Mary Magdalene responded.

"To what do you owe that relationship?" Joseph asked.

"Joseph, Jesus has changed my life. You see I was involved in a sinful life, a life I was not proud of," Mary Magdalene answered, shifting her eyes down. "As I said before, Jesus cleansed me of my demons—seven demons, in all."

Seven demons, Joseph thought to himself, why not six or eight? Joseph didn't mean to be flippant about the young woman's life. But he always gauged his own reaction against the potential reaction of a jury. And coupling her words with the diverse reactions of the woman and the man on the street when he asked for directions along with Mary's willingness to allow him inside her dwelling unchaperoned, brought Joseph some clarity about the young woman. Joseph was a gentleman and he would not press Mary Magdalene about her past. However, her past life potentially presented another dimension of obstacles in case the woman was called by the prosecution. Joseph wistfully wondered if any of Jesus's witnesses would ever present a bright spot in the case, effective and free of controversy. Then again, were Joseph to pursue the defense of Jesus as the Messiah, Son of the Living God, Mary Magdalene's testimony could support his ability to heal the sick or, in her case, the sinful. But on the other hand, of course,

Caiaphas could destroy Jesus's reputation if he tried to make a sinister connection between Jesus and Mary Magdalene.

After a prolonged silence, Mary Magdalene smiled slightly at Joseph.

"I may not have been proud of the years before I knew him, but I have been one of his strongest advocates. He told me so himself. I have spread the word of his mission. It is not with hubris that I tell you I was called by Simon Peter and some of the other disciples, an equal of the apostles. I'm proud of that, Joseph. In fact, I have helped other downtrodden women to abandon their sinful ways. I am establishing safe houses for them. My work pleases the Lord."

Joseph returned Mary Magdalene's smile and scratched many notes on his parchment. As he wrote, Mary Magdalene looked kindly upon the gentle man.

"Joseph of Arimathea, please excuse my boldness, but I understand that you volunteered to defend Jesus with no compensation and at risk of harsh criticism from the Pharisees. Tell me, why do you help Jesus?" Mary asked.

Joseph looked intensely at Mary Magdalene. "I felt Jesus had so much stacked up against him that he didn't have a chance without representation. I sensed that he must have felt that the world had turned against him."

"This world? Perhaps, "Mary Magdalene responded. "But there are more important matters that are not of this world. In that other world, he will be at peace and be able to look over all of us."

"One thing that strikes me is that most of his followers feel his fate is sealed," Joseph responded, slightly annoyed by the fatalist attitude of those who should be positive and supporting him.

"His destiny is set, Joseph, which is what gives us, his devoted followers, our hope," she said.

"Your hope is in his death?" Joseph asked, confounded by the obvious conflict in Mary Magdalene's words.

"I think you'll understand someday," Mary Magdalene said simply and quietly.

Joseph gathered himself. It wasn't like him to become emotional over his clients—especially since most were fat, old rich men.

"Mary, you're a young woman and you are obviously very bright," Joseph said, "I do not want to suggest that you be anything but truthful but do you see that by speaking of Jesus's ability to make miracles and making references to his power in the afterworld that… that testimony will help prove the case of the prosecution—the blasphemy charges?"

"I understand what you are saying and I see that perhaps Jesus could be spared from execution in this life but it would not be God's will," Mary Magdalene responded. She paused a few moments before she spoke again. "Joseph, I could never deny that Jesus was the Messiah, that he was not the Son of the Living Good. Saying that would truly be blasphemy."

"Of course," Joseph said, once again frustrated by one of his own witnesses.

***

After Joseph left Mary Magdalene, he headed back to his office even though his home was nearby. He wanted to make sure that no fires had erupted in his absence and to learn if anyone was looking for him like the Governor of Judaea, perhaps. Yakir was just closing up shop when Joseph arrived. And to Joseph's surprise and delight, everything had gone smoothly and no one of authority was seeking his counsel or demanding his presence.

After looking over a few matters that had been saved for him, Joseph felt satisfied that he had left his practice in good hands. Dusk was turning to dark and Joseph would be very late for two consecutive nights. But at least he now had an ally in his wife. After learning details of the Jesus trial, Irit could not have been more understanding. Joseph decided he would not tell Irit about his visit to the lovely Mary Magdalene who apparently had a background of ill-repute. Irit probably wouldn't be as compassionate about her story and as understanding about his visiting with her for hours.

Tomorrow would be another long day. Joseph would be seeking the depositions of four men that Simon Peter had mentioned: Matthew, Mark, Luke and John.

Chapter 11
The Gospels

Joseph headed off early for the Garden of Gethsemane. He had found it difficult to sleep the night before so he rose early from his fitful rest. While it was dark and Irit was still fast asleep, Joseph furtively left the house and began a morning that he hoped would yield positive results for the case. He was anxiously anticipating the discussions he planned to have with several more close followers of Jesus of Nazareth. Simon Peter told Joseph that each of the men was maintaining logs about the life and ministry of Jesus and their experiences and relationships with them. He hoped that their notes would not present many conflicts. But he was realistic. He knew that if there were four people who observed the same crime being perpetrated or a run-in between two carts, there would be four different interpretations. There were four apostles Joseph would be talking to and the possibility that there would be four different stories. He just hoped that Matthew, Mark, Luke and John could provide some solid defense for his client. He also held onto the hope that any talk of angels, miracles and demons would be at a minimum.

Joseph reached the garden just as the sun was peeking over the horizon. It was pleasant that morning in the shaded garden. Joseph picked out a large ash tree to sit under. The lush dewy grass that surrounded the trunk made a comfortable and inviting resting place for the weary man. Joseph, exhausted from a combination of the long walk and lack of sleep, leaned his head back against the tree trunk and closed his eyes. He didn't want to get too relaxed, lest he drifted off into a deep sleep and missed meeting with the disciples.

But drowsiness took over and soon Joseph was making a noisy spectacle of himself with the snores and snarls of a deep and much needed sleep. Just as Joseph's slumber came to its most sweet and mesmerizing height, he was awakened by a gentle tugging on his arm. Joseph's eyes shot open and he looked into two friendly hazel-colored eyes.

"Uh... sorry, I must have fallen off," Joseph said as he forced himself into a measure of lucidity. "My dear wife claims I'm quite a snorer. Hope I didn't disturb anyone's peace."

The gentle eyes were now smiling. "Your slumber was no bother to me or my friends but I do believe there were a few cross squirrels and birds that were driven away. But they'll return."

Joseph chuckled at the stranger's humorous reference to what was probably quite a noisy display. He stood up and bowed to the man.

"I will certainly make my amends with the forest denizens, Joseph said good-naturedly. "I'm Joseph of Arimathea, kind sir."

"I had thoughts that you were he," the man said, "My colleague Simon Peter told me you wanted to speak with me about a mutual friend." The man bowed slightly to Joseph. "I am a disciple of Jesus of Nazareth. I am Matthew of Galilee, son of Alpheus."

"My pleasure, sir," Joseph responded. "And, yes, I do indeed need to speak with you—if you would be so kind. As you may know, I am defending Jesus against the charges leveled at him by the Jewish High Court."

"I am gratified by your efforts and I will do whatever I can to help you," Matthew responded.

The two men strolled around the sumptuous gardens as Joseph learned a few basic things about Matthew. He learned that Matthew had been, like his father before him, a tax collector for Herod—not the most popular of positions to hold. Having that position indicated to Joseph that Matthew was more highly educated than the general masses since being literate in Aramaic and Greek was a requirement for the task. It was while Matthew was performing this function in an area north of the Sea of Galilee that Jesus called Matthew to serve him, to become one of the disciples in his ministry. Jesus responded to the criticism of the Pharisees for his association with a tax collector but Jesus responded that he "came not to call the righteous" but to call the sinners.

Matthew said he had heard tales of Jesus for years before he met him.

"When Jesus was only two years old, the Magi from the East came to honor him," Matthew began.

Joseph was a little taken aback. "The kings didn't visit him upon his birth?"

"Jesus was a young babe able to toddle around when the Magi brought him gifts honoring him as the Messiah," Matthew responded.

Matthew explained to Joseph that Jesus, his twelve disciples and his other followers had entered the city of Jerusalem less than a week before Jesus was arrested.

Joseph asked that they find a comfortable place to sit. He had brought along some parchment and needed to take notes. Joseph was particularly interested in Jesus's ministry in Jerusalem and didn't want to miss any important details. Matthew knew of a grove of trees that provided both privacy and shade. Matthew led Joseph to the spot and they sat down under the largest tree.

Matthew explained that several of the disciples were able to locate a young donkey for Jesus to ride. It was on a bright Monday morning, Matthew told Joseph, that Jesus first rode into the city. Jesus was greeted with the love of many who already believed in him. After Jesus was in the town but a few days, he became upset with the money changers in the temple.

"One of the charges that Caiaphas has brought against Jesus is his alleged threat to destroy the temple and then rebuild it," Joseph said. "Is this perhaps the incident he referred to?"

"Yes. Jesus was quite upset with the show of greed by the rabbis in the temple," Matthew responded.

"Did he threaten to destroy the temple?" Joseph asked.

"Jesus was quite angry and rightly so," Matthew responded. "In his anger, he broke some items and threw over some stands."

"Was he arrested?" Joseph asked.

"Not right then," Matthews responded, a sad look came over his eyes as he recollected the last few days. "Even though Jesus's outrage was warranted and he was right to rid the Temple of evil, the Pharisees made note of his actions and now they are being held against him."

"When you say that Jesus was right, what exactly do you mean?" Joseph asked.

"The rabbis were allowing greedy money changers to operate in the temple," Matthew responded.

"I assume that is against Jewish religious laws?" Joseph asked, already knowing the answer.

"Yes, sir."

"Hmm. Well, then we have evidence of Jesus defending Jewish law against rabbis who were breaking it, don't we?" Joseph asked rhetorically.

Matthew and Joseph shared a warm smile. Maybe there is hope, Joseph thought to himself.

"I'm sure Caiaphas will not appreciate a public airing of the actions of his rabbis that were tantamount to blasphemy," Joseph commented.

Matthew's face grew stoic. He recalled to Joseph how trouble began to emerge in the intervening days. Perhaps the rabbis were avenging their embarrassment over the temple debacle but they began making trouble for Jesus.

"What trouble?" Joseph asked.

"They began to question Jesus's authority," Matthew responded. "And the Pharisees complained to the Jewish High priests that Jesus was disparaging their reputation, calling them hypocrites."

"No doubt that was connected to the temple incident," Joseph commented as he scribbled furiously on his parchment.

"I'm sure you're right, sir," Matthew replied. "There was no initial complaint of Jesus claiming to be God. What Caiaphas and the others were concerned about was how they would be viewed by their congregation. They saw Jesus as their competition and a person who was not afraid to confront them publicly about their behavior and motivations." Matthew paused for several long moments.

"Tragically, the Jewish elders were able to corrupt one of our own," Matthew offered.

"Who was that?"

"Judas of Iscariot—one of the disciples," Matthew answered. "Caiaphas himself gave Judas silver pieces to lead the guards to Jesus."

"How much was he paid?" Joseph asked.

"Thirty silver pieces."

"Sounds like a bribe," Joseph mused. "Perhaps I'll have to call Caiaphas as a witness. Where was Jesus arrested?"

Matthew looked around and gestured with his hands. "Right here in the Garden of Gethsemane where we sit. He was praying to God."

A chill went through Joseph's body thinking of that morning and how distressing it must has been for Jesus. He looked at a clearing beyond a clump of trees and sensed that it was there in that solitary spot that Jesus had selected to pray.

"Jesus was very disappointed in Peter and John who he asked to keep watch for him." Matthew offered.

"Simon Peter? I believe the man suffers from great guilt over that failing," Joseph replied.

"Judas led the rabbis and the guards and kissed Jesus's cheek as a means of identifying him," Matthew told Joseph.

"Deception disguised by affection?" Joseph commented.

"The disciples tried to defend Jesus. Simon Peter cut off the ear of one of the Jewish guards during the scuffle," Matthew said. "Jesus healed the man and..."

"Wait, please. How did he heal him?" Joseph asked, interrupting Matthew for what seemed to him an important event, even a miracle.

"Jesus pressed the man's dangling ear to his head and healed his wound," Matthew responded.

"The ear was back in place?" Joseph asked, not attempting to hide his astonishment.

"Yea, as though it had never been wounded," Matthew responded.

"What is the man's name?"

"Maluch. He was the head of the Sanhedrin guards. He became a believer and is in hiding from Caiaphas and the others for obvious reasons."

Joseph quickly took notes about the event with the intent of finding this man. Matthew continued speaking about the night of the arrest.

"Jesus was upset by the violence, even in his own defense. He warned us that if we lived by the sword that we would die by the sword."

"Wise words," Joseph responded as the speed and fury with which he was writing increased.

"I feel pity for Judas," Matthew said as he turned and looked intensely at Joseph. "He offered to give the silver back to the Pharisees but they wouldn't have it. Sadly, his fate was sealed."

Joseph finished up his notes from his conversation with Matthew and then asked him if he could help him find one of the other men on his list—the names he had been given by Simon Peter. Matthew was happy to help Joseph and asked him to follow him. He would know where to find John who wasn't one of Jesus apostles but was ardent follower of him and had been taking notes about Jesus's ministry. John might be able to enlighten Joseph about some of the details of Jesus's life and ministry.

The sun was shining brightly as Matthew led Joseph through the dusty streets of Jerusalem to a settlement near the southern edge of the city. Joseph's short legs took two gaits to every one of Matthew's long strides and by the time they arrived at John's apartment, Joseph was breathing heavily. Matthew knocked on the door several times before it slowly swung open. John, like some of the other followers of Jesus, were keeping out of sight. After all, it would do no good for them to be arrested just because their leader was. They could stay free to continue his ministry—albeit in secret—while Jesus was incarcerated. John smiled widely when he saw Matthew. He trusted that the person with his friend was not an enemy.

"Hurry, Matthew," John said, "Step inside quickly... your companion as well."

Matthew and Joseph immediately entered John's apartment. It was dark inside; the shutters were drawn and only a dim ray of light made its way through. John offered them a seat at the table but Matthew declined his hospitality.

"John, this is Joseph of Arimathea."

"My pleasure, sir," John said. "You've volunteered to help Jesus, have you not?"

"Yes. I am defending Jesus in the Roman Court," Joseph responded.

John seemed to be visibly shaken. He looked at Matthew. "That sounds so ominous. How did it come to this, Matthew?"

"The Lord works in mysterious ways, John," Matthew responded, trying to comfort the younger man.

"John, I understand you have kept a sort of journal about Jesus and his ministry," Joseph said.

"Yes, sir. I have kept many notations during our time together... which seems to have ended."

Joseph made a mental note that John seemed to be especially distraught over Jesus's ordeal, more so than the others. Emotional witnesses can be a benefit to the defense but they can be detrimental due to their volatile natures. Joseph sensed that Matthew was potentially the most valuable witness he had thus far. He had a clear and concise way of speaking and his tone was one of authority lending his words credibility. One matter nagged at Joseph. There were a few statements he made that seemed at odds with what Mary, Jesus's mother, had told him. But Joseph put that thought to the back of his mind. He'd worry about that later.

Matthew told John he would not stay that it was best for him and Joseph to speak privately. John's wife was at the market so they had the small apartment to themselves. Matthew bid the two men good day and told Joseph he was willing to do whatever he could to help him. It struck Joseph that no one close to Jesus pleaded with Joseph to save Jesus from his impending fate. It was unusual and generally the first thing family and friends were concerned with but Joseph dismissed the thought. Perhaps they didn't fully understand the seriousness of the charges.

John told Joseph of his relationship with Jesus and his knowledge of the man. He first heard of Jesus when he was in Galilee where Jesus had caused quite a commotion in a temple. Greedy money changers had been allowed to corrupt the temple. Joseph set his marker down and looked intently at John.

"Was this incident not at the temple here in Jerusalem?" Joseph asked.

"There was a slight dustup here but the most controversial incident happened in Galilee," John responded.

"Jesus is accused of threatening to destroy the temple. Did he display violence at this incident?" Joseph asked.

"Not at all. Jesus is a peaceful man," John replied.

"It was after that when Jesus felt called to this city." John smiled remembering. "Most kings ride atop a mighty steed. But Jesus was happy with the donkey we found for him. His followers walked behind him just last Sunday as he rode triumphantly into town."

Sunday? Joseph thought to himself. Another discrepancy—minor but still a discrepancy.

"Tell me about when Jesus was... was apprehended, John," Joseph said in a gentle tone not wanting to stir too many emotions from the sensitive young man.

"That was the worst day of my life, Joseph," John responded, his face had a faraway look as he recalled the incident. "Judas, one of our own betrayed him. He identified Jesus for the priests and guards. He did the bidding of the Jewish High Priests."

"Was he paid for his betrayal?" Joseph asked.

"Perhaps. I've heard rumors but not sure of what they may have paid him," John responded.

Joseph sighed and scratched down several more notes on his parchment.

John turned and looked earnestly at Joseph. "I'm very close to Jesus. Perhaps because we're near the same age. He confided in me perhaps more than the others."

"That's very interesting and could be very important to his defense," Joseph responded. "Can you elaborate?"

"Jesus talked with me at length about his divineness and his purpose," John responded, the reverence was obvious in his voice and tone. "Through our talks, Jesus taught me that salvation was meant for everyone and that it was available just for the asking."

"If I may. . . how were you convinced?"

"You see, kind sir, Jesus conquered death. He proved the miracle of his being by resurrecting the dead," John answered.

Joseph did not allow his countenance to reveal how stunned he was by John's words as he wrote down every one of them. "Was there someone specific—evidence of such a miracle that would stand up in court?"

"Lazarus of Bethany. Jesus made Lazarus live after death," John told Joseph.

"Can you tell me something about Lazarus?" Joseph asked controlling his tone to make sure it was neither mocking or doubting.

"Jesus was called to the bedside of Lazarus who was ailing" John said. "By the time he arrived, Lazarus had passed away from his illness. His family was upset that Jesus had delayed his visit but Jesus comforted them and they believed in him." John looked intently at Joseph. "I'll tell you his exact words. Jesus said to Lazarus's family, "'I am the resurrection, and the life: he that believeth in me, though he were dead, yet shall he live: And whosoever liveth and believeth in me shall never die.'"

Joseph was completely engaged in John's retelling of the event. "Well, did the man rise from his grave then?"

"Yes, he is alive as we speak."

It occurred to Joseph that one defense strategy could be simply that Jesus was indeed the Messiah. But as quickly as the thought ran through his mind, he dismissed it. Such a scenario was bizarre and a certain loser.

"Can we find him? Would he be willing to testify?"

"I'll seek him out, Joseph," John responded.

"Lazarus would literally be living proof of Jesus's powers," Joseph responded. "Please do track him down and perhaps family members who could support this claim. I'll have my assistant contact you."

John looked slightly offended, even hurt. "I do tell you the truth, sir. I defend Jesus but he taught us that truth is beauty in his world. I would never violate God's laws."

"Of course not, John," Joseph responded. John's reaction confirmed his first impressions that John was very emotional, even fragile. He did not want to upset John since his testimony could be vital to Jesus's defense. Joseph was quick to soothe John's feelings and convince him that Joseph's words were not an effrontery to him or Jesus.

"I believe your words, John, "Joseph continued. "But unfortunately it is not me who has to be convinced. We will be facing a jury and a very discriminating judge in Pontius Pilate. Please understand that we need as many people as possible on our side to build a case so that no one can tear it down including and most importantly the Prefect of Judaea."

"I understand. It's just... that it's been so disturbing," John said. "Jesus means so much to me. To see him in this horrid circumstance has made my heart raw and my spirit on the edge of collapse."

Joseph gently grasped John's arm. "I know that you are a good friend of Jesus and that you only have his welfare in mind. We need you to stay strong because his defense needs you."

"There is something else that disturbs me," John said tentatively as he looked askance from Joseph.

"Please tell me what that is, John."

"Jesus told me many things. He foretold of his future," John responded. "I was in tears when he told me he would not be on this earth for many years. I tried to reject his words and hoped against hope that they were not true. But now, with all this, I fear that his words are coming true."

Joseph thought to himself about the destiny so often spoken of by Jesus's followers which continued to loom over the case. Was there something to the prophecies about Jesus? Would he ever be able to structure a strong defense from all this mysticism?

A slight smile washed across John's face. "There is one bright ray of hope, Joseph."

"Those words are music to my ears," Joseph said, smiling back at John. "Lift up my heart. Please make haste and tell me what that bright spot is."

"Jesus told me that he had life eternal and that all those who believed in him did as well."

Joseph took down his last notes with John all the while thinking with more than a little trepidation that yet another witness would be on the stand talking in terms of the eternal life of the living god. The scales were tipping in that direction for the defense strategy but it would never work. First, Joseph himself couldn't support it and secondly, it was folly.

***

John was good enough to walk with Joseph the short distance to where Mark could be found. He was staying out of the public eye with relatives. John rapped on the main door with what appeared to Joseph to be a coded knock. Soon a small, wrinkled woman with huge dark eyes and no teeth creaked open the door and seeing John allowed the two men to enter. She quickly shut and bolted the door behind them. John explained that he and his companion needed to speak with Mark in private. The woman, not saying a word, quickly disappeared to an interior room.

A few moments later, Mark who was a few years older than John emerged from the hallway. Mark had a serious look on his face and piercing dark green eyes. His face had the look of wisdom possessed by people who were never surprised by anything and always seemed to know everything. This day was no exception.

Mark bowed to John and Joseph. "Are you Joseph of Arimathea?"

Joseph bowed slightly to Mark who was nearly half a meter taller than he. Mark had quite an impressive bearing and Joseph was already sizing him up as a potentially powerful presence on the witness stand.

"Yes, Mark, this is Joseph," John interjected. "He is defending Jesus in the Roman Court. He needs our help."

"Destiny needs no help, John," Mark said, his words as wise as his countenance. Mark looked intensely at Joseph. "I mean not to disparage you, Joseph. I know you are a good man and have the best intentions. Of course, I will do everything possible to help you. Today I am committed to my family. I will meet you tomorrow in the garden at sunrise if that suits your day." He looked pointedly at Joseph again. "Sometimes fate is dynamic. We can only hope that will be what results."

Joseph was a bit confused by Mark's words but gathered that destiny was once again interjecting itself into the defense of Jesus of Nazareth. But no matter—Joseph was in for the long haul. He felt as though he was but a small leaf in the palm of God who was walking along to a destination that only He knew. But, Joseph thought, all of us were but leaves and we were all in the hand of God and tied to a destiny that He would take us to. Even Jesus.

Chapter 12
Mark and Luke

Joseph was once again fatigued from lack of sleep when he set off to meet Mark in the garden. He didn't mind at all that he was exhausted. His fatigue told him that he was fully engaged in the case. His mind was swirling day and night with details and legalities. The testimony he had received thus far was at its best conflicting and at its worse detrimental to his defense. But he would figure it all out. While he may not relish the challenge the case presented, he would meet it without hesitation.

Joseph scurried into the shady, secluded area where he was to meet Mark. Joseph declined his wife's kind offer to make him breakfast and left home early. He brought along a jug of water and a crust of bread figuring he'd have to wait for Mark. It would give him time to formalize the myriad of thoughts in his head into questions for Jesus's friend. To his surprise, Mark was already at the meeting site when Joseph arrived, sitting under a large ash tree. He probably would have to forego partaking in his food as he would never be disrespectful to Mark by eating and drinking in front of him. As he drew closer, Joseph was relieved to see that Mark was munching on some fruit. Joseph, after all, would not have to starve himself until dinner.

After the two men finished their repast, Joseph began the deposition.

"Please be so kind as to tell me about your relationship with Jesus, Mark," Joseph began.

"I, like the others you've already spoken to, am dedicated to Jesus," Mark began, his rich voice resonating in a manner that made Joseph smile, thinking how impressive it would sound in the open court. "Jesus is the Living God. If it is deemed blasphemous for me to state publicly, then so be it. Let anyone with ears to hear, listen."

Joseph smiled to himself. His spirits were buoyed by Mark's statement and the boldness and confidence with which it was delivered. People naturally admired those who stood up for their beliefs. That attitude would go far with the jurymen, Joseph thought to himself. He scratched a note on his parchment, referencing Mark's statement.

Mark recounted Jesus's baptism by John the Baptist at Bethany in the Jordan River. He told how both Jesus's words and deeds convinced him that He was the Son of God. It was Mark's strong belief that Jesus had performed many miracles. Mark himself had actually witnessed Jesus driving the devil out of the possessed and healing the sick. He relayed to him how Jesus was approached by a band of lepers during his ministry. Others had claimed that Jesus was angry with the lepers, but it was not true. Jesus was touched by the plight of the lepers and to demonstrate that those sick people were not evil or contagious, Jesus laid hands upon them. The skin on the lepers immediately began to heal before everyone's eyes. The cause for Jesus's anger was how cruelly those poor sick people had been treated by others in the village.

"When did Jesus first arrive in Jerusalem?" Joseph asked Mark.

"It was on a bright Sunday morning," Mark responded. He then trained his intense gray eyes on Joseph. "It was a triumphant moment and one that God beckoned him to do."

Mark replied to Joseph's question about Jesus's problem with the money changers in the temple. Mark replied that Jesus kept a cool head and took a peaceful approach to forcing the evil from the temple.

Mark's response about Jesus's arrival agreed with John's account. Mark's version of Jesus's confrontation with the money changers in the temple disputed Matthew's version which portrayed Jesus as angry and even violent. Joseph scribbled down a reminder to address that inconsistency. Trials were known to turn on lesser disparities.

Mark remarked about how the multitudes followed Jesus after being in his presence and witnessing his good works. He looked intensely at Joseph.

"Joseph, once a man has observed the works of Jesus and his goodness and purity, it is impossible for him to turn his back on him," Mark said with great emphasis. "I predict that you too, Joseph, will one day have the same reaction once you have come to know him."

Joseph and Mark had been sitting under the big ash tree for nearly two hours and needed to stretch their legs. Mark suggested that they take a walk around the shaded garden. Just then, they heard a commotion and some loud voices nearby. Mark, a protective sort, immediately turned on his heel and rush toward the sound of the voices. Joseph followed right on his heels. As they grew nearer, it was immediately apparent that several Jewish guards were having a verbal confrontation with some of Jesus's followers who had gathered to pray for him.

"What is your business here?" Mark called out loudly to the men, his booming voice wafting over the air and gaining their immediate attention.

One of the guards, a tall rather stocky man, smirked when he saw Mark. "We're looking for another holy man who thinks he's a god," the guard said. "Can you help me out with that?"

"If you come here to belittle us and our beliefs, I would advise you to turn around and spread your venom elsewhere," Mark said. "We are a peace loving people but we have our limits."

"This garden belongs to no one, your holiness," the guard said, laughing with his two other companions. "It is not for you to tell us to leave."

"Very well. You have a point," Mark said. He used his foot to draw a line in the sandy turf. "But each person has a right to his own space. I dare you not cross that line."

The anger on Mark's face, his confident tone, powerful bearing and deep, throaty voice caused the hectoring guards to lose their bravado.

"I too have a line that you dare not cross," the guard responded but his demeanor had softened and his voice was stilted, unsure.

"Have every confidence, sir, that any line you stand behind is not one that I would ever wish to cross," Mark responded as he glared intensely at the man.

Mark stood his ground. Just his sheer size was intimidating, not to mention the ire in his eyes and the angry timber of his voice.

Wisely, the guards decided to move on for Mark was not known to make groundless threats. The innocent followers who were merely praying when they were verbally assaulted by the guards, were grateful for Mark's intervention. Most of those gathered were women. One young woman spoke for the group.

"Mark, thank you for chasing off those bothersome guards," the young woman said. "We were merely praying our hearts for the Lord."

Mark patted the woman on the arm. "It is I who thank you for your prayers," he told her.

Joseph was impressed with how Mark handled himself. Perhaps, since he prevailed over the bullying guard, Mark could have the same impact on a more bothersome bully, Jesus's prosecutor.

***

After that bit of mid-morning drama, Joseph and Mark proceeded on their walk. Joseph's short legs took twice as many steps as the loping long strides of Mark. Mark volunteered some personal thoughts that, he said, he didn't often share. Joseph was anxious to hear what Mark, who Joseph observed to be a very thoughtful and introspective man, would reveal. Joseph stayed ever-hopeful that one of his witnesses would give him a golden nugget that would rock the court and prove Jesus's innocence.

Mark told Joseph that he was certain that Jesus was the Son of God. He reiterated again his good works and the miracles he performed on behalf of the poor and downtrodden. But there was another element, a deeper dimension which struck Mark to his very heart and soul. Jesus had taken Mark aside and told him that new knowledge would come to his followers after his death.

Joseph was stunned. There were inferences by the others that Jesus's death was his destiny and tied to his being the Son of God. Joseph didn't fully understand why death was Jesus's destiny and silently refused to believe it. Joseph was defending Jesus and his goal was to keep him alive. As much as his followers seemed to be resolved to Jesus's ultimate death, Joseph was just as committed to seeing to it that his life was spared. But now, with Mark's words, there was another disturbing element that was being heaped upon Jesus's dedicated counsel. How could new information come to Jesus's followers after his death, Joseph wondered to himself. What was Mark intimating? Would Jesus be leaving behind a secret cache of documents that would reveal more about his ministry and about God? Would the spirit of Jesus visit his loyalists? Or was Mark saying that Jesus would somehow defeat death and live again? That thought recalled to Joseph the case of Lazarus… he made a mental note to learn what progress his assistant had made in locating this man who had reportedly risen from the ashes. Joseph remained confused over Mark's words and needed him to clarify his statement.

"Mark, please help me," Joseph began using his most tactful tone and demeanor. "I mean no disrespect to you or to Jesus. I hope you can understand my need for clarification. What is your interpretation of what Jesus told you? How would you receive word from him after his death?"

Mark stopped and turned to Joseph and spoke to him in a low tone.

"Joseph, Jesus is the Lord our God, the Living God who never dies."

Joseph gazed back at Mark whose intense eyes reflected his sincerity. Joseph realized the enormity of what Mark was relating to him. He also knew that Mark's words were tantamount to proving the prosecution's case. Well, he thought, at least there is consistency among Jesus's followers. They were all blasphemous—at least in the eyes of Caiaphas.

Joseph still needed to press Mark further.

"I understand the concept of the Living God," Joseph began, ever mindful of the respect he must show to his prospective witnesses. "How would more knowledge be given to his followers after his earthly demise? What would be the instrument of this transfer?"

"The Lord works in wondrous ways, Joseph," Mark responded. "It is not for me to understand how the Lord will continue to teach us. Perhaps he will inspire some of us to write a tome that encompasses his wisdom that will be a legacy for all time. The only certitude I have about his words is that I know they will be forthcoming and that I will be inspired and know what actions he wants me to take to spread the word of his ministry."

***

Joseph enjoyed his talk with Mark and even though his revelations about Jesus's role after his death were jarring and unclear to him, he felt certain Mark could be an impressive witness. Joseph would just have to strategize how he could temper the explosive nature of his deposition.

As the two men walked back toward the path that led out of the garden, Joseph asked Mark how he could find another of Jesus's followers—the disciple named Luke.

"I'll take you to him now," Mark responded. He knows of your work and he wants to offer his help."

Joseph proceeded to follow Mark out on the path that led to the inner city. Before the stepped onto a small foot bridge that crossed a dry stream, Mark stopped and looked intensely at Joseph.

"Joseph, we all know that you have taken on a task that is... next to impossible," Mark said. "We all appreciate your efforts and the risk you take yourself. Your heart is in the right place. And, I would venture to say, your heart has been touched by Him."

***

Joseph was growing weary by the time he and Mark arrived at the building where Luke had a small apartment. It was oppressively hot as usual and, coupled with his lack of sleep, Joseph was near to collapse. He thought to himself that it would have been more sensible for him to see Luke the next day yet it was vital to get this last, important deposition from the closest followers of Jesus. He'd still have others to interview but the disciples were decidedly among the most crucial.

Mark rapped on the door in what seemed to be a pattern: one knock, followed by two quick knocks, a pause and then a third knock. Joseph knew that their caution wasn't paranoia having witnessed the treatment of Jesus's followers earlier in the day.

Soon the door squeaked slowly open and a small boy peeked around the edge of the wooden door.

"Aviv. I and my companion are here to see your father," Mark said quietly.

Without saying a word, little Aviv slammed the door. Mark smiled. "Children are so naturally uncouth! That's why the Lord made them physically charming—so we could bear them."

A few moments passed and Luke opened the door. He had a small stature and deep-set, dark eyes. His eyes were so black that they appeared to have no pupil. He looked nervously between Mark and Joseph—of course, trusting his friend but wondering who the stranger was.

"Luke, this is Joseph of Arimathea," Mark told him quietly.

Luke smiled warmly at Joseph. "Ah, wonderful. I was looking forward to meeting you. Bless you for your work and courage."

"Please let us in so we do not draw attention to ourselves," Mark said.

Luke showed the men into his small apartment which was dark, stuffy and sparsely furnished. He motioned for the men to sit on a large rug in the middle of the main room. It seemed apparent to Joseph that Mark was going to stay while he spoke with Luke. Joseph would never insult Mark by asking him to leave but it was always his experience that deposing a witness was much more successful and useful when the person was alone. But, Joseph would have to make the best of it.

"Firstly, thank you for meeting with me without forewarning, Luke," Joseph began.

"We are all grateful, Joseph, for your efforts on behalf of Our Lord Jesus," Luke said.

Joseph realized that Luke's black eyes belied the kind spirited man beneath.

"First, if you could tell me of your relationship with Jesus," Joseph said. "Where you met and how? Perhaps your first impressions of him—in fact, anything you'd like to offer.

"Certainly, kind sir," Luke said, "I will help however I can. I heard about Jesus's ministry and good works before I met him."

"Ah, so his reputation preceded him," Joseph added.

"Yes, you could certainly say that," Luke responded. "Jesus was truly the Light of the World and was known as the Good Samaritan, an example to us all. While my fellow disciples prefer to focus on Jesus as the Son of God—which I completely subscribe to—I am most taken with the humanity of Jesus. My heart stirs for the compassion he has for the poor, the sick and the downtrodden."

"We all agree with your sentiment, Luke," Mark interjected. "But the miracle of Jesus is that he is the Son of the Living God."

"Of course, my friend," Luke responded. "But it his acts of compassion and the love in his heart that draws us to him."

Joseph was sorry to be proven correct so early-on in the conversation about his suspicion that this deposition would be difficult and that the assertive and opinionated Mark would contest any detail with which he found the slightest disagreement.

"We are not here to debate the blessings of Jesus for there are many," Luke said. "Joseph needs our words to help in his preparation to defend the Lord."

Mark conceded to Luke's point but Joseph was quite sure from what he had observed about Mark thus far that his latest comment would not be the last helpful remark that he would offer. Luke seemed to be more introspective than the others about Jesus. He seemed to be offering his heart—how Jesus impacted him. Luke focused on the human side of Jesus which was exactly what Joseph needed to emphasize at the trial. Perhaps it would be Luke who would emerge as the star witness, Joseph mused.

Luke provided a chronology of Jesus's life story. He broke his account into two basic portions. The first covered his birth up to his baptism by John the Baptist which Luke presented as a pivotal event in Jesus's life. Luke then discussed Jesus's ministry and the good works that he performed. Many of the stories of Jesus's deeds were the same or very similar to those related to Joseph by the others. But Joseph appreciated Luke's unique perspective. He spoke of Jesus's ministry itself—not just the man. He stressed the goodness of Jesus's message. While Luke portrayed Jesus's word as divine, he also emphasized that it was respectable and law-abiding and for one and all. The term, "law-abiding" grabbed Joseph's attention. Joseph could craft Luke's testimony to showcase his view that Jesus's teachings were law-abiding, respectful of the law which was contrary to how Jesus was being portrayed by the prosecution and what Jesus was being charged with—indeed the driving force that had placed his very life at risk. Joseph did not reveal his satisfaction with Luke's words, rather, he chose to appear neutral to the testimony of the two men but within Joseph was enthralled.

"Joseph, what is most admirable about Jesus is the care he shows the needy and for women who sadly are often mistreated in our society. That is why Jesus has so many female followers. He teaches that women have the same rights to the blessings of the Lord as do men," Luke said. He then turned and looked intensely into Joseph's eyes. "We feel that women are just as worthy as men, Joseph."

"Well, I know that is not a popular concept in many circles," Joseph replied. "But you can trust that in my house it is quite popular." Joseph snickered. "Believe me, my wife wouldn't see it any other way."

The men shared a good laugh and all agreed that the women in their lives were very important to them and that they revered and appreciated them. Luke explained that it was Jesus's philosophy to allow all people to become followers of his ministry—Gentiles as well as the much-despised Samaritans were all welcomed. Luke stressed that Jesus's plan was God's plan and that since God created all men, all men were welcome to join his ministry.

"Luke, I do think your testimony will be quite helpful," Joseph said. "Tell me about the last few weeks, starting with Jesus's arrival into Jerusalem."

"When I look back to that time, it seems to be a thousand years ago, though it has been less than 20 days when Jesus first rode into the city."

"It was on Sunday, two Sundays ago," Mark interjected.

"Sunday?" Luke shrugged. "Some say Monday?" Luke responded. "I think that the day is immaterial. Jesus came to Jerusalem because he was called here by the Lord. I don't think we serve Jesus by bickering over minor details. The history I write may vary from the one you may write but I dare say the love and devotion that we feel for Jesus will shine through those differences and render them inconsequential."

Joseph silently cheered for Luke's refusal to get into a debate about the minor details. But Joseph would not ignore the differences among his witnesses, minor though they may be. A good prosecutor like Caiaphas would not hesitate to exploit them.

So, Joseph had to be aware of each and every inconsistency that arose among them.

Luke gave his account of the arrest of Jesus. He told of a slave's ear being cut off in the battle.

"Joseph, Jesus healed the man's ear," Luke said with great reverence. "I saw it with my own eyes! Quite naturally, the man immediately became a devotee. This episode illustrates the wondrous works Jesus accomplishes and the effect that he has upon people."

Mark cleared his throat in such a manner that Joseph sensed he was about to utter an opposing view of the incident.

"But, Luke, it was Matthew who heard Jesus say that one who lives by sword shall die by it," Mark said.

"Our statements are not necessarily mutually exclusive of one another," Luke responded.

"No, but we need to portray Jesus as the peaceful man that he is," Mark said. "Jesus does not condone violence although he healed the ear of a violent man. By his healing a warrior, one could construe that he condones the warrior's actions."

Joseph knew that Mark was speaking of Maluch. He was happy to have a confirmation of Matthew's story about the incident. He would indeed try to find Maluch and convince him to testify for the defense.

"Well, I see both your points and I think we will be able to include both of them in testimony," Joseph said. "We do not want to appear to have conflicting evidence but conflicting views of the same incident are normal human responses."

The two men seemed satisfied with Joseph's attempt to reach a compromise about the incident. Joseph agreed in spirit with Luke who was a person who looked at the larger, all-encompassing aspect of an issue.

Luke brought up a rather touchy subject, one that Matthew had certainly attested to in his deposition. According to Luke, after the last meal that Jesus shared with his disciples in the Garden of Gethsemane, Jesus went off on his own to pray. It was apparent to Luke that Jesus was in quite an internal, private struggle as he prayed. Luke looked intensely at Joseph.

"Joseph, I was worried about Jesus and was watching him from just a short distance away," Luke said. "I swear on my children that I witnessed the sweat of blood on Jesus's brow as he prayed to the Father."

Mark shifted his position on the rug, signaling his discomfort with Luke's words. Joseph was sure that the very bright Luke sensed the same thing about Mark but he continued on making an even more startling statement.

"There was a swirl of light around Jesus as he prayed—a soft glow that Jesus seemed to interact with," Luke said, his face stoic. "I am quite certain the light was an angel sent from God to help Jesus through this… this phase of his life on earth."

Chapter 13
Lazarus and the Wayfarer

As Joseph bid Luke and Mark goodbye, he felt both relieved and a sense of accomplishment. He had set out to gain the depositions of those closest to Jesus of Nazareth and he had been successful. He was hopeful that he would perhaps be able to rest that night and actually sleep more than a fitful hour or two. Joseph was more fatigued than he could ever remember, more fatigued than even the most complicated case for his richest client had ever brought about. Joseph had a long walk home ahead of him which would give him time to think… to sort out how to best use the testimony he had gathered since some of it could decidedly be inflammatory and even injurious to the case.

First, there was the issue of the women. Women were rarely called upon to testify in open court. Joseph had always been of the opinion that this policy was ludicrous. Women were as smart as men, perhaps even more so. He recalled the recent moment of solidarity when Mark, Luke and he had agreed on how important the women in their lives were. He was sure that Pilate, who was known to be fair and judicious, would allow the testimony of the two Marys. But Joseph had to evaluate just how beneficial their testimony would be.

Mary, mother of Jesus, could come off as daft with her tale of becoming a mother while still a virgin. Joseph could envision the smirks and laughter that those comments could evoke in open court. Mary would be seen as a mother defending her son which would be a positive moment and one to which the jury panel, or anyone else for that matter, could relate. As with the others, Joseph would have to determine the most strategic way in which to thread Mary's testimony into the case.

Then there was the other Mary—the Mary allegedly of ill repute. Joseph did not judge people on moral issues. There were undoubtedly whispers about Mary Magdalene but Joseph had no intention of participating in a debate about her behavior. His only concern was what impact the young woman would have on a jury of all men. To be sure, the panel members would find Mary attractive. She was an alluring and beautiful woman. Joseph knew that women like that can make a man forget everything, even a vow to seek justice. That could be a plus. However, the men on the panel could not be painted with a broad brush. Some may be orthodox and judge her as despicable, essentially putting her on trial. Such ill-will toward Mary Magdalene could poison their decision about Jesus. They might even think that Jesus was involved with her and find him not only to be a blasphemous holy man but a hypocritical and immoral one. Joseph, who had a controlling and suspicious wife himself, also knew that the wives of some of the jurors may have an influence on how the men view the young woman. The wives could well badger their husbands to not believe a thing that the wanton woman had to say.

And then, there were the disciples. There was some conflict to their accounts, mostly minor in nature, yet still contradictory. Joseph would have to be careful to blur those lines as best he could by either omitting them or presenting them to appear as inconsequential. Just as with the Marys, Joseph would have to adapt the testimony of the disciples as best he could.

But the overarching problem that loomed over the entire case was that each of his witnesses would be vulnerable to charges of blasphemy themselves. Joseph had to approach Pilate about this aspect of the trial. He was certain that Pilate would give his witnesses immunity. If not, there would be no trial. Joseph knew that Pilate was a dedicated justice and would do everything within his power to see that a trial he was charged to hear was carried out.

Hadas and Yakir were trying to locate Lazarus, Simon Peter's mother-in-law and some of the people that Jesus reportedly healed, including and especially Maluch. But there again, in the eyes of Caiaphas and the Jewish High Priests, their testimony would also be public displays of blasphemy. There was another major problem. Joseph was at a loss as to what his overall defense strategy would be. There were many possible scenarios—in fact, potential defenses were in abundance. But Jesus would have to approve of them and Joseph did not have much confidence that

Jesus would be cooperative especially if the normal legal maneuver employed by attorneys of bending the truth to point in one direction or another would be part of it. He would have to get his thoughts together and the arguments he would present to Jesus in an effort to convince the man to agree to one of them. Would he have to take Jesus by the arms and shake him?! He could see himself pleading with Jesus in his cell: *This is your life, man! You have to help me save it!*

But there was one more witness that Joseph knew he must speak to. He must find out what motivated Judas Iscariot? Was it the thirty pieces of silver that Matthew alluded to? Surely there was more to this man who had been a devotee of Jesus? Joseph would have to find out because Caiaphas was sure to call Judas to the stand. Joseph had to cover everything, be prepared for any challenge the prosecution may present.

***

As fatigued as he was, when Joseph reached the fork in the road he chose the one that led to his office as opposed to the one that would have taken him home. He had to tell Yakir to begin looking for Judas. Joseph had thought of asking one of the disciples but there was so much bad blood over Judas's behavior that Joseph rightly sensed it would be the wrong move. He needed to keep the disciples on his side.

Joseph wearily climbed the stairs to his second story suite and slipped into his office. It was late afternoon and he was slightly annoyed to hear the gentle snoring of Yakir in the outer office. But Yakir had been working hard recently and the late hours and the long days had probably caught up with him. Joseph was the forgiving sort. But he did have to talk to his assistant. Joseph cleared his throat loudly several times, heard several loud snarls and a few expletives and knew that Yakir was now awake and preparing the excuses he would make to Joseph for sleeping at his desk.

Joseph's prediction of his assistant's behavior was right on the mark. Yakir soon stumbled into Joseph's office. Joseph was reviewing some parchments on his desk and did not look up. He'd allow Yakir to hang himself.

"Sir… I was finally getting to that pile of filing…" Yakir began but was interrupted by Joseph.

"Were you using it for a pillow?" Joseph asked.

Yakir's face fell. He was embarrassed and fearful. He had a young family to feed. He could not withstand a job loss.

"Never mind about all that. You're human," Joseph eased his mind. "Have you found Lazarus?"

"Oh, yes. Yes, sir," Yakir responded, relieved that he apparently was still employed. "I have the word of two good shopkeepers that Lazarus lives in a village just outside Jerusalem. He comes into the city for work most every day. I asked my contacts to have Lazarus stop by the office the next time he visits. I told them that it was important."

"Excellent work," Joseph said. "I have another important assignment for you."

"Yes, sir, anything," Yakir responded enthusiastically.

"There's another person we need to depose. His testimony could prove to be crucial," Joseph said. "But this man, Yakir, may be a little more elusive than the others. He may not want to talk with us. You'll have to use your wits to get him to cooperate.

"I'm up for the task, sir!"

***

That evening Joseph was quiet at dinner. Irit was happy to see her husband at home for dinner on time for the first time in days. But she was not happy that he seemed so remote, his mind wandering off somewhere else. Since he was physically present, she would have loved that his mind would have been there as well.

"You're so quiet, Joseph," Irit said, as she eyed her husband closely. She was always concerned that her dedicated husband would over extend himself. She knew the case of Jesus of Nazareth meant a lot to him but she prayed daily that it would not do him in.

"Just some things on my mind, dear," Joseph said and then focused more squarely on his wife. "I apologize for my preoccupation."

"How is the case proceeding, Joseph—the case of Jesus?" Irit asked.

"The depositions are nearing an end. Although I have several other important ones still to take place," Joseph replied. "For one, Yakir is trying to track down Judas Iscariot."

"Is he a follower of Jesus as were the others?" Irit asked.

Joseph gazed intently at Irit. "He was a follower."

"Was?" Irit asked.

"Apparently, this man, this Judas, is the person who turned Jesus over to the Jewish guards. At least he's accused of doing so," Joseph responded. "And, I was told that he was paid thirty pieces of silver to betray him."

"Oh my! What kind of friend could he have been?" Irit responded. "What on earth could have possessed him?"

"You know, my dear that is probably a very good question," Joseph answered. "The use of the word 'possessed' may have been very astute of you, my wife."

***

Joseph was grateful that he had a good night's sleep for once. It wasn't that he had no worries. It was just sheer exhaustion that finally allowed him to slip into a deep, rejuvenating sleep. He arrived at the office early, even beating the always prompt Hadas. Yakir was not in yet. He had hopes that he was trying to locate Judas. Hadas popped his head into Joseph's office.

"Have you completed your depositions, Joseph?" Hadas asked.

"I've taken the majority of them. Now I just have to make sense of them," Joseph responded. 'I'll probably ask you to depose some of the people who claim to have been healed by Jesus."

"You'll be calling upon such dubious witnesses?" Hadas asked.

"You know Hadas, you go with what you have," Joseph responded. "This case is a patchwork of angels, demons, miracles and mysticism. I just have to take all that and mold it into something that does not appear to be a madman's folly."

Hadas turned to leave the office but Joseph stopped him.

"Hadas, one more matter," Joseph said. "When Jesus was born, Mary claimed that three wealthy kings came to Bethlehem to honor her son and mark the coming of the new Messiah. They brought him gifts such as gold and frankincense and myrrh."

"Three kings?" Hadas responded. "From where?"

"That's the problem," Joseph responded. "Mary knew only that they were from the East, Persia I believe. The testimony of these men or any one of them would be a fait accompli but... it's been thirty years and they're probably all dead."

"Did Mary know their names?" Hadas asked.

"I believe I scratched them down on a scrap," Joseph responded. "Why?"

"I know a wayfarer who travels to the East on frequent occasions," Hadas responded. "Find those names and I'll give them to this man. His name is Cyrus. If these men are still alive, Cyrus will find them."

Joseph looked through his myriad of papers for several minutes and then pulled out a small jagged piece of parchment and peered closely at it.

"Here it is Hadas," Joseph said. "Let's see if I can read my writing... I believe the names are Balthazar, Casper and... Melchior." Joseph looked up at Hadas and handed the scrap of paper to him. "Not much to go on."

"You don't know Cyrus," Hadas said with a smile.

"Pay him well, Hadas," Joseph said.

Suddenly there was a light rapping on the front door.

"I'll see who it is," Hadas offered. "Hopefully it's not a demon."

Hadas rushed to the front door and a few moments later, he returned and informed Joseph that a man named Lazarus was at the door asking for him.

"Very good!" Joseph said and was up on his feet heading for the front door.

***

In a compact meeting room, Lazarus was seated at a small wooden table across from Joseph. As Joseph was told, Lazarus was a young man, tall and slender and healthy looking. His appearance was reminiscent of Jesus's.

"Thank you for coming by to talk," Joseph said. "Your words may well be very important for Jesus's defense."

"It is I who thanks you, Joseph," Lazarus responded. "Your defense of our beloved is brave and heroic."

"It's not about me, Lazarus," Joseph said. "But it is partially about you. Can you tell me about your relationship with Jesus?

"Of course. I am a devoted follower of Jesus. I live in the town of Bethany which is just outside the city," Lazarus began. "I fell very ill. In fact my family feared I would not survive the disease that struck me. My sisters, Martha and Mary, sent word to the disciples that I was near death and needed Jesus's powers to save me. I was in and out of consciousness and the next thing I knew, I was awake looking into the peaceful and loving eyes of Jesus."

"Did you wake from a sleep or a suspended unconsciousness?" Joseph asked.

"No, sir, I awoke from death."

Even though Joseph knew what Lazarus was going to say, hearing the words from the man himself was astounding. Joseph quickly took a few notes on a large scrap of parchment.

"You do realize that such a tale would be... well, difficult for people to believe," Joseph responded gently. "What proof do you have that would be convincing to those who doubt your story?"

"Mary and Martha told me that I was dead and that Jesus raised me."

"Please believe me that I am not disrespectful when I ask you where you were when—as you say—you awoke from the dead? In your sick bed, perhaps?"

"Why, in my tomb, of course, sir," Lazarus said, responding as though he wondered where else Joseph would think a dead man would be.

Joseph furiously scratched more notes.

"You see, he did not come immediately when he was called," Lazarus said. "Jesus has so many people to tend to. I feel no bitterness that he was not able to come to me before I died." Lazarus lowered his voice a bit. "Truthfully, my sisters were a little upset. I'm their younger brother and they're overprotective of me."

"Did they blame Jesus for your... death?" Joseph asked, feeling a little silly asking a living man details about his "prior" death.

"Yes, but Jesus came and made everything fine as you can see," Lazarus said with a smile. "My sisters harbor no ill-feelings toward Jesus. They follow and love him, too."

"Can you tell me, Lazarus, exactly what happened?" Joseph asked. "Of course, you were... dead. What I mean is what have been told about the incident? What happened before Jesus brought you back to life?"

"I was in my family tomb and there were mourners all around—family and neighbors," Lazarus said. "Then there was a peaceful feeling among the people and Jesus walked quietly up to the tomb."

"What did he say or do?" Joseph was becoming completely engaged.

"Against the objections of my sisters, Jesus insisted that the large boulder that covered the tomb be moved," Lazarus explained. "He then called to me and said, I am told, 'I am the resurrection, and the life: he that believeth in me, though he were dead, yet shall he live: And whosoever liveth and believeth in me shall never die.'"

"Then I assume that you... uh...," Joseph was uncharacteristically stuck for the right words.

"Then I rose from my tomb and I've been alive ever since!" Lazarus told Joseph gleefully. "Please know that I am sincere when I say that when my eyes opened, I saw Jesus right before me. And Jesus wept."

"Did any authorities learn of this event?" Joseph asked.

"Yes, I am certain that the leaders in my village reported my return to life to the Jewish High Priests," Lazarus responded.

"To Caiaphas?" Joseph asked, intrigued.

"I'm not sure who that is," Lazarus responded.

"No worries. The fact that it was reported could be very important," Joseph responded.

Joseph fantasized a moment about the possibility of calling Caiaphas to the stand as a hostile defense witness. *"Answer this rabbi! Were you not advised by the family of Lazarus that*

Lazarus did indeed return from the dead?! Did you fail to take the appropriate actions according to Jewish religious laws as leader of the temple?!" Joseph knew it probably would never happen yet he refused to rule it out and it gave him a bit of pleasure to contemplate the possibility. This case was proving each day to be like no other case he'd ever been involved with or ever heard of.

"I did hear, sir, that the chief priests did speak of putting me to death—I mean for the second time... you understand because I was already dead once and..."

"Lazarus, I understand. Why did the priests speak of putting you to death?" Joseph asked the question but was beginning to wonder if the case of Lazarus was the final straw on the camel's back that led Caiaphas and Sanhedrin and the others to persecute Jesus.

"I understand the priests were upset that so many people began to follow Jesus because of... what happened to me," Lazarus responded. "I was concealed at a friend's farm until the threat appeared to pass. Of course, for all I know they could be thinking about killing me right now."

Joseph looked off in the distance. "No, Lazarus. I think they're thinking about killing someone else right now."

***

In the heat of the day, Hadas hurried down the narrow, dusty road that led to the heart of Jerusalem. He passed through the throngs of shoppers and vendors who were swarming in the market place. The bright sun reflected off the shiny brass helmets belonging to several tall Roman guards who were dispersed throughout the crowd. Hadas craned his neck and smiled as he spotted a light-colored camel tied to a post in front of a small eating and drinking establishment.

"Cyrus!"

Hadas pushed his way into the noisy, cramped tavern and scanned the room. He spotted Cyrus holding a cup of wine and talking with several men. Hadas began to make his way over to him. Cyrus was stocky and robust and taller than most Persian men. His thick black hair hung to his shoulders. He was distinguished by a scar than ran from one side of his forehead across his face down to the opposite cheek. On one occasion, he told Hadas that he was looking for the vagabond who was man enough to make another scar from the opposite direction to form a giant "X" on his face. Cyrus didn't really think that man existed.

"Cyrus," Hadas called out over the loud voices and tugged on his arm.

Not knowing whether it was friend or foe who tugged on him, Cyrus pulled a dagger from his sleeve and turned with a scowl on his face to see the frightened countenance of Hadas. Cyrus smiled widely and returned his dagger to its sheath.

"Hadas!" Cyrus boomed. "I'm happy I didn't cut your throat!"

"Not as happy as I," Hadas smiled, wiping a few drops of perspiration from his brow.

"I have a favor, Cyrus. Can we talk? Outside?"

Outside Cyrus stood petting and stroking his camel as Hadas told him the story about Mary and the three Magi. He told him about the trial of Jesus and the importance of tracking one of these kings down so they could testify about Mary's story. He asked Cyrus if he would try to find the men. When Cyrus hesitated, Hadas pulled out 25 aurei from his vest and offered it to Cyrus who smiled and took the coins.

"They'll be twice this much for you if you find at least one of the men," Hadas said.

"Trust that I will find at least one and convince him to come back with me," Cyrus responded.

Hadas pulled the scrap of paper out of his pocket. "Here, Cyrus. Here are their names."

"I don't read. Just tell them to me. I won't forget," Cyrus responded.

"Balthazar, Casper and Melchior."

Cyrus patted Hadas on the shoulder and mounted his camel. He moved slowly through the crowd then turned and waved to Hadas. When he arrived at a clearing, Cyrus whipped his camel and was soon galloping out of the city in an easterly direction.

***

When Joseph returned to his office that afternoon, he was nearly stampeded by Yakir. Joseph walked down the narrow hallway to his office, passing Yakir's small nook. Yakir nearly jumped straight up when he saw Joseph. He rushed after Joseph, nearly knocking him over.

Joseph scowled. "What spirit has possessed you this day, Yakir?"

"Sir, I got him!" Yakir said, a huge smile across his face.

"If I may know who is it that you got?" Joseph asked, mocking and slightly annoyed.

"Oh, sorry! I tracked the important man down. I've arranged for you to meet Judas Iscariot!" Yakir said with more than a bit of pride.

Now Joseph joined Yakir in celebration, a big smile crossing his face. "How on earth did you accomplish the feat so quickly, Yakir?"

"I went to the garden where Jesus's followers gather. I sought out Mary Magdalene and told her of my—our—dilemma. She was kind enough to seek him out. He's been in hiding and she knew where to find him. I waited at the park for her and she returned later with the news that she convinced him to talk to you."

"I wonder how she did that. The thought of now helping Jesus's defense after betraying him places Judas in quite an unusual position," Joseph said, more to himself than to Yakir.

"I gather that Judas is feeling remorseful, guilty for his actions," Yakir said, then smiled coyly. "And since it was Mary Magdalene seeking his help, perhaps he couldn't resist. Mary is ravishing."

"Oh, I hadn't noticed," Joseph responded. Then recognizing a dubious look on Yakir's face, Joseph amended his statement. "I hadn't noticed her beauty, Yakir," Joseph said quite deliberately then winked at Yakir. "At least that's the official story as far as my wife is concerned."

Both men enjoyed a moment of merriment before Joseph turned to the serious matter at hand.

"Where and when do I meet him?" Joseph asked anxiously.

"There is a small eating place that is owned by a relative of Judas. He'll feel safe meeting you there. I have written down the directions on this parchment," Yakir said, handing Joseph the scrap of parchment.

"Judas apparently tries to stay out of sight most days. He agreed to meet you but only if you can meet him there after sunset," Yakir told him.

"Irit will not be thrilled but I have no choice," Joseph said as he rushed on to his office.

Joseph faced a pile of new scrolls and parchments on his desk but he found it difficult to concentrate. He had neared the end of the deposition portion of his work and had done so in record time. He looked quickly over the pile of work on his desk and decided whatever it was it could wait.

"Yakir! Yakir!" Joseph called out to his assistant.

Yakir rushed in. "Yes, sir."

"Please put these all away in one of your baskets. Make sure to mark the basket as things I have not seen yet," Joseph said as he headed for the door. "I have a little time before my meeting with Judas. I'm going to go home for a short spell. I decided I best tend to my marriage before my wife makes my bed on the portico."

***

Joseph's sensibilities were right on target as usual. His wife was once again growing tired of his absences and, when he was home, his remote, incommunicative behavior. But on this night, Joseph made sure he gave his wife his undivided attention, raved over every bite of supper he ate and repeatedly told her just how lovely she looked. Irit was very smart—Joseph himself would claim smarter than he—so she no doubt figured out why she was getting all the special attention when he mumbled that he had to meet someone. She was annoyed mainly because she didn't like him out at night. There were beggars and thieves and murderers who roamed the dark streets of Jerusalem. Naturally, she feared that her husband might become a victim. She insisted that he take a small torch with him because the few torches that lit the streets were either weak or burned out. Joseph assured her that he would be fine and that this meeting would mark the end of his major depositions. She was happy to hear that news and that he planned to dispatch Hadas to any other depositions that needed to be taken.

Joseph took off with what his wife called a small torch but which he thought of as a beacon in the night. It might even draw thieves to him, he thought. But he wasn't focused about anything other than his meeting.

***

Joseph held the small scrap of parchment up to his torch as he neared the meeting place. He thought he found the right door but there was no marking on it. He pulled on the door but it was locked.

"For the love of all that's holy!" Joseph said, as he wrapped angrily on the door, thinking that he had been sent on a fool's journey. Then the door swung open and a voice spoke from within.

"Joseph of Arimathea, please enter."

Chapter 14
Judas Iscariot

Joseph stuck his torch down in the sand and entered the dark room. There were only a few flickering candles to illuminate the room. The five dining tables were all empty. Thus far, there was no one in the abandoned room who Joseph could connect to the voice who bade him enter. Suddenly, a tall, slender figure emerged from the dark shadows.

"Please, share a table," the man said, his voice thin and tight.

"Are you..."

"I am Judas Iscariot. The man you seek," Judas said.

Sitting on the table that Judas led Joseph to was a large wine jug and two wooden cups. The two men sat at the table across from each other. Joseph remained quiet, allowing Judas to take the lead. Judas poured dark red wine into each cup and picked up his vessel, downed its contents and immediately poured another draught of wine into his cup. He focused an intense gaze on Joseph who could see anguish in his narrow, dark eyes.

"Word has traveled you have sat with friends and supporters of Jesus," Judas began. "Now you sit with his betrayer."

The usually glib Joseph was silent. He could not think of the right words. Judas sensed his discomfort.

"Fret not, Joseph. Take comfort that I am not a demon but rather a man who has been plagued by demons," Judas said, bitterly. He threw back his head and emptied his cup and slammed it back down on the table. "I am not proud of what I have done..." his voice trailed off to a whisper.

Joseph was upset with himself, struggling to utter a word. Finally, he was able to respond to Judas.

"I am not here to judge you, Judas," Joseph offered.

"I understand that, kind sir," Judas said. "I know my judge."

Joseph absorbed the full meaning of Judas's words. Joseph made no judgments about Judas, not even silently. He felt an overwhelming sorrow for the man. He sensed that Judas had been swept into something beyond his control.

"It was not just for money, Joseph," Judas said quietly.

"Then what?" Joseph asked, gently.

"I believed in this man. I was a loyal follower," Judas said. "But I am also a patriot—a lover of my city and country. I thought he would abolish Pilate and the lot."

"Overthrow the Romans?" Joseph asked rhetorically. "Such change most probably could not be done overnight, would you agree?"

Judas did not respond. Instead he poured more wine. Joseph watched carefully as Judas's hands trembled and beads of perspiration formed on his brow. Joseph would be patient and allow Judas to reveal his heart in his own time.

Finally, after another stiff drink, Judas refocused on Joseph.

"There's no reason not to be honest now, is there?" Judas asked softly, more to himself than to Joseph. "Yes, it is true that I was disappointed that Jesus did not rout the Romans out of our city... but I had problems, too... of a personal nature. When Caiaphas approached me asking that I lead him to Jesus, I was at a vulnerable point in my life. My disillusionment over what I perceived to be Jesus's failure coupled with destitution was the brew from which my betrayal was wrought." Judas said in a voice broken with emotion.

"Each of us have valleys that we come upon and..." Joseph began but Judas interrupted him.

"But that was not all, Joseph," Judas said, his voice stronger now. "I was weak and allowed evil to overcome me. It was the weakness of my convictions and my soul that spawned this tragedy. I take full blame."

There was nothing Joseph could say. There were no words that he could add—Judas had said them all.

"You know that my peers, Luke and John, claim that Satan was within me on that foggy morning," Judas said. "I had once been called by the Lord. Little did I know I would be summoned by the devil who commanded my betrayal."

Joseph poured himself a bit of wine. He took a sip all the while keeping a careful eye on the broken man before him. The lawyer in him wondered what kind of witness Judas would make. The human in him asked whether Judas would last that long.

"Jesus knew," Judas blurted out suddenly, his voice stronger and louder.

"Jesus knew of your..." Joseph found it difficult to say the words.

"Betrayal, Joseph, my betrayal," Judas finished his thoughts. "His countenance and the knowing look in his eye told me so. From the beginning, we all feared that Jesus wouldn't be with us long, that his parting was inevitable and preordained." Judas buried his head in his hands. "Little did I know that I would be a tool for his demise. I was not a corrupt man. It wasn't my plan, wasn't my wishes."

Joseph watched the young man before him being punished by his own guilt and shame. In terms of a court appearance, Judas's testimony would not be without its faults. Undoubtedly, the jury panel would not have sympathy or understanding for the man. On a more philosophical level, Joseph wondered whether Judas had been used as a means to an end, to a predetermined end. Was there justice in the obvious agony that engulfed him? Was he used to promote an ideology?

But what about his free will? Didn't God bestow that gift upon us all, Joseph wondered to himself. He reflected on Judas's own words about his weakness of spirit and mind which apparently rendered him unable to make the true and noble choice. The disciple, Judas Iscariot, represented a paradox. Was Judas's will his own or was he predestined to damnation?

***

On his way home, Joseph had an unsettled feeling. His meeting with Judas Iscariot had not been a pleasant experience and not particularly illuminating as had the other depositions. What had been jarring was the emotional state to which Judas had apparently devolved. Judas was a wretched man. Had he been an instrument of a more powerful force—either good or evil? Joseph had a nagging foreboding about Judas Iscariot.

It was very late and on this night he would not be heading to his office. The torch he carried had nearly spent itself, burned downed to just embers. He threw it on the side of the pathway and stomped on it until it flickered out. The moon was waxing and large and bright enough to guide him home.

Joseph breathed a sigh of relief that the depositions were completed—and the most harrowing completed just that night. The larger task of deciding on a line of defense, the witnesses he would use and his line of questioning for defense as well as prosecution witnesses lay before him. He would soon be given the names of the witnesses that Caiaphas would be calling. There was so much to do and so little time. Pilate was riding herd over the entire process, insisting that the trial begin without delay.

There were several important matters he would have to settle and one would be with Pilate. He decided he would seek immunity for all his witnesses. From Mary, mother of Jesus, to Lazarus, all of his witnesses could be seen as blasphemous. He would not put it past Caiaphas to charge them on the spot, right on the stand, with violating Jewish Law.

The second important matter he would have to resolve would be with another individual—Jesus. He had been formulating several different defense strategies but he'd have to discuss them with Jesus. Jesus would have to approve of the defense that would be presented for him. He wasn't sure how Jesus would react. Jesus hadn't been a fountain of cooperation up to that point but Joseph planned to interject a sense of urgency into his conversation with Jesus. He needed to stress vehemently that his very life was at stake that he was walking on a path to his death! Of course, Jesus seemed to understand that already. In fact, Joseph had the eerie sense that Jesus understood that better than he did.

***

The next morning, Joseph was at the Roman Court early before any sessions were underway. The Roman guards eyed Joseph as he approached the courthouse just at the crack of dawn. Joseph had experienced yet another night of restless, fitful sleep. There was too much on his mind. Someday—when this trial concluded—Joseph would be able to sleep like a babe. He would, that is, if the trial turned out in his favor. If not, perhaps he would never sleep again, he thought sardonically to himself.

The Roman guards remained silent as Joseph bowed slightly to them as the large courthouse doors were held open for him. He walked slowly down the middle aisle of the large room and scanned all facets of the courtroom: the two large wooden tables, one for the defense and one for the prosecution; the towering bench where Pilate would preside; the raised platform for the jury panel; the witness stand; and, the narrow benches of the gallery where citizens were allowed to observe public trials. He envisioned the upcoming trial—himself seated with Jesus at the defense table at the upcoming trial, Caiaphas posturing before the jury and the imperial Pilate gazing down at the proceedings with the cold eyes of justice. The scene of his imagination was at once exhilarating and intimidating. Although he was unable to formulate exactly why, Joseph had no doubt that this trial would be the most important of his career.

As he felt the room and all its ghosts of past and future, he was lost in the moment. Life changing decisions were made in this room—some right and some wrong. He prayed that he would do his best to see that the right decision was made in the case of Jesus of Nazareth. His thoughts and prayers were suddenly interrupted by the presence of Liberius who had emerged from the back hall.

"Welcome, Joseph of Arimathea," Liberius said. His naturally loud speaking voice respectfully tempered sensing that Joseph was deep in thought… or prayer.

Joseph turned toward Liberius's voice that marked the end of his reverie. Joseph bowed slightly toward Liberius.

"Good day, Liberius. My imagination just placed me in the trial that I will soon be part of." Joseph scanned around the distinguished room for several moments more. "Many important things are resolved in this room, aren't they?" Joseph asked rhetorically.

A serious look came over Liberius's face. "Yes, sir, I certainly echo that sentiment." But the old veteran of hundreds, nay thousands, of trials knew that it was not that simple. "But despite decisions made, kind sir, some things are never resolved."

Joseph returned Liberius's steady gaze. He knew the truth in Liberius's words. And Liberius was well aware that his words were no revelation to the seasoned lawman. A trial was a gamble, a risk. The outcome favors one side or the other and often says nothing about the truth. But court trials were generally civilized events and a level or two above scrapping in the streets.

***

After consulting with Pilate, Liberius emerged from his office.

"He'll see you now," Liberius told Joseph. "Please be mindful that he's very busy and doesn't have much time."

"Of course," Joseph responded as Liberius showed him into Pilate's office.

Pilate did not look up from the parchments he was reviewing when Joseph entered. Joseph did not want to rile Pilate's famous temper so he stood quietly near the door.

"Please, sit, counselor," Pilate said after a few moments without looking up from his reading.

Joseph complied and found himself once again gazing at the countenance of Pontius Pilate, Governor of Jerusalem. His judicious bearing was impressive as always. The thought ran through Joseph's mind that Pilate's aquiline features were remarkable and quite fitting for posterity and replication in marble.

Finally, Pilate shoved his parchments aside causing several scrolls to roll across his table and onto the floor. Joseph bent to retrieve them.

"Leave them, Joseph," Pilate ordered. "Liberius loves to clean up after me. Let's not spoil his fun." Pilate focused his intense gaze on Joseph.

"What may I do for you on this fine day?" Pilate asked.

"I believe I briefly mentioned to you, sire, that there were some issues, some conflicts with some of my defense witnesses," Joseph replied.

Pilate's eagle-like eyes narrowed and peered closely at Joseph. "And these would be witnesses in the case of...?"

Joseph was almost annoyed, which was unusual for him. It took much to test his patience. Perhaps it was his fatigue from lack of sleep and his inability to stop thinking about his case that had lowered his boiling point. Pilate knew full-well what case he was referring to. He was quick to criticize others for game playing but apparently allowed himself to engage in the practice with impunity. But Joseph was a gamesman, too, and knew how to play. He smiled and bowed slightly to Pilate.

"Why it is the case of Jesus of Nazareth of which I speak," Joseph replied in his most respectful manner. "Forgive me for not speaking with clarity."

"Go on..." Pilate ordered as he had the sudden need to inspect his cuticles.

"Sir, the defense for my client—for Jesus of Nazareth—includes his mother and his closest followers," Joseph offered

"That alone is prosaic," Pilate said, gamesman that he was.

"Allow me to explain, sire," Joseph bantered back. "His followers all believe in him. They believe he is the Son of the Living God."

"Good for them," Pilate, the pantheist, responded.

"My point, sir, they could all be called down for blasphemy by Caiaphas," Joseph replied. "Charged with the crime against Jewish religious laws and facing the death penalty by making the public assertions that they would have to make in their testimony."

"Hmm. So, you're saying that if you call these persons to the stand, they could face prosecution," Pilate said. "And, if you don't call them..."

"Sir, if I don't call them I have no case, no defense for my client," Joseph said.

Pilate turned and looked out his window, kicking the shutter to the side with his sandaled foot to allow more light to filter in. He knew politically speaking he had to ensure that Jesus had a fair trial. He had to make every effort to see that it took place. He knew where this was going but he'd allow Joseph to take him there.

"Your honor, Jesus has a right to a defense," Joseph said quietly.

"You are aware of my position, Joseph, and that I would know that primitive fact, I pray," Pilate said in an even-tone that did not reflect the reproach implied by his words.

"Of course, I meant no disrespect," Joseph answered.

"What do you suggest, counselor?" Pilate asked.

"Immunity," Joseph said. "I suggest that all of Jesus's witnesses be granted immunity from prosecution by the Jewish High Priests."

Pilate turned back toward Joseph, a bemused look on his face. "Brilliant!"

Just as Pilate thought—Joseph was seeking immunity for his witnesses. There was an unintended pleasure personally for Pilate in this strategy. It would enrage Caiaphas and send him into a near-death swoon.

Joseph somewhat taken aback, remained silent. He waited for the possibility that another shoe might drop. Instead Pilate's smile grew broader as he refocused on Joseph.

"Brilliant."

***

Joseph scurried down the hall behind the tall Roman guard who was escorting him to the holding cells located underneath the courthouse. Joseph had never represented a defendant who was imprisoned in the deplorable conditions of the courthouse jail. Joseph normally held strategy meetings with his clients in fine parlors and luxurious bath houses of Jerusalem. Joseph tried to hold his breath as he walked through the putrid area. He kept his eyes forward as he walked, not responding to the calls and whispers he heard as he passed the rows of forgotten men pleading for the eyes of a free man to fall upon them and his ears to hear their soulless cries.

But as sympathetic as Joseph's heart was, his mission was to save but one of these prisoners. When he first contemplated his meetings with Pilate and Jesus, he presumed that the more difficult would be that with Pilate. But he was wrong. The judge would prove to be much more cooperative than the defendant.

Seeing Jesus in the miserable cell never failed to tug at Joseph's heart. He struggled to look past the conditions that this kind, peaceful man was forced to live under. Instead, he focused on getting him out of there and back to his tranquil life as a minister. It had had only been a few days since he had last seen

Jesus but he was stunned by his appearance. He struggled to hide his astonishment that the already lithe figure of Jesus had been reduced by a stark loss of weight. But as Joseph looked upon the countenance of Christ, he felt a warmth that generated from his deep, soulful eyes—eyes that were at once strong and kind and wise. It was never lost on Joseph the immediacy of the comfort he felt when he was in Jesus's presence. How could Jesus lift Joseph's spirits given the conditions he was forced to endure and do so without speaking even a word?

"Joseph, it is heart-warming to see your pleasant face," Jesus said, a smile spreading across his thin face.

Joseph bowed to Jesus. "As always, my spirit is buoyed by yours," Joseph responded.

Jesus's eyes glistened with understanding at Joseph's words.

Joseph pulled the small stool over closer to Jesus who sat on his mat and leaned against the rough limestone wall at the back of the cell.

"I have completed the interviews with all our witnesses," Joseph told Jesus. "Depositions. I feel we have the bones of a good defense."

Jesus gazed silently at Joseph, his eyes knowing and kind.

"You are loved," Joseph said.

"So are you," Jesus replied.

Joseph felt touched and inexplicably humbled by Jesus's simple words. Slightly taken aback by his own reaction, Joseph fiddled with the parchments he had brought with him.

"I believe there are several scenarios, several options for a strong defense," Joseph began. "I hesitate to characterize these stratagems as creative, let's just say they all have tactics that are based in facts but that are... pliable, bendable."

"The truth is not bendable, Joseph," Jesus said quietly.

"Please, hear me out, Jesus," Joseph responded, feeling defensive. "There's so much at stake, Jesus."

"More than perhaps any of us know," Jesus responded.

"Let me share with you my thoughts about your defense. There are several possibilities," Joseph said. "I spoke with Judas Iscariot."

Joseph glanced quickly at Jesus. He saw no sign of anger or bitterness so he continued.

"As you can imagine, he would not be the most sympathetic of figures in this case. No one likes a disloyal friend. My thought was that we could suggest to the jury that it was Judas who spread the rumor that you were a god. We could present the possibility that Judas envied you and that that envy had turned into hatred and resentment and eventually drove him to harm you—to make it appear as though it was you who was promulgating the blasphemous words."

"But that would not be true," Jesus responded simply.

"Our need is to plant doubt about your guilt. Perhaps you don't fully understand the legal process..." Joseph began.

"Perhaps not but I do understand what truth is," Jesus said and smile. "Truth is beauty."

That scenario was apparently out, Joseph thought to himself, for now at least. But he wouldn't abandon it completely.

Jesus may be forced to accept an imperfect defense. No defense is perfect, Joseph thought to himself.

"Then another possible approach to your defense occurred to me when I spoke with your friend, Mary Magdalene. She apparently had things in her background, that, well... perhaps she was less than proud of," Joseph said. "My thoughts were that Mary could testify that she recovered from her past foibles due to the positive influence of her association with you."

Jesus watched with a bemused looked on his face as Joseph stood and paced back and forth, much like a defense lawyer at trial.

"Mary thought so much of you that she thought of you as a "god" and, you know, a miracle worker and perhaps related those expressions and opinions to others. Maybe others got the... wrong impression."

"Mary Magdalene knows me," Jesus responded. "She gave no one the wrong impression."

Joseph was beginning to feel more than a little frustrated. Here he was trying his best to save Jesus's life but Jesus barely listened before he rejected his advice. Joseph then thought of Lazarus. He was not a disciple or close follower of Jesus. Perhaps twisting the story of Lazarus a bit would not be as objectionable to Jesus. Joseph was running out of ideas.

"I spoke with Lazarus, the young man..." Joseph began but was interrupted.

"I know the young man," Jesus interjected.

"His claims... well some would find them implausible, even unbelievable," Joseph weighed his words so that he would not offend his client.

But Jesus remained silent, waiting for Joseph to continue.

"We could suggest that Lazarus was overzealous in his claims that he... uh..." Joseph just couldn't say the words. But Jesus could.

"Rose from the dead," Jesus completed Joseph's words. "And he did."

"Jesus, all these scenarios I present to you are not bending the truth as much as they are ways to raise reasonable doubt within the mind of the jurors," Joseph, said. "In other words, the bar is low in that we don't have to prove our defense we just have to present plausible explanations that will makes the jurors consider that the charges against you may not be true."

"Joseph, I know your heart is pure," Jesus responded. "I caution you not to present this case or any other based on falsehoods. Don't get caught up in the politics of winning. Truth is more important. It's all any of us have."

Joseph was suddenly overcome with emotion. Tears formed in his eyes and his heart was racing.

"Jesus, please, I'm trying to save your life!" Joseph pleaded. "I am dedicated to your defense. I fear for the outcome. I fear that you will be found guilty. You are such a kind man. The world needs you to be alive, Jesus. I beg you to help me save you!"

The tears streamed down Joseph's cheeks as Jesus rose from his mat and gently embraced him.

"Joseph, I am ever grateful for your help and your caring," Jesus said tenderly. "But there are limits as to what a man can do."

Joseph wiped his tears away with his sleeve, recovered his decorum and reached into his quiver for one last possibility that he knew, on its face, was ludicrous. But as Jesus's defense attorney, it was his responsibility to present every possible defense to his client. He gently touched both of Jesus's hands.

"There is only one more defense I can think of," Joseph said. "I have doubts that you will take to it."

Joseph paused a few moments and gazed intensely in Jesus's eyes.

"Insanity."

Jesus laughed. "You bring me joy, Joseph."

Joseph sighed. That was it. Joseph was out of ideas.

"I feel I am failing you," Joseph said, defeated.

"The love you have in your heart could never lead to failure, Joseph."

"At this point, I honestly don't know what your defense will be, Jesus," Joseph said not hiding his frustration.

"The truth, Joseph" Jesus replied. "The truth."

A very sober expression came over Joseph's face. "What is the truth, Jesus?"

"The truth is within you."

Chapter 15
The Truth

Joseph had much to think about on his way home from the Roman jail. Jesus had challenged him to his core with just a few simple words. Joseph frowned as he walked along—after all his work on the depositions and after all the sleep he lost and time he spent away from his family struggling with what defense he would present for Jesus, his client was not interested in any of them. And, he was to appear before Pilate the next morning with a brief summary of the defense he planned to offer. He had no idea what that would be.

Humph, Joseph thought to himself, Jesus says the truth is within me. *All I feel within me is defeat. How can I save a man's life who speaks in riddles and rejects any semblance of a defense?* Joseph viewed Jesus as naïve and almost child-like in his refusal to cooperate. Did he think that he'd escape Caiaphas's punishment by the sheer magic of his presence? Jesus was in store for quite an awakening.

Joseph recalled his conversation with Jesus. He had offered some viable, plausible scenarios but they were all roundly rejected by Jesus without as much as polite discussion. Judas Iscariot had betrayed him yet Jesus wouldn't even consider suggesting to the jury panel that perhaps some of the rumors and speculation about Jesus had come from him. It very well could have. *Why didn't that qualify as the truth that Jesus spoke of—the one that's in me?*

Joseph was happy when his house appeared on the horizon. It was a beautiful night. The stars had never looked so bright and so large. It was as if glowing lamps had been strung across the skies. But Joseph was in no mood for the beauty of nature. He scoffed at the stars and planets. They seemed to mock him as they twinkled and winked at him. It was rare for Joseph to feel deflated and uncertain. It was at those times when Joseph sought counsel with his most reliable advisor.

***

The house was quiet when Joseph entered off the veranda. It was late and he didn't want to disturb his wife or children. He especially did not want to rile his mother-in-law who was staying with them on an extended visit. Joseph lit some candles from the burning embers still flickering in the stone oven. They illuminated the room enough for him to make his way around and spot a pot of food that was sitting on a side table.

"Ah, dinner," Joseph said quietly to himself.

"Yes, dinner, my husband," Irit's voice filtered into the eating area as she emerged from the hallway.

"Irit! I didn't intend to wake you from your slumber," Joseph said. He glanced around behind her in hopes that her mother, Binah, wasn't following.

Irit never missed any signal that emanated from her husband.

"Rest assured that Mother still sleeps," Irit said, a sharp edge to her words.

"I am glad to hear the old lady rests," Joseph said. "It is good for her health."

"And good for yours," Irit responded. "You feel much healthier when she is not about."

Joseph remained silent as Irit took a bowl and spoon from the dish safe and scooped several heaping ladles of lamb and chard stew from the still-warm pot. She quickly tore a crust from the loaf of brown bread sitting on the counter and sat the food in front of Joseph.

"I could have gotten that," Joseph said quietly and insincerely.

"You are efficient in the courtroom and I am efficient in the kitchen," Irit said, a smile curling the corners of her lips. "How is the trial of the century progressing along?"

Joseph was in the middle of a bite of stew. He swallowed his food, sighed and focused on Irit.

"What's wrong, Joseph?"

"I'm not so sure your words are accurate... that I'm proficient in the courtroom especially considering my ineptitude in developing a defense for my current client," Joseph replied. He resumed eating and diverted his eyes from Irit who was focused on him like a hawk.

Irit was not of the mind to let his comment go unaddressed. She never let anything Joseph said get by her and linger in her thoughts as a question or a doubt. As domineering as Irit could be, she was sensitive to her good husband's moods. On this late evening, she could see that Joseph was upset. She also knew that when Joseph failed to hide his distress that it was a signal that he needed her help and counsel. Irit sat down across from her husband.

"Joseph, tell me what distresses you," Irit said in a gentle voice.

"I am a failure," Joseph responded.

Irit was successful at repressing her smile and stifling her laughter. Joseph was truly feeling sorry for himself, Irit thought to herself. Joseph was the best attorney in all of Jerusalem among all lawmen, both Hebrew and foreign, who practiced in the city. Normally Irit would scoff at Joseph's ridiculous statement but Joseph didn't need to be scoffed at. He needed her support and advice and Irit always gave Joseph what he needed.

"Tell me why you speak such unexpected words, Joseph," Irit persisted.

"In the day when I was a good attorney..." Joseph began until he was interrupted by his wife.

"Let's get something straight, Joseph," Irit interjected. "I know you are feeling particularly low on this night but your premise is wrong-headed. You are still a good attorney and always will be—the best in all of Jerusalem. Just tell me what's going on right now without wasting time by mischaracterizing yourself."

Irit's predictable support was as always a comfort to Joseph and immediately lifted his spirits. Joseph put his spoon down and wiped his mouth on a cloth scrap.

"Irit, I have a client—Jesus of Nazareth to be precise—who rejects every defense that I present to him," Joseph said. "I am trying to save his life! Pilate expects me to present to him a summary of the defense I plan to offer before the court. But Jesus is a stubborn man and without discussion dismisses every potential defense."

"Hmm. Why do you think that is, Joseph?" Irit asked thoughtfully. "You tell me he is stubborn but you have also told me and I have heard from others that Jesus is quite a brilliant person."

"Brilliant? I thought so, too, but now I'm not so sure," Joseph responded.

"But again, Joseph, why does he reject your counsel?" Irit persisted.

"I suggested that we infer to the judge and jury that it may have been Judas Iscariot, the man who betrayed him, who spread the word that Jesus was God," Joseph replied. "But that was unceremoniously discarded by Jesus. And then I suggested that Mary Magdalene or perhaps Lazarus could have misled the people with talk of Jesus's miracle works. Again, Jesus would have no part of these scenarios."

"What is the truth, Joseph?" Irit asked sincerely.

The question though simple literally sent a chill down Joseph's spine. It recalled to him Jesus's last words to him: "The truth is in you, Joseph."

"He said that... that I knew the truth," Joseph responded.

"And I'm sure that you do," Irit said. "And that, my husband, is what you must follow."

***

As Joseph lay in his bed next to Irit that night, he was more than a bit annoyed. Once again he couldn't sleep and the woman who never failed to give him the best advice had this time failed him. She had echoed the mysterious words of Jesus. Somehow the truth dwelled within him. *Ha! If it's in me, why on God's good earth do I not know it then?!*

Joseph finally fell asleep but it was not a restful sleep. His dreams were filled with images of Jesus, his mother Mary, the disciples, Mary Magdalene, Judas Iscariot. They all swirled before him like wild chaotic ingredients that he was charged with making into an edible stew. He could not rein them in and he was reduced to standing before them, helpless and defeated. The image of Jesus then overwhelmed the others. Jesus was reaching out to Joseph, his eyes kind and wise. The confusion and conflict seemed to disappear in both the dream and in Joseph's mind. As Joseph reached his hand out to Jesus, he woke. He shot up in bed, a smile on his face.

"I know. I know what the defense must be!"

***

The next morning, Joseph was up bright and early and bustling around the kitchen even before Irit had risen. He was in the process of making tea when he was joined by Irit.

"My, you are up early and your mood seems to have changed for the better," Irit said.

Joseph kissed his wife on the cheek and hugged her.

"Thanks to you my dear. The seed you planted in my mind grew quite robustly overnight and now, the day is new and the sun is bright and I, my dear wife, know the defense that I will present to Pilate. It was there all along before me but I refused to see it," Joseph said, the tone of his voice reflected his high spirits.

"And is the defense... the truth?" Irit asked.

"That it is, Irit. That it is." Joseph smiled as he poured tea for Irit and himself.

***

Joseph stood before the raised bench where Pilate would soon be seated. Had Joseph been in the same frame of mind that he had been after speaking with Jesus the day before, he would have been absolutely panicked in presenting a defense strategy to Pilate. But after Jesus's words and those of his loving wife had time to sink in, he could not have been more confident to speak before Pilate. In fact, he looked forward to it.

Joseph waited for quite a while before he heard the sound of a few doors slamming and the swish of Pilate's robe as he walked brusquely into the courtroom.

"All rise, the court is in session," Liberius's voice started out in its usual robust tone but trailed off as he looked around the room, slightly embarrassed, and saw that it was empty save Joseph who was already standing.

Pilate took his seat at the bench and after looking over a few parchments on his table focused on Joseph.

"Joseph of Arimathea," Pilate began. "What brings you here this fine day?"

Game playing again, Joseph thought to himself. But on this day Joseph would not be thrown off balance and would not play. Joseph smiled and bowed respectfully to Pilate.

"And a grand morning it is," Joseph responded. "It is at your request that I come here, sire."

It was Pilate who was thrown off balance. He looked at a few papers and then glared at Liberius.

"Why didn't you remind me, Liberius?" Pilate barked.

There was no one more loyal to Pilate than Liberius and this trusty court clerk had undoubtedly reminded Pilate of his day's schedule. But Joseph was unperturbed. He would allow Pilate to soothe his ego and proceed as he saw fit.

"I recall that you needed to assure me that you are prepared to defend Jesus of Nazareth and ready for the trial to proceed. Is my recollection correct, Joseph?" Pilate asked.

"Sir, of course, your memory is as perfect as your integrity," Joseph said, as he bowed slightly again.

"Well, tell me," Pilate responded. "What defense have you concocted for the young minister? How do you propose to save this Jesus of Nazareth from the death knell that Caiaphas rattles before him?"

Joseph paced a few times in front of Pilate's bench—all the time a smile on his face and all the time a scowl on Pilate's.

"Get on with it, man!" Pilate said, raising his voice and signaling his impatience.

Joseph stopped in his tracks and turned toward Pilate.

"It is a simple matter, your honor," Joseph responded. "I simply plan to defend Jesus of Nazareth... with the truth."

Pilate's eyes flashed. He stared at Joseph for several long moments.

"That is all you have to say. The truth?" Pilate demanded.

"That's all there is, your honor," Joseph replied.

Pilate appeared a bit uncomfortable. "And do you, Joseph of Arimathea, believe in this truth?"

"With all respect," Joseph responded, "It matters not if I believe it or nay. My job is to present the evidence and prove my case."

Pilate glared at Joseph as though he had more questions and wanted more answers but he remained silent a moment until he remembered who he was and regained his composure. "As you well know, I must have entered into the public court records the defendant's response to the charges," Pilate lectured Joseph. "The charge is blasphemy against Jewish Religious Laws. The punishment is death! Are you telling me, man, that you wish to have the public record indicate that your response is that you will simply tell the truth?"

"Sir, with all respect, you know me to be a man of good repute," Joseph responded, his eyes locked on Pilate's. "I vow to provide the best defense possible for my client. Do you trust me, your honor?"

Pilate hesitated for a few moments, averting his steely eyes from Joseph's beseeching ones. He drew in a deep breath and sighed. He did know Joseph and he knew him to be an honorable man and a celebrated attorney, his ethics beyond reproach. He did trust him but he was not keen on allowing an absurd defense to be entered into the public rolls of his court. It had been hot lately. Perhaps Joseph was suffering from overheating—his brains a boil. He had been wearing quite a silly smile on his face during most of his presentation. Whatever it was, Pilate was well aware that Caiaphas was bent on convicting Jesus. Pilate had hoped that

Joseph would devise a way to get Jesus out of the mess he was in. But, perhaps it was not to be.

"Very well. I will have my clerk enter into the rolls that your defense will be the *truth*," Pilate said, pronouncing the last word with much derision.

"Please be assured that this defense is the best and only one possible," Joseph said, bowing once again.

"As you say," Pilate rose from his seat. "The trial will begin in tomorrow's morning court session. Be prepared to present your... truth."

Joseph watched as Pilate descended the steps from the bench and disappeared down the hallway. He realized that he had not made a very good impression with his defense summary but he was sure that Pilate would understand more clearly once the trial actually began. Liberius, who had been standing at the back of the courtroom, suddenly reappeared alongside Joseph.

"We'll see you tomorrow, Joseph... after sunrise."

***

Irit made Joseph a large platter of cheese, bread and melon early the next morning. But Joseph could only pick at the food, his mind on the courthouse, musing about how everything might turn out. There was so very much at stake. While Joseph had confidence in his abilities, he also had confidence in Caiaphas's skill. And, the determination in Caiaphas's eyes was daunting and undeniable. Joseph was up against a worthy opponent and one that obviously held much personal meaning for him. But Joseph was up for the challenge, in both regards. His legal skills would certainly match those of Caiaphas. As far as a personal stake in the case, Joseph had become involved on an emotional level. Joseph had become increasingly engaged with each story he was told about Jesus and was more drawn in with each word of love and devotion expressed about him. But more than the stories and the words of praise, it was Jesus himself—his presence, his goodness... his eyes always kind and wise. Yes, he had as much to lose on a personal basis as Caiaphas did—perhaps even more.

Those thoughts ran through Joseph's mind as he walked in the still dark morning to his office. He hadn't been there in several days and felt compelled to stop by and see if there were any emergencies he had to deal with. When he lit his office lamp and saw the pile of parchments and scrolls on his desk he wished that he had just gone straight to the courthouse. But being the dedicated and ethical person he was, he sat down and decided to go through as much as he could before he had to leave for court. And if he missed anything of an urgent nature, Yakir would be in court and could relay the information to him. At any rate, he wouldn't dare be late for the first day. In fact, he would be early, before sunrise, so he could speak with Jesus. He wanted to tell him that his defense would simply be the truth, something that Jesus had known all along.

Joseph waded through some of the pile of documents then focused on a note that Hadas had scratched out on a scrap of parchment. The note said that he had located a man whose sight had been restored by Jesus and a woman whose leprosy was cured by him. He also talked with Simon Peter's mother-in-law who was still very much alive. She was eager to testify. Joseph was perplexed by the final words on Hadas's note indicating that he might have a surprise witness for him. Joseph shrugged and shoved the scrolls and papers into a large basket and rose to leave. He had to be on his way. Destiny awaited him.

***

The guard unlocked Jesus's cell to allow Joseph to enter. Jesus was asleep on the thin mat that was shoved against the far wall. Joseph sighed as he looked at him. He was gaunt, his cloak was caked with dried blood and mud from the filthy cell. His long dark hair was matted and unkempt. A deep sadness overcame Joseph as he looked upon Jesus, seemingly peaceful in his sleep. Joseph closed his eyes and said a brief prayer that Jesus was dreaming of better times and more pleasant days. When he opened his eyes, Jesus was sitting up, leaning on his elbow and gazing at Joseph.

"I hated to wake you," Joseph said softly.

Jesus looked kindly upon Joseph. Joseph pulled the small stool over closer to Jesus so that he could talk quietly with him.

"Today the trial begins, Jesus," Joseph said.

"Very well," Jesus replied.

"I want to assure you that I will be presenting the... the only defense I could," Joseph said. "You were right. It was within me all along."

Joseph returned the warm smile that crossed Jesus's face.

***

Joseph had been at the defense table in the main courtroom for over an hour when he heard a soft jingling. He recognized the sound and turned slightly to see Caiaphas walking down the main aisle toward the prosecution table. Caiaphas was dressed in a white tunic covered by a dark blue cloak. At the bottom of the cloak were embroidered chrysanthemums alternating with small golden bells—the source of the gentle jingling—that hung between them.

Out of respect for Caiaphas's position in the community, Joseph stood immediately and bowed toward him.

"Good morning, Caiaphas," Joseph said, a slight smile on his face.

Caiaphas turned toward Joseph, his imperial visage reflected wonderment as to why in heaven's name Joseph would be standing there.

"Why, Joseph... Joseph of Arimathea," he said in mock surprise as he returned the bow. "It is a pleasure to see you." Caiaphas smiled, wanting to appear unfazed that he had already lost one battle. When Pilate informed Caiaphas that he was extending immunity to the defense witnesses, Caiaphas vigorously argued against it but to no avail. Pilate's word on the issue was final.

Crafty as always, Joseph thought to himself. Joseph considered himself fortunate to know the nature of the man who was to be his opponent in this legal proceeding. It might be impossible to stay one step ahead of Caiaphas but Joseph was determined to at least stay apace with him.

"Please know that though you are my opponent in this legal proceeding," Joseph began, "I have nothing but respect for you as a person and religious leader of our community."

"I appreciate the kind words, sir," Caiaphas responded. "It is my understanding that you volunteered for this... task—that you were not court-appointed?" he added in a reproachful tone.

"That is correct, Caiaphas," Joseph said. "I felt it only fair that Jesus be afforded a defense. Besides, it is Roman law."

"Even the devil should have his due," Caiaphas responded, averting his narrow eyes from Joseph's gaze.

"But it is from God's goodness that has inspired fairness in this world," Joseph responded gently.

At Joseph's words, Caiaphas stopped in his tracks as he headed for the prosecution table. Joseph watched him as he seemed to fully absorb his words. Since Joseph had said nothing that he could disagree with, Caiaphas resumed walking to his table, lay his parchments down and offered no response.

***

As the sun continued to strengthen, the courtroom continued to fill. Spectators and officers of the court filled the gallery. Yakir appeared in his finest tunic and cloak and sat at the defense table with Joseph who needed him there to act as courier for him when the need would arise. Caiaphas was joined at his table by Annas, the Jewish High Priest of the same rank as Caiaphas who would serve as his co-counsel and by Mered who would serve as Caiaphas's runner.

The crowded room was filled with raucous chatter and laughter. The ambiance in the room was more like that of a crowded bazaar than the expected decorum in a courtroom, especially when a capital trial was about to get underway. Liberius rushed into the room, the scowl on his face reflected his anger at the disrespect that was being shown to Pilate's court.

"Silence!" Liberius's booming voice brought an immediate hush across the room.

But the silence was short-lived and the once loud boisterous voices were lowered to whispers as two Roman guards escorted Jesus into the courtroom. Joseph and Yakir rose as Jesus was led to the defense table. The guards turned to leave but Joseph stopped them.

"Guards! Untie this man's hands!" Joseph demanded as he glared at the unthinking dunces.

"We have no orders from our commander to do so," the elder guard responded.

"You do now! Untie him!" Joseph snarled, his eyes burning with rage.

"I take no orders from you, sir!" the guard replied.

Everyone in the room was focused on the conflict, waiting on the edges of their seats to see its outcome. Liberius was also watching. Liberius was a loyal court officer who would never allow a defendant to sit through his trial bound up. It would be a deplorable reflection upon the court itself. Besides, Liberius had a kind heart and was a humane person. He looked into the peaceful face and the soft eyes of the defendant and decided to solve the conflict himself.

"Guards! Untie the defendant's hands! At once!"

Chapter 16
Opening Statements

Joseph stood erectly before the bench beside his client. On the other side of the aisle, Caiaphas and Annas stood as well. While Joseph looked straight ahead, waiting for Pilate's entrance, Jesus looked downward, his lips moving ever so slightly. Although Caiaphas also seemed to be watching for the Judge, his narrow eyes looked to the side toward the defendant. His hatred for the accused had never been so intense. It was finally time for the minister of the people to meet the executioner of the people. It would simply be a matter of time. Caiaphas knew that his case was solid and that Joseph's witnesses were all either daft or blasphemous themselves. He would make short shrift of them all.

"All rise," Liberius shouted, his voice reaching every corner of the courtroom.

The spectators dutifully complied with Liberius's announcement and rose abruptly in their chairs. A group of citizens who comprised the jury pool were cordoned off in one section of the gallery, separating them from the general public. It would be from these individuals that the jury would be created.

Pilate swept into the room with his usual grandeur. His gold crown of leaves was perched firmly atop his head, his dark coarse hair in stark contrast to the gleaming official headwear. Pilate's countenance was stoic and serious. He sat at the bench and looked over a stack of parchments. Not a sound was heard throughout the room while he pored over the documents. Finally, Pilate pushed the stack aside and peered down at Liberius who was at the ready alongside the bench.

"Liberius, what case do we have on the top of the docket this morning?" Pilate asked, of course, already knowing the answer.

In his finest and strongest voice, Liberius answered. "The case of the Jewish High Council versus Jesus of Nazareth is before the court this good morning, sire."

"Very well," Pilate said, as he peered out over the courtroom, his eyes finally resting on Jesus. "The defendant is present and represented?"

"Yes, sir," Joseph answered. "Jesus of Nazareth is present and I, Joseph of Arimathea, am present and represent him in the proceeding.

"And the prosecution is prepared to..." Pilate began to address Caiaphas but was interrupted by same.

"The prosecution in this case is ready to proceed; however, I shall allow the defense to be the first to call its witnesses," Caiaphas said, his head tilted with an arrogant bearing.

"It would be a pleasant experience if we allow one another to finish a sentence before we answer it, would you not agree, Caiaphas?" Pilate said. He did not like to be interrupted mid-sentence. Caiaphas was showing disrespect in hour one of day one. It was a mark against him but not necessarily a mark in favor of Joseph.

***

Pilate did not delay in ordering the questioning of members of the jury panel to begin. He ran his courtroom with dispatch and efficiency. Pilate's goal was to get through panel selection that day with the prosecution and defense agreeing upon twelve jurors and two alternates. He hoped to get through that process with enough time allowed for opening statements. Pilate was more than a little curious about exactly how Joseph would present his "truth" defense. He thought that while the courthouse was where truth and justice should prevail, ironically very often neither was ultimately the victor. Perhaps Joseph would change that but the odds were not in his favor.

"We shall now begin the process of selecting a jury," Pilate said in an off-handed yet imperial manner. The trial had finally begun.

Liberius led the prospective jurors, all men, one by one from their segregated area to the witness stand to be questioned by both the prosecution and defense.

There were two farmers who grew produce for the marketplace. After a smattering of light questioning from both sides, there were no objections to these men. They were designated as jurors one and two. The next man was the owner of a small shop that sold household items. Again, neither side saw an objection to this man, juror number three.

Potential juror number four was a little more controversial than the preceding three candidates. He was a Jewish man who had become secular in his philosophy. He rarely attended temple services. Caiaphas had a problem with him.

"Sir, can you explain why you do not attend the temple on the regular, required basis?" Caiaphas asked, his tone snide and reproaching.

Before the man could answer, Joseph interceded.

"Objection!"

Pilate's had snapped toward Joseph. "Knowing the reason for your objection, counsel, would be helpful."

"Begging your pardon, your honor," Joseph responded. "Religion should have no bearing on this matter."

Annas, sitting at the prosecution table, stifled a laugh. Caiaphas found no humor in Joseph's words.

"Religion has everything to do with this case," Caiaphas countered. "It is the heart and soul of the matter."

"This man does not have to be religious to consider and decide the truth in a matter, your honor," Joseph responded.

Pilate absorbed both sides of the disagreement and gave them both serious consideration. Although the defendant was accused of blasphemy, a crime against Jewish law, the truth in the matter, as Joseph asserted, was a standalone issue from religion. Caiaphas was a fanatic and believed that every issue had its roots in religion. Joseph was right.

"Sustained," Pilate said.

"But your honor..." Caiaphas said, who actually seemed hurt.

"Sustained and proceed. I'll waste no more time on this," Pilate said, raising his voice nearly unperceptively.

Jury selection was based on a triune comprised of the prosecution, defense and the judge. The vote in the case of juror number four was two in favor and one against. He was thus approved to be part of the panel much to Caiaphas's consternation.

There were several men who were passed by both. One man was known to be a public drunk and another was known to be slightly demented. Another man was a religious fanatic who was a follower of neither Jewish law or of Jesus of Nazareth. He was seen by both sides as biased and an individual with his own agenda who may want to make his own mark. A politician was rejected because of speculation that his decision was possibly for sale.

An upstanding physician and a retired shoemaker both made it easily onto the panel. There was no objection from either side in adding a medical man and a reputable businessman to the panel. They each had reputations as honest men who seemed to have no preconceived notions about the case against Jesus.

The empanelment of an elderly rabbi was objected to by Joseph. Caiaphas's argument was that if the rabbi were rejected, the court would be shown to publically harbor bias against a religious figure, suggesting that such a personage could not render a fair decision. Joseph argued vigorously that the charges against Jesus would evoke prejudice due to the panelist's heartfelt ideas and tenets.

Pilate was in a spot he had hoped he would not be placed in—at least not so early-on in the process. Agreeing with Caiaphas fundamentally went against Pilate's grain on many levels. But above all else, it was Pilate's responsibility to show no bias and he knew he could not allow the personal animosity he felt for Caiaphas to compromise the proceeding. Finding with Caiaphas in his argument against Joseph's objection was not pleasant but it was the right thing to do.

"Overruled," Pilate declared.

The burn that Joseph felt from Pilate's rebuke was uncomfortable. But he had to be tougher than that. There would certainly be many more rebuffs and losing battles ahead that would render more profound wounds.

The rest of the jury panel and two back-up jurors were selected without much objection. There was an unspoken agreement among the principals to get the trial moving. Pilate wanted nothing to tarnish the reputation that he reined over an efficient courtroom, one that stayed on schedule and one that did not tolerate theatrics or posturing by the attorneys which would not serve justice but only serve to prolonging the process.

For Caiaphas, he was near salivating to begin so he could ultimately emerge victorious in the case that would call for one punishment and one only—the death of Jesus of Nazareth. The defense counsel, Joseph of Arimathea, of course saw it differently. He was anxious to begin the trial of the century, perhaps of all centuries, where the truth would emerge—perhaps a truth for all time.

Pilate spoke to the chosen jurors, admonishing them to listen to all the evidence with an open mind and to have no preconceived assumptions about the defendant's guilt or innocence. He had them vow to no less than Roman Emperor Tiberius that they would adhere to Pilate's instructions. With the jury set, Pilate announced that it was time for the prosecution to lay out its charges against the accused and for the counsel for the accused to explain the basic defense that would be presented to the jury.

It was at Pilate's discretion which side would be the first to speak. Pilate had considered the question and decided to call for Caiaphas to begin the proceeding with his opening statement. Only the closest observer would have noticed the slight look of annoyance that registered on Caiaphas's face upon hearing that he would speak first. He felt the side that was allowed to speak last was at an advantage. Caiaphas could not object, of course, but he didn't like it. He was somewhat placated by Pilate's pronouncement that the defense would be presenting their case first allowing the prosecution to have the advantage of presenting its case last.

"With your permission then, your honor, I shall proceed," Caiaphas said. Not waiting for a response, he walked stridently up to the jury panel.

"Speaking for the Jewish High Council, please know that your service in this endeavor is much appreciated," Caiaphas began.

Joseph maintained his demeanor but he resented Caiaphas beginning his remarks with a direct reference to his religion and, of course, everyone in the room, the jury included, knew that Caiaphas held a high position with the Council and that most of the panelists were in his congregation. Retribution was definitely a word that Caiaphas would not omit from his lexicon. Whether the threat was implied by Caiaphas or inferred by members of the jury panel, it was floated in the air and Caiaphas would allow it to linger there. Pilate knew that Caiaphas was exploiting his position and half-way expected Joseph to object. But Joseph held his tongue. There was certain to be many other opportunities for objection.

"Gentlemen, the defendant that you see before you and that you will judge is accused of committing the ultimate crime against God and our Jewish laws," Caiaphas began.

Caiaphas turned and walked toward the defense table. He focused his black, bird-like eyes upon Jesus who returned his look with one of gentle kindness. Caiaphas caught Jesus's sincere gaze for just a moment and quickly averted his eyes. Although he would never confess to it, it seemed that Caiaphas had the same reaction that everyone had when Jesus looked upon them. He, too, felt the strength and goodness of that penetrating gaze. Joseph watched closely and detected the reaction that Caiaphas had to his client. It could prove to be helpful to Joseph.

"You will learn, gentlemen, over the course of the next few days that the accused, Jesus of Nazareth, has claimed to be the Son of the Living God," Caiaphas said, projecting his thin voice with as much strength as he could muster.

The jurors seemed to have a range of reactions to his words from curious to confusion and even to anger. Just what Caiaphas wanted! From the gallery, which now included many citizens who were standing and crammed behind those who filled the seats, a rush of whispered comments and remarks swelled to a muffled crescendo.

Liberius scowled at the gallery. "Silence!" he shouted.

Pilate banged his gavel angrily. "I will clear this court of all spectators if there is another outburst. You harp and complain at the risk of not hearing one more word of this proceeding."

Pilate surveyed the room. The red glow on his cheeks and his narrowed eyes immediately quieted the room. Pilate meant his words and would follow through with his admonition. He would not tolerate such behavior in his court. His job was to oversee a fair and swift trial. He would not let the dregs of the city who had come to be entertained by the proceedings keep him from fulfilling his responsibilities.

"Go on," Pilate said, looking at Caiaphas. He banged his gavel again for further emphasis.

Caiaphas paced slowly in front of the panel. After making a few turns, he stopped and looked pointedly at each one of them.

"Jesus of Nazareth, the son of simple peasantry, has illusions of greatness. He has bolstered his reputation with claims of miracle-making," Caiaphas said, his words hissing from his mouth.

"Yes, gentlemen, Jesus of Nazareth, the accused who sits here before you, has made claims that he has the powers that only God has. He has claimed to cure deadly diseases."

Caiaphas stopped and drew closer to the panel. He grasped the banister in front of the jury and bent toward them. A sneer curled his lips.

"But there is worse," Caiaphas said, now whispering angrily. "This man violated our laws by claiming to turn water into wine. He even claimed to have brought the dead back to life!"

Not a sound was heard in the entire room. As Caiaphas scanned the room, he remained silent allowing his words to linger in the air and gain a stranglehold on the room. It was apparent that the spectators struggled with great difficulty to adhere to Pilate's warning to remain quiet. It was obvious that Caiaphas's words had shocked them. Jesus looked straight ahead with no reaction to those words. His face remained calm and his eyes kind. His countenance was bereft of any shame or guilt. Joseph maintained his calm with sheer willpower. Even though he knew that Caiaphas would twist the words from the depositions, the manner in which he was doing so was infuriating. Joseph battled to control his rage and did not yield to it. Doing so would show a sign of weakness to his opponent and he wasn't inclined to cede that advantage to Caiaphas. As for Pilate, he was disinterested in Caiaphas's dramatics. He had seen them before. He had to tolerate Caiaphas's drawn out opening statement and had no choice but to maintain a serene exterior.

Caiaphas turned slowly and took a few paces in front of the panel again. His head was slightly bent and he grasped his chin with one hand as if in deep thought. His image was that of the wise sage who was considering all sides of an issue. Of course, nothing could be further from the truth. Caiaphas's focus could not be narrower. His entire being relied upon seeing Jesus of Nazareth convicted and sentenced to death. But along with being a Jewish High Priest and a barrister, Caiaphas was an actor. His dramatic flair was on full display as he gave his opening remarks. His histrionics ranged from anguish to mock astonishment that any man would be such a pretender to his beloved God.

"You will hear testimony from witnesses who will swear that the miracles this man purports to have performed were shams," Caiaphas said. "They will tell you that they witnessed a fit man pretend to be lame and then carry out the farce by walking again after the defendant placed his hands on the man—like he was a god!"

Caiaphas let the panel absorb that revelation.

"Further a blind man who was reportedly made to see again will testify that he was never blind," Caiaphas said. "The man was hired by followers of Jesus to play a part. And there will be others who will prove beyond the shadow of a doubt that Jesus did not perform miracles, that he is a sham, a fraud, a criminal and above all that he is not the Son of the Living God!"

Caiaphas had shouted so loudly that his frail body trembled from the effort expended. He regained his bearings for he had much more to say.

"Society cannot tolerate a man who would take on the mantle of the very God who created him, who created us all," Caiaphas said, getting to the heart of the matter. "Such a man cannot be allowed to continue his immoral and sacrilegious ministry. If we permit this man to continue in his sinful ways, we will all be held accountable for the evil that results."

Caiaphas paused for dramatic effect. It was so quiet in the room that every scratch made by a scurrying mouse across the wooden floor could be heard. Then Caiaphas bowed his head, closed his eyes and grasped his hands as if in prayer. Everyone except Jesus was watching his every move. Even Joseph kept a sly but steady eye on Caiaphas, making sure not to appear to be impacted by his words.

"Death!" Caiaphas said, now shouting as loudly as his weak voice could summon.

"It is death that our God has prescribed for blasphemy! And it is blasphemy that Jesus has committed!" Caiaphas raged.

Caiaphas spun quickly around toward the panel once more, his blue over-smock flying parallel to the floor from the speed and momentum of his move, creating the image reminiscent of a lank bird of prey. He focused his frenetic gaze on the men of the jury.

"You cannot allow this man to live so that he can violate our God again," Caiaphas said as he walked back toward the prosecution table.

Almost as an afterthought, Caiaphas spoke over his shoulder as he walked away from the jury.

"Jesus of Nazareth must die," Caiaphas said in a venomous whisper.

Caiaphas' performance had been disturbing—dazzling in a sense, but disturbing. Joseph glanced sideways at Jesus whose demeanor and countenance remained unchanged. Joseph was still recovering from the impact of the prosecutor's words when several light bangs of Pilate's gavel brought him back to the present. Pilate sensed Joseph's reaction to Caiaphas. He had a similar reaction but he would never allow his steely image to reflect it. Of most importance, Pilate had to oversee efficacious proceeding so he had to draw Joseph out from his daze. The gentle tapping of his gavel signaled Pilate's sensitivity to Joseph and his grasp of the challenge before him. Joseph shot up to his feet like a date palm sprout in spring.

Joseph strode to the bench. Although he was short in stature, he stood as straight as he could so he would appear to fill a larger space. He wanted to portray an image of strength and confidence. He was starting to gain confidence in this case. He hoped that strength would accompany it. He understood that he was up for quite a challenge—even with the truth on his side. Caiaphas had just delivered a shot across the bow, but it wasn't a killing blow. This was just a battle—the war was still ahead of them.

"Your honor, I am ready to proceed with my opening remarks," Joseph said, bowing slightly to show his respect to the court.

Pilate nodded, signaling for Joseph to proceed. Joseph took a deep breath and turned to face the jury, the body of the twelve men who would decide the fate of Jesus of Nazareth.

"We appreciate your service, gentlemen," Joseph began. "My honored opponent has aptly laid out the prosecution's case to you. But the presentation was fundamentally flawed because the presumption that Jesus of Nazareth conducted his ministry on a lie... is a lie."

Caiaphas did not look at Joseph. Even the adversarial words that Joseph spoke did not seem to ruffle his feathers. The only indication that Caiaphas was angered, was the crook of one eyebrow as he feigned interest in the stack of parchments before him.

For his part, Pilate paid apt attention. He knew that Joseph promised to base his defense on an intangible that he categorized as the truth. Wasn't that the point of all trials? Pilate was not naïve and was well aware that arriving at the truth was not always the result of a judicial proceeding. Pilate was anxious to see just how Joseph proposed to use the "truth" to his benefit especially in face of Caiaphas's promised testimony that was potentially devastating to his client. If Caiaphas was right, Pilate thought to himself, perhaps Jesus was a magician and entertainer and not a minister at all. Therefore, if Jesus were an actor, he could not be considered a blasphemer at all. Could something that simplistic be Joseph's defense? Pilate smiled slightly at the thought of Caiaphas's reaction to such a scenario.

"The defense will show through witnesses and evidence that Jesus is not guilty of the charge of blasphemy that has been brought against him by the Jewish High Council.

"The honorable Caiaphas promises to bring witness after witness to refute the claims that have been made about the miracles performed by Jesus," Caiaphas said. "The defense will refute each of those witnesses with our own who will testify that… Jesus actually did perform those miracles."

A few whispers brought Pilate's gavel down again. Pilate's eyes were focused like a goshawk on Joseph. Even Caiaphas snuck a few furtive, angry glances at Joseph as did Annas who sat beside him.

Joseph paced back and forth a few times in front of the panel himself then stopped and turned toward the men.

"What will your opinions be about the witnesses that I propose to call? Will you think they are lying? Or perhaps you may think they're daft or committing blasphemy themselves. Those are all possibilities, are they not?" Joseph implored rhetorically.

"But there is one more possibility. You must consider that what these individuals will be testifying to is… the truth," Joseph said.

Joseph turned and walked to the defense table and stood directly behind the seated Jesus.

"For what they will tell you is the truth," Joseph proclaimed with great deliberation. "And the truth is within all of you."

Joseph continued to stand behind Jesus who was focusing that unique and intense gaze upon the members of the jury.

"The truth, gentlemen, is that Jesus of Nazareth is the Son of the Living God!"

The room was thrown into chaos. Caiaphas and Annas both shot to their feet. As they did, they disturbed the stacks of documents on their table and parchments went flying everywhere. The spectator's gallery was out of control, with any thought of Pilate's admonishment completely abandoned. Pilate rose and stared at Jesus. There was a look of deep sorrow on his face as he turned and swept out of the courtroom. Liberius was calling for order but no one was listening.

Joseph remained standing behind Jesus.

The members of the jury seemed disturbed and confused.

Jesus's face was peaceful and his eyes were kind.

Chapter 17
Preposterous!

"Preposterous!" Caiaphas raised his fragile voice to a volume that even he didn't realize he could attain. The two Jewish High Priests were livid as they stood before Pilate who was sitting sprawled out behind his table. Joseph of Arimathea was in the chamber as well. Out of respect for Pilate and the court, he stood there silently waiting until it was his turn to speak.

After Joseph's disturbing presentation and the resultant chaos, Caiaphas and Annas had immediately demanded that Liberius arrange for them to meet with Pilate in his chambers. Liberius looked over his shoulder at the out-of-control courtroom with great dismay. It was not like him to allow such disrespect but it seemed that Joseph's words had launched a tumultuous commotion that had a vitality and life of its own. He'd have to call in the Roman guards if this continued, he thought. The tips of their spears would be more convincing that his demands for order. But now he had the angry glares of Caiaphas and Annas to contend with and their consternation took precedence over the riotous gallery.

Liberius scurried back to Pilate's office and rapped lightly on the door that was partly ajar.

"Come!" Pilate shouted from within.

"Your honor, Caiaphas and Annas request an immediate audience with you," Liberius said.

"I expected as much," Pilate responded, as he sat gazing out his window, his elbow crooked on the arm of his chair and his chin resting in the palm of his hand. "Send them in."

Liberius turned to go but was stopped by Pilate.

"Have Joseph of Arimathea come in as well," Pilate ordered. "I'll allow no private words with that snake Caiaphas and his lizard companion."

Liberius bowed slightly, "Very well, sir."

"Oh, Liberius," Pilate stopped his clerk again. "What is the mood of the courtroom?"

"I regret to report that it is chaotic and the citizens are in an uproar and behaving in a disrespectful manner, sir," Liberius responded, ashamed to concede to his personal failure. "I contemplate that the presence of the guards and their sharpened spears may be necessary."

Pilate quickly turned away from the window and faced Liberius, waving off his last words.

"The presence of the guards will not be necessary—not at this juncture," Pilate said. "There is great passion about the matter presently before this court. Allow the spectators to vent their feelings. However, I will expect decorum when the trial resumes." Pilate hesitated for a few moments, listening with great attention to his own words as though they were unknown to him. "But you know Liberius, passion cannot be truly eradicated, only repressed. In this instance, I judge that we will not be able to stand in the way of passion for it may be passion that decides the fate of Jesus of Nazareth."

***

Caiaphas was less than pleased when Liberius announced that he and Annas could speak with Pilate but that the Governor insisted that Joseph of Arimathea be present for the discussion. Caiaphas could say nothing about it. Pilate held the power in the courtroom. But Caiaphas could sneer and sneer he did. Pilate looked unfazed when the trio of attorneys was shown into his chambers.

"What is on your mind, Caiaphas? I ask you because I know there is always something crawling around in there," Pilate said, the almost imperceptible glint in his eye reflected his bemusement that the words of the humble and gracious Joseph had so perturbed the old dilapidated camel.

"Preposterous!" Caiaphas screeched.

"Preposterous? Why I would think a holy man like you would think that every day that your god blesses you with another is nothing short of a blessing," Pilate said, continuing his unsympathetic game of words.

But Caiaphas was in no mood for games. He regained his composure, took on his usual haughty demeanor and began to make his case.

"Your honor, the rubbish that the defense counsel just spewed was totally out of order!" Caiaphas responded, his voice louder and his tone angrier than he had planned.

"I believe it is I who determines what is in and out of order," Pilate responded. "And, I daresay your bellowing is out of order for this small chamber. If I had a gavel, I would rap it. I'll have Liberius remind me to bang my gavel an extra time on your behalf when I return to the bench."

Caiaphas was growing all the more disconcerted but managed to rein his frustration in.

"I apologize, your honor," Caiaphas said, his voice much softer. He glanced at Joseph who was standing a few steps behind, his eyes lowered to the floor.

"Sir, I never like to be the bearer of bad news—even to an opponent—but Joseph has not only boldly lied to the court with his nonsensical words—he has committed blasphemy against the laws of the Jewish Council, the very charge that he defends Jesus against."

"I must apologize to you, Caiaphas. I thought you enjoyed sharing bad news. I must have misjudged you," Pilate shot back. "Hear me now, High Priest, the immunity that I have granted to the defense witnesses is hereby extended to the defense counsel himself."

Caiaphas was shocked into silence. But he burned and seethed. After a long pause, he gathered himself and had one more question.

"You, sir, are a much more knowledgeable legal scholar than I," Caiaphas began.

"I bow to your wisdom, Caiaphas," Pilate said, enjoying his own repartee.

"My point, sire, do you consider the defense that Joseph has presented as a viable and, dare I say, a legitimate one?" Caiaphas asked cautiously.

"Joseph is a legal expert of excellent repute," Pilate began, in a professorial tone. "Joseph, I assume that you have discussed your defense strategy with your client, have you not?"

It was the first time that Joseph was called upon to speak in the impromptu meeting. He bowed slightly to Pilate to show his respect.

"Yes, sir," Joseph said.

"And the defendant is in agreement with the defense you have planned?" Pilate asked.

"It was the only defense that Jesus would agree to," Joseph responded.

A strange noise came out of Caiaphas. It sounded like a cross between a sniggle and a snort. Pilate shot darts at him. It was enough to have to look at the swine without having noises to match. The room grew silent for a few moments. Pilate looked out on the street again. The sun was gaining power and the heat was drifting upward from the stone street. Pilate seemed to be mesmerized by something outside his window and continued to gaze for what seemed like a very long time. Since duty was calling, Pilate finally rose. He straightened out his tunic, readjusted his golden crown and turned to the men.

"We have much to do. We shall work until the sun sets and the heat dissipates." With that Pilate swept out of his chambers, his sandaled feet surprisingly silent on the marble floor. Without exchanging glances, Caiaphas, Annas and Joseph followed behind. It was time to hear the sworn accounts of the witnesses.

***

When Pilate re-entered the court, Liberius shouted for silence. The crowd had settled down and this time obeyed the clerk. There was total quiet as the attorneys took their places again. Pilate looked over some documents that were stacked on the bench. He scratched down a few notes and then looked up expectantly.

"Joseph of Arimathea, shall we proceed?" Pilate asked.

Joseph rose from his chair and quietly approached the bench.

"I am ready to proceed, your honor," Joseph responded.

"Please. . . call your first witness," Pilate directed.

"The defense calls Mary, mother of Jesus of Nazareth," Joseph said as he nodded to the Roman guard who stood before the door that led to the anteroom where the witnesses were required to wait.

The guard, with great dispatch, opened the door and loudly called the defense's first witness.

"Mary, mother of Jesus, your presence is required in court," the Roman guard announced.

The guard held the large door open as Mary, small and fragile appearing, walked tentatively in the room. Joseph smiled and motioned to her to come forward. Mary, whose hands were trembling noticeably, felt some relief when she saw Joseph's kind face. Mary picked up her pace and was met by Joseph at the end of the aisle leading to the witness stand. Joseph sensed that she needed some assistance and offered his arm to Mary who gratefully slid her arm into his. Mary glanced at Jesus as she passed the defense table. He returned her look and smiled broadly, uplifting her spirit.

Joseph and Mary walked toward the bench and stopped before Pilate who looked down at the small woman, blanching at the ethereal nature of her countenance. The thought ran through his mind that mother and son had a similar impact on him, one which made him feel inexplicably uncomfortable.

"Your honor, may I present to you Mary, mother of Jesus of Nazareth," Joseph said quietly.

Pilate narrowed his eyes as he spoke directly to Mary.

"Mary, mother of Jesus of Nazareth," Pilate began, "Do you swear to this court of the Roman Empire that what you tell the jury and the public will be the truth, without omission or embellishment?"

Mary bowed deeply. "Yes... yes sir," Mary spoke so softly it was difficult to hear her.

Joseph whispered in her ear. "Mary, tell him, 'Yes, sir, I swear my words will be truthful.'"

Mary nodded to Joseph.

"Yes, sir, I swear my words will be truthful," Mary said, her voice a little stronger now.

Pilate nodded toward Liberius.

"The court hereby recognizes Mary, mother of Jesus of Nazareth, as a witness for the defense," Liberius bellowed.

Jesus watched his mother carefully, concern for her was obvious on his face. Joseph led her the rest of the way to the raised platform where she would stand to testify about the life and times of her son. Joseph gave her arm a gentle squeeze, signaling that all would be well.

Joseph stood at his table and consulted a few papers. He then walked toward Mary. He decided that he would strike first and begin the defense with an explosive issue.

"Mary, can you tell the court about the birth of your son, Jesus?" Joseph asked.

Mary swallowed hard. "Yes, sir," she said and then took a deep breath. "My son was born in a manger in Bethlehem."

"Hmm. Bethlehem?" Joseph asked. "Is that where you resided at the time, ma'am?" Joseph asked.

"No, sir," Mary responded.

Joseph furrowed his brow in mock puzzlement. "Then why did you travel to Bethlehem for his birth? How did that come to be, Mary?"

"I... I was told to travel there for his birth," Mary responded.

"By whom?" Joseph persisted.

"Gabriel had come to me and told me that my son must be born there," Mary replied.

"So you were acting upon the advice of Gabriel and...," Joseph began but was interrupted by Caiaphas's first objection.

"Objection! Hearsay!" Caiaphas screeched. "No such man—no 'Gabriel'—has been identified before this proceeding."

Joseph looked to Pilate. "If I may ask Mary to provide the identity of Gabriel, it will clarify the matter."

Pilate looked warily at Joseph. "Overruled... for now."

"Mary, can you identify 'Gabriel' for the court?" Joseph asked.

"Yes, sir," Mary said quietly. "Gabriel came to me in the night. He is an angel of God."

Caiaphas recoiled like he had been struck across the face. Annas's mouth dropped open. The crowd stirred—the spectators expressed themselves in both whispers and shouts. The guards, holding their swords before them, advanced toward the gallery.

"Blasphemy!" Caiaphas hissed.

Pilate banged his gavel. "Halt!" he shouted at the guards.

The guards froze in place, waiting for further orders. Pilate scowled as he scanned the spectator's gallery.

"I will not tolerate these outbursts. They will only serve to bias the jury and prolong the trial," Pilate said. "I allowed you some freedom earlier to express your passion but now we all have to get down to the business of the day which is to allow this process to continue without undue interruption."

You have three choices. Stay and be quiet and witness the trial. Stay and be rowdy and feel the sharp spears of my guards as they expel the guilty from the courtroom. Or, with one more outburst I may choose to clear the courtroom. Be warned that I do not make idle threats."

There was one more matter that Pilate had to straighten out before it got out of hand.

"Caiaphas... approach," Pilate ordered.

Caiaphas rose from his chair. His countenance took on an indignant look as he walked brusquely to the front of Pilate's bench.

"The crowd is not allowed to have impassioned outbursts and neither are you," Pilate said, speaking in a private tone. "I suggest you don't humiliate yourself by making any further such improper remarks."

Caiaphas bowed to Pilate. "Henceforth, my decorum will be above reproach." But Caiaphas was not one to give up too easily. "But your honor," Caiaphas whispered, "the woman is claiming an angel of God came to her."

"And you can ask her about that, can't you?" Pilate responded. "That's what cross examination is designed to accomplish."

Although he maintained a calm demeanor, Caiaphas resented being scolded by Pilate who he considered imperious and contemptuous. But he was practical and disciplined and would not allow his acrimonious feelings toward Pilate to jeopardize the case. Caiaphas took his seat and vowed to maintain a professional demeanor and a face of stone throughout the rest of the trial.

Joseph returned to his direct questioning of Mary.

"What was the identity of your husband when you were with child?" Joseph asked.

"Joseph of Nazareth," Mary responded.

"And can I assume that he accompanied you from Nazareth to Bethlehem for the birth of your son?"

"Yes, sir."

"You traveled quite a distance. Was it difficult to find your way?" Joseph asked.

"No, sir. We went by the light of...," Mary said, but was interrupted.

Annas shot up from his seat. "Judge Pilate, the honorable Joseph of Arimathea did not ask how she found her way, only if she found her way."

"Brilliant!" Pilate said sardonically. "Sustained," he added almost as an afterthought.

"If you will allow me, sire, I shall rephrase," Joseph said. "Mary, how did you find your way to Bethlehem?"

"Sir, Joseph and I followed the bright light. It was the Star of Bethlehem that led us there," Mary answered.

The murmurs that floated around the courtroom quickly dissipated with several bangs of Pilate's gavel. Caiaphas lowered his eyes and scratched several notes on a scrap of parchment with his stylus. Thus far he had kept to his vow not to react to the testimony.

It was probably a combination of fear and interest that kept the spectators quiet. Everyone was on the edge of their seats to hear what Mary would say next. But it wasn't fear and interest that kept Caiaphas silent. Rather, it was anger and determination to win the case and send Jesus of Nazareth to his death.

"And how did you know to follow that bright star?" Joseph asked.

"It was Gabriel. He told me to look for the bright star in the East and to follow it," Mary said. "We followed it to a manger where Jesus was born." Mary smiled at her son.

"Did this bright star bring anyone else, other than you and your husband to this manger?" Joseph asked?

"Yes, sir," Mary responded. "Three kings from the East came to pay homage to Jesus as the new Messiah."

"Objection, your honor!" Caiaphas said as he rose from his seat. "There has been no evidence that these individuals even existed—other than in the mind of this woman. No one of this description is listed on the witness list for the defense."

"Sustained," Pilate said.

Joseph decided to end his questioning of Mary at that point. He could have rebuttal after Caiaphas questioned her if need be. Or he could call her back later. Testifying was such an ordeal for Mary and the circumstances of the day—the possibility that her son could lose his life—it was just all so much for her to bear. Joseph was sensitive to Jesus whose eyes implored him not to prolong his mother's agony.

"Your honor, I have no further questions at this time for Mary, Mother of Jesus," Joseph announced. "However, I do retain the right to question her at a later time as circumstances dictate."

"Very well, Joseph, you may sit," Pilate said as he turned slightly toward the prosecution table. "Caiaphas, do you have any questions for Mary, Mother of Jesus?"

Caiaphas quickly stood up. "Yes, your honor."

Caiaphas walked toward Mary, who trembled slightly as the Jewish High Priest approached. Mary's eyes rested on Jesus. His smile comforted her and gave her strength.

"In your testimony, ma'am, you claimed that your son, Jesus, is the Son of God, did you not?" Caiaphas asked.

Mary fiddled with her hands, lowered her eyes and nodded.

"I didn't hear your response," Caiaphas said loudly.

Pilate leaned over toward Mary. "Your head makes no noise when you shake it, ma'am."

There were a few stifled chuckles until Pilate glared at the gallery.

"Sorry, sire," Mary responded and looked up meekly at Caiaphas. "Yes, sir. My son is the Son of God."

Caiaphas fixed a look of incredulity upon the jury panel. He paced back and forth a few times in front of it. Mary's knees were shaking. She was praying that she could endure the torturous process.

"From your testimony, I recall that you had a husband," Caiaphas said, now peering at Mary. "Please tell me what your husband's name is again."

"Joseph—Joseph of Nazareth," Mary responded.

"Ah, Joseph of Nazareth. Of course." Caiaphas said as he walked toward the defense table and focused on Jesus. With his back to Mary and glaring at Jesus, he asked Mary another question. "Is Joseph of Nazareth also a god?"

There was a rustling in the gallery but not a word was uttered. All eyes were on Mary including Pilate's hawk-like eyes; the judge was as anxious as everyone in the room to hear her response.

"No, sir, Joseph was not a god," Mary answered.

"Does not a god beget a god?" Caiaphas said triumphantly, feeling proud that he was chipping away at what he considered Mary's bizarre and sinful testimony. "I am a learned man in all things that my God has revealed about himself."

"Objection!" Joseph rose to his feet. "The court does not need to hear about counselor's religious credentials!"

"Sustained."

"I apologize, sir," Caiaphas said, the anger just simmering below his mien. He walked back toward Mary who visibly cringed as he neared her.

"Ma'am, pray tell, in your vast knowledge of god, is it your contention that a human could beget a god?" Caiaphas hissed?

"No, sir. It is not," Mary replied quietly.

"Then what?! How did we get Jesus?! How was the world blessed with this Christ?! You claim him to be the Son of the Living God but how could that be true since he was sired by Joseph of Nazareth who, you admit, is not a god?" Caiaphas demanded.

Mary stood up straight and looked directly into Caiaphas's black eyes for the first time. No longer would she humble herself before this horrid man. A strength came over her that she did not understand but nor did she question it. Mary was resolute.

"The Holy Spirit came to me and told me that I was with child, sir, that I had conceived God's child," Mary said, her voice strong and steady. She looked upward and began praying quietly as the tension in the room was palpable and the silence deafening. Pilate watched nonplussed as Mary prayed. Jesus joined in Mary's silent prayers. Caiaphas was aghast, turning several shades of red and purple thus breaking his vow not to react to the testimony. Annas jumped to his feet.

"Objection!"

Pilate swung around in his chair and glared at Annas. "On what grounds do you object to your fellow prosecutor's cross examination?"

"I... I'm not sure," Annas said tentatively, doddering like the old man that he was.

"Well, sit down then!" Pilate boomed.

Joseph stood. "May the witness stand down, your honor?"

Pilate watched as a visibly shaken Caiaphas took his seat at the prosecutor's table.

"I assume you have finished questioning the witness, Caiaphas?" Pilate asked.

"Yes... yes," Caiaphas said without rising from his chair.

With that Joseph rushed to the witness stand and helped Mary step down. He took her arm and escorted her to the witness anteroom doorway. He took Pilate's warning about extraneous talking seriously but assumed the risk and whispered quietly to Mary.

"You were wonderful, Mary. Just wonderful."

Mary smiled up at Joseph and then craned her neck to get one last look at her son. He was looking back at her. His face was peaceful and his eyes were kind and loving.

Pilate called Liberius over and then swept out of the courtroom.

"His Honor Pontius Pilate has called for a brief interlude," Liberius shouted across the room. "Harken to the sound of the Roman trumpets that will signal Judge Pilate's call to order!"

The spectators filed out. The heat was rapidly escalating and everyone was in need of a drink of water. The jurors were led to a waiting room by two guards. Caiaphas and Annas were content to sit at their table. Liberius had two jugs of water brought to them.

Joseph gently touched Jesus's arm.

"Are you in need of drink, Jesus?" Joseph asked.

Jesus smiled. "A taste of water would be pleasurable."

"Come with me, Jesus," Joseph said.

Jesus rose and walked with Joseph toward the side exit where he had spotted a fountain. As they began to walk through the threshold, a tall Roman guard stopped them, placing his spear across the doorway and barring their passage.

"The prisoner cannot leave," the guard said.

"But he is parched. You must allow his passage," Joseph responded.

"I do not take orders from a Jew," the guard said, a slight smile revealed that he had more missing teeth than those still in his head.

Suddenly, the swishing of Liberius's fast-moving legs was heard rapidly approaching.

"Let him pass," Liberius ordered.

"But he is the defendant. He might escape through the terrace," the guard responded. "It is my orders to keep him here."

"Stand aside, now, man," Liberius growled. "I speak for his honor Pontius Pilate. Your own head will dangle on the tip of your own spear if you do not heed my word!"

The guard immediately withdrew his weapon and allowed Jesus and Joseph to leave the room. Joseph turned back to Liberius as they left.

"Thank you Liberius," Joseph said. "You are a kind man."

"It is not kindness, Joseph," Liberius responded. "It is just fairness."

Chapter 18
The Trumpets Sound

Liberius stood like a sentry at the front of the court as trumpeters at each doorway signaled with their sharp staccato that Pilate had ordered that the trial was to resume. Many of the spectators had already returned to the gallery so they'd be assured of a seat. Jesus was already seated at the defense table, hands folded and eyes closed.

When the trumpets sounded, Joseph was in the anteroom where the witnesses awaited their time on the witness stand. Simon Peter was next and Joseph was aware that he had a very anxious witness on his hands. Joseph assured him that his testimony was important and that speaking the truth in public would be a cathartic experience for him. At the second sounding of the trumpets, Joseph had to return to the courtroom. He certainly didn't want to be in contempt of court which was not out of the realm of possibility since Pilate was known to have no mercy with those who broke his rules. Joseph patted Simon Peter gently on the back then rushed off with great dispatch back to the courtroom.

Joseph hurried to the defense table just in the nick of time as Pilate was gliding into the room and heading for his seat. After taking his seat, Pilate scanned the courtroom and was pleased to see that the spectator gallery was exhibiting proper decorum and that the jury was filing in and taking their seats. He glanced at Caiaphas, who as usual had his nose buried in a stack of papers and at Joseph who has just taken his seat next to Jesus. Pilate hoped that the rocky start to the trial was only that—and that the rest of the trial would go much more smoothly. Deep down Pilate knew he was being a dreamer considering the explosive nature of the case and the personalities involved.

"Joseph of Arimathea? Might you call your second witness?" Pilate said.

Joseph rose and bowed to the court. "Yes, your honor, the defense calls Simon Peter."

Liberius scurried over to the Roman soldier who was guarding the witness area and spoke with him quietly. The guard squeaked open the door and stuck his head inside.

"The court demands the presence of witness Simon Peter," the guard shouted loud enough for the entire courtroom to hear.

A disoriented-looked Simon Peter walked to the threshold of the door and stopped. The guard took it upon himself to shove him the rest of the way into the room, bringing a scowl to Liberius's face. Joseph rose and met Simon Peter, escorting him to the front of the bench. In his stern and cold manner, Pilate elicited Simon Peter's vow to tell the truth, swearing to do so in the name of Tiberius and the Roman Empire.

Joseph motioned Simon Peter to take the witness stand. When he did so, his gaze fell upon Jesus who sat in front of him with an expression of kindness and love as always on his face. Looking at Jesus lifted Simon Peter's spirits and gave him confidence that he would be able to endure the ordeal of testifying.

Joseph approached the jury panel then turned slightly toward Simon Peter.

"Sir, you are Simon Peter, are you not?" Joseph asked in a gentle tone.

"Yes, sir. Yes, sir, I am Simon Peter. Yes, sir," he said.

Simon Peter's over-zealous response brought a few snickers from the gallery. Pilate ignored them, slightly amused by Simon Peter's repetitive answer himself.

"Sir, do you know of Jesus of Nazareth?" Joseph asked.

"Yes, sir," Simon Peter said. "Just as I told you when we met, I do know. . ." Peter was interrupted by none other than Pilate who decided the witness needed a quick lesson in courtroom protocol.

"Kind sir, if I may, Joseph of Arimathea is just *pretending* he doesn't know the answer," Pilate explained. "A good attorney—who Joseph of Arimathea certainly is—always knows the answers to the questions he plans to ask in open court before he asks them."

Pilate nodded at Joseph to proceed.

"How would you describe your relationship with Jesus?" Joseph asked.

"As I told...," Simon Peter began but then glanced at the attentive Pilate and changed his answer. "I am a follower of Jesus. He is the Messiah, Son of the Living God," Simon Peter said with obvious pride.

Annas scowled and began to stand but Caiaphas grabbed his arm and stopped him. With the slight shaking of his head, Caiaphas cautioned Annas to remain silent. There was a sense that the spectator gallery was literally bursting at its seams. Pilate was privately enjoying the drama.

"Can you elaborate for the court about your personal relationship with Jesus of Nazareth?" Joseph asked, knowing that he was nearing an area of Peter's testimony that would be most challenging for him.

"I first encountered Jesus through my brother, Andrew, who was a follower of John the Baptist," Simon responded. "He told us of a man he baptized who was called Jesus. He referred to him as the Lamb of God."

Someone in the gallery mimicked the bleats of a lamb causing Pilate to abruptly rise to his feet.

"Guards find that animal and put him out to pasture at once!" Pilate bellowed.

Liberius and the guards walked around among the gallery but no one volunteered the identity of the animal. Pilate was livid. He contemplated clearing the gallery but something stopped him. His conscious or perhaps it was an internal voice, told him to allow the public to witness the trial. Despite his unwillingness to shut the gallery down, he was determined not to allow his courtroom to deteriorate into a farce.

"I will pay two denarii to the man or woman who comes forth and identifies the culprit," Pilate announced.

The room fell silent for a few moments. Then a young street vendor timidly stood and pointed to a grungy beggar who sat on the floor next to the back bench. Liberius nodded toward the man who the guards quickly removed from the courtroom. His painful moans were heard throughout the courtroom as he was thrown onto the street. Surely the consequences of misbehavior would convince the other spectators to maintain their decorum in order to avoid facing a similar painful banishment.

"This offers stand throughout the length of this proceeding," Pilate said, as he glared at the gallery.

"Proceed, Joseph," Pilate said as he retook his seat.

"Simon Peter, did you have doubt about that Jesus was the Messiah?" Joseph asked.

"Perhaps at first, but Jesus told me and my brother who are both fishermen the exact height at which we should run our fishing nets. We caught hundreds more fish every day after we followed his advice," he responded.

"Were there other incidents that convinced you of Jesus's specialness?" Joseph asked.

"Yes, sir," Simon Peter replied, "The mother of my wife was very ill. We feared she was near death. But after Jesus tended to her, she recovered and is fine and healthy to this day."

"That's a miracle, is it not?" Joseph asked.

Caiaphas stood up, "Objection! Leading!"

"Sustained."

"Strike the question," Joseph responded.

Joseph took a few strides back and forth in front of the jury panel. He would be broaching the subject that would be most difficult for Simon Peter and the one he dreaded. But it would be more damaging if Caiaphas brought up the issue during cross than if defense laid it out on the table first. Joseph made the decision to hold back on what was potentially the most painful aspect of his relationship with Jesus.

"Simon Peter, were there ever any... problems between you and Jesus?" Joseph asked in a tone most gentle.

Simon Peter beaded his eyes on Jesus whose peaceful mien gave him strength.

"I... I failed him," Peter said.

"Can you elaborate?" Joseph asked.

"I was to guard his safety the very night he was arrested by the..." Simon Peter turned and looked at Caiaphas whose face was a serene mask.

"... by the Jewish High Council," Simon Peter completed his answer. "It was late and I drifted off. When I woke they were taking him away."

Joseph remained silent, allowing Simon Peter's words to linger. The sympathetic look on the faces of several jurors as they observed the witness's personal agony did not escape Joseph's notice.

"Your honor, that's all the questions I have for Simon Peter for now," Joseph said.

Caiaphas seemed to be slightly surprised that Joseph had ended his questioning. It seemed Joseph avoided a potentially explosive subject with Simon Peter. But Caiaphas would not. Without a moment's hesitation, Caiaphas was on his feet, ready to take his turn with Simon Peter. He quickly approached the witness stand.

"What is your definition of loyalty, Simon Peter?" Caiaphas asked.

Joseph stood up quickly. "Objection! Simon Peter is not here today as a scholar or a scribe!"

"I'll rephrase," Caiaphas offered.

"Sir, did you have occasion to identify Jesus on the night of his arrest?" Caiaphas asked?

"Yes, sir," Simon Peter answered in a quiet voice.

"Were you able to identify this defendant as Jesus of Nazareth?" Caiaphas persisted.

"No."

"Why could you not identify him?" Caiaphas asked in mock surprise but like a good lawyer, knew the answer.

"I... denied him," Simon Peter answered.

"You denied you even *knew* him?" Caiaphas said with feigned incredulity as he scanned the jury panel in an effort to evoke their distaste.

"Perhaps it was dark and you couldn't see him in the mist?" Caiaphas offered trying to be his most helpful. "Anyone could have a lapse... once."

"Sir, it was three times," Simon Peter said, his eyes lowered to the floor.

"You, a devotee of the Son of the Living God, denied him three times?!" Caiaphas stormed.

"Yes," Simon Peter answered, his voice barely perceptible.

"Is it your habit to lie?" Caiaphas asked, peering closely at Simon Peter.

Simon Peter looked up at Jesus, gazing intensely into his eyes and then knew what to say. Caiaphas walked to the jury panel and leaned both hands on the bannister in front of it.

"I knew it would happen," Simon Peter said.

Caiaphas's snapped his head at Simon Peter and scowled, confused by his answer.

"That... that doesn't answer my question, sir," Caiaphas said. "I repeat, is it your habit to tell falsehoods?!"

"No. It is not."

"Do devotees of Gods generally lie about knowing them?" Caiaphas said.

Joseph stood up quickly but before he could speak, Caiaphas withdrew the question, a triumphant and sardonic look on his face as he walked to his table. "The witness is dismissed."

"Your honor, I have another question for the witness on redirect," Joseph said. He remained standing by the seated Jesus.

"Simon Peter, did you know in advance that you would deny knowing Jesus?"

Pilate frowned. It was a strange question. There was no objection from the prosecution but both Caiaphas and Annas listened intently as did the entire courtroom.

"Yes, sir," Simon Peter answered.

"And how did you have this prior knowledge?" Joseph asked.

"It was Jesus. He told me that before the cock crowed...," Simon Peter began but stopped when he noticed Pilate shifting in his seat.

Pilate glared at the gallery daring anyone to make the call of a cock. When he was sure that silence would be maintained, he sat back in his seat. Joseph nodded at Simon Peter signaling him to continue.

"The night before his arrest, Jesus told me that I would deny him three times before the cock crowed," Simon Peter responded.

"And how on earth would Jesus know that?" Joseph asked, feigning astonishment.

"Only God can know the future and Jesus is the Son of God," Simon Peter responded.

"Objection!" Caiaphas shouted.

"Sit down, Caiaphas!" Pilate boomed. "You failed to object to Joseph's question so you cannot object to the witness's answer just because you don't like it."

***

Pilate ordered a much-needed pause after Simon Peter's shocking testimony. Jesus was allowed to stay at the defense table and Joseph remained there with him. Joseph wrote down a few notes and allowed his eyes to wander to the prosecution table which he discovered had been abandoned. Blessings, Joseph thought to himself. The old snake had slithered away allowing Joseph to speak freely with Jesus without fear of being overheard. He turned and looked at Jesus.

"Jesus, we have only questioned two witnesses and already our case has made quite an impact," Joseph said, the corners of his mouth turning up in a slight smile.

"The truth has a way of doing that," Jesus responded.

"I plan to call Mary Magdalene as our next witness," Joseph whispered as he looked around behind him. "I fear that Caiaphas's questioning could prove to be brutal for the young woman."

"Mary will only speak the truth," Jesus replied, "And the truth will withstand any abuse."

Joseph absorbed Jesus's words as his eyes fell on the slashes and bruises on Jesus's arms and the dried blood on his robe. Joseph looked into Jesus eyes and gently patted his hand.

When the trial reconvened, Pilate ordered that Joseph proceed to his next witness. The length of time already devoted to the trial with just two witnesses was annoying Pilate. He had planned for the trial to finish in a matter of days but the dynamic nature of the testimony was setting that possibility on its end. Pilate was well aware of the unique nature of the proceeding. With everything from animal sounds to virginal births to talk of gods, it was indeed no ordinary trial. As Joseph rose to call his next witness, Pilate's eyes fell upon Jesus. Although his head was bowed and his long hair hid his face, Pilate still felt the intensity of the man's eyes. It was in sense disturbing.

Mary Magdalene entered the quiet courtroom with all eyes upon her. Her shiny wavy dark hair cascaded over her shoulders and down her back. Her dark eyes glistened contrasting attractively against her porcelain skin. Mary Magdalene was a beauty.

Joseph took a few steps down the main aisle and met Mary as she walked toward the front of the courtroom. It was obvious from the reaction of the male portion of the gallery that Mary was a pleasant sight to behold. Joseph smiled kindly and took her arm to lead her the rest of the way.

At Pilate's behest, Mary swore to tell the truth. Pilate had never laid eyes on Mary Magdalene before. Her beauty and allure was not lost on the Governor of Jerusalem. The lovely Jewess could almost make him forget fidelity to his wife, Pilate thought to himself.

"Mary Magdalene, would you describe for the court your relationship with Jesus of Nazareth?" Joseph asked.

"Sir, I am a devoted follower of my Lord, Jesus Christ," Mary Magdalene said, speaking in a loud and firm voice.

Although Caiaphas and Annas were becoming accustomed to what they considered irreverent testimony from the defense witnesses, it was still unsettling to them. By sheer will power, Caiaphas controlled his reactions while the less disciplined Annas scowled and glowered.

"Did you know him on a personal level?" Joseph asked.

At just that moment, Caiaphas was compelled to clear his throat—rather loudly. Pilate focused on Caiaphas who refused to return his glance.

"Yes, sir. I was part of his inner circle," Mary Magdalene replied.

"Was it unusual for you, as a woman, to be part of his ministry?" Joseph asked.

Mary Magdalene smiled warmly at Jesus who returned her smile in kind. "Jesus is fair and holds no biases," she said. "He treats women as equals because we are all His children."

"How did Jesus effect you, on a personal level?" Joseph asked.

"He saved me and inspired me," Mary Magdalene answered.

"I understand how a religious man inspires one, how did Jesus save you, Mary?" Joseph asked.

"I led a sinful life," Mary answered, then turned directly to Pilate. "A life that I was not proud of." Mary turned back to Joseph. "Jesus cleansed me of my sin. He chased the demons from me."

There was a stirring in the gallery, shifting in seats and involuntary sighs that created a tenseness that was palpable. Pilate banged his gavel lightly. He nodded at Joseph to continue.

"Mary, what was your position in the ministry?" Joseph asked.

"I have spread the word of Jesus to the forgotten people," Mary said.

"Please elaborate."

"Jesus sees all people as good and worthy," Mary responded. "I reached out to those who society has cast asunder—the homeless, the wretched, the criminals and… the wanton."

"How did you come to assume this outreach role in Jesus's ministry?" Joseph asked.

"I knew these people... I had been one of them." Mary responded.

"And what were your successes?" Joseph asked.

"Simon Peter considered me an equal among the apostles," Mary said proudly. "I have helped people, particularly women I knew, to abandon their sinful ways."

Joseph felt Mary Magdalene's testimony went well. People were generally moved by stories of redemption. Mary, the erstwhile profligate, was the epitome of such narrative. He hoped that she had had a positive impact on the jury. Joseph bowed slightly to Pilate and told him he had no further questions of the witness for the time being. He knew there were more tantalizing tales to tell and inferences to make about Mary Magdalene. That would be Caiaphas's job—a job he would be happy to take on. He had already trapped Caiaphas; in fact, with both of his first witnesses. Perhaps his luck would hold so he could trip up Caiaphas for a third time.

Caiaphas walked toward Mary Magdalene. His countenance was stern. He was the only man in the room who was not taken with her. Even old Annas seemed to be a bit enchanted from the dotty look on his face. Caiaphas stayed his distance almost as if she had the plague. He began to focus on the young woman on the stand.

"In your last statement, you claimed that Jesus chased away the demons from your soul," Caiaphas began. "What was your sin, madam?"

"As I said I was not proud but I led a sinful life..." Mary said but was interrupted.

"What was the nature of your sin?" Caiaphas said in a loud screeching voice.

"I lay with men," Mary Magdalene said defiantly, showing no sign of shame.

Caiaphas cringed and drew back as if struck, horrified by her words. And this was no act. It was real—Caiaphas was appalled. This woman was a shameful sinner, a woman he was loathe to even look upon. He turned his back to Mary and faced the jury.

"Do gods lay with sinful women?" Caiaphas asked.

Joseph objected. "Counsel is calling for a conclusion from the witness."

Pilate was intrigued by the testimony. He waved Joseph off. "I'll allow the question."

Caiaphas's back was still to Mary, his histrionics intended to underscore the vile nature of the woman. Mary Magdalene's eyes were lowered to the floor.

"I repeat," Caiaphas said. "Do gods lay with sinful women?"

"No... no but..." Mary said but was interrupted.

"That's all. No further questions," Caiaphas said as he brusquely walked back to the prosecution table.

"But I...." Mary began.

"You've answered the question," Pilate instructed.

Joseph rose. "I have a question for the witness." He rushed to her. "Mary, did you lay with Jesus?"

"I... I only rubbed his tired feet with ointment and...," Tears began to stream down Mary's face.

"Your honor, the witness can stand down," Joseph quickly interjected.

Joseph was upset. He did not handle this witness well. He broke the most basic rule of all good attorneys which Pilate had referred to. He didn't know the answer to a question before he asked it. When Mary Magdalene said she rubbed his feet, he didn't know what she might say next so he was compelled to stop her. Her testimony ended in disaster and would require some repair work later.

Pilate looked annoyed. The jury looked nonplussed. Caiaphas looked pleased with himself which was his usual bearing. Jesus looked peaceful and his eyes were kind.

***

Pilate announced that he needed to see to other matters before the court. Actually, he was hungry and instructed Liberius to clear the courtroom until the sun reached its apex. He ordered his court clerk to have the servants bring food and drink to his chambers.

Joseph was relieved to have some time to plan his next move and reflect on what had already transpired. The testimony with Mary, mother of Jesus, had gone well as had that of Simon Peter. Caiaphas had been caught off balance in both instances. Joseph hoped that the jury noticed that the old specter had been tripped up. Joseph sighed at the thought of Mary Magdalene's testimony. He needed to re-interview her and make some sense of why she was rubbing Jesus's feet with ointment. He was sure that the image had caused some consternation among the jurors.

While Jesus was taken away by the guards to have a crust of bread and a drink of water, Joseph remained at the defense table plotting his next move. He scratched down a few names on his parchment then crossed them out. He would save Matthew, a potentially very strong witness for later. Mark was a bold speaking man. It would be wise to leave him for later in order to end on a strong note.

Joseph wrote the name, "John," and did not cross through it. John seemed to be the most emotionally distraught over Jesus's plight. Perhaps John would evoke sympathy from the panel and make them forget about what Mary Magdalene did or did not do with Jesus.

Chapter 19
Pilate in Charge

"Your honor, the defense calls John, a follower of Jesus of Nazareth," Joseph announced when the trial resumed.

As John emerged from the witness waiting room, he looked unsure and, Joseph thought, smaller than he remembered him to be. Other than the click-clack of John's sandals on the wooden floor, there wasn't a sound in the courtroom as John made his way to the front where Joseph awaited him. John glanced at Jesus for a moment before his attention was required by Pilate to whom he swore to tell the truth. Joseph nodded toward the witness stand and John quickly took his place there, standing before his Lord and ready to defend him. John's trembling hands told Joseph that the young man's testimony could well be wrought with emotion.

"John, what is your relationship with Jesus of Nazareth?" Joseph began.

John took a deep breath and looked at Jesus who gave him a warm smile that seemed to immediately erase the tenseness on John's face.

"I am a devotee of Jesus of Nazareth," John responded, his voice surprisingly strong and loud.

"Under what circumstances did you first learn of Jesus or hear of him?" Joseph asked.

John smiled. "I first heard of Jesus when he made quite a commotion in a temple in Galilee," John responded.

"Do you know why he made this... this commotion?" Joseph asked, careful not to lead.

"The house of God was being violated," John replied. "The avarice of the moneylenders who conducted their business there was corrupting the temple."

"Jesus was defending the temple?" Joseph asked.

"Objection!" Annas rose. "The witness cannot know the motivation of the defendant."

"Oh, but I do, sir," John said, speaking directly to Annas in a tone most sincere.

"Kind sir," Pilate interjected. "I address the objections, not you."

"My most humble apologies," John said. The red streaks of humiliation that crossed his face indicated that he truly was sorry.

"Sustained," ruled Pilate.

"But you do know of Jesus's activities, do you not?" Joseph asked.

"Yes, sir," John replied.

"Do you rely on your memory in recalling these activities?" Joseph asked.

"Sir, I keep a diary, a daily log of my experiences with the Lord..." John responded but then was interrupted.

"Objection!" Caiaphas screeched. "No one called 'The Lord' has been introduced into these proceedings."

"Sustained," Pilate ruled. He then turned to John. "Young man, when you refer to the defendant you may only call him 'Jesus of Nazareth,' 'he,' 'him' or 'the defendant.'"

John nodded. "Yes, sir."

"Why do you keep this daily log?" Joseph asked.

"I plan to write a book, or more accurately, a gospel about my association with him," John said.

Joseph paced back and forth in front of the jury a few times, a thoughtful look on his face.

"In your writings, sir, do you recall making a notation about a disturbance in the temple here in Jerusalem?" Joseph asked.

"No, not here in this city," John replied. "It was in Galilee."

Caiaphas glared at John. His charge had been that Jesus had become a disruption in the temple in Jerusalem. John's testimony cut at the heart of the charge. But Caiaphas remained silent. Just because he didn't like the answer gave him no grounds for objecting. He had already been admonished by Pilate for attempting to use that tactic.

"One of the charges against Jesus is that he threatened to destroy the temple," Joseph said. "Did Jesus show any signs of such violence during this disturbance in Galilee?"

"No, sir," John responded. "Jesus is a peaceful man."

"Objection!" Caiaphas rose to his feet. "The witness was not asked what his impression of the defendant was."

"Hmm. It seems that he, indeed, was not asked that specific question," Pilate said as he focused on Joseph. "Would you agree, counsel?"

"If I may continue, your honor," Joseph replied. "What is your impression of Jesus of Nazareth?"

"Jesus is a peaceful man," John responded.

"I assume you withdraw your objection, Caiaphas," Pilate said, directing his attention to the prosecutor.

"For the record, I hold to my objection," Caiaphas said as he sullenly sank back into his chair.

"Perhaps the witness will include that historical tidbit in his gospel," Pilate shot back.

There were a few muffled giggles that were quieted by a quick glare from Pilate. Although he would never display his pleasure, he had privately enjoyed that little exchange with Caiaphas.

"Objection overruled! Please continue, Joseph of Arimathea," Pilate said, banging his gavel for emphasis.

"Were you present when Jesus of Nazareth was arrested?" Joseph asked pointedly.

The emotion on John's face was obvious to one and all. Tears welled up in his eyes as he struggled to regain his composure.

"Take your time, young man," Joseph said. Although his comment was sincere Joseph also knew that a prolonged pause would draw the jury's attention to the obvious impact that Jesus's ordeal was having on John.

After several minutes, John nodded at Joseph to indicate that he was ready to proceed.

"What were the circumstances of the arrest, John?"

"I failed to protect him," John began, tears brimming in his eyes.

"Your honor," Caiaphas interrupted as he rose and walked toward the bench. "Do we have to endure a melodrama in order to get to the truth?"

"Come to my sidebar, counselor," Pilate ordered Caiaphas.

As he approached, Caiaphas had a scowl on his face that he was not at all successful in hiding.

"Honorable Caiaphas," Pilate began, talking in a quiet voice, "I strongly advise you to remember that I am in charge of this court. If this case devolves into a melodrama, I am in charge of that as well. And if it does so deteriorate, keep in mind that you are one of the actors responsible for it."

Caiaphas detested every word that Pilate spoke and he detested that it was Pilate who spoke them to him. He nodded in acknowledgement and returned to his table.

Joseph approached the witness to continue his questioning. "What were the circumstances of Jesus's arrest?"

"One of his disciples, Judas Iscariot, led the...," John stopped and glanced at Caiaphas. "Judas led the Jewish guard to Jesus."

"You indicated that it was the worst night of your life. Why was that so?" Joseph asked.

"We were very close. We are very close I should say," John said and returned the smile that flashed across Jesus's face. "We are near the same age."

"Tell the court about your relationship," Joseph said.

"Jesus shared his inner thoughts with me. He told me that salvation was available for everyone," John replied confidently. "He told me it was there for the taking, that he had life eternal and that all those who believed in him did as well."

John turned to Pilate. "Sir, I know what I am required to call him Jesus but might I say that to me he is my Lord and Savior?"

Caiaphas was livid and objected. For his part, Joseph could not contain the smile that curled his lips. The tenseness in the courtroom was palpable. Pilate stared back at John as he gave due consideration to his request.

"Overruled," Pilate declared then directed his attention to John. "You may state that you considered him your Lord and Master. You just can't call him that in this proceeding." Pilate turned in his chair and fixed his gaze on Caiaphas. "I hope the compromise of words suits our esteemed prosecution."

Caiaphas remained silent and averted his eyes. It was obvious that the "compromise" did not suit him.

"John, how were you convinced that Jesus was, as you say, your Lord and Master?" Joseph asked.

Caiaphas fidgeted in his chair but he wisely suppressed any urge to object.

"I saw him perform miracles," John said earnestly.

Joseph did not immediately respond. He walked slowly back to the defense table and pretended to be looking at his notes while he purposely allowed John's words to linger in the air. Caiaphas was doing his best to contain himself although his leg was shaking involuntarily under the table. Pilate was intrigued by John's response but his stoic face revealed no sign of interest. Right when Caiaphas was ready to jump out of his own skin, Joseph finally approached the witness stand again.

"John, can you please describe the miracles that you saw Jesus perform?" Joseph asked.

"I attended a wedding in Cana of Galilee," John began. Jesus was also at the celebration to bless the newly-wed couple. The bride fretted that she had only water to serve her guests." John looked admiringly at Jesus as he recalled the incident. "Jesus wanted to spare the couple of any shame about their meager offerings so he walked over to the feast table, closed his eyes, prayed and held his arms open wide. Suddenly the water in all the jugs were at once turned into red wine!"

There were mumblings of surprise that ran the breadth and width of the gallery but soon disappeared with an angry glare from Pilate and the gleaming swords of the guards who patrolled the aisles. As soon as silence dominated the room once again, Joseph continued.

"Were there other miracles performed by Jesus that you can attest to, John?" Joseph asked.

"Most certainly. A young man named Lazarus of Bethany had died from an illness." John responded. "The family called Jesus to his side. And... uh... Jesus brought Lazarus back to life from death."

Even the stringent rules and admonitions of the imperial governor had no effect on the crowd that now buzzed and gasped. Caiaphas was shaking in rage as he objected. Pilate ignored the prosecutor, rose and scanned the courtroom. There it was—that emotionalism that he cautioned Liberius about, that he predicted would be part of the trial. Pilate swept out of the court. He'd allow his court clerk and the Roman guards to settle the crowd down. Pilate would not admit even to himself that after John's last statement, he felt an irresistible urge to quench his thirst with a cup of wine and that's exactly what he intended to do.

Liberius, red-faced and livid, stood before the courtroom and shouted for order. No one listened. Not even the Roman guards who looked as confused as everyone else.

***

Finally, the courtroom settled back down. Liberius swore to himself that his heart would not serve him much longer if the chaos in his courtroom continued. It was a failure on his part that the gallery had gotten so out of control. But Pilate didn't blame him, he assured Liberius. He blamed the emotionalism that was inherent in the case. After comforting Liberius thusly, Pilate reentered the courtroom. He sat down as if nothing unusual had occurred. Perhaps it was the cup, or rather the two cups, of red wine that he consumed on the impromptu break in proceedings. After reviewing a few parchments before him, Pilate looked out across the courtroom with a face as blank as a marble slab.

"Where were we?" Pilate asked.

It was obviously a rhetorical question and no one dared offer a response.

Pilate pretended to consult with some of his paperwork again and then looked up.

"Oh, yes. There was some mention of a dead man, or rather a man who was once dead," Pilate said, obviously enjoying the torture he was inflicting upon Caiaphas.

But Caiaphas wasn't about to enter into Pilate's silly parlance. He rose to his feet; his face never more pompous.

"Your honor," Caiaphas began in his most respectful tone, "I have not yet had the opportunity to cross examine the last witness who spoke. Might I recall him now, sire?"

"Of course," Pilate responded. "I would not disallow you that right and opportunity." Pilate directed his attention to Liberius. "Recall defense witness, John."

John took the witness stand again and was reminded by Liberius that his oath to the Empire to tell the truth must still be adhered to. Caiaphas walked toward the witness stand, but stayed back a few steps. He refused to stand too close to a blasphemer.

"Are you, sir, a doctor?" Caiaphas asked?

John looked alarmed and glanced at Joseph who nodded slightly to encourage him to answer.

"Uh, no, I am not," John responded.

"You are **not** a doctor," Caiaphas reiterated John's statement. Caiaphas paused for a moment, appearing to be in deep thought. "Well, then are you a mortician?"

Once again John looked unsure. He trembled a bit and remained silent.

"I am curious as to your response," Pilate interjected. "Are you a mortician?"

"No... uh... sir. I am not a mortician," John answered.

Leaving a totally flustered John, Caiaphas turned from him. "That is all, your honor."

Joseph shot up from his seat. "Your honor, I have one further question."

Pilate nodded has ascent. Joseph remained standing at his table.

"John, do you know the difference between a dead person and a living person?" Joseph asked.

"Uh... I do, sir," John responded. "My grandmother and my grandfather both died and I saw their bodies. And they didn't move and they were blue and stiff and..."

"Objection!" Caiaphas shouted.

"You object, Caiaphas?" Pilate asked sardonically. "I could have my legal scribe dig for the precedence that a person must either be a doctor or mortician to determine if a person is dead. I could have him look for court records that characterize the status of a person who is stiff and blue but I think we all know what the outcome would be. Overruled!"

The scowling Caiaphas sat back down and glared at his honor.

"The witness is excused," Pilate said, a slight smile emerging on his lips.

John stepped down from the stand and stood awkwardly in front of Jesus for a few moments. After a smile from Jesus, John smiled widely and headed toward the rear of the courtroom where he planned to stay as a spectator for the rest of the trial. As he walked down the main aisle, there was a smattering of applause which Pilate chose to ignore. Pilate called Liberius over and talked quietly with him for a few moments after which Pilate quickly exited.

"The court session is hereby ended for today," Liberius shouted over the increasingly restless crowd. "The court will resume with the trumpeting of the Roman Guard shortly after the sun rises in the morning."

Two Roman guards immediately approached the defense table to escort Jesus back to his cell. Joseph stood in front of Jesus and focused on the guards.

"If you would be so kind, I just need a moment with the defendant," Joseph appealed to the guards.

The guards stood back and did not dispute the counselor. Joseph sat down next to Jesus and assured him that things were going along well. Jesus smiled and told him that he is most thankful for Joseph's bright mind and kind heart. Joseph was moved by Jesus words as he gazed into his intense eyes. But the guards were growing impatient and it was time for Jesus to go. The two friends—because they were friends now—bid each other a good night.

***

Joseph felt good about the trial but he also felt hungry and when he felt hungry he thought of only one person. When he entered the front door off the veranda, Joseph picked up the unmistakable aromas of stew and baking bread. Irit was happy to see him. Irit not only had food for her husband, she had a warm hug and kiss.

"Well, things are going quite favorably," Joseph said. He laughed. "Tomorrow might just do Caiaphas in for good. Lazarus will be in to testify tomorrow. Caiaphas will have to question a dead man who has returned to life."

A serious look comes over Irit's face. "Joseph, I don't know if it would be proper, but..."

Joseph took Irit's hand into his. "Now, now. What is it? I have never known my wife to be too shy to tell me her thoughts."

"Well, I would like to be in court tomorrow," Irit said. "Would that be improper or make you nervous, husband?"

"You always make me nervous, Irit," Joseph said warmly. "In a good way, that is. Of course, you may come to the gallery. I am always blessed by your presence no matter what the circumstances."

Irit smiled and got up quickly from her chair. She went to the pantry and brought out a flaky plum tart. "Here is your dessert, dear Joseph."

"Wait a second," Joseph said, in a teasing tone. "Would I have gotten this fine dessert if I had refused to let you come to court."

Irit smiled coyly. "Now that is something we'll never know, will we?" She said.

Joseph and Irit both enjoyed a hearty laugh together. "One thing I know about my wife, is that I will never really know her."

They laughed again and dug into their fine dessert.

***

Early the next morning, Joseph was ready for court and waiting for Irit on the veranda. He was patient, understanding that Irit was fussing with her appearance a bit more than usual. The sun had not yet dawned which explained why he hadn't noticed the approaching figure until the man was almost upon him. Joseph froze for a moment as the man, who was quite tall and full-bodied, came clearly into view and was obviously heading directly for his home. The case was controversial and causing a full spectrum of emotions. Was this friend or foe? Was he in danger?

"Joseph?" The tall, man called to him.

"Yes, I am Joseph of Arimathea," Joseph responded in a voice so strong that it surprised its owner. Being a man of small stature, Joseph had acquired the ability to display a booming voice when circumstances called for a show of might. This was one of those occasions.

"I understand you are looking for me. My name is Maluch."

A sense of relief came over Joseph. "Yes, sir, my men have been looking for you."

Joseph descended the stairs from the veranda and met Maluch as he walked up the pathway to his house.

"Since my men could not find you, I am grateful that you found me," Joseph said.

"I am sure you know my story and understand why I am not easy to find," Maluch said. "I assume you want my testimony at the trial about the miracle that Jesus performed in healing my wounded ear."

"Precisely, Maluch. Are you willing to testify publically about the incident?" Joseph asked.

"I am a devotee of Jesus of Nazareth and would do anything in my power to help him. Although I will be placed at great risk, I could never deny testifying about what is the truth."

There it is again—the truth. Joseph had always honored the truth. Now he was beginning to experience a sheer rapture for it. The two men talked for a few minutes more. Joseph confirmed the story that both Matthew and Mark had told him. Maluch told Joseph not to expect any of the Sanhedrin guards to confirm his story. Caiaphas had threatened them all with their lives if they would dare to come forward. Maluch said that it would be impossible to find him because he moved locations often to stay ahead of those who were trying to track him down. But he assured Joseph that he would appear at the trial. Joseph had no choice but to settle for those arrangements. Irit stepped out on the veranda and waited there until Joseph finished his conversation with Maluch.

Joseph told Irit about his visitor as they walked to the court. It was early but Joseph wanted to make sure he didn't miss the call to order by the trumpeters. Irit was excited. The case held her fascination and she was eager to see the principles in the case—especially Jesus of Nazareth. Just as he thought, when Joseph walked in there were very few people present. Liberius was buzzing around and there were a few citizens already seated so they'd be assured of a good seat. Joseph led Irit to a seat a few rows behind the defense table.

***

The time passed quickly and soon the entire gallery was filled. The spectators were all eagerly awaiting the appearance of the principals. There was a stirring among the gallery when the jurors filled in as it was a sure sign that the proceedings would soon begin. Almost on cue, the trumpeters sounded the call to order. Caiaphas and Annas took their places and Pilate was the last to enter.

"All rise!" Liberius commanded.

Irit almost jumped straight up. She wanted to make sure she followed all the rules and did nothing to embarrass her husband. She was thrilled to be there and did not care how oppressively hot it might get in the courtroom although it was already as warm as mid-day.

"Joseph of Arimathea," Pilate began. "Are you prepared to present your next witness for the defense?

"Yes, your honor," Joseph responded. "I call Lazarus of Bethany."

If there was such a thing as a silent scream, Caiaphas was emitting one at that very moment. Despite the urge to rant and rave, he maintained his calm as best he could. Soon, the young Lazarus was sworn in and was taking his place on the witness stand.

"Please state your name, sir," Joseph began.

"Lazarus of Bethany," Lazarus responded.

"How do you know the defendant, Jesus of Nazareth?" Joseph asked.

"I am a right follower of Jesus?" Lazarus responded.

"Was there anything in particular that convinced you to become a follower of him?" Joseph asked.

"He... he came to see me when I was actually... dead," Lazarus responded. "Jesus laid his hands on me and gave me life again."

The man who claimed to have been returned from the dead through a miracle performed by Jesus of Nazareth was alive and well and speaking in court. The courtroom came alive and buzzed. Pilate banged his gavel several times but then refocused on the man who claimed to have recovered from death.

"Can you elaborate for us?" Joseph asked.

Pilate accidentally banged his gavel absentmindedly. Everyone looked at him expectantly. Pilate realized that he had unintentionally stopped the proceedings with his errant rap. He used the opportunity to offer his opinion.

"It seems that elaboration, indeed, would be the order of the moment," Pilate said. "Proceed."

"I had been very sick," Lazarus continued. "My family was quite worried about me and sent word for Jesus to come to my side and minister to me. But his visit was delayed. I died before he arrived."

"How did your family know of Jesus?" Joseph asked?

"My older sisters were followers of Jesus," Lazarus responded.

"And were you a follower?" Joseph asked.

Lazarus smiled widely. "No. Not then. But I surely am now!"

"Now that you're not dead any longer?" Pilate asked rhetorically. He knew it wasn't an appropriate comment but it was just too rich to resist.

Guffaws and snickers were heard throughout the room. The Roman guards advanced with their spears and soon took all the fun out of the moment.

"Sir, as you can judge from the reaction in this room, you do understand that the claim that you returned from the dead is a difficult one to believe?" Joseph asked.

"Yes, sir, I do," Lazarus responded.

"Since you were... uh... dead, how did you know you were dead? Joseph asked awkwardly. But there was not a way to ask the question that was not awkward. It certainly had never come up before in Joseph's vast legal career.

"My sisters called a physician in who verified that I was dead," Lazarus responded.

"Was this event noted in your village records?" Joseph asked, knowing that he was getting into some treacherous territory for Caiaphas.

"My sisters told me that the incident was so unusual that the village leaders reported my return to life to..." Lazarus hesitated and turned toward Caiaphas for a moment then quickly refocused on Joseph. "... to the Jewish High Priests."

"So, your sisters had no fear of retribution in making such a claim since the village leaders obviously accepted the report?" Joseph asked.

"Objection! Calling for a conclusion." Caiaphas screeched.

"Withdraw," Joseph responded. Now it was time to get to the heart of the matter, he thought to himself.

"What was the response from the Jewish High Council?" Joseph asked. He glanced at Caiaphas whose dark eyes were smoldering.

"Nothing. None of us ever heard from them," Lazarus responded.

"They had no reaction to such an incredulous event?" Joseph asked feigning incredulity.

"They had a reaction all right," Lazarus said. "I heard they wanted to kill me... again. So I went into hiding."

"No further questions, your honor."

There was such an uproar that there was nothing that Pilate could do but call a recess. But it was good timing because his mouth was thirsting for another taste of wine. *Was this trial driving him to drink more red wine than was his usual habit?* He'd let Liberius deal with the spectators. Caiaphas was livid. Joseph busied himself at his table trying not to appear too pleased. Irit was fully engaged in the proceedings.

Suddenly, Jesus turned around in his seat and looked directly at Irit. Never before in her life had she felt such an impact from anyone's presence. Tears welled in her eyes as her heart filled with emotion.

Chapter 20
Lazarus and Maluch

After a sip or two of dark red wine, Pilate summoned Caiaphas and Joseph to his chambers. As much as he'd enjoy humiliating Caiaphas, propriety dictated that he handle the rather indelicate issue that had just emerged in open court with discretion. Caiaphas entered Pilate's room with Joseph trailing a few steps behind.

"Sit," Pilate told both men.

After taking seats across from Pilate who was sprawled out in his throne-like chair and fanning himself as the heat was beginning to win the day. Pilate focused on Caiaphas.

"How do you respond to the statement of the young man... the formerly dead young man?" Pilate asked.

"I have no recollection of such an incident being reported to the council," Caiaphas responded haughtily. "The man does not tell the truth."

"You are saying, sir, that my witness is lying under vow to the Empire?" Joseph asked.

"An intelligent man would make such an interpretation," Caiaphas replied.

Joseph felt a rising anger but he managed to keep his temper in control. He had gathered that Pilate did not seem to hold the old Jewish Priest in exaltation and figured that Pilate would handle the situation better than he could. He'd let the maestro take the lead.

"Do you wish to take the oath and enter your statement into the court record?" Pilate asked Caiaphas, knowing he was on the periphery of shattering the prosecutor's ego and self-importance.

"I would hope that your honor would trust the word of an officer of the court over that of a country lummox," Caiaphas responded, making no attempt to hide his agitation.

"Presumably all words spoken in court have the same weight," Pilate said. "According to high-minded idealists; that's the beauty of the justice system. It, like death, is the great leveler."

Caiaphas skulked and did not respond. Pilate knew that Caiaphas was fully capable of uttering falsehoods and his gut feeling was that the young man, Lazarus, was probably telling the truth or rather what he thought the truth was. But the issue, to Pilate, was a minor one and not worthy of delaying the trial any longer than it already had. Pilate rose from his chair. The other men followed suit.

"Do you wish to question the dead fellow?" Pilate asked, almost as an afterthought.

Caiaphas felt insulted in being forced to answer such a ridiculous question. "I will question the witness called Lazarus of Bethany."

***

Once the courtroom was back in order, Lazarus took the stand again. Caiaphas approached him but stayed a comfortable distance away.

"What condition were you suffering from when you fell ill?" Caiaphas asked.

"I had a terrible fever and a case of the vapors, sir," Lazarus responded.

"How would you characterize your fever?" Caiaphas asked?

"Raging. My sisters couldn't control it," Lazarus responded.

"Please describe how you felt as this fever overwhelmed you."

Lazarus locked eyes with Joseph who nodded slightly signaling him to proceed.

"I... uh... I don't remember," Lazarus replied.

Caiaphas seized on the young man's answer. He twirled around and glared at the witness.

"Why? Why don't you remember?" Caiaphas demanded.

"I was delirious," Lazarus responded. "Out of my head from what I was told."

Caiaphas paced in front of the jury panel, allowing them to fully absorb Lazarus's words. While he slowly scanned the members of the panel, he resumed his cross-examination.

"Could it be that you were so delirious from fever that you imagined things?" Caiaphas began in a soft even tone then spun around and faced Lazarus.

"Might your delirium have endured, even until this day?!" Caiaphas boomed as he walked quickly back to his table.

Joseph began to object but Caiaphas withdrew the question before he could. Caiaphas had accomplished what he had intended to. He planted the seed in the minds of the jurors that Lazarus may not be in his right mind. Joseph had wanted to bring the sisters in to testify that their brother was resurrected by Jesus but Yakir couldn't locate them. He'd have Yakir try again. But for now the damage was done. Caiaphas had hopes that the jurors were at least dubious about Lazarus's story. By getting Lazarus to admit that he was not in his right mind when he was sick did not lend any credence to his bizarre story.

Pilate excused Lazarus and looked to Joseph to call his next witness.

"The defense calls Luke, follower of Jesus of Nazareth," Joseph called out.

Luke was sworn in and took his place on the witness stand. Like the others his spirit seemed buoyed when he looked at Jesus who smiled warmly at him. Luke missed Jesus. Even under the horrid circumstances, Luke's heart was fulfilled to see his Lord once again.

"Luke, how do you know Jesus of Nazareth?" Joseph began.

"I am a follower of Jesus's ministry," Luke said, his small dark eyes looking back and forth between Jesus and Joseph.

"How did you come to be his follower?" Joseph asked.

"I had heard of his good works and was eager to meet him," Luke responded.

"What good works were attributed to Jesus to make you want to know him?"

"People referred to him as the Light of the World," Luke responded. "I had heard the tales of how he helped the poor and the sick and the forgotten. He taught us the lesson of the Good Samaritan who came to the aid of his enemies."

"Did you think of Jesus as a god?" Joseph spoke in a soft tone when asking this most sensitive of questions.

"Jesus was the Light of the World," Luke replied. "What drew me to him was his heart. He had compassion for the sick and the poor."

"What message did Jesus stress in his ministry, Luke?" Joseph asked.

"His message was one of pure goodness," Luke responded. "He preached to us to be good, law-abiding citizens."

"He advocated adherence to the law?" Joseph asked.

"Yes, sir," Luke quickly answered. "He respected the law."

"Hmm. Respected the law." Joseph repeated his words.

Caiaphas shot to his feet. "Do we need to waste time and energy with the defense counsel repeating the responses of the witnesses?"

"Strike my words," Joseph interrupted the prosecutor. He was pleased that he was able to bring focus to Jesus's respect of the law. It was a subtle point for the defense. There were a few more issues that Joseph needed to draw from Luke.

"How was Jesus known to treat women?" Joseph asked.

"Jesus felt women were just as good as men," Luke responded. "He treated them kindly and well, just as he did the rest of us."

Irit looked at Jesus. She was impressed with this young holy man who was kind to women. So many men, even the rabbis, treated women as though they didn't count. Her admiration for Jesus was growing.

"It seems as though you looked at Jesus as your friend, as a good man but not as a god at all. Is that an accurate statement?

"Oh, no, sir. Not at all," Luke said emphatically.

"I saw him praying alone just before his arrest. The sweat that beaded on his brow was blood. The light glow around him wasn't the mist of the night. It was an angel who was sent from God to see him through the night."

Was there any example of, as you say, Jesus's goodness during the night of his arrest?" Joseph asked.

"During the conflict, we defended Jesus and clashed with the Jewish guards. One of the guards lost an ear. It was sliced off," Luke responded.

Pilate hid his repulsion at the imagery of Luke's words and was sympathetic to the smattering of groans and gasps emanating from the crowd so he did not admonish them.

"But how did this incident demonstrate Jesus's goodness?" Joseph asked.

"Jesus took the guard's head in his hands, the man's ear reappeared all in one piece," Luke said, becoming emotional recalling that night. "Even though the man was his enemy, Jesus healed him. The man immediately knelt down and became a follower."

Once again, Joseph let the drama linger in the air while he paused for a few moments at the defense table. Caiaphas busied himself reading through some papers but in reality he was seething inside.

"That's all I have, your honor," Joseph said, ending his questioning of Mark.

Caiaphas sprung up immediately and nearly charged at the witness stand.

"Sir, you referred to Jesus telling the story of the Good Samaritan, did you not?" Caiaphas asked pronouncing the words, "Good Samaritan" with much derision.

"Yes, sir."

"Were you aware that it is the considered opinion of the Jewish High Council that the Samaritans are evil?" Caiaphas asked.

"No, sir."

Joseph was tempted to object although he wasn't sure on what grounds he would be able to do so. He decided to have patience and see where Caiaphas's line of questioning would take Luke.

"Since it is a fact that the council has found the Samaritans to be evil, doesn't it follow that Jesus of Nazareth was in fact really lauding the actions of the Evil Samaritan?!"

"Objection!" This time Joseph had no hesitation.

"Sustained," Pilate said lazily.

"In your testimony, you indicated that Jesus of Nazareth was kind to women," Caiaphas began. "If this is so, can you characterize for the court just how kindly Jesus was with the wanton woman known as Mary Magdalene? Or was their relationship intimate beyond your knowledge?"

Joseph was angry and showed it. He started to object but Caiaphas withdrew the question. The prosecutor sat down feeling satisfied that at least some damage had been done.

***

After Luke stepped down from the witness stand, Pilate called for a recess. He told the principals to stay close. The break in the proceeding would not be a lengthy one. As he headed back to his chambers, he felt that Joseph was making a compelling case for the defense. Although he would, of course, remain impartial he felt that Caiaphas looked sniping and cruel. He wondered if the jurors felt the same way.

Jesus was allowed to stay at the defense table but a Roman guard stood nearby fixing a steady gaze upon him. Joseph assured Jesus that things were going well. He then turned and motioned to Irit to meet him in the aisle. But she didn't move. He rushed over to her.

"I don't want to lose my seat," Irit told her husband.

Yakir was milling about in the aisle leading to the witness waiting room. Joseph called him over.

"Yakir, sit in my wife's seat to save it for her. We will be away only a few moments."

Joseph told his wife that it would be good to stretch her legs. Since she was his most trusted advisor he also wanted to learn what her opinion of the trial was thus far.

"You are making a splendid case for Jesus of Nazareth, husband," Irit told him. "I am proud of your skills."

They strolled around the back of the court which was crowded and oppressively hot from the body heat and the increasing temperature. When Joseph noticed Liberius dashing back into the courtroom, he knew it was time to return to the courtroom. He put his arm through Irit's and started back inside. But Irit stopped him. She saw a small fragile looking woman who appeared to be frightened. Her large brown eyes had a familiar look, although she couldn't say why. She asked Joseph if he knew the woman. He whispered that the woman was Mary, Jesus's mother. Irit felt a pang in her heart and headed right over to Mary. Joseph had no choice but to go in alone. He didn't want to rile Pilate.

"Mary, I am Joseph's wife. My name is Irit."

Mary smiled and clutched Irit's hands. "Bless you and bless your wonderful husband. I am so grateful for his generous heart."

"I am learning from the trial that it is your son who has the generous heart," Irit replied. "The proceedings are about to begin," Irit told Mary quickly. "Won't you walk in with me?"

"Oh, no, ma'am. I have no seat. I am standing here," Mary replied.

Mary didn't know who she was dealing with. Irit wouldn't take no for an answer. "Mary, you must come with me."

Without further explanation, Mary was swept into the courtroom by Irit who walked her to the row where Yakir was holding her seat. When Yakir saw Irit, he stood up to let her have the seat.

"Mary, you sit here. I will stand," Irit said.

Mary protested. She didn't want to take Irit's seat. But Irit would have her way. She patted Mary gently on the back and told her she would stand. As she turned to head back to the standing area, the man who had been seated beside her throughout the session had been listening to the two women and rose.

"Kind lady, you take my seat," the man said. "I will stand."

The man also wouldn't take no for an answer and was soon making his way toward the back of the courtroom. Irit sat down by Mary and smiled. She took Mary's small hand in hers and squeezed it. Irit thought to herself that there certainly seemed to be a kind and blessed presence in the courtroom. Jesus turned just then. He was pleased to see his mother sitting nearby.

Joseph was prepared to call Mark as his next witness but a breathless Hadas ran into the courtroom just before Joseph was preparing to do so.

"Joseph, Maluch has arrived to testify," Hadas told him.

"Maluch? Wonderful! I will call him immediately." A smile stretched across Joseph's face in anticipation of the explosive testimony that was about to be heard. He rose to call his witness.

"Your Honor, the defense calls Maluch of Jerusalem," Joseph said in that booming voice that showed might.

Joseph glanced at Caiaphas who appeared as though he might implode at any moment. Maluch's appearance was a surprise to Caiaphas but his testimony would not be. After swearing to tell the truth, Maluch took the stand.

"Please tell the court, Maluch, of your association with Jesus of Nazareth."

"I am a devotee of Jesus. I first became acquainted with him when I was a commander of the guards of the Sanhedrin. I led a brigade to the Garden of Gethsemane to arrest him," Maluch said, his last words trailing off in sadness.

"Did you fulfill your mission? Did you arrest him?" Joseph asked.

"No, sir. I was injured in a violent confrontation with his disciples. My ear was nearly sliced off."

Joseph displayed a dramatic flair as he very carefully looked at each of Maluch's ears several times.

"I see you have both ears and I detect no battle scar on either," Joseph said.

"I was grasping my head in pain, blood was spewing all about. Jesus rushed to my side and clutched my dangling ear to my head," Maluch said. "I'll never forget the look in Jesus's eyes. It was the kindest I had ever seen."

Maluch looked directly at Jesus who smiled at him.

"He was pulled away by the other guards and my ear was reattached and completely healed in that instant."

Pilate was so fascinated with the testimony that he failed to notice the outbreaks from the gallery sparked by Maluch's charged testimony.

"Your witness, Caiaphas," Joseph said.

Caiaphas rose and glared at the witness, a man who was once his trusted commander. Caiaphas was too proud to approach Maluch or call him by name. He remained standing at the prosecution table.

"Are you a loyal person?" Caiaphas asked. His black eyes seemed even blacker.

"I became one after I found out what loyalty really meant," Maluch said.

Caiaphas didn't like his response and decided on another tact.

"Who of your former men would corroborate the claim about your ear?" Caiaphas asked.

"None. Someone has frightened them into withholding the truth," Maluch responded, matching Caiaphas's glare with his own.

Joseph was cheering inside. He had always been of the opinion that Matthew and Mark would be his strongest witnesses. He was as surprised as anyone in the courtroom how strong his surprise witness turned out to be.

Caiaphas walked to the jury box and looked directly at the jurors, a smirk on his face. "Since there is no verification of this fantastic tale, how could you expect anyone to believe it?"

"I don't except anyone to believe it," Maluch responded. "What matters is that my Lord Jesus of Nazareth knows the truth. I do not need anyone else."

Caiaphas spun around and headed to the prosecution table in a huff. He took his seat and buried his head in his documents. Pilate watched him for a moment then turned to Maluch.

"If I am not mistaken, sir, I believe that the prosecution has completed its questioning of you."

***

It was time to call the imposing Mark to the stand. Mark presented an image of wisdom and confidence. After seeing Mark again, Joseph was sure he'd be right about Mark making a good witness. Joseph approached the witness.

"Kind sir, what was your relationship with Jesus?" Joseph began.

"Is. What *is* my relationship with Jesus," Mark said, unafraid to correct the defense counsel.

Joseph smiled. "Forgive my misstatement. What *is* your relationship with Jesus?"

"I worship Jesus. He is the Son of the Living God," Mark responded with a casual tone, one that he would use to state his name or comment that the sky was blue and the grass was green.

There was a slight noise that came from the direction of the prosecution table. Joseph was unaware of the source of the noise but under the table, Caiaphas leg was shaking quite violently.

"You understand that such a statement is one that some would meet with derision?" Joseph asked.

Mark looked pointedly at Caiaphas and responded. "Yes, I know of some people who would have that exact reaction. Would you like me to name them?"

Pilate leaned over in his chair toward Mark. "Kind sir, we all have different roles here. The prosecutor and defense counsel ask questions, the witness—your role—answer questions and the judge, well, we tell people when they are playing the wrong roles."

Mark turned away from Pilate, choosing to ignore his imperial governor. He looked at Joseph ready for more questions.

"What led you to believe that Jesus was, as you characterize him, the Living God?" Joseph asked.

"I personally saw him perform miracles," Mark answered and without prompting or hesitation provided some examples. "While traveling with Jesus, we ran across a group of lepers. I am not hesitant to say that I didn't want to get anywhere near them. But Jesus—well, his heart is so generous and giving—he laid hands on the lepers and right before our eyes a mist arose around the sick. It swirled around them and when the mist dissipated..."

Mark hesitated and as he leaned closer to Joseph, several of the jurors leaned forward as well. Joseph knew that was a good sign—a sign that the jurors were fully engaged. Irit was on the edge of her seat as well. Mark finally continued.

"...when the mist dissipated, the lepers were cured. Their skin was new and gleaming with no sign of disease."

Caiaphas fumed silently. He didn't know how many more tales of miracles he could take. Joseph decided to move toward the precise area where he needed to make his strongest case.

"Mark, you stated earlier in your testimony that Jesus of Nazareth was the Son of the Living God," Joseph said. "Can you please define exactly what those words mean?"

"It would not only be my pleasure it is my responsibility to do so," Mark answered. "Jesus was born of a woman and inherited human characteristics like his passion, joy and curiosity. But from his father, our God, he inherited the ability to make miracles, understand events far beyond what we humans can." Mark turned and this time glared angrily at Caiaphas, "No matter what happens or who wants to crucify him, Jesus has life eternal and will never die!"

The room seemed to echo with the words from the booming voice of Mark and the gallery was eerily non-responsive to Mark's provocative statement. Joseph sat down. Pilate glanced at Caiaphas who quickly diverted his eyes. Caiaphas seemed thrown off balance as if he didn't know how to proceed. But Pilate was there to help him.

Joseph next asked Mark about Jesus at the temple. Mark testified that Jesus saw no sign of violence. He was there with him and felt that Jesus did the right thing by accusing the money changers of violating the temple. It seemed that those in charge were not living up to their responsibilities, he told Joseph as he again looked pointedly at Caiaphas and Annas. Joseph smiled, that arrow was meant for Caiaphas and it did not miss. Joseph controlled himself from being too happy about Mark's testimony. Matthew's version of the incident was different. In his deposition, Matthew had claimed that Jesus was angry and violent. He didn't plan to ask Matthew about the temple incident when he testified. He hoped that Caiaphas wouldn't ask him either. Joseph indicated he was through with his questioning of the witness. But Caiaphas seemed frozen.

"If I remember the process correctly, I believe it is now time for the prosecutor to cross-examine the witness if indeed he feels so inclined," Pilate said as he gazed out over the courtroom and the sea of faces that seems to be frozen in wonderment.

Annas hurriedly elbowed Caiaphas and whispered to him. Caiaphas quietly responded to him. Annas stood and indicated he would question Mark. Apparently, Caiaphas was overwhelmed and was allowing his deputy prosecutor to question Mark. But Joseph would not be fooled. Caiaphas may be down but would rebound and, if Joseph's instincts were correct, would rebound with a vengeance.

"What are your qualifications, sir, to testify that a person has been cured from a serious condition like leprosy?" Annas asked Mark.

"The eyes in my head," Mark answered sharply.

There were a few snickers from the gallery that Pilate chose to ignore. He was enjoying the confident bearing of the robust man who was testifying. Even if he was misguided and thought that Jesus was a god, he seemed to believe it himself, Pilate thought, and had no trepidation in voicing his beliefs. Jesus was either a very convincing individual, Pilate deduced, and had a way with words or he was somehow able to round up a bunch of gullible or even deranged people to propel his ministry.

Annas was a lot less aggressive in his questioning than was his senior partner. He allowed Mark to win the first point. But he hadn't given up.

"How can you be so certain that Jesus has an eternal life? Was he like Lazarus of Bethany?" Annas asked animatedly. "Did Jesus of Nazareth return from the dead?"

"No," Mark responded as he locked eyes with Annas. "But if you snakes have your way, he probably will!"

Both Caiaphas and Joseph rose quickly to their feet as if to prepare for battle. Mark fumed on the witness stand—his eyes bulging and his face a deep red. The decorum in the room vanished. Pilate sighed heavily. He knew the case would be an emotional one but had no idea that its drama would virtually be without pause. Although Mark was somewhat aware of Jesus's destiny, he was naturally resistant to it and opted to blame the preordained instruments of that destiny.

Pilate banged his gavel and nodded at Liberius who immediately unleashed the guards on the crowd. They settled down immediately not because anyone feared a lashing but because no one wanted to be thrown out of the courtroom and denied the opportunity to witness what would happen next.

"I have no more questions, your honor," Annas sat down. He seemed deflated. The Jewish High Priest had been defeated by a peasant man with highly developed principals. Mark stepped down and nodded to Jesus. The two men exchanged a smile. As Mark walked down the aisle to exit the courthouse, he could not control the overwhelming feeling that he'd never be with Jesus again and neither could he control the tear the tracked down his face.

Pilate had had enough for the day. He was exhausted—exhausted from the heat, the long day and most of all the dramatics of the trial. In an instant, he disappeared down the back hallway. Liberius dismissed the jurors and told the guards to ensure that all the spectators immediately cleared out.

Joseph walked back to where Irit and Mary were seated. They rose and he offered an arm to each lady and led them down the long aisle that led to the outside.

Chapter 21
The Betrayer and A King

The next day, Joseph planned to call Judas Iscariot to the stand. It was still his strategy to have Matthew appear last because he would be a strong witness and would enable Joseph to end the defense case on a strong note. While Judas Iscariot's testimony would be a difficult and complicated one, Joseph was aware that loyalty meant a lot to the Jewish citizenry and that Judas's betrayal of Jesus would shine a sympathetic light on the defendant.

Joseph empathized with Judas's plight. While he was disloyal to the man who he had once dedicated himself to, Joseph sensed that the man was suffering greatly from internal demons. As Joseph walked into the courtroom that morning, he recalled the tense meeting he had with Judas and knew it best that he speak with Judas before his testimony to encourage him with some simple advice. Just tell the truth, he would tell Judas—as dark as that truth was there were no options.

After going over a stack of parchments that Yakir had brought to the court for Joseph to review, Joseph sighed and looked toward the witness waiting room door. It was time to speak to Judas. As Joseph walked from the defense table he saw that Irit and Mary were walking down the main aisle to get a seat close to the front. He gave them both a friendly wave and a big smile. He was grateful for Irit who has turned out to be such a comfort for Mary. He sensed that it gave his client consolation to see that his mother was being comforted by Irit's loving friendship. Today's testimony from Judas would be particularly difficult for Mary but Irit would be there to hold her hand.

As Joseph approached the waiting room door, the Roman soldier guarding the door opened it for Joseph who was by now a familiar figure to the soldiers assigned to guard the courtroom. When Joseph walked into the room he at first did not see Judas. Panic came over him for a moment. Perhaps Judas had betrayed his word and would fail to appear. Joseph had sensed how desolate Judas was from the overwhelming agony he suffered under. It was just a matter of time, Joseph had thought, before Judas's guilt and misery would end in tragedy. Joseph moved further into the darkened room and spotted the gaunt figure of Judas, sitting on the floor in the far corner of the room. Joseph was relieved although it seemed that Judas's emotional state had deteriorated. Joseph approached Judas slowly and respectfully.

"Judas," Joseph spoke softly.

Judas looked up quickly, startled and obviously confused. Is the man in his right mind, Joseph wondered to himself? He seems to not know where he is. Judas gazed at Joseph for more than a few moments, as if he was trying to recollect exactly who he was. Judas was a lost man dazed by a deep understanding of his reality.

"Judas, it's me, Joseph of Arimathea."

"Yes...," Judas said. "I recall."

"Are you prepared to take the stand this morning, Judas?" Joseph asked in his most gentle tone.

"Yes. I suppose that's why I'm here," Judas responded as he gazed forlornly off in the distance.

Joseph kneeled down by Judas. He felt a deep sorrow for the young man and wanted him to feel he had Joseph's support and understanding.

"Remember, I don't judge you Judas," Joseph, said, trying to be reassuring. "Your task is merely to answer my questions and those of the prosecutor and respond with the same answers that you provided to me during our meeting. Judas, it is not you who is on trial today."

Judas turned and looked intensely at Joseph. "You are a kind man, Joseph. But you are wrong. I am on trial today... every day."

The courtroom was eerily quiet when Judas Iscariot walked down the long aisle to the front of the bench. Being the perfect justice that he was, Pilate's countenance did not change as he swore Judas in even though, through Joseph's court submissions, he was aware of the integral role Judas had played in Jesus's arrest. As Judas took his place on the stand, Jesus tried to catch his eye but Judas refused to look his way. Indeed, his only gaze was downward, at the floor. Shamed and filled with self-hatred, Judas was withdrawing from life as though he were rotting from within. Joseph glanced at Jesus and then at Mary a few rows behind them, there were no signs of bitterness or anger on either face. The sight of the kindness on the faces of mother and son pulled at Joseph's heart.

The only annoyance that Joseph experienced about Judas's appearance was seeing the slight glimmer of joy in Caiaphas's bird-like eyes. But he could expect no more from the soulless rabbi.

"Judas Iscariot, may I call upon you to describe for this court what your relationship was with Jesus of Nazareth?" Joseph began.

It was several long silent moments before Judas responded. Finally, his thin, tight barely perceptible voice emerged.

"I was a follower, a believer..."

"You are here to address the court, sir," Pilate instructed. "Not the vermin that dwell beneath the floorboards."

Judas raised his head and gazed toward the open courtroom, looking at nothing and no one. He repeated his response but this time in a clear and robust voice.

"I was a follower, a believer of Jesus of Nazareth."

"Was there a point when that relationship changed?" Joseph asked.

Judas took a deep breath and for the first time dared to lay eyes upon Jesus. But it was just a glance and for just an instant. Judas could not bear to allow his eyes to linger on him. But even though brief, Judas seemed to be strengthened by once again looking upon Jesus's face.

"I became disillusioned in Jesus," Judas responded.

"Please elaborate and tell the court why your feelings about him began to change," Joseph said.

"It was my perception that when Jesus rode into Jerusalem, he would rid the city of..." Judas stopped and turned to Pilate.

"Please, sir, proceed," Pilate said. "I can take it."

"... rid the city of the Romans." Judas concluded.

"What happened and how did you react?" Joseph asked.

"He failed to accomplish this task," Judas responded. "And I felt profound disappointment."

"What did this disappointment that you characterize as profound lead to?" Joseph asked.

"I turned Jesus into the Jewish High Priests," Judas said, his voice trailing off to a whisper.

"Were you compensated?"

"I am not proud to admit that I received 30 silver pieces for this act of betrayal."

Joseph could sense the tenseness in the room. He allowed Judas's words to linger in the air before he continued.

"May we learn what you did with that silver?" Joseph asked.

"I found the highest mesa in the desert and threw them to the devil from whence they came," Judas responded, his voice for the first time breaking from the emotion and agony that resided within him.

"That's all I have, your honor," Joseph announced and took his seat. He could have asked more questions but instead decided to set another trap for Caiaphas. The prosecutor bounded up and displayed a distorted smile, which was a first for the entire trial.

"Good morning, Judas," Caiaphas began in a manner most effusive. "When you spoke of your disappointment in Jesus not ridding Jerusalem of our Roman friends, did you consider that a failure?"

"Yes," Judas responded, now glaring at Caiaphas.

Caiaphas stood in front of the jury panel and scanned each face. "In your knowledge of God, is there any possibility that He could ever fail?"

"No," Judas responded. "I..." Although he attempted to explain his answer, he was cut off and summarily dismissed by the prosecutor.

"The witness may be excused," Caiaphas said in a self-satisfied and haughty manner.

"Your honor, if I may. I have one further question for the witness," Joseph said, who remained standing behind the defense table next to Jesus.

"Judas, do you think Jesus is the Son of the Living God?" Joseph asked.

"Yes."

"Did Jesus fail?"

"No!" Now Judas looked directly at Jesus, his face pleading for a sign of forgiveness. "It was I and Destiny who failed Him!"

Caiaphas shot up from his seat to object but thought better of it. He knew it would be an exercise in futility. Judas hung his head, once again overcome by the haunting desolation that was ever present.

"You may step down, sir," Pilate said.

Judas failed to move. Out of empathy for his fellow man, Joseph walked to the witness stand and gently guided Judas off the stand and escorted him down the aisle where he would be free to go. But as Joseph glanced at the broken man, he sensed that Judas would never be truly free again.

***

On a break from the proceedings, Liberius led Joseph to a small back room where he could meet with Hadas and Yakir to go over some pressing issues that were bubbling up in the office. As Hadas presented each matter, Yakir took quick notes of Joseph's instructions. There was quite a stack and the three men got through only half when Joseph decided he needed to focus on the trial that would be resuming in just minutes.

"Yakir, I pray that Matthew is poised to take the stand when we return?" Joseph asked the question but it was more an assumption.

"Yes, sir, Matthew is primed and anxious to testify," Yakir responded.

"Matthew dropped by the office just yesterday," Hadas said. "He registered his dismay that he had to wait so long to testify and had not been allowed to sit in and observe the proceedings."

"You did explain...," Joseph began but was interrupted by Hadas.

"Not to worry, Joseph," Hadas responded. "I explained that a witness waiting to testify was not allowed in the court so that there was no issue of his being biased by the on-going testimony. I also tried to appeal to his pride and told him that we thought he was such a powerful witness that we were saving the best for last."

"How did he respond?" Joseph asked, curious.

"I found that Matthew could not be thusly flattered," Hadas responded.

"I think that's a common characteristic among all of Jesus followers," Joseph responded with a smile. "Their behavior mimics that of their idol."

Joseph rose and told his assistants to gather up their documents. He promised to stop by the office that night after court—no matter how late it might be—and go over the remaining of the issues at that time.

Back in court, the spectators and principals were already gathering. Joseph was slightly annoyed when Yakir came rushing through the courtroom to return to the office with the huge stack of parchments. The young office assistant failed to look where he was going and tripped on someone's foot and the documents went flying. There were a few gasps and chuckles as the red-faced young man raced around to pick all the papers up before court began. And he did so with no room to spare. But all was well in the end and Joseph was ready to end his defense by calling Matthew as his last witness.

Pilate peered down at Joseph. "Well, counselor, shall we proceed?"

Joseph rose and hurried to face the bench. "Yes, sir, the defense calls...," Well, Joseph couldn't get the complete sentence out before Yakir was back in the courtroom making mischief for Joseph and putting a halt to the proceedings. Yakir was motioning to Joseph in such a manner that he feared he couldn't ignore him. Irit frowned and glared at Yakir as well. She had always held the opinion that Yakir was too young to be given the responsibilities that her husband assigned to him. Now, she would be proven right in the worst way—he would publicly disgrace her husband.

"Your honor, I pray for your tolerance and allow me to consult with my runner," Joseph said. "It appears that a matter of urgency has possibly occurred."

"I pray that it is indeed a matter of urgency," Pilate responded with more than a little pique in his tone.

Joseph turned on his heel and headed for the back of the courtroom to see what the young irresponsible empty-headed boy wanted.

***

In the seclusion of the courtroom, Joseph had no idea that while he met with Hadas and Yakir, that outside an event was occurring that was astounding and confounding the townspeople. Cyrus galloped into town on his trusty camel and was followed by a group of fellow travelers. The dust that covered the Bedouins' garbs was evidence that they had just traveled through the desert.

Days before when Cyrus first accepted the mission, he carefully contemplated the best route for his journey. There were many different paths in the desert familiar to Cyrus, routes that he chose to take depending on what he needed to accomplish. But on this occasion he would be taking the most direct path that led from Jerusalem to the Persian kingdom of Shushan. The mission on this trip was to convince one of the three kings of the Magi, Balthazar, Casper or Melchior, to return to Jerusalem with him. Since it had been over thirty years since the birth of Jesus, it was Cyrus's considered opinion that the three old royals probably were no longer alive. If that were indeed the case, his goal then was to bring back an heir or relative of one of these men. There was a caveat, however, whoever he brought back with him had to have been told the story of the Magi visiting the child in the manger in Jerusalem so many years before. He would have to recall the details of that night as told directly to him by one of the kings. Cyrus's task was not an easy one—but few of his missions were.

Cyrus had been determined to find the witness that Hadas asked him to find. It was a challenge but Cyrus lived for challenge. As it turned out, Cyrus was able to find the son of Balthazar who was now a king who ruled over the people of a small region in southern Persia. Although the young King Sharaman at first refused an audience with Cyrus, the nomad had a way of interjecting himself into the inner circle and eventually made his way to Sharaman. Just how Cyrus was able to reach the young King, has been lost on time. Suffice it to say that as crude as Cyrus could, he could be just as charming when charm was the order of the day. But once Cyrus asked about the story of his father and two other Eastern kings who paid homage to a newborn in the city of Bethlehem over thirty years before, a look of recognition washed across his face.

"I recall the story, nomad," King Sharaman said. "My father told me of his journey."

"Why did His Highness, King Balthazar, travel such a distance to honor a peasant's baby?" Cyrus asked, curious himself.

"My father told me that he and the other rulers from nearby kingdoms interpreted the bright Star of Bethlehem that night as an omen," Sharaman said. "It called to them. It told them that Jesus Christ, the King of Kings, had been born."

Suddenly the inappropriateness of his having a discussion about his father with an unknown dusty wayfarer struck Sharaman. He was young to the nomad's years but he was a King.

"Why are you so bold as to ask me about my father?" Sharaman asked.

Cyrus realized that to get the rest of his bounty that he would have to stay on the good side of the young ruler in order to convince him to return to Jerusalem for the trial. He made a deep bow to Sharaman.

"I do apologize," Cyrus said. "I meant no disrespect. But there is an urgent matter. That baby that your father saw fit to honor—that King of Kings—is now in a fight for his very life."

Sharaman was now intrigued and concerned. His father had passed away many seasons ago but the young king would never cease to honor his father's memory and beliefs.

"Why does this man, this Jesus Christ, find himself in such dire circumstances?" Sharaman asked.

"There are those who want to sabotage him," Cyrus responded in a tone that hinted at treachery and conspiracy. "These powerful men—rabbis of the highest order—have determined that his claims of divine origin are fraudulent." Cyrus sensed that Sharaman would respond most vehemently if his father's story was being perceived as a lie or myth. "And, perhaps worst of all, they dispute the story that the three Kings of the East paid honor at his birth. I even heard that one of these men implied that only a foolish man would believe in such a holy birth."

"Well, my father was not a fool!" Sharaman responded in exactly the manner that Cyrus had hoped for. "He was a wise man who had the gift of vision."

"Jesus's very life is at stake, Your Highness," Cyrus said. "We need a brave and wise person from the east to once again ride to the side of Jesus of Nazareth."

"I do not know this Jesus of Nazareth," the King responded. "But I will not allow my father's name to be besmirched. It is I who will ride on behalf of my father's legacy. I will tell these arrogant rabbis that my father did indeed travel to honor the new born King."

Cyrus bowed to the King again and a smile of satisfaction stretched across his face. Cyrus had genuinely impressed himself with his crafty wiliness.

"I will escort you across the sand and guard your safety, Your Highness," Cyrus said in a tone most grateful and respectful.

Early that next morning, Cyrus mounted his faithful and stalwart camel and led the King and his entourage toward the desert path that led to Jerusalem. King Sharaman guided his fleet-footed camel directly behind Cyrus. Behind and alongside the King was a brigade of palace guards who served as the King's protectors. The commander of the contingency rode a stately white Arabian steed while his men were all mounted atop sleek black Arabians. The King's mount was a pale, tan camel of above-average height. Its coat had been transformed into a silky spun gold from the extraordinary care given to it by the King's groomers. The saddle cloth was a rich brocade of interlaced silver and gold. The bridle was made of fine leather and trimmed with small golden bells that chimed delicately at every movement of the rein. The saddle itself was a glorious and opulent work of art. The leather saddle was adorned with precious ores as well as diamonds, rubies and emeralds. The camel's saddle and the other accessories were of more value than that of all the ordinary families of Jerusalem combined.

All the travelers wore heavy robes and face coverings to shield them from the dust they would encounter on their journey and would offer protection in the event a vicious sandstorm swirled up from the desert floor.

But the King was not concerned with sand or wind. His mission was a singular one and one that overrode any inconvenience or discomfort he might encounter. He was traveling to Jerusalem to defend his father's good name.

***

An angry and red-faced Joseph tramped down the main aisle to the waiting Yakir. Joseph became even more irritated when he saw the silly smile on his young assistant's face.

"What is it?!" Joseph whispered hoarsely.

Joseph's tone and obvious frustration did not take the smile off of Yakir's face.

"Sir, we have another witness who has just arrived in all his splendor," Yakir said.

"This is no time for games," Joseph fired back. "Pilate is ready to nail my arms to a cross. What on earth do you speak of?"

Just then a bright beam of sunlight appeared as the great outer door opened. Yakir turned toward the sound.

"I speak of a King, Joseph," Yakir said still smiling and motioning toward the door.

As the door opened further, King Sharaman stepped in and, as Yakir promised, in all his splendor. His gold and silver brocaded royal robe had been kept pristine from the dust of the journey by his outer travel robe which he had shed outside. Sharaman's white turban was set off with a large ruby that held the tail feathers of a silver falcon in place. A cluster of diamonds and pearls was clasped to his satin over-robe of purple. Jeweled rings and necklaces of every description adorned his hands and body. The monarch's shoes were made of leopard skin and adorned with large sapphires.

Well, Joseph nearly swooned. And his conscious state was further challenged when in stepped the imposing figure of the wayfarer Cyrus, still dusty and crusty from the trip. He spotted Joseph and deduced that he was the man to whom he should speak.

"Sir, I am Cyrus. Hadas hired me to bring you one of the Eastern Kings who paid honor to the new born Jesus Christ."

"Ah... so this is..." Joseph began as he looked at Sharaman patiently waiting nearby with his security contingent.

"This is King Sharaman," Cyrus explained. "He is the son of Balthazar, one of the Magi. He is prepared to swear before Caesar that his father visited Jesus of Nazareth who the Magi had heralded as the new born King of Kings."

Now Joseph had the same silly smile on his face as the one that Yakir wore.

"Very good," Joseph said and leaned closer to Cyrus. "Go see Hadas. Tell him to pay you triple the amount he owes you.

Now with a smile on his scarred face, Cyrus turned quickly to leave. He bowed graciously to King Sharaman and was gone.

***

After a brief meeting with Pilate and Liberius, Joseph returned to the defense table and stood next to Jesus. He turned slightly and smiled at Irit. He knew she would be enthralled with the next witness.

"The defense calls King Sharaman of Persia," Liberius called out loudly.

With that, King Sharaman entered the courtroom to the gasps and hushed surprise of the gallery. Even Pilate, Caiaphas and Annas stood at their seats to watch the King enter the courtroom. He was accompanied by two guards who waved large fans of ostrich feathers over the monarch to cool him in the oppressively hot room. Irit and Mary both watched with wide eyes and mouths agape as the young king passed by. Sharaman stood before Pilate who treated him with due respect and did not require him to swear to tell no falsehoods. The King took his place behind the stand. He gazed off in the distance—looking at no one in particular.

"Your highness, if you would be so kind as to tell the court your name and from where you hail," Joseph said.

"I am Sharaman, King of the Shushan Realm of Persia."

"And, sir, what relationship do you have with Jesus of Nazareth?" Joseph asked.

"My dead father King Balthazar told me the story of Jesus of Bethlehem," Sharaman responded. "My father was one of the three kings of the orient who paid him homage when he was but a babe. He told me this story many times over the years."

Caiaphas stood up. "Objection. Hearsay!"

Pilate looked at Caiaphas's scrawny face and then at the resplendent king who now glared at the man who for some reason had objected to what he was saying.

"Overruled."

Caiaphas did not take his seat but remained standing until Annas politely pulled him back down to his chair.

"And, Your Highness, what caused your honorable father to visit Jesus on that occasion," Joseph asked.

"My father was a visionary and knew that the bright Star of Bethlehem beckoned to him. It told him to honor the birth and bring gifts to the new King of Kings."

The gallery became loud and unruly for a few moments until Liberius and the guards convinced them to be silent. Joseph excused the witness to the prosecution. Caiaphas wondered to himself why Joseph had missed asking the most obvious and important question. But Caiaphas would not be so foolish.

"Your highness," Caiaphas addressed the King and bowed deeply before him. "Who was this King of Kings?"

"The baby born that night was Jesus Christ," Sharaman responded.

"How did your wise and esteemed father know that this baby was a King, or in your words, King of Kings? Did the little infant have a tiny crown on his head?" Caiaphas asked, sarcasm dripping from every word.

Sharaman glared at Caiaphas then like quicksilver looked at Jesus who was sitting slightly bent over at the defense table.

"My father was a King as I am a King," Sharaman said, his voice gaining volume. He pointed at Jesus. "As a King I know that that man is a King and that in fact and in deed he is the King of Kings!"

***

After the King's fiery testimony, the courtroom was in such disarray that Pilate ended the day's session. Joseph expressed his gratitude to Sharaman who quickly left with his entourage. Caiaphas and Annas rushed from the room in an apparent attempt to escape the evil that had permeated the room from the King's presence.

Later, Joseph wondered how the Young King was so sure that it was Jesus sitting there in the afternoon shadows and that Jesus was the King of Kings who his father had visited. Irit, in all her usual wisdom, told him that he probably would have to be a King himself to understand that.

Chapter 22
Matthew and the Physicians

The next morning, Joseph and Irit arrived early to the courthouse. Irit remained in the lobby area to wait for Mary. Joseph hurried up to the defense table and went over the notes he had from his talk with Matthew. He took a deep breath. At last it was time for Matthew's testimony. Matthew would be his last witness. Joseph squeezed his eyes shut and recollected the trial thus far. Had he done enough? What surprises would Caiaphas have for him? He said a quick prayer that all would go well. Just as he finished, he heard a rustling nearby and looked up into the peaceful face of Jesus. He immediately stood.

"Good morning," Joseph said cheerfully. "Today, Matthew will testify. He will be our last witness."

Jesus smiled and sensed the worry that Joseph was suffering under. He assured him that all would be well and thanked him for his dedication to his defense. Jesus saw his mother approaching and turned and smiled at her. Mary's face lit up and she returned his smile. As usual, Irit had Mary in tow and led her to the row where they always sat. Irit's face fell when she saw that two men were already sitting there. But her concerns were soon dashed. The two men stood up.

"Madam, here are your seats," the older man said. "We noticed that you always sat here. My son and I saved them for you."

The kindness of the two men touched the hearts of both Mary and Irit.

"Blessings to you and your son, kind sir," Irit said as she led Mary into the row. Mary smiled and bowed to the men.

Joseph had observed what the kind men had done for his wife and Mary. Things were starting out on a positive note. Perhaps it was a good omen for the difficult day to come.

Just as Joseph had hoped, Matthew made an imposing figure on the witness stand. When Pilate swore him in, his voice resonated clear and strong.

"Yes, I will tell the truth, your honor," Matthew said, "I never lie."

"I am heartened," Pilate said sardonically. "Joseph please proceed."

Well, thought Joseph, that was certainly a positive and robust way to begin one's testimony. Joseph approached the witness stand.

"Kind sir, if you will please provide for the court your name and your association with Jesus of Nazareth," Joseph began.

"I am Matthew of Galilee, son of Alpheus, a disciple of Jesus of Nazareth. I am Matthew."

"When did you first encounter Jesus?" Joseph asked.

"I was working as a tax collector near the Sea of Galilee," Matthew responded. "Jesus called to me." At those words, sadness washed over Matthew's face. He turned to look upon Jesus's face and recalled those first times with Jesus when there was peace, before the troubles began.

Matthew explained to the court that Jesus and he and the other disciples had just arrived in Jerusalem a week before his arrest.

"Were you a witness to any miracles performed by Jesus?" Joseph asked.

"Of course!" was Matthew's robust response. "Jesus instructed all the disciples to board a ship that would take us across the Sea of Galilee. Half way through the journey, we encountered a powerful storm. We were terrified of the wind which we were barely able to stand up against. It was wreaking havoc with our ship."

"Was Jesus with you?" Joseph asked.

"He wasn't on board the ship," Matthew said with a smile. "But he was with us."

"Please explain," Pilate interjected.

"At the height of the storm we were certain that we would not survive," Matthew responded. "Suddenly off in the distance we saw Jesus. He was surrounded by light. We heard his voice over the storm. He told us not to be afraid. Then in an instant the storm subsided and we were no longer frightened. Jesus led us ashore to safety."

"You indicated you saw Jesus ahead of you," Joseph followed up. "Was he on a ship ahead of you?"

"Oh, no, Joseph," Matthew responded quickly. "He wasn't on a ship. He was walking on the water!"

The courtroom came alive with gasps and whispers. Caiaphas was furious. He stood to object but was met with Pilate's gavel and his ill-temper."

"Silence!" Pilate shouted as Liberius and the guards made the rounds to quiet the gallery. "And Caiaphas you may take your seat." Pilate glared at Caiaphas and continued in a sardonic, taunting tone. "I'm sure you know by now how this works. Joseph asks the defense witness questions first then you get your turn."

Caiaphas sat down his face streaked with anger, obviously struggling to maintain basic decorum. The courtroom quickly quieted down since no one wanted to be thrown out even temporarily; no one wanted to miss even a minute of the proceeding. Joseph resumed his position in front of the witness stand and again addressed Matthew.

"Are you familiar with a visit that Jesus made to the temple?" Joseph asked.

Matthew smiled a little. "Do you refer to the time when Jesus became upset with the goings on there?"

The very engaged Matthew had suddenly taken over questioning, something that Pilate was duty-bound to correct. He bent over toward Matthew. "Sir, your role is to answer questions. We have counsel to handle the questioning."

There were a few guffaws. Joseph didn't mind that Matthew had asked him a question. It would just demonstrate to the jury how bright his witness was. He smiled warmly at Matthew who, knowing his own aggressive personality, was enjoying the moment.

"Matthew what happened when Jesus went to the temple?" Joseph asked, returning the court to proper order.

"Jesus was upset with the actions of the rabbis that day," Matthew said and pointedly looked directly at Caiaphas who refused to return his look.

"Why was Jesus upset?" Joseph asked.

"The rabbis were allowing greedy money changers to execute their evil deeds in the temple and defile that holy edifice!" Matthew said with emphasis.

Caiaphas was on his feet. "I object!"

"I'm sure you do object," Pilate said barely able to control the smirk that fought to curl his lips.

Pilate looked at Matthew. "Is it your truthful testimony that the rabbis were allowing the activities you describe to be conducted in the temple?"

"With no doubt and no lie," Matthew responded, his voice booming over the courtroom.

"Prosecutor, your objection is overruled!" Pilate said. He looked at Caiaphas who was still standing, obviously shaken. "You may sit down, Caiaphas."

Caiaphas slumped back down in his chair but the fury in his face did not abate.

"Do you consider yourself an expert in Jewish Law?" Joseph asked.

"Yes, my entire day is devoted to reading the Holy Scriptures," Matthew responded. "I know them in my heart."

"So when Jesus became upset that day, was he defending the evil money changers?" Joseph asked.

"Of course not, sir." Matthew said, slightly annoyed at Joseph's question.

"Then what was he defending?" Joseph asked.

"Jewish Law," Matthew responded.

Joseph walked to the defense table, pretending to consult some notes, in order to allow Matthew's answer to float in the air for a few moments before he resumed.

"Who was breaking the laws?" Joseph asked.

"The money changers... the money changers and the rabbis!" Matthew's voice grew loud. He turned and looked directly at Caiaphas and Annas and pointed at them.

Caiaphas was completely exasperated. He didn't say a word, only looked at Pilate pleadingly. Not one to ever feel much sympathy for the prosecutor, Pilate thought Caiaphas was about to collapse or explode and decided to call a brief recess. The spectators were getting rowdy anyway. Besides, it was time for Pilate's mid-morning cup of red wine. The trial of Jesus of Nazareth has made his imbibing part of his daily routine.

***

Pilate was lounging in his chambers with a cup of wine when Liberius scurried in.

"When shall we resume, sire?" Liberius asked.

"After my wine," Pilate responded. A sardonic smile came over Pilate's face. "Did you see the look on Caiaphas's face? I thought the old boy was going to keel over."

With that, Caiaphas, who had just been standing outside Pilate's door, knocked.

"Come." Pilate said, raising his voice.

Caiaphas came in and stood respectfully before Pilate's table.

"I was buoyed to hear your words," Caiaphas said. "Your concern for my health is heartening."

"Were you eavesdropping, prosecutor?" Pilate asked, more than a little annoyed that Caiaphas had the arrogance to reproach him about his words, even though he tried to disguise his intention.

"Your voice is rich and carries," Caiaphas responded.

"Enough of this absurdity," Pilate said, now peeved. "What is it you want, Caiaphas?"

"I beg that you strike the words of the witness, Matthew, from the public records," Caiaphas responded.

"Why?"

"Such words will cause a problem with my congregation," Caiaphas answered, resenting that he had to grovel to the governor.

"I'm sure it would be a problem," Pilate said, staring intensely at Caiaphas.

"I am aware of your desire to maintain peace among the Jewish community," Caiaphas said, intentionally hitting upon a vulnerable area for the Governor of Jerusalem.

"I'll give it my consideration." Pilate said, annoyed that his weak heel was being exploited by the calculating rabbi. He rose and looked at Liberius who was still in the room, standing by the door. "It's time to resume the trial, Liberius. Put the word out to reassemble."

***

Joseph had just a few more questions, then his defense case would be concluded. Next, it would the prosecutor's turn. Joseph did not look forward to that. However, from the witness list that had been given to Joseph by the prosecution, there apparently weren't a great number of witnesses that Caiaphas planned to call upon to testify.

Once Matthew retook the stand, Joseph planned to make short order of the rest of his business with this witness.

"Matthew, what led to Jesus's arrest on that night in Gethsemane?" Joseph inquired of his witness.

"One of our own, the disciple Judas Iscariot, turned him in," Matthew responded. "Sadly, I and the other disciples ate too heartily and drank too much wine. We became drowsy after our meal and fell asleep and... failed to protect him." A tear welled in Matthew's eye as he looked forlornly at Jesus. Joseph decided to push on and focus on Judas's role in the capture.

"What was this disciple's reward?" Joseph asked.

"He was paid thirty silver pieces by the Jewish High Priests for his act of betrayal," Matthew responded.

"Was the silver paid to him for his trouble? For the time it took him to find Jesus?" Joseph asked.

"Not at all. It was no trouble for Judas to find Jesus he knew where he was just as we all did," Matthew responded, then offered more. "The payment was a bribe."

"Is paying a bribe a legal act under Jewish law?" Joseph asked.

"It is permissible in our laws for officials of the Jewish High Council to offer a bounty for the capture of a wanted criminal. But of course, Jesus was not a criminal," Matthew answered.

"Bribery is legal then, Matthew?" Joseph asked.

Matthew stood up as straight as he could and puffed his chest out. He responded to Joseph's question in his loudest voice.

"If a law is confounded and manipulated to bring about evil, its legality is rendered meaningless," Matthew said as tears brimmed in his eyes.

Joseph thought it best to end Matthew's testimony on those dramatic words. "I have no further questions for Matthew, your honor," Joseph told Pilate.

Caiaphas stood. He would ultimately try to redeem himself and his fellow High Priests; however, he would begin by attempting to tear down some of the more minor testimony. By doing so, he hoped to damage Matthew's overall credibility.

"Matthew of Galilee, do you have knowledge of a visit of Kings from the East to the newborn Jesus in Bethlehem?" Caiaphas asked.

"Well, he wasn't new born," Matthew responded. "He was two years old."

"Yet others have testified that he was but a babe when the Persians came," Caiaphas said. "You declare your expertise in Jewish Laws. Is not the simple law of honesty corrupted when two proclaimed disciples of a visionary relate different versions of the same event? Is this the kind of followers that the Messiah leads?"

Joseph literally leaped to his feet. "Objection! It is not the prosecutor's place to lecture the witness much less the court."

"Withdraw the question," Caiaphas said.

"It wasn't a question now was it?" Pilate said. He then focused on the court recorder. "Omit that last diatribe by the prosecutor, scribe."

Caiaphas appeared unaffected by the exchange and resumed his questioning.

"You testified that Jesus walked on water, did you not?" Caiaphas began.

"Yes," Matthew responded. "I said that because I was a witness to it."

"You also testified that in the Garden of Gethsemane, you failed to protect your... your friend, Jesus of Nazareth because you had drunk too much wine," Caiaphas continued. His eyes narrowed and a barely detectible smile crossed his lips. "Since you are therefore known to drink too much by your own admission, perhaps you had too much wine and just imagined that you saw Jesus walk on water..." Caiaphas raised his screechy voice to its highest volume to finish his thought. "... something that no man has ever done or is capable of doing!" Caiaphas looked at the jury panel, a sneer of derision on his face.

The red blotches on Matthew's cheeks chronicled the anger that Caiaphas's inference engendered but he responded in a controlled manner. "Rabbi, I had not imbibed on wine on that occasion, on the ship that sailed the Sea of Galilee. You are correct to assert that no man has ever walked on water." Matthew leaned forward, glared at his questioner and spoke with heightened emotion and increased volume. "Only a god can do that!"

Pilate was prepared for the outburst that followed. He stood and banged his gavel down on his table with such rage that it redounded throughout the courtroom. The people quickly settled down save one man who out of utter astonishment could not stop his chatter; he was immediately escorted from the proceedings with the point of a spear at his backside. Caiaphas took a deep breath and continued before Pilate could chide him for any perceived delay. Besides he wanted to push forward so the jury would get past the last words of Matthew that portrayed Jesus as a god.

"In the temple incident that you referred to in your original testimony and in your deposition did Jesus become violent and dangerous?" Caiaphas asked Matthew. "Did he threaten to destroy the temple and thus break sacred Jewish laws?"

Matthew glared at Caiaphas. He knew that the old rabbi was trying to force him into a corner. This time Matthew answered in a soft, more reticent voice. "He... uh... may have broken a few items."

"Is defiling a holy temple a violation of Jewish religious laws?" Caiaphas asked, already knowing the answer.

"Normally, it is, sir," Matthew answered, his voice stronger. "But in the case we speak of, it was not."

Caiaphas's face took on a haughty mien. "Oh? And why was the destruction of the temple not a violation of law on that occasion?"

"Because, Caiaphas, it was not a holy temple on that day because your money changers had made it a den of thieves!" Matthew boomed, his voice reverberated to every corner of the large courtroom.

Caiaphas spun around and headed for his seat.

"Jesus was defending Jewish law on that day while the High Priests were in collusion with the criminals who were destroying its holiness!" Matthew, his face red with anger, continued his words now escalated into a tirade.

The gallery reacted with gasps and whispers. Liberius immediately ordered the Roman guards to calm the crowd.

Caiaphas turned back toward Pilate. "I did not ask the witness a question. I demand that his statement be removed from the record!"

"You demand that?" Pilate asked in a tone that reminded Caiaphas who exactly was in charge of the courtroom.

Caiaphas bowed deeply. "I apologize to the court, your honor. I request that the last words of Matthew of Galilee be removed from the record."

"I shall comply with your request," Pilate said. He then turned to the jury panel. "You are to disregard the unsolicited statement last made by Matthew of Galilee. But the court understands that words can linger in one's mind even when the Governor of Jerusalem tells them not to."

Pilate's ambivalent instructions angered Caiaphas but he had no recourse. He could only hope that Matthew's words would fade over time as they were a threat to his authority and that of the other Jewish High Priests. Caiaphas was angry. He and the other rabbis weren't on trial. It would not be the Jewish High Priests who would be castigated throughout the width and breadth of history—it would be Jesus and his sins.

***

After a much-needed break, the gallery, followed by the principals and the jury returned. Pilate was eager for the trial to move along more quickly. It was already stretching out longer than he had ever imagined. At least the process had reached a milestone. The defense had rested. It was now Caiaphas's turn to present his case.

Caiaphas called Rabbi Gideon Levi a highly respected physician of Jerusalem. After he swore to Pilate that he would tell the truth, he took the stand.

"Rabbi Levi, please describe your medical practice for the court," Caiaphas began.

"I have been a physician of general ailments and conditions for more than twenty-years," Dr. Levi responded.

"Did your practice include the delivery of babes?" Caiaphas asked.

A big smile crossed Dr. Levi's face. "I've delivered hundreds of babies." Dr. Levi looked at the jury and the spectator gallery. "I daresay that some sitting here today were babes that I delivered."

The spectators laughed and looked around, wondering who those former babies were. Pilate didn't mind the lightness that Dr. Levi's remark interjected into the proceedings. Pilate tapped his gavel gently a few times to bring focus back the questioning.

"I can assume you understand how the human female conceives a child," Caiaphas said.

"It does not take a physician to know that," Dr. Levi responded, evoking a few more snickers.

"Is it possible for a woman to be with child by any way other than the one... we all do know?" Caiaphas asked.

"No," Dr. Levi responded.

Caiaphas had no more questions. Joseph stood and approached the physician who he knew quite well.

"Good afternoon, Dr. Levi," Joseph greeted the witness. "Is it possible for a child to be conceived by divination?"

Dr. Levi stared at Joseph and looked puzzled. "Divination is not my area of expertise."

"Please, kind physician, answer the question." Joseph urged Dr. Levi.

"I cannot answer for I do not know," Dr. Levi responded.

"No more questions, your honor," Joseph said as he took his seat pleased at having destroyed Caiaphas's strategy.

Caiaphas was on his feet again. "Dr. Levi, could Mary of Nazareth have conceived a child by divination?!"

Dr. Levi hung his head for a moment, then looked up earnestly at Caiaphas. "Counselor, my answer remains the same. I do not know."

Caiaphas's first witness was arguably a disaster for the prosecution. Joseph was silently enjoying the fact that his opponent started off on such wobbly footing. But it was just a battle, the war was still proceeding. And unknown to Joseph, Caiaphas was about to strike back with a vengeance. The prosecutor requested permission to speak with Pilate. After the two men spoke for a few moments, Pilate signaled Joseph to join them.

"Joseph, Caiaphas has made an unusual request, one that I tend to approve," Pilate began. "The trial is a protracted one and its length is unsettling to me and causing conflicts on my court docket. Caiaphas has suggested a way to speed up the proceeding."

"I favor as quick a resolution as possible myself," Joseph responded. "What is the honorable Caiaphas's suggestion?"

"Caiaphas plans to call five townsmen to testify at one time," Pilate responded, in a hushed tone. "They will all testify that they paid Mary Magdalene silver denarii to lay with her."

Joseph felt his knees beginning to weaken. He was bowled over by the hubris of the prosecutor and his reckless disregard for the transformed young woman's reputation and feelings.

"Your honor, such a move would disgrace the court," Joseph responded, trying to appeal to Pilate's own stake in the matter.

"Well, as Caiaphas pointed out, he plans to have all five men testify as a group to shorten the time necessary to present their testimony," Pilate said. "Their testimony will be presented in a succinct manner and thus save the court precious time. I see no way that the words of these men will be more or less damaging presented as a group or individually." Pilate hesitated a moment, thoughtful. "I hereby concur in Caiaphas's request. All five of these witnesses will be sworn in at once. Caiaphas has assured me that he will only require simple responses from the men and will not pursue prolonged exchanges with them."

"But, your honor, the image of the five men lined up in front of the jury will evoke undue prejudice upon my client," Joseph said in a pleading voice. "Through his association with Mary Magdalene, my client's reputation will be unduly sullied."

My decision is made, Joseph," Pilate said with finality. "You will have the chance to redeem your client through the cross-examination process."

Joseph hung his head knowing he was defeated. As he walked back to his seat, he scanned the gallery and was relieved when he did not see Mary Magdalene's face. But she was known to stand in the back. He prayed that she was otherwise engaged.

The five men were called to the front and sworn in by Pilate. It was obvious that Caiaphas was anxious to present these stellar witnesses. Joseph figured that Caiaphas probably had to pay these men dearly to reveal their nefarious activities publicly. He hoped that they were married and that their wives would have due revenge on them.

Caiaphas approached the five men who stood in front of the witness stand.

"Gentlemen, do you know Mary Magdalene?" Caiaphas asked.

The men answered "yes" in unison.

"How do you know Mary Magdalene?" Caiaphas asked with an eagerness that was appalling.

One man, Shimon, spoke up. "She was a bought woman."

"Please explain what you mean sir, by 'a bought woman.'" Caiaphas said.

"She's a prostitute," Shimon said. "Her flesh was for sale."

There was quite a bit of buzzing in the crowd and a little stir in the standing area. Joseph turned and looked just in time to see Mary Magdalene turning and fleeing toward the door to leave the building. Joseph's stomach was in a knot. There was a stoic look on Jesus's face but he seemed to have no bitterness toward the men.

Caiaphas confirmed with the others that they agreed with Shimon's description of Mary Magdalene and their relationship with her.

"Did you, as you infer, buy her?" Caiaphas asked, unwilling to allow any doubt to linger.

The men all indicated that they had lay with Mary Magdalene and had paid for sexual pleasures.

Caiaphas indicated he had completed his questioning of the witnesses. He could not help but get in one more slur as he walked back to his table.

"Thank you, your honor, for allowing the men to appear together," Caiaphas said. The volume of his thin voice increased as he finished his thought. "There were more men but I assumed that five was all the court could accommodate at once."

Joseph had never felt more angry. "Your honor!" Joseph said in the loudest voice the courtroom had heard from him to date.

"I withdraw my statement," Caiaphas said, relishing the moment.

Pilate saw that Joseph was still livid. "I'm sure the gentlemen of the jury will take into account only testimony, not the barbs of a struggling prosecutor."

Caiaphas didn't like Pilate's comment but it didn't ruin the moment for him. Joseph approached the five men. He stood in front of them and looked at each one intensely.

"Have you had the relations you described with Mary Magdalene in the last year?" Joseph asked.

They men all said they had not.

"Have you pursued Mary Magdalene for that purpose in the last year?"

Three of the men said they had. Joseph pursued the line of questioning and the three men admitted that Mary had refused them. Shimon was the last to speak up.

"Mary told me she had found the Lord and he had relieved her of all her demons," Shimon volunteered.

Caiaphas objected to the exchange but was told by Pilate that all of their testimony would be allowed, not just the bits and pieces that he found acceptable. Joseph was still upset by the appearance of the five men but felt he had salvaged it as best he could.

Next, Caiaphas called another physician, this time a younger one, named Nachum Hysh.

"Dr. Hysh," Caiaphas began, "Can you tell the court of your medical profession?"

"Of course," Hysh responded. "I am a physician of a general nature here in the township of Jerusalem. I have been in my practice for near nine years."

Joseph observed that Dr. Hysh had a demeanor that was self-important and boorish.

"In all your experiences with patients, has one ever died only to live again?" Caiaphas asked.

"Yes," Hysh answered in a matter-of-fact manner.

There was some rustling in the courtroom. Were they about to hear of other miracles and would it confirm that Jesus could well have been involved in one? But why would Caiaphas call forth such testimony?

"Do such returns to life have to do with the spiritual world?" Caiaphas asked.

"Of course not. Let me explain," Hysh responded sardonically. "Some inexperienced and inept physicians fail to recognize that a person is in a somnolent condition—a deep sleep. This is a condition where a person could appear to be dead to the untrained eye."

"How long do these periods of deep sleep last?" Caiaphas asked.

"They could endure for days or even weeks," Hysh replied. "After that, the person would die from lack of nutrition."

"So, you would not categorize such an event as a miracle?" Caiaphas asked.

"There are no miracles," Hysh responded, a sly smile curling his lips.

"I have no more questions," Caiaphas said in an almost joyful manner.

Joseph approached the witness stand. He would take his turn at the arrogant physician although he had little hope that he'd made much of a point.

"Why do people in these somnolent conditions wake up?" Joseph asked.

"They recover from what ailed them," Hysh responded.

"What makes them recover?" Joseph persisted.

Hysh appeared perplexed for a few moments before he spoke.

"I have no idea."

Chapter 23
Another King

It seemed that Caiaphas was not going to allow the defense to have the only royal witness. The next morning Joseph was notified that King Herod would be testifying for the prosecution. With King Sharaman of Persia, the kings involved in the trial would total two. Of course, some would say that the real King was sitting at the defense table in a tattered and bloody robe but at that time those with that opinion were not large in number.

Joseph arrived at court early as usual and was dismayed to hear that the proceeding would not begin until Herod arrived. The Jewish King was known to be a self-absorbed individual who always kept people waiting. Even though Pilate detested Herod, he had no choice but to allow the delay. Joseph used his time to continue writing his closing statement which he had been working on for days. Although the trial seemed to have been going on forever, looking back now it seemed to Joseph that it had raced by and he could hardly believe that it was coming to a close.

**

As it turned out Joseph had plenty of time to write. The sun was nearly straight up in the sky when there was a stirring in the back of the courtroom and whispers soon spread the news that King Herod and his entourage had arrived. Liberius hurried back to Pilate's chamber to give him word of Herod's arrival and the Judge soon swept into the courtroom and took his perch on the bench. Although Herod was not a popular figure among the citizens of Jerusalem, he was a king and the gallery was abuzz with anticipation as the spectators had awaited his arrival. Joseph knew that his entrance would not be a modest affair.

The crisp click-clack of Herod's leather sandals resounded on the gleaming ebony floor. He was adorned in his finest garb: a black and red brocade vestment covered a white linen tunic embroidered with silver and golden silken threads. Necklaces of beryl and onyx hung around his neck. A woolen robe of deep magenta covered his under garb and was held in place by a jewel encrusted brooch. On his balding head, Herod wore a gold crown sprinkled with sapphires and rubies. Herod advanced toward the front followed a few steps behind by two palace guards. Bringing up the rear were two barefoot slaves who were in attendance to tend to any personal needs that the King might have during his testimony.

Herod looked straight ahead and made no eye contact with anyone, even Caiaphas who had eagerly awaited his arrival. Pilate gazed upon the Jewish King with a skeptical eye. He had no more respect for this "king" than he had for the slaves he brought with him. Pilate addressed Herod instructing him that he was required to vow that he would present only truthful testimony. Herod refused to recognize Pilate and only mumbled something unintelligible to Caiaphas.

"Your Honor, His Highness agrees to your request," Caiaphas offered nervously.

"Well... please tell His Highness that Your Honor requests that His Highness take the stand," Pilate said, not attempting to hide his contempt for the porcine king. This filthy Jew was no King to him and he would hold no pretense that he bestowed such honor upon him.

Caiaphas escorted Herod to the stand. His guards followed behind. Caiaphas motioned to the guards to stand to the side so they would not obscure the view of the jury. The two slaves sat on the floor on either side of their master.

"King Herod, may I welcome you to our court and express my gratitude for your willingness to participate in this proceeding," Caiaphas said, his patronizing was turning at least two stomachs—those of Pilate and Joseph.

"It is not my normal habit to stand for prolonged periods of time," Herod announced to circumvent any lengthy questioning.

Caiaphas, who could not stand the sight of Herod any more than Pilate could, bowed to his witness. He detested him but he was a key witness and one whose words would linger in the thoughts of the jurors.

"Do you know Jesus of Nazareth?" Caiaphas asked.

"Of course not," Herod answered with noticeable annoyance.

The answer caught Caiaphas off guard. He stared at Herod trying to get his bearings. If Herod testified that he didn't know Jesus, there would be no testimony. Pilate, of all people, realized that Caiaphas's question was slightly off target and decided to bail the rabbi out.

"King Herod," Pilate began, "Do you know *of* Jesus of Nazareth?"

"I suppose," Herod answered, still not looking directly at anyone.

Pilate had dealt with Tiberius Caesar and knew how to handle egocentric rulers. Caiaphas bowed to Pilate to show his appreciation and daresay his admiration for his ability to interpret royal thought processes.

"Uh... how is it, King Herod, that you know *of* Jesus of Nazareth?" Caiaphas asked, taking back the reigns of witness examination.

Now Herod stared intensely at Caiaphas. "Why it is your own guards who brought him to me! I'm sure you have the capacity to recollect that you sent him to me so that I would sentence him to death."

Caiaphas figured the best way to get past this rather awkward moment was to just plunge ahead.

"Sir, what occurred when Jesus was brought to you?" Caiaphas asked.

"As a King I was asked to judge whether this man was also a king or indeed even a god of all things," Herod responded. "I will confirm to you that he is no more a king or a god than you are."

"How did you determine that Jesus was a fraud?" Caiaphas asked, ignoring the insult.

"Objection... leading the witness," Joseph interjected.

"I shall rephrase," Caiaphas responded.

But Joseph's interruption annoyed Herod. "Why is this common man allowed to slow the process with his inane comment?"

Caiaphas decided to ignore Herod's question since the King would refuse to even try to understand the process. "King Herod, how did you determine that this man was neither a king or god?"

"I ordered him to perform a miracle. I heard tales that this man was the King of Miracles, that he could turn water into wine, heal the sick, walk on water and make the blind see again!" Herod responded. "But the man was a charlatan. He could do none of this!"

Caiaphas smiled and bowed to Herod once again. "Thank you your highness." Caiaphas headed to the prosecution table. Without even a glance at Joseph, he told the defense counsel that Herod was his witness. Joseph rose and walked slowly to the witness stand. Suddenly, Herod looked at him an annoyed look on his face as Joseph neared him.

"And who might you be?" Herod asked.

"I am Joseph of Arimathea, Your Highness," Joseph responded. "I am the counsel who defends Jesus of Nazareth."

"Really? Since this man obviously has no defense, may the fortunes be with you," Herod replied with more than a few scattered snickers heard about the room.

"Since you found Jesus guilty of being a fraud, why did you send him away?" Joseph asked.

Because... because I did not agree that his crimes merited the death sentence," Herod responded, his face growing more serious. "His actions were petty and mean-spirited but not worthy of death on the cross."

"Did you have any compunction that you did not save him from crucifixion since you deemed him innocent of high crimes?" Joseph asked.

Herod puffed up, his chest appeared to grow twice as large, his face red and sweaty. "I will not be reproached by the likes of you."

Joseph took Herod's angry words in stride and did not react to them, surprising Pilate and Caiaphas and surprising himself the most.

"I meant no disrespect, Your Highness," Joseph continued. "If I may rephrase... as the King of the Jewish people of Jerusalem do you believe that Jesus of Nazareth, one of your subjects, should be executed for what the prosecution characterizes as blasphemy?"

"Blasphemy is being a pretender of God," Herod focused on the defendant sitting at the table before him. "This man is not even a pretender of a pretender of a pretender of God. This man is nothing. As such, I deem him to be no threat to our society. To execute him would give him an importance and credibility that he does not deserve. The last thing this kingdom needs is a false prophet who is transformed by death into a spurious martyr."

Joseph excused the witness while Caiaphas fumed silently. He knew having Herod on the stand was a huge risk. The man was arrogant and knew no limit to his words. Joseph sat down at his table quite satisfied that the prosecution's royal witness had turned out to be a royal pain in Caiaphas's backside.

Herod made his way out of the courtroom with as much aplomb and overwrought majesty as with his entry. Pilate eyeing the monarch with disdain grew tired of Herod's procession's slow and protracted exit and called a brief recess.

***

After the court resumed, Joseph saw from the witness manifest that Caiaphas would be calling a blind man next—a man who would allege that Jesus had claimed he could restore his sight but had failed to do so.

As Caiaphas's runner accompanied the blind man down the aisle from the witness room, the click of the man's walking stick alternated with the sound of his footsteps. Joseph eyed him closely as he walked slowly by. He wouldn't put it past Caiaphas to pay someone to pose as a blind man to make his case. But Joseph saw no sign that the man was feigning blindness. Joseph turned to Jesus and asked him if he knew the man but Jesus did not.

Caiaphas walked up to the man who had been sworn in by Pilate.

"Sir, what is your experience with Jesus of Nazareth?" Caiaphas asked.

"Friends of this man came to me and said that he could cure my eyes, make them see again," the man said. "I was brought before this man. He laid hands upon me and ordered me to see. But I could not!" The man was plainly angry at the outcome.

"Were you required to provide remuneration for this... miracle?" Caiaphas asked in his signature snide manner.

"Remuner...?"

"Did you have to pay him?" Pilate interjected.

"Yes. I was forced to give him all my silver," the man said, obviously outraged.

"And, your sight has never returned since that occasion?" Caiaphas asked.

"Never."

"Your witness," Caiaphas said in conclusion.

Joseph spoke quietly with Jesus for a few moments before he rose and approached the witness stand. Upon closer inspection, he confirmed that the man's eyes were opaque and unseeing.

"Sir, where did this incident take place?" Joseph asked the man.

"Why here in Jerusalem, of course," the blind man said.

Joseph thought to himself for a few moments then returned to his table pretending to consult his paper that contained the notes he took when he talked with Matthew.

"How do you respond to the fact that Jesus cured only four men from blindness, one in Bethsaida, three others in Jericho and not even one in Jerusalem?!" Joseph almost screamed at the man.

"It is a lie. A lie!" the blind man yelled angrily.

Caiaphas was on his feet. "Your Honor, there is no evidence that Jesus did not attempt to heal this man!" He glared at Jesus. "There is only one person who could testify to the contrary. The accused one who sits here now among us. Jesus of Nazareth is the only one who can testify to this!"

Pilate told Caiaphas to have a seat. He called Joseph up to the bench and asked if Jesus would testify about this blind man's claim. Joseph told Pilate that Jesus would not defend himself. He would not take the stand to refute the man's words.

"Sustained!" Pilate ruled as Joseph walked back to the defense table, shamed that he could not provide a better defense for his client. He had failed him. He knew the blind man was lying and he would have wagered all his wealth that Caiaphas decided to once again use silver pieces to get his way. He should have been more prepared for the inevitable manipulation and maneuvering of the prosecutor. But his hands were tied. Jesus would not defend himself. The only defense he had—at least on earth—was Joseph.

Just as Joseph feared, Caiaphas marched a cavalcade of the sick and maimed before the court. Each one claimed that he'd been duped by Jesus. Caiaphas had smelled blood and was taking advantage of Jesus's refusal to testify in his own defense. There was a crippled man and sick woman who claimed that Jesus had taken money from them with the promises that he would cure them—promises that were broken. Jesus sat stoically by. He knew the people were lying. At one point, Joseph turned to Jesus to discuss one of the witnesses. But Joseph decided not to disturb him. His eyes were closed and he was praying silently— undoubtedly praying for the souls of those who had brought lies against him.

The coup de gras for Pilate was the appearance of a prosecution witness who was very ill. Caiaphas didn't warn anyone that someone that sick was coming into open court. He relished the potential dramatic effect that the witness would have on the jury. The man emerged not from the witness waiting room but from a side door. As soon as gallery spectators got a glimpse of him they gasped and recoiled. The man was covered with a linen wrap from the top of his head to his sandaled feet. Only the man's eyes were exposed. He was a leper.

As the man walked further into the courtroom, spectators in the gallery began to leave en masse. Pilate rose from his chair and glared at the man.

"Halt!" Pilate roared. "Not a step further, witness!"

Caiaphas spun around and looked a Pilate who was now glaring at him.

"You have marched the lame and the blind and the addle-brained before us," Pilate snarled angrily. "Now you bring us a leper! The court and, I trust, the jury understands the pattern that you are establishing and the point you are trying to make. More of the same is not necessary! Now you expose everyone to disease!" Pilate banged his gavel angrily. "I order that you, Caiaphas, personally escort this man out of this courtroom!"

With that Pilate was gone. Most of the courtroom was cleared save Mary, Irit, Liberius, the guards and a few loyal hangers-on. Caiaphas could not disobey Pilate's direct order and walked slowly toward the man who had frozen in place. Caiaphas walked as far away from him as possible as they walked to the door. The bandage around the leper's leg loosened a bit and the end caught on a brad in the floor partially pulling the wrapping off the man's leg. The leg was exposed and looking as healthy as Yakir's who was watching a short distance away. Caiaphas flung the door open wide.

"Get out!" Caiaphas screeched at his star witness.

Yakir immediately reported the incident to Joseph who informed Pilate about the apparent chicanery. Pilate took note of it but his patience had disappeared and he was bent on concluding the trial. Joseph was fairly certain that Pilate would not allow the issue to go further.

As the curtain fell on that drama, the day's session was ended. Pilate did not reappear and Liberius ambled over to Joseph and Jesus and told them what they already knew—that court had ended for the day. When Jesus saw the soldiers approaching, he stood and met them. He smiled at Mary, Joseph and Irit as they escorted him away.

***

Irit made a big supper that evening and sent word for her older children and their families to join Joseph, their younger children and her for what was an unannounced celebration. The trial was not over but it soon would be. Joseph enjoyed the company of his large family that evening but his mind was filled with thoughts of the trial. The usually insatiable Joseph merely picked at his meal and lost his place in on-going conversations. His mind was in one place only and it would stay there. Joseph's state did not go unnoticed by Irit who fussed about him, worrying that he might collapse under the strain and pressure. Irit served a special dessert, Joseph's favorite, and gave a big portion of it to her husband first. When he barely ate a bite of that, she knew that her husband would not fully return to her until after the trial.

Joseph excused himself early from the family dinner. He had to once again go over his closing argument which he would be presenting to the jury first thing at tomorrow's proceeding. Irit knew to leave him alone. He needed this time dedicated exclusively to only his words and thoughts. Joseph knew his closing words from front to back without missing a beat but it was crucial that he get it just right. There was so very much riding on it.

Understandably, Joseph did not sleep well that night. As he lay on his pillow, the entire trial flashed before him. Joseph was a skilled and talented attorney. He knew that he had won the case on merit. But there were so many other factors. What duplicitous actions had Caiaphas taken? He paid thirty silver pieces to find a peaceful holy man and send him to his death. That the prosecutor was not above bribery was a given. And, what biases did the jurors hold? There were so many followers of Jesus who loved and worshiped him. But there were just as many, nay more, who detested him and felt threatened by him. Whatever answers awaited Joseph, one thing was certain they were not far in coming.

***

As it turned out the prosecutor opted to present his closing words first. He waived his chance to have the last word. Joseph was surprised. It seemed Caiaphas was confident—but perhaps overly so. Caiaphas rose and asked for Pilate's permission to proceed with his closing argument.

Caiaphas walked to the front of the jury panel. He thanked the jurors for their service and attention to the case. He had confidence, he told them, they would deliberate in good faith and send forth a just and thoughtful verdict.

"Jesus of Nazareth is accused of committing the vilest crime against our laws and against our God," Caiaphas began. "This man, the defendant, has declared himself to be God. His followers have either been placed under a magical spell or they have been paid to spread the word of his divinity."

Caiaphas paced back and forth a few times, allowing his dramatic words to have their full effect.

"Our children and our children's children will all suffer if this man would be allowed to continue to perpetuate his evil. A deadly and poisonous snake has slithered into our innocent community. If the head of that snake is not ripped from its body, the results will be devastating for generations to come."

Again, Caiaphas paced.

"Consider the witnesses that the defense called forth to testify," Caiaphas resumed. "One is a wanton woman who had an intimate relationship with this supposed man of god. This loose woman is bound to be as careless with the truth as she was with her chastity.

"Another witness, a young man, was obviously not in his right mind. He claimed to have been dead at one time but brought back to life through a miracle performed by Jesus. The defendant is known as a charismatic and bright man, a teacher. But he's conniving and calculating. He took the young Lazarus and convinced the poor boy that he had been dead! You heard our physician tell you that such an occurrence is not possible. Another witness showed the true nature of Jesus's followers. Judas Iscariot illustrated that the defendant's devotees were for sale.

"Recall the testimony of our other witnesses who swear that they paid for cures that he could not deliver. He has a band of followers who were either corrupt or mesmerized by Jesus or perhaps a little of both who would testify to anything that Jesus bade them to. Their testimony can be thrown out as self-serving and untruthful. I do have pity and empathy for the defendant's mother. She is a sympathetic figure who was drawn into this diabolical scheme when just a young woman. The evil of the conspiracy has preyed upon her over the years and obviously rendered her without reason."

"King Herod and even the Honorable Pilate had a turn at acquitting them but they did not," Caiaphas said.

The scowl on his face revealed Pilate's displeasure with those words. But he could not interrupt during the closing statements. Besides, the proceeding would soon be over. Pilate decided to focus on that positive certainty.

"The entire town, in fact, refused to save him," Caiaphas continued. "The people sensed his evil and chose to release a serial murderer rather than allow Jesus to continue his wickedness."

Caiaphas spun around and pointed at Jesus. He looked directly at him, something he had avoided during the entire trial. However, he could not maintain his glare and diverted his eyes.

"All you really need to know is that this man committed blasphemy against our laws and of most supreme importance, against our God," Caiaphas said as he walked away from the intense gaze of Jesus. "Those words are all you need. He stabbed our Loving God in the heart. Don't help him plunge his dagger in deeper and destroy us all. This man must be convicted and sentenced to death!"

The words were crushing and devastating to Mary and to Irit and to Joseph.

Jesus's peaceful face did not change not even once.

Chapter 24
Joseph's Closing Words

The next morning Joseph was at court before sunrise. The sleepy soldier who pulled night duty on that occasion was surprised to see Joseph at that early hour. The soldier straightened to an erect posture, trying to convince himself as much as Joseph that he was alert and attending to his duties. Joseph wasn't judgmental since he was intimately acquainted with physical exhaustion. After all, he'd been sleep-deprived since the trial began. It had become his normal state.

Today was a monumental day. It would be his last day speaking before the court—his last chance to make his case. His final argument would end the presentation portion of the trial. Next it would be up to jury and judge. But just because his own efforts would be completed didn't mean that sleep would be forthcoming. Joseph knew himself so well. He would be twisting and turning and thinking and pacing the night away until there was denouement. But after that—what? What if the jury concluded that Jesus was guilty of the trumped-up charges by the Pharisees who feared the young man's impact on their own power? How would Joseph ever sleep through the night again if such a verdict was rendered?

But lack of sleep was not at the forefront of Joseph's mind. His focus that morning was on his closing words. He had won the trial so far on points and merits—of that he was sure. Now those final words, that final statement had to successfully confirm that which had been presented to the jurors. Under Roman law, the burden was on the defense not the prosecution. This is why Joseph felt the weight of the entire trial on his shoulders as he sat there alone in the still dark courtroom?

Joseph went over his argument again. Was it for the hundredth time? It was that or more, he thought. But it would soon be the telling time. No more rehearsals or wordsmithing.

***

When the guards entered the court and began to allow the few spectators who were already outside before sun-up, Joseph felt renewed energy when daylight began to seep into the room, proof that time was actually advancing toward the grand conclusion. He'd soon present the statement, words that would mean that the entire trial would soon be behind him.

Joseph was reading his statement when the guards escorted Jesus to the table. A knot always formed in his stomach when he watched the guards take the ropes and chains off the defendant. Once settled, Joseph brought a smile to Jesus's lips when he confessed how obsessed he was with his closing remarks. He'd read them repeatedly, he told him, but it was a needless exercise since he knew every word by heart. Jesus once again told him how he appreciated his dedication to him. He apologized again for not being able to compensate him for his efforts. Joseph said he was being rewarded in ways he'd never imagined. Jesus only smiled; his eyes lit up with a twinkle.

Liberius made his way into court and after a few moments, Pilate appeared. There was a buoyancy to his gait which reflected his anticipation of the trial's end. Caiaphas and Annas took their seats and commiserated quietly with one another. Joseph wondered if they were contemplating the end of the trial or just contemplating the end of Jesus.

A chill went through Joseph as he thought of another who was contemplating the trial's end. Almost as if he sensed their approach, Joseph turned in his chair just in time to see Mary and Irit walking down the aisle. The seats were so identified with the two women that no one dared sit there. He smiled wistfully at the two women as Irit wrapped one arm around the smaller, frailer Mary as they approached their seat. Jesus turned to see his mother. Joseph could have sworn a soft white aura encompassed Mary for an instant when their eyes met.

"Joseph, we have reached the moment for the last official words of the trial to be spoken," Pilate said. "Are you prepared?"

Joseph rose and walked to the bench. He looked up at Pilate, a remote man but one whom Joseph felt he had gotten to know on some level. There was much that he respected about the man who wanted to run his court in a judicial manner. Joseph bowed slightly to Pilate.

"Yes, sir." Joseph responded. "I am prepared to present my final statement for Your Honor and for the jury."

Joseph walked to the jury and looked at each of the men.

"May I first of all thank you for your service. I know this has been a lengthy proceeding. My best hope is that I made my case, the case for Jesus of Nazareth, as clear and understandable as possible, least while that was my full intention."

Joseph walked over to Jesus and stood behind him.

"The story of Jesus of Nazareth has been told to you from the instant of his blessed conception through to this very moment which finds him just as blessed."

Caiaphas stirred in his seat, bursting to speak but knowing that he could not.

"You heard the testimony of King Sharaman whose father trekked for miles with other Persian monarchs to pay their homage to the New Born King in Bethlehem. The birth of this babe was a prediction that they held in their hearts for decades. And when that moment came, when that star burst into the black sky over Bethlehem, they knew it was heralding the birth of the King of Kings.

"And what these revered Kings of Persia knew was that the child who was born was a very special child which was underscored by Mary's testimony when she told of the angels who visited her to tell her about the blessed child she was bearing. So, what is compelling about the testimony of these two important witnesses is that they independently verify the divine nature of Jesus of Nazareth. I think we'd all agree that a royal monarch like

King Sharaman and a peasant woman like Mary could not be from more diverse backgrounds. But in this one event, the birth of Jesus of Nazareth, they came together and told the same story. There was not even the possibility of a conspiracy existing between these two people who were worlds apart.

"You heard the testimony of young Lazarus who told us of his very unusual experience. He was considered dead by his family. But when Jesus ministered to him, he returned to life. Caiaphas would have you think that Lazarus was daft or a fraud. The physician who testified for the prosecution told you that what Lazarus claimed was impossible. Most of us would have agreed with that assessment. However, although the physician was able to describe a man in a state of deep sleep, he could not say with any certainty how that person could recover. What could be a deeper sleep than death? And who could be more vital than the young Lazarus who appeared before you? The doctor could not tell us why he woke from his deep sleep. When things occur that seem impossible that no one, not even experts, can explain, I believe they are often referred to as miracles.

"Our prosecutor tried to use a young woman's past against a man who befriended her and saved her from herself. Although the esteemed counsel saw fit to dredge up men who were from her past, they were under a sworn oath and could not testify that the young woman, Mary Magdalene, had anything to do with them in the last year which is when she first encountered Jesus of Nazareth. Not having any way of knowing, of course, that these matters would come to court, Mary told the men that Jesus had rid her of her demons. I don't know about you gentlemen, but I would not begin to know how to rid someone of demons. It seems such talent is restricted to a special person—like the ones the Persian Kings were certain was born that night so long ago under an uncommonly brilliant star."

Joseph paced slowly in front of the jury allowing the descriptions of the miracles of Jesus to linger in their thoughts. Now it was time, he thought to himself, to have a little revenge against the calculating Caiaphas.

"It is unusual that in this case the prosecutor became part of the proceeding. We know from the testimony of Judas Iscariot and others that the Jewish High Priest, our most revered prosecutor, paid 30 silver denarii to Judas to lead him to Jesus. Our defense has been effective and it gains its strength from associating one testimony with another. It is no different in the case of the prosecution's presentation of an array of individuals who claimed they had been bilked from money for miracles promised but not received. Since it was sworn testimony that the High Priests had bribed Judas to lead them to Jesus, it makes one wonder if more denarii may have exchanged hands for testimony that would bolster the prosecution's case."

Caiaphas went from ashen to red to purple. He half-rose from his chair until Pilate gave him a cautionary look an implicit warning to remain silent. Pilate ruled the courtroom absolutely and Caiaphas had learned not to challenge him.

"The credibility of the witnesses who accuse Jesus of stealing their silver and not healing them comes into question. The woman who claimed to have been duped by Jesus made the mistake of claiming that Jesus had performed his miracle in a locale where he hadn't been at the time. The alleged leper who the prosecution dramatically marched in here covered in tape from head to toe was accidentally revealed as a fake and fraud and perfectly healthy underneath his wrappings."

Joseph glared at Caiaphas daring him to reject the statement but Caiaphas refused to acknowledge Joseph's stare.

"Was there a pattern of chicanery and a willingness to win through bribery on the part of the prosecutor? It's a serious matter and something to consider as you deliberate."

Joseph took another breather at the defense table and glanced at Caiaphas. He smiled at the prosecutor's bitter face. Not only would he hopefully lose the biggest case of his career, Caiaphas' reputation would suffer, as in all fairness it should. As he stalled a moment longer, he urged himself not to be over-confident. Although all signs were good, there was always the possibility of a guilty verdict. An attorney can never be assured of the outcome of any trial. And when human nature was involved, the many variables precluded prediction. And, there was that frequent nagging in the pit of Joseph's stomach that he tried but failed to ignore. The destiny that Jesus seemed to believe was awaiting him, a destiny that would give Caiaphas his way. Joseph had to shake that thought off for now. He had a statement to complete and could not show any lack of confidence in tone or demeanor.

"Jesus's ministry began just three years ago. Although he had been that special person since birth, his life went in different directions before he began to live out his purpose on earth. He cared for his mother, he worked as a carpenter, and he exhibited the gift of teaching from a young boy on— astounding the rabbis with his knowledge and wisdom. In these brief three years, his following only grew. Of all his close associates with whom I spoke in preparation for this trial, none had anything but praise and adoration for him—save the one who was paid to betray him. But those who associated with him and were devoted and dedicated to him had nothing but good and loving words for him.

"As a defense counsel I seek the truth. I could not adequately represent a client unless I knew the bad and the good. I'd have to be prepared to explain anything that was damaging to my client. I stand before you now, as a sworn officer with a sterling reputation with the Roman Courts, as I tell you that I did not find one scrap of anything that shed a nefarious light on him.

"To be honest, I found that curious. Everyone has something—something to hide or be ashamed of. Why, then couldn't I or my investigative staff find even one iota of evidence of fault or guilt? It was a pressing issue which I could not ignore and with which I had to grapple."

Joseph walked closely to the jury and look at each one. "Defending someone's life is a huge responsibility," he said, his voice rising in tone and emotion.

"I shared with you in the opening statement that our defense would be that Jesus was not guilty of committing blasphemy and did not falsely claim to be the Son of the Living God. After all my time, all my words and thoughts and those of all the witnesses and my staff and my most favored counsel, I could honestly come to only one conclusion.

"Jesus of Nazareth was the Immaculate Conception. He was honored by the Persian royals whose lore taught them to await and watch for the birth of the King of Kings. You heard testimony from John that Jesus did turn water to wine. Matthew testified under oath that Jesus calmed a storm and walked on water. Others testified that he healed the blind and the sick and the lame... he brought the dead back to life. He stands for goodness and light. He is kind and humble and all-powerful. He is the blessed Son of God. Jesus is the Messiah. Jesus of Nazareth is Jesus Christ."

By the time Joseph said his last words, his voice had reached crescendo level. As Joseph walked back to the defense table, the only noise was Joseph's footsteps on the floor. The room was still and silent and the humanity in the room was collectively on the edge of its seat. Joseph glanced at Pilate who was just as rapt and engaged as was the homeless man who sat on the floor in the aisle. Joseph looked at the jurors so that his last words were said directly to them.

"You must find Jesus of Nazareth to be the innocent Lamb of God!" Joseph said.

"You must find Jesus of Nazareth is the Son of the Living God and therefore did not commit any acts of blasphemy. There is no other answer from all that has been laid before you."

Seemingly by rote, Pilate gave his final instructions to the jurors. He reminded them to take all the evidence into consideration and to deliberate without prejudice. Pilate left immediately after his spare statement. It seemed he couldn't wait to leave the trial behind him.

Chapter 25
The Verdict

Joseph was fidgeting at the defense table the next morning. He pretended to be reviewing some documents that Yakir had brought to him but it was a hopeless pursuit. Joseph's mind was on the jury and when they would begin to file back into the courtroom with their verdict. Joseph's life would not be his own until that happened. He envied how relaxed Caiaphas and Annas appeared as they strolled into the courtroom. Did they know something he did not? Did they have good news which would surely translate to very bad news for his client?

The day wore on and the sun had already peaked and was on decline when Pilate walked briskly into the courtroom and took his seat at the bench. The moment of final resolution had arrived Joseph speculated. Pilate would soon be ordering the principals to be front and center for the jury had reached a decision. Joseph's stomach was churning with the prospect but it was all for naught. Pilate was simply conducting other court business, business that had gone by the wayside since the Jesus trial had begun.

By late afternoon, there still was no movement no progress. Inertia had set in. Joseph had a debate with himself as to whether it was a good sign or a bad sign for the defense that the jury was taking such a long time to arrive at a verdict. Most certainly, their decision was not cut and dried—hopefully another plus for the defense. The image of Caiaphas's uncommonly placid appearance and nearly pleasant countenance came to Joseph's mind. The prosecutor had entered from the rear hallway that day. Did he have a clandestine meeting with a juror or jurors? And if so, had he brought silver denarii to the meeting? All through the afternoon, Joseph wrestled with the thoughts about what Caiaphas may have done behind the scenes. His thinking became so out of control that he worked himself into a dither. In the end, he calmed himself down a bit. He would probably never know what Caiaphas did and it was a waste of time to be obsessed about it.

All the fretting and worrying in the end wouldn't do anything but put his innards in disarray Irit had told him that morning. But she didn't push it. Joseph was a very sensitive man and he had never been in a more emotional situation in his entire life. But the good news was that it would soon be over. Irit and Joseph had prayed that morning that the verdict would free Jesus. As he said goodbye to Irit, Joseph was slightly deflated that the sparkle that was always there in Irit's huge brown eyes had vanished. Was she beginning to believe in the destiny that Jesus's followers always alluded to? If that were the case, perhaps it was her close association with Mary that was bringing her a new understanding of Jesus. Joseph was glad that Irit had been there for Mary and would be there for her on this last day.

The courtroom was near dark which was Joseph's signal to give up for the day. A verdict was apparently not forthcoming. He'd have to go through yet another miserable night and wait again the next day for it. Yakir had waited with him and the two began to gather all the parchments and materials that were strewn about on the table. They didn't stop when they heard the click-clack as Liberius scurried into the courtroom. He was always there, it seemed, and he always scurried about. He was probably going to tell them to pack it in for the night. But he had different news.

"Joseph, don't leave," Liberius said in a hushed tone. "The jury is ready to return."

Joseph's knees weakened and he plopped down in his chair. He looked up at Liberius.

"Did someone send for...," Joseph began but Liberius finished his thought.

"The guards are on their way to the cell to bring Jesus in," Liberius informed him. "Pilate will be out soon and a messenger has been sent to bring Caiaphas and Annas."

Joseph's eyes widened as he spun around and looked at Yakir.

"Yakir, hurry go and find Mary and Irit and bring them back," Joseph said.

The time had come. The decisions had been made and soon the word "guilty" or "innocent" would be heard in open court. Joseph was lost in his thoughts and watched as court slaves worked around the perimeter of the courtroom lighting torches that were attached to the walls. It was almost dark and the dancing light from the glowing flames created an eerie backdrop to the drama that would play out in either freedom or death for Jesus of Nazareth.

Joseph was alone in the courtroom for what seemed forever. There was part of him that wished that time could magically freeze and the moment of final reckoning would never come. But that was fantasy, of course. His reverie was soon interrupted by the footsteps of the jurors as they filed into the room and took their seats in the panel area. Word had spread to the community that a verdict was in and townspeople began to quietly enter and sit in the spectators' gallery. Joseph noticed that Liberius had arranged for extra Roman guards to be on duty. He probably feared that the verdict—whatever it may be—might cause an outburst or even a riot. As Pilate had said from the beginning, this was a very emotional proceeding.

Joseph rushed up to Pilate as soon as he swept into court.

"Your Honor. May we await the appearance of Mary, Mother of Jesus, before the verdict is read?" Joseph asked.

"We can wait," Pilate responded. Joseph thought Pilate even seemed a bit unnerved. Perhaps he was struggling to maintain his decorum and rein in the happy anticipation of finally ending the trial. Pilate would be free to go back to his normal life and, if speculation was correct, he would soon be returning to Rome for a promotion and eventual retirement. Joseph recognized that the trial was just one of many for Pilate and would have no lasting impact on his life or legacy.

Just when it was obvious that Pilate was growing impatient, Joseph saw that Mary and Irit were hurrying to their seats. The guards then brought in the shackled Jesus.

"Joseph, shall we leave the prisoner shackled in case we must return him to his cell?" one of the soldiers asked him.

"Take the chains and ropes off of him at once!" Joseph responded, literally shaking in rage. Joseph wasn't about to prevent Jesus from having one last moment of freedom should the verdict go against the defense.

As soon as everyone was settled in, Pilate addressed the court.

"To one and all in hearing distance, it is my duty to announce that the jury has arrived at their decision."

Silence.

"Liberius, fetch the verdict and bring it to me," Pilate ordered.

Liberius hurried over and took the small parchment from the main juryman and brought it to Pilate who read it over, handed it to Liberius and bade him to read it aloud. Joseph and Jesus stood for the reading of the verdict.

There were sixteen separate charges against Jesus, five of which were for blasphemy which all carried the death penalty.

"For the charge of blasphemy in that Jesus of Nazareth considered himself to be the Son of the Living God—Guilty as Charged!

"For the charge of blasphemy in that Jesus of Nazareth claimed he could destroy and rebuild the temple in three days—Guilty as Charged!"

Joseph was reeling. At the first guilty disposition, his knees grew weak. With the second one, he thought he would surely faint. Each guilty verdict—and they were all guilty—was like a stab in Joseph's heart. Jesus sensed how upset Joseph was and put his arm around his back to brace and comfort him. The irony that Jesus was comforting him was not lost on Joseph. Joseph stole a glance at Mary—she and Irit their hands clutched together, were comforting each other. After the horrid few moments that it took to read the entire verdict, the guards were binding up Jesus in ropes and chains to take him away but Pilate had one last duty—one that he, Joseph sensed, was not relishing.

"Jesus of Nazareth, you are condemned to die by crucifixion which will take place at sunrise." Hardly anyone heard Pilate's words since the room was in total chaos and everyone was already well-aware of the punishment that the Judge was required to hand down. Pilate rose quickly and left the courtroom and this trial behind him forever. Once back in his private chambers, he poured himself a grog of red wine. Pilate was uncharacteristically shaken by the verdict of the Jesus trial. Normally, a judgment rendered by a jury—whether in his mind fairly or unfairly—vanished from his thoughts as soon as he left the courtroom. But this time it was different.

On edge from the outcome of the trial Pilate took quite a long drink from his grog and slammed it back down on his table, wiping away a dribble of wine from his chin. A sudden noise outside his door startled him causing his hand to hit the goblet that was still half-filled with wine. Attempting to catch the goblet before it spilled, his hands were suddenly covered in the red liquid. For just a moment there was a fearful look in his otherwise steely eyes as he gazed down upon his hands. He recovered from his lapse and quickly reached over and plunged his soiled hands into a nearby basin which instantly turned the water to red. He pulled his hands out but inexplicably the water had not washed away the stain.

Pilate gazed out the window and focused on the blazing sunset that was heralding in the darkness. At that very moment, he wondered if he'd ever see his homeland again.

***

Joseph, in an almost trance-like state, walked with Jesus to his cell. Joseph could not keep his eyes dry.

"I don't know what to say, I am so devastated and so, so sorry...,"

"You could not have done more, Joseph," Jesus told him. "You were up against impossible odds."

The guards forced Joseph to leave. He kept looking back over his shoulder to look upon Jesus as long as he could. The last image was of Jesus in prayer as he sat on the floor of his cell against the filthy back wall.

The Aftermath

Early the next morning just before Jesus had to lug his cross to Golgotha to meet that destiny that had so often been floated around in the air, Judas Iscariot committed suicide. He was found hanging from a Joshua tree on a hill outside the city. The news shook Joseph—the young man's tragedy was so complete.

Joseph and Irit followed Mary to Golgotha, walking with Jesus's followers—for they were now a part of them. Joseph and Irit stayed with Mary until the end. Joseph provided a piece of property he owned for Jesus's tomb. In the middle of the next night when no one else was about, Joseph walked alone to the burial site. He sat by the tomb and prayed. He prayed for Jesus and for Mary and for all those who loved him.

Of all his prayers, Joseph's most fervent prayer was that the world would not forget Jesus of Nazareth.

***

Several months after everything was over, Joseph was struck with the idea of petitioning the appellate court in Rome for a ruling on the case. True, Jesus was gone but Joseph wanted to appeal the case in an effort to burnish Jesus's reputation. Perhaps the higher court would remand the case back to Pilate which would stain the guilty verdict, leaving Jesus's case in limbo and removing the cloak of guilt from him.

Things moved slowly in Rome and even slower across the terrain and the desert to Jerusalem. The appellate court, uncertain of its jurisdiction over the matter, had passed the case onto the Supreme Court for review. A little over a year after Joseph had submitted his appeal, a decision on the matter was dispatched to Pilate's court.

The Supreme Court had found errors in the case—many of them minor: Jesus should have never been seen by the jury in shackles; and, he should have been allowed to wear clean clothing in good repair in court, not the shredded and bloodied shift that he wore. The Court questioned Pilate's judgment in allowing a principal—namely Caiaphas—to prosecute the case. Further, upon investigation, the Court was concerned about rumors of the prosecution's nefarious dealings with witnesses and perhaps even jury members.

Joseph knew all these things and felt slightly disappointed at their less than monumental findings but read on. An astonished yet joyful look came over Joseph's face as he came to the last page and the high court's final disposition: "In the case of Jesus of Nazareth, the preponderance of evidence favored a not guilty verdict. The defendant is hereby released and no record shall exist of the initial guilty finding."

The Supreme Court had no idea that the defendant had already been crucified. Pilate was admonished for his errors and was ultimately reassigned for another three years to Jerusalem where he continued what many considered his maladministration. Joseph would have a quite different stance were he asked about Pilate's competency. Joseph believed that Pilate conducted the proceeding by the book and was dedicated to the law. It was Joseph's feeling that Caesar wanted to defer any criticism that may befall his empire resulting from the Jesus trial to Pilate; Pilate would take the blame for the ages.

Pilate had initially been ordered back to Rome by Emperor Tiberius. However, Pilate's fate was to be decided by Caligula who succeeded Tiberius after his death. The crucial decision to have Pilate remain in Jerusalem came with his orders to slaughter thousands of Samaritan pilgrims. Pilate considered his additional time in Jerusalem as punitive and forever connected it to the trial of Jesus of Nazareth. Some who knew Pilate in his last years claimed that he lamented more over the death of one man than over the deaths of the thousands he had been responsible for.

Caiaphas was censured by the court and his certification to serve as counsel for the Jewish High Council was revoked.

Joseph finally got his "not guilty" finding but this "victory" was bittersweet. The real victory was the life of Jesus of Nazareth. A melancholy feeling washed over Joseph. He thought back to the trial and all that had gone on.

But as a devotee of Jesus Christ, Joseph now understood that the trial had turned out the only way it could have.

About the Authors

Kathleen Keithley is a screenwriter and author who lives in Los Angeles.

Daniel T. Doyle is a defense attorney who lives in Boston and in addition to *The Jesus Trial* is the author of *Keeping Teens on Track: A No-Nonsense Guide for Heading Teens in the Right Direction*

Books by Kathleen Keithley

The Jesus Trial

The Myrmidons: A Police Tale
Book 1, Subterfuge

The Myrmidons: A Police Tale
Book 2, Counterplay

OMNI I: Supercomputer

OMNI II: Legacy

Dreams of Yesterday and Tomorrow

One Thousand Showers

Ildico, the Last Bride of Attila the Hun

Son of Dracula

Emerson's Hat

Tooth Galaxy Mission

Genetically Modified Werewolves

Made in United States
North Haven, CT
13 May 2022

19154626R00192